# BATTLE FOR AN LOC, 1972

UNDAUNTED VALOR
BOOK 5

## MATT JACKSON

# INTRODUCTION

In 1972, the United States was departing South Vietnam. Ending the war in Vietnam was one of Richard Nixon's campaign promises in 1968, and soon after taking office in 1969, he began ordering the withdrawal of US forces. The drawdown was a very orderly, planned drawdown, with goals and objects as to the number of personnel that would be in-country on certain dates and the amount and type of equipment that would be withdrawn or left for the South Vietnamese government to use on our departure. The first unit to be withdrawn was the 27th Marines on 12 September 1968, followed by the 9th Infantry Division in July 1969. Over the course of the next three and a half years, men and equipment were sensibly withdrawn. By January 1972, there were only two brigades of US combat forces in-country, a few Army aviation units scattered across the country, some US Air Force assets, and US Army and Marine advisors with South Vietnamese units.

At the height of the war, US advisors were assigned at all levels of the South Vietnamese Army and Marines. US Army advisors were at the battalion level, with usually two to four advisors with each battalion. At the brigade level, there was a senior advisor for the commander advisors with almost every staff officer. It was not uncommon for a division advisory team to have seventy advisors on the team in the mid- to late 1960s. Besides being divisional advisor teams, advisory teams were also mobility teams moving to Regional/Popular Forces and advising. There were logistical advisor teams and district advisor teams working with district and province chiefs on pacification projects. The US Marine Corps also had advisors with each South Vietnamese Marine Corps battalion. However, as the drawdown deadlines came, the advisor teams were reduced.

The US Army reduced the number of advisors so much that in divisional units, the advisors were only located at the brigade and division levels. Airborne and Ranger battalions continued to be manned with two advisors, an officer and a noncommissioned officer if possible. Attempts were made to maintain two advisors with each province chief and cover the districts as well. The US Marines continued to provide advisors down to the battalion level. When the Easter Offensive of 1972 began, these were the links that held the North Vietnamese Army at bay.

By 1972, an advisor had to be a jack-of-all-trades, advising his Vietnamese counterpart in tactical operations and the employment of forces in combined-arms operations and requesting and directing close-air support. At the battalion and brigade levels, those advisors were on the front line with the South Vietnamese forces. They were also a morale booster to the South Vietnamese soldiers and marines, who believed if the American was there with them, there was hope.

I would be remiss if I did not pay tribute to the Army Aviation and US Air Force crews that supported the ground advisors at An Loc. When South Vietnamese helicopter crews refused to support their own, US Army Aviation did the job. The US Air Force FAC pilots, C-130 crews, fighter pilots and B-52 crews were the difference between defeat and victory for South Vietnam.

This historical novel is my attempt to honor those who served in any capacity in the Battle of An Loc and Loc Ninh. All the events presented happened in the sequence offered. All the characters whose names have been used are those that participated in the events, with three exceptions. I hope you enjoy *Undaunted Valor: Battle of An Loc.*

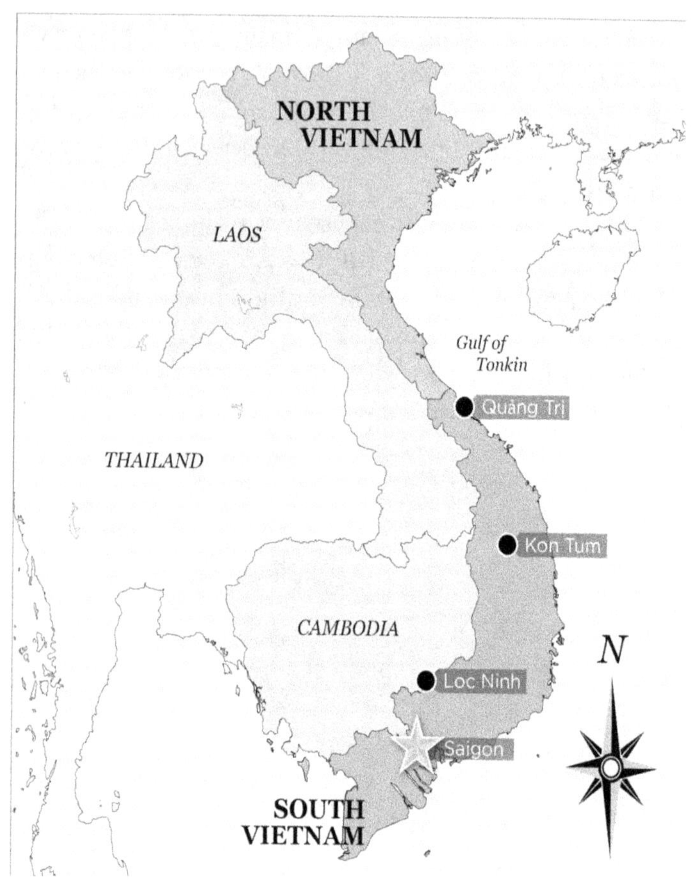


*Map. South East Asia, 1970, Created by Infidium LLC for Matt Jackson Books.*

1

1

---

## PRELUDE TO BATTLE

**13 MARCH 1972**
  **Central Office of South Vietnam**
  **Snoul, Cambodia**

Rain pelted the stucco roof of the building. The rumbling penetrating the walls was not the sound of thunder but the sounds made by one-thousand-pound bombs being dropped from a flight of three B-52 aircraft. Since the Cambodian Incursion in 1970, South Vietnamese forces had frequently returned to Cambodia. Each time, they would call upon US airpower to strike known and suspected People's Liberation Army of Vietnam (PLA) ammunition and supply sites as well as troop concentrations. General Hoang Van Thai, Deputy Secretary for the Central Office of South Vietnam or COSVN, paused in this briefing. Before him stood General Tran Va Tra, Commander B-2 Front, and his three division commanders and key regimental commanders. They encircled a table with a map spread out of the northern part of Military Region III. The area encompassed Tay Ninh to the southwest, An Loc in the north center, and Song Be to the northeast. Also scattered along the landscape was Lai Khe, south of An Loc. Running through An Loc and Lai Khe was Highway 13, which crossed the Vietnam-Cambodian border outside the border town of Loc Ninh and terminated in Saigon.

Loc Ninh sat fifteen kilometers south of the Cambodian border. Surrounded by high hills covered in heavy vegetation, the bulk of the town was on the northeast side of Highway 13. An airfield was located on the southwest side of the town, oriented northeast-southwest. At the southwest end was the advisors' compound occupied by the 9th Regiment command post, 5th ARVN Division. The compound for the province chief was located on the northern end of the runway. An artillery compound was positioned between the two compounds.

"Gentlemen, our mission is to seize and secure An Loc. Once that's accomplished, a provisional government will be established there. Be prepared to exploit success to Saigon. To do this, we will attack with the 5th VC Division crossing into Vietnam and seizing Loc Ninh and destroying the forces there," General Thai indicated, looking up at Colonel Bui Thanh Van, the 5th VC Division commander. "At the same time"—he paused to look at the 9th Division commander, Colonel Nguyen Thoi Bung—"the 9th Division will attack and seize and secure An Loc." Colonel Bung smiled and nodded his head in acknowledgment of being given the prize. General Thai continued, "The 7th Division will move south of An Loc and establish blocking position on Highway 13, preventing reinforcements from reaching An Loc. I would recommend that a strong position be established in the vicinity of Dong Phat, where this rubber-processing plant is located, or in the hills around there just to the south. I will leave the final location up to you, General Nguy, as you will be the man on the ground." His gaze shifted to the western portion of the map. "Now we must use some deception here to maximize the element of surprise. We should allow the enemy to rely upon their assumptions. They will assume that we will attack on traditional avenues of approach through Tay Ninh in the west as we did in Tet '68. They will think we are attempting to control people as we did then instead of the true purpose of this attack, which is to destroy the South Vietnam Army."

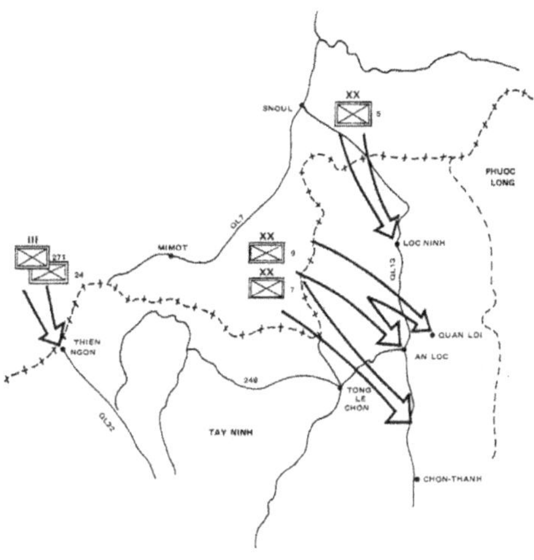


1

General Thai looked over at the commander of the 24th Independent VC Regiment. "Colonel, you will attack in this area and overrun this firebase at Lac Long. Prior to your attack, we need a soldier to be captured who will state that he is part of a reconnaissance unit and that they were reconning a road from Tay Ninh to the border. We should also let the enemy find a cache site in the area to further convince them we are making our main attack towards Tay Ninh. Understood?" The commander acknowledged. Turning to the commander of the 271st NVA Regiment, he went on, "The action of the 24th will trigger a reaction, and I anticipate that will be an order to move the forces at Thien Ngon. When they start to move, you are to ambush them, but do not become decisively engaged. Understood?"

"Yes, sir," was the 271st Regimental commander's response.

Looking up from the map, the 24th Regimental commander asked, "What is the date for my ground attack, sir?"

"The second of April will do nicely. That will give the ARVN command time to shift forces towards Tay Ninh before we launch our main attack on April fifth against Loc Ninh," General Thai explained. "Any other questions?"

"Sir, do we know the distribution of forces around Loc Ninh?" It was the 5th VC commander.

"Yes, right now in Loc Ninh is the headquarters for the 9th Regiment, 5th ARVN Division, which two days ago replaced the 7th Regiment, 5th ARVN Division. The commander is a Colonel Nguyen Cong Vinh. He is well liked because he is very easy and does not enforce high standards of discipline amongst his soldiers. The 9th Regiment has two battalions as it left one battalion at Bu Dop. There are two batteries of artillery at Loc Ninh. Two companies of the 2nd Battalion with two 155 artillery pieces and four 155 tubes are located at the Cam Le Bridge south of Loc Ninh," Thai said, pointing to that location on the map. "There is the 1st Armored Squadron with two companies of infantry and some 105 and 155 artillery located just south of the border at Firebase Alpha along with the 74th Border Ranger Battalion.

They are calling this organization Task Force 1-5. We have intelligence that indicates that a unit is coming from Xuan Loc to reinforce the 5th ARVN Division. They plan to have this unit they are calling Task Force 52 located at this firebase here, Hung Tam Base, approximately ten kilometers to the southwest of Loc Ninh. The commander is Lieutenant Colonel Nguyen Ba Thinh. He is considered very capable. The task force is composed of 2nd Battalion, 52nd Regiment, and 1st Battalion, 48th Regiment. It has a reconnaissance company, a battery of 105mm artillery, a platoon of 155mm howitzers and an engineer company," General Thai explained, pointing out each location on the map as he spoke. "As the 9th settles in, our reconnaissance must determine the final disposition of his forces," General Thai said.

"One other important piece as well," he announced, breaking everyone's train of thought. "There are, at Loc Ninh, members of the American Advisory Team 70, which is located in Lai Khe. There is also an advisor team to the district commander, part of Advisory Team 47. They will no doubt have the ability to call upon the US Air Force for support with air strikes. Their command post must be eliminated quickly, and their communications cut off even quicker. If we can capture the advisors alive, all the better. Any other questions?" Thai asked.

"Sir, what is the disposition of forces in An Loc?" the 9th VC Division commander, Colonel Bung, asked.

*He should already know what he will be facing in An Loc. Why is he asking now?* General Thai thought.

"An Loc as of right now is occupied by two battalions of Binh Long Regional and Popular Forces. The 7th Regiment is six kilometers west of An Loc in a fire support base with two 155mm howitzers and four 105mm howitzers. Two companies from the 7th's 1st Battalion are located at Quan Loi here, just east of An Loc. The division also has the 8th Regiment, which is Binh Duong Province, and only has two battalions as one is at their national training center. An Loc can be reinforced from Lai Khe, so we need to be sure and block Highway 13. Understood?" General Thai emphasized, looking at Colonel Dam Van Nguy, the 7th Division commander, who responded with a nod.

"On Highway 13, south of An Loc is the 92nd Ranger Battalion, located here at Tong Le Chon," Thai said, pointing at a hamlet southeast of An Loc. "They have artillery with this unit that could support An Loc and anyone moving up Highway 13." Thai's message was clear.

"Our biggest threat to success is going to be the American Air Force and their helicopter forces. These we must neutralize and do it effectively," Thai indicated as he looked at an officer with air-defense markings on his uniform. "The 271st Anti-Aircraft Regiment will reinforce your regimental anti-aircraft forces. In addition, members of the regiments will begin training on the new Soviet anti-aircraft missile system, the SA-7 shoulder-fired missile. These will be effective against the American attack helicopters, especially as they slow and attack from altitude. Worst case, this missile will force them to fly very low and be subject to our direct-fire weapons such as the 12.7 and 23mm guns. Questions?" he asked. As there were none, he continued. "Colonel," he said, catching the immediate attention of the air-defense officer, "how do you intend to array your weapons?"

"Sir, we will create a series of rings around An Loc. The outer ring will consist of spotters who can tell us when aircraft are approaching. They will be twenty kilometers out from An Loc. The next ring will be our 37mm and 57mm self-propelled guns. These will be six kilometers out from An Loc village. Each of our large guns will have its own rings of 23mm guns, with each of those having a ring of 12.7 guns. In this manner, we will have early warning of approaching aircraft, defense in depth for our troops and our major guns," the commander explained.

"Good," was all Thai said. "Now, any equipment you can capture, do so. Tanks, armored personnel carriers and artillery pieces are all valuable assets. If you can capture rather than destroy, do so. Codebooks and radios are other important items that we want to seize and utilize if we can. Capture if possible. Understood?" Everyone answered in the affirmative.

"Alright, then, let us move forward and prepare ourselves for this victory," General Thai announced before he turned and left the room.

**2**

---

# ONLY AN OBSERVER

**28 MARCH 1972**
  **Advisory Team 70**
  **Lai Khe, Vietnam**

Lai Khe sat astride Highway 13, approximately seventy kilometers south of Loc Ninh. Formerly it had been the main base camp for the 1st US Infantry Division before that unit had rotated back to the United States in April of 1970. Since that time, the 5th ARVN Infantry Division had moved in and occupied the base camp. Adjacent to the base camp were the village of Lai Khe and the larger town of Ben Cat. The base sat on the edge of the area known as the Iron Triangle and had been the recipient of numerous rocket and mortar attacks over the years.

"Show them in," Colonel William Miller directed as he stood. Colonel Miller was the commander of the Military Advisory Team 70, and the senior advisor to the 5th ARVN Division. His immediate superior was Brigadier General Hollingsworth, whose 3rd Regional Assistance Command headquarters was located in Bien Hoa, fifty kilometers to the south. Colonel Miller had seen action in World War II and Korea. He was no stranger to the advisor role, having served previously as an advisor with the 5th ARVN Division. He was prior service enlisted for ten years before receiving a commission. As General Hollingsworth walked into Miller's office, he noticed an Army major behind the general.

"Morning, sir, good to see you," Miller said, extending his hand, which Hollingsworth accepted.

"You too, Bill. I want you to meet Major Hank Sabine," Hollingsworth introduced as he gestured towards the major.

"Morning, sir. Glad to meet you," Hank said, accepting Miller's outstretched hand.

"Gentlemen, let's have a seat and get down to business," Hollingsworth said, taking charge of the meeting. "Bill, Major Sabine has been sent here by the DoD IG to look into how well the Vietnamization Program has done. He's been in Saigon and my headquarters for the past month, looking at the logistical system that the Vietnamese have and how the transfer of supplies and equipment is working as well as the maintenance. He's now ready to look at the combat training of the Vietnamese Army. He has a counterpart in each of the four military regions, although the guy up north is a Marine looking at the Marine regiments. We're giving him our full cooperation." As Hollingsworth spoke, Miller occasionally glanced at Hank.

"Certainly, sir, and I look forward to reading your report, Major," Miller expressed as he looked at Hank.

"Well, that's just the thing," Hollingsworth cut in. "Major Sabine's report is close hold, which means no one, not even Abrams, gets to read it before the major and his group head back to Washington."[1] The look on Miller's face was one of confusion. Hollingsworth continued, "Apparently, the president wants a report that no one can say was tainted by those of us executing the program. So, we've been ordered not to attempt to influence the group in any way but to provide them with full support. Understood?"

"Yes, sir," Miller replied and turned to Major Sabine. "Major, mind telling me a bit about yourself and your qualifications for this assignment?"

Miller had been assessing the physical characteristics of the major since Hank had walked into the room. First, he'd noted Hank's uniform, displaying his crossed rifles infantry insignia, Combat Infantryman Badge, Senior Airborne Wings and Ranger Tab and a MACV combat patch. *So he's had some experience on the advisor side of the Army*, Miller immediately thought. Physically, Hank was an impressive man with a touch of gray at the temples. Standing five foot eight and probably weighing in at one hundred and seventy pounds, he was "ordinary" for an infantry officer but notably not carrying any fat. In fact, he looked pretty solid, with a square face and brown eyes to match his hair. The scar down the right side of his face from just below the eye to his chin didn't do wonders for his appearance.

"Well, sir, I'm prior service, infantry for five years, where I learned Vietnamese at the Defense Language Institute in Monterey and then did a two-year tour as an interpreter out of Pleiku with Advisory Team 36. After I was commissioned, I served my platoon leader time with the 101st at Fort Campbell but came back to Vietnam after that year to serve with the 1st ARVN Airborne Division Advisory Team for a year. After that, it was company commander time in-country with the 101st, battalion operations officer, then back to the States for CGSC and a tour at the Pentagon, where I got tagged for this assignment. Not married and no family," Hank explained.

"I see you wear a MACV combat patch and not a 101st patch," Miller noted.

"I figured with this assignment, the MACV patch would

give me more credibility with the Vietnamese offices and sergeants I would be dealing with."

"How are your Vietnamese language skills?" Miller asked. He quickly learned that Hank's Vietnamese was as close to fluent as an American could get.

"I keep my ability quiet so I can eavesdrop on conversations between Vietnamese officers," Hank admitted with a smile.

"Satisfied, Bill?" General Hollingsworth asked.

"Yes, sir. The major has the qualifications for the job and we will be glad to assist. Let me give you a quick rundown of our disposition." Miller stood and moved over to a wall map. "The 5th ARVN Infantry Division is responsible for military operations in three provinces, Phuoc Long, Binh Duong and Binh Long. In Binh Long Province, we have three districts: Loc Ninh in the north, An Loc in the center and Chon Thanh in the south. At Loc Ninh is a small element of the team with Lieutenant Colonel Schott, the senior advisor for the 9th Regiment, aided by a Captain Smith, Major Carlson, Sergeant First Class Lull, and Sergeant Wallingford. Captain Wanat is the assistant district advisor with Major Blair, who's on leave right now. The 9th Regiment command is located there at Loc Ninh, with a couple of units on outlying outposts.

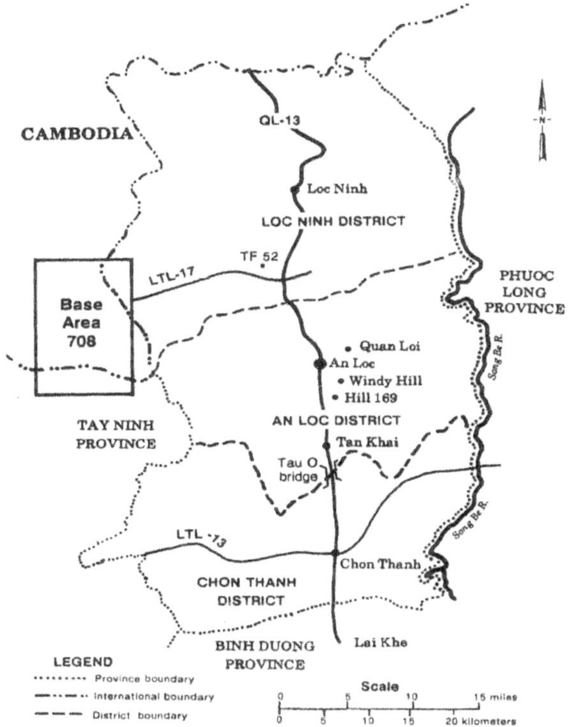


Source: Lieutenant General Ngo Quang Truong, *Indochina Monographs: The Easter Offensive of 1972* (Washington, DC: U.S. Army Center of Military History, 1980).

"When you get up there, Schott can give you a rundown on this unit. At An Loc is Team 47, under Lieutenant Colonel Colby, who's the province senior advisor. He has Major Davidson, here with him and Major Blair up at Loc Ninh. They advise the province chief and the Regional-Popular Forces or Ruff-Puffs, as some refer to them."

"Who is the province chief?" Hank asked.

"That'd be Colonel Tran Van Nhut, one tough man. He was a Marine and came here in 1970 to take the job as province chief. Very aggressive in patrolling, putting two-thirds of the Ruff-Puffs out and only keeping one-third at a time in garrison. He was awarded a Silver Star by General Abrams back in '68 for his actions against the 5th VC Division. He's from this area and asked to come to this assignment."

"Sounds like a warrior. What's opposing the 5th ARVNs now?" Hank asked. He noticed Miller and Hollingsworth exchange looks. Hollingsworth answered the question after a sigh.

"Truthfully, Major, a lot more than we care to think about, and building every day. We know that operating over in Cambodia are the 9th VC Division, the 7th NVA Division and the 5th VC Division. There are also a couple of tank regiments, an artillery regiment and an air-defense regiment. They're well supplied from several cache sites, one being Site 708 just across the border, which is just west of the province in the Fishhook area. There are a couple of smaller ones around Snoul. We have had intel reports of a bridge built across a stream on the border up north and another bridge built under the water as well. We have a buildup across the border in front of the firebase at Lac Long. Traditionally, the NVA have attacked towards Tay Ninh in an attempt to move towards Saigon."

"How are you getting the intel?" Hank asked.

"We get some from MACV and some from ARVN JCS. However, we also get good immediate hard intel from D Troop, 229th Aviation Battalion. They run up along the border with scout teams and come back and brief us. We pass their stuff up the chain. Truthfully, I trust what intel we get from them much more than what we get from MACV," Miller said.

"Why's that, sir?" Hank inquired.

"These are our guys that are up there every day snooping and pooping. They come back in here and give us exact coordinates of what they're seeing and where they're taking fire. Someone shooting at you is a good indicator that someone is there and they don't want you there. They're giving us reports on a daily basis of finding tank tracks in the jungle. They found the underwater bridge. If what they're giving me is accurate, then something big is across that border. General Hung doesn't believe it as he thinks if they attack, it will be the traditional route to Tay Ninh," Miller said.

"Excuse me, sir, but who is General Hung?" Hank asked.

"Brigadier General Le Van Hung commands the 5th ARVN Division. The previous commander was relieved by General Minh, the corps commander, for poor performance, and Hung was brought up from the Delta to take command recently as he was General Minh's fair-haired boy down in the Delta. He doesn't think much of advisors, and we're working to change that perception. I've tried to get him to move some forces in an operation north of Tay Ninh, but he says he can do nothing unless General Minh orders it. The guy won't take a dump unless Minh says it's okay," Colonel Miller said in exasperation.

"Let me add that Minh's strategy is for a standoff defense along the border. He's not going to authorize any strikes across the border. He has complete autonomy from Saigon to do as he sees fit, but he doesn't want to move against those base camps," Hollingsworth added with some frustration in his tone.

"I'll have a talk with Minh and see if I can get him to move Hung. Just tell me what you want Hung to do. Okay?" Hollingsworth asked.

"Sure, sir," Miller replied.

"Well, I have to get over to Xuan Loc for a ceremony at the 18th Division. Major, I'm going to leave you here with Colonel Miller," Hollingsworth said, standing. "Good luck, and if you need anything, give me a call."

"Thank you, sir," Hank said as Hollingsworth departed the room. He turned back to Miller, who motioned for him to sit back down. "Seems like a good man to work for."

"Who? General Hollingsworth? The best. You know he personally writes a letter to every child of the men assigned under his command, thanking them for allowing him to use their father for a year and apologizing because some dads wouldn't be home for Christmas," Miller said.

"Sir, you're joking, right?" Hank asked in amazement.

"Nope. He's old-school. Served with Abrams in the Second World War and was wounded five times. He was the assistant division commander of the Big Red One under DePuy in '66 and did a stint back in Washington, evaluating the National Guard leadership after the Detroit riots. The Vietnamese respect the man, but they fear him as well because he tells it like it is. If something stinks, he'll let you know about it. Got himself in trouble a couple of times telling the press just how it is when people back in the puzzle palace don't want to hear it. Well...where do you want to go from here?" Miller asked.

"I'd like to spend a day or two watching the ARVN division staff and then move up north to Loc Ninh and work my way back down to here if that would be alright, sir," Hank stated.

"That should work fine. Let's get you settled in the team hooch and introduced to the rest of the team. I'll arrange to get you up north in a couple of days. That okay?" Miller asked as he stood and picked up his hat.

"That would be great, sir, and thank you," Hank replied as he moved towards the door ahead of Colonel Miller.

**3**

---

# FIRST SIGNS

**31 MARCH 1972**
   **Team 70**
   **Lai Khe**

Major Sabine had been observing the outer perimeter around Lai Khe since first light. He had arrived even before dawn. Discipline would usually break down between 0300 and sunrise as those were the longest hours for anyone standing guard. The caffeine had worn off as everyone ran out of coffee at about midnight. Fresh coffee wouldn't be ready until 0530 and wouldn't get to the guys on guard duty until 0600. Hank expected to see soldiers sleeping on their posts. NCOs would be hanging around the command posts and not out walking the line. This was the most dangerous time, as the NVA were noted for night attacks. Sapper attacks usually occurred between midnight and 0200 hours, with ground attacks starting at 0300.

Hank was pleasantly surprised as he made his way around. Almost every post was manned and ready. Several times he was challenged as he approached. His response was always in English, which the guards recognized immediately as he would always answer with "lollipops and lilies." Vietnamese had real trouble pronouncing the letter L. It always sounded like an R. It invariably made the guards laugh when he responded. Arriving back at the division command post, he immediately noticed tension in the air.

Approaching Colonel Miller, he said, "Morning, sir. What's going on?"

"Where have you been? I was a bit concerned about your absence," Miller expressed with concern on his face.

"I was walking the perimeter. They were all pretty much on their toes. Didn't see any lack of discipline in the ranks. Why? What's going on?" Hank asked, looking around.

"We're getting reports that there's a lot of activity up north along the DMZ. Nothing that Saigon is worried about, as it appears that four of the outposts along the DMZ are in contact. Saigon has been saying for some time now that a major offensive is going to start soon. They thought it would be at Tet this year, but it didn't materialize. General Hollingsworth isn't too concerned and General Minh is mildly concerned. Hung, on the other hand, is shitting bricks that a major attack may be coming this way. I'm not sure how much of a warrior spirit Hung has. He won't do anything without clearing it with Minh first. The problem is worse in that he won't even recommend any action up to Minh."

"He has his forces arrayed to repulse an attack, doesn't he? With the 5th Division, that is?" Hank asked.

"Come over here and look at this map," Miller indicated, pointing at a map spread out on a table with hard plastic over the top. "This is Binh Long and Phuoc Long Province, which the 5th has responsibility for. To the west is Tay Ninh Province, which is the responsibility of the 25th Division. To the southeast are Bien Hoa and Long Khanh Province, which are the 18th Division AO. We here in Lai Khe are actually in Binh Duong Province. Highway 13 runs north to south from Snoul, Cambodia, right through the middle of our province straight to Saigon. It's the only road that does so. Highway 1 in the southern portion of Tay Ninh Province also runs straight to Saigon out of the Parrot's Beak and Base Camp 713 in Cambodia, but the bulk of their base camps are here around Snoul," Miller said, pointing at the locations of Base Camps 708, 712, 711, 714 and 715. "Base Camps 711, 714, and 715 are all well north of Tay Ninh Province, but 712 and 708 are right above us. We have the best road and avenue of approach to Saigon. If you were going to launch an attack, would you choose to attack through restrictive terrain on the expected route through Tay Ninh Province or take the high-speed and unexpected route straight to Saigon?" Miller asked, drawing his finger down Highway 13.

"I see your point, sir. What local intelligence has Hung provided?" Hank asked.

"Hung says that they've uncovered some underwater bridges on the streams up north along the border. An air cav team confirmed this. Said it was made of stones placed just below the surface but wide enough to support a tank. In addition, the air cav is reporting tank tracks through the jungle that just seem to suddenly disappear. Hung reported capturing an NVA officer, artillery, who was surveying firing positions in preparation for a major attack. Reconnaissance teams are reporting hearing tank engines and movement west of Loc Ninh as well. All this has been passed up to III Corps," Miller explained.

"So what has he got laid out to slow and stop them if they decide to attack this way?" Hank asked.

"Despite my best efforts," Miller started with a sigh of frustration, "to get him to move the bulk of the 5th to An Loc, he won't move. Here at Loc Ninh, he has the 9th Regiment with two infantry battalions, one battalion of Ruff-Puffs and a battery of 105 howitzers."

"Where's his third battalion?" Hank asked.

"It's in Bu Dop to the northeast. He gave up a battalion to 18th Division and received what's being referred to as TF-52, which is located here at Hung Tam Base. It has two infantry battalions, one from the 52nd Regiment and from the 48th Regiment. It's a pretty robust outfit, with a reconnaissance company, an artillery battery of 105s and a platoon of 155s as well as an engineer company. About a thousand soldiers altogether," Miller exclaimed. As he did so, he was tapping his finger on Hung Tam Base, located twelve kilometers northwest of An Loc.

Continuing his dissertation, he said, "Up north, the 9th Regiment has two companies from the 2nd Battalion located at this bridge at Cam Le, and they have two 155 howitzers and four 105 howitzers for support. Cam Le is about equal distance between Loc Ninh and An Loc," Miller indicated, pointing at the point on the border between the Loc Ninh District and the An Loc District. "Way up north there is the

1st Armored Cav Squadron with two attached rifle companies from the 9th Regiment and a mix of 105 and 155 howitzers. We refer to this as Task Force 1-5, and their location is Fire Support Base Alpha."

"Sir, Alpha is what? Nine klicks south of the border?" Hank observed.

"More like seven," Miller corrected him, "and the 74th Border Ranger Battalion is collocated there as well and OPCON to the cav."[1] Colonel Miller moved his finger to An Loc. "Here we have the 7th Regiment." He pointed at a location six klicks due west of An Loc. "It's minus one battalion, which is at Phuoc Binh in Phuoc Long Province. The 1st Battalion has two companies located at Quan Loi up here northeast of Loc Ninh," Miller said, pointing at Quan Loi. "The 8th Regiment is located at Dau Tieng in Binh Duong Province, overwatching the Song Be River area. One of the battalions that's at the national training center. Advisor Team 47 is located here in An Loc and provides support to the Binh Long Province chief."

"So what's here at Lai Khe, sir?" Hank asked. He had his suspicions at this point.

"Here we have the Ruff-Puffs and the 3rd Ranger Group's cooks, bakers and candlestick makers as well as 5th Division Headquarters and all logistic and communications people. Actually, Team 70, you may have noticed, are advisors to the operations, logistic and communications people. Team 47, located at An Loc, is the advisor team to the province chief. There are some additional forces in the AO that the 5th doesn't control, such as the 92nd Ranger Battalion located here at Tong Le Chon, southeast of An Loc. There are also some special operations people over here at Quan Loi," Miller said, pointing at the location on the map. "The division maintains a tactical command post at An Loc as well, although seldom will you catch Hung up there. He likes his creature comforts too much. We used to have advisors with each of the infantry battalions, but we lost them a while back, unfortunately. I think they made a real difference in the overall training of the battalions. Now, advisor teams are just at the division and regimental levels. Have you had breakfast yet?" Miller concluded.

"No, sir, and I could use a cup of coffee."


## 4 April
## 0530 Hours


Colonel Miller had just woken up to sounds of activity outside the team hooch. It was still dark, but from the sounds outside, it appeared that the entire command group was up and anxious about something. Pulling on his pants and boots, he got up and headed to the door with the intent of taking a quick piss, then finishing dressing and heading over to the command post. As he stepped into the hall, he saw Hank coming back inside.

"What's going on out there?" Miller asked.

"Not sure, sir. Something about Lac Long," Hank said, reaching his sleep area.

"Get your shirt and come with me," Miller ordered, returning to his room and coming out a moment later with his shirt and hat. As they walked out the door, Miller set a fast pace to the command post.

"Lac Long is a small firebase close to the Cambodian border in Tay Ninh Province. It has artillery and at least a battalion of infantry there. Part of the 25th Division. What was said about it?" Miller asked.

"I think they're in a fight, from what I heard," Hank replied as they entered the command post. Hung was already there, listening to the radio traffic. The communication was one-sided as he could monitor what the 25th Division was responding to from the unit in the field but couldn't hear the unit that was at Lac Long. He was smiling slightly as he turned to see Miller.

"See, Colonel Miller? We have nothing to fear. We have no need to reposition forces. It appears that any attack will be in Tay Ninh Province and not in my AO. Good thing I did not listen to you and your advice," Hung said, spitting the word *advice* out. "Some advice. I would have wasted fuel and energy to reposition forces if I had listened to you. American advisors do not know it all."

Miller was ready to punch Hung's lights out but remained a professional soldier. Miller had been a professional soldier his entire adult life, first as an enlisted soldier for ten years and then commissioned, having risen from a second lieutenant to a full colonel.

"Well, General, I'm glad for you, but may I say, this is just the opening round." Miller turned to Hank. "Let's get some breakfast."

Walking out of the command post, Miller turned to Hank. "Major, you're here to observe and that's what I want you to do. Captain Smith and Major Carlson are going to drive up to Loc Ninh this morning. Along the way they're picking up Major Davidson in An Loc. He wants to head into the province chief's compound up at Loc Ninh as Major Blair is on leave in Thailand right now. Lieutenant Colonel Schott is the team leader up at Loc Ninh, but he lets Smith handle most tactical stuff. Smith is on his fifth tour over here, fluent in Vietnamese and a hell of a combat officer. Go up, see what's going on and come back and brief me. How does Loc Ninh look to repulse an attack of a regiment or more? Can you do that for me?" Miller asked.

"Sure, sir, that's right in line with what I'm supposed to be doing over here anyway. Observing the actions up there will give me a good start on evaluating the combat effectiveness of the Vietnamization Program. Let me find Smith and I'll join them."

## 0800 Hours

"Hey, Captain Smith, thanks for the lift," Hank said as he tossed his rucksack into the quarter-ton trailer that the quarter-ton jeep was towing.

Major Carlson was the senior officer between him and Smith, but it was evident to Hank right away that Smith was in charge. Miller had told Hank that, although this was Smith's fifth combat tour in Vietnam, he had also been wounded five times over the years and had every award up to and including the Silver Star, more than one. Just looking at Smith, Hank saw a warrior. Not an ounce of fat on his five-foot-seven frame, with short-cut hair and hollow cheeks. His face was narrow and long. His eyes were sunken sockets. *I'd hate to meet this guy in a dark alley at night*, Hank thought.

As Carlson approached, he likewise tossed his rucksack in the back of the jeep and took the front passenger seat. Hank took the back seat and Smith assumed the duties of driver. In no time, they were heading up Highway 13 north towards An Loc.

Highway 13 was a dirt road, albeit a well-maintained dirt road. Easily wide enough for two vehicles to pass each other and room on the shoulders for oxcarts, bicycles, and pedestrians. Little girls stood on the side of the road selling vegetables, fruit and sodas. If you purchased a soda, you had to drink it right there as the bottle was too valuable to allow it to leave. With few Americans traveling the road, business was way down from the 1960s, when the 1st Infantry Division along with the 1st Cavalry Division and the 11th Armored Cav Regiment had patrolled this stretch of road. As they rolled north, the dust wasn't bad as it was still the rainy season. Not enough rain to turn the road into a mud field, but enough to keep the dust down. Along the sides of the road, some vegetation was beginning to grow back, Hank noted. The 1st Infantry Division had used very large bulldozers with massive plows on the front to clear trees and brush back one thousand meters from the sides of the road when it had occupied the area. This action had cut down on the number of ambush possibilities the local VC had. Without stopping, Hank noticed a compound off to the right side of the road. There was a small airstrip adjacent to the compound.

"What's this place?" Hank asked.

"This is Chon Thanh. It sort of controls the intersection of Highway 13 and Route 14, which goes off towards Tay Ninh Province," Carlson answered. "That's a Regional-Popular Force compound. Whenever the district chief comes and visits, Lieutenant Colonel Corley will accompany him. Colonel Conley is the senior advisor for Team 47. The Binh Long Province chief is Colonel Tran Van Nhut. Damn fine officer. He's down in Vung Tau right now for a province chief meeting but should be back in a couple of days."

As they passed, Hank's attention turned back to the countryside they were passing through. It wasn't a pretty sight. The areas cleared by the bulldozers, or Rome plows as they were referred to, had torn up the ground, leaving behind rotting stumps, skeletons of downed trees and stripped brush.[2] Some new growth was coming up as it had been over three years since the plows had come through. The jungle would reclaim the area eventually; it always did. Shortly after leaving Chon Thanh, Hank could see the outline of a sizable town to the north. He also noticed an increase in the terrain elevation on the sides of the road.

"That's An Loc up ahead," Smith called out, pulling up in front of a building in the center of town.

Major Davidson was standing in front with his rucksack. Smith made the introductions as Davidson climbed in the back next to Hank, tossing his rucksack in the quarter-ton trailer. Smith maneuvered through the streets of An Loc along Highway 13, which passed through the center of town. As he did so, Hank noticed that the buildings were mostly concrete block with stucco and a mixture of one- and two-story buildings with a few three-story. Upper floors appeared to be apartments, with storefronts and shops on the ground floors. Some wooden structures were also present. There were no thatched roofs, however, most being concrete or metal. It appeared that there was central electricity and some telephone communications. Typical of Vietnamese rural towns, chickens were present everywhere, along with kids and dogs. Shops were open and life was normal, or so it seemed.

As they cleared the town, Smith picked up speed and explained that they were on a twenty-kilometer stretch up to Loc Ninh. Along the way and shortly after clearing An Loc, he pointed out the town and base camp of Quan Loi to the east.

"Quan Loi used to be the base camp for one of the brigades of the 1st Cav when they operated up here. Has a good airfield. Right at the end of the airfield is a really nice home for the manager of the rubber tree plantation. Even has an in-ground pool and an attractive wife, or maybe that's a girlfriend. He pays the VC to leave him and the plantation alone. He knows they're in there but can't afford to have the rubber trees blown to pieces, so when they're in the plantation, they generally behave themselves so we don't bomb the crap out of them," Smith said. "Well, shit…"

"What's the matter?" Carlson asked, looking around.

"Isn't that the plantation manager at Loc Ninh's car coming towards us?" Smith noted as a car approached and slowed to a stop. The car was a Citroën, French-built. The driver appeared to be a European gentleman with a rather attractive woman in the front seat next to him. Their faces were masks of apprehension.

"Good day, Mr. Gaudeul," Smith said in English.

"Good day, Captain Smith. We are going to Saigon. I think it is good time to go now. You should consider going to Saigon today too," the plantation manager said, looking in his rearview mirror.

Smith looked up and noticed several people coming down the road from Quan Loi, carrying belongings.

"Sir, is there something you would like to tell me?" Smith asked as his apprehension rose.

"I am telling you it is a good time to vacation in Saigon, now. I must go." He paused. "Good luck to you, Captain Smith. Be safe. You have been a good friend and I wish you well. I go now." And with that, he put the car in gear and hastily departed.

Smith turned, as did everyone else, to watch the car pick up speed and disappear down the road in a cloud of dust. Smith turned back to look at Carlson.

"I've never seen him like that nor had that conversation with him. Not like him to drive down to Saigon. He usually has a plane come in and pick him up for trips there," Smith mumbled to himself.

"What do you make of it?" Hank asked.

"I'm not sure, but let's get up to Loc Ninh," Smith replied. The rest of the trip passed pretty much in silence, but with a sense of heightened vigilance on the part of each officer. Smith mentally noted what he thought was an increase in civilian traffic moving south.

Arriving at Loc Ninh, Smith turned down a road just short of the town that led to the airfield located on the southwest side of town. The town of three thousand people appeared to be deserted for the most part. As he passed the district police station, he noticed the total force of six placing sandbags around doors and windows. The airfield was laid out northeast to southwest. The tree line had been pushed back three hundred meters on the west, and to the south was open terrain with good fields of fire. A slope fell away from the eastern side of the runway towards Highway 13. On the northwest side of the runway, the first compound they came to was the district compound, where Major Davidson hopped out.

"You joining us for dinner tonight, sir?" Smith asked.

"Let me see what George has planned and we'll let you know," Davidson replied. He was referring to Captain George Wanat, the assistant district advisor. "Want me to see if the district chief wants to join us?"

"If you want, Major Sabine should meet him," Smith replied. "Until then, sir."

Smith moved away past the second compound where the artillery was located. Hank took note of the battery of 155mm howitzers and another battery of 105mm howitzers. Arriving at the regimental compound and 9th Regiment command post, Smith pulled up in front of the advisor bunker.

Just then a young Vietnamese soldier trotted up the Smith. He was all smiles. "Dai'uy, you come back okay?"[3] It was more of a statement than a question.

"Yes, Hen, I come back okay," Smith said, almost laughing when he turned to Hank. "Sir, this is Corporal Hen. He's my bodyguard, sort of. Speaks passable English. Follows me like a puppy dog," Smith acknowledged. "Hen, in trailer is package with your name on it. Something I got you in Lai Khe. Enjoy," Smith said, watching Hen's face light up as he started digging through the trailer.

"Thank you, Dai'uy," Hen said, grabbing the small box, which was about the size of a cigar box.

"Hen has a thing for cigars," Smith told Hank. "Okay, Hen, I go advisor hooch. You can go. I no need you anymore today, okay?

"Okay, Dai'uy," Hen responded and took off running to his bunker on the perimeter.

Turning back to Hank, Smith chuckled. "Welcome home, Major Sabine. Grab your gear and I'll show you your accommodations, all very five-star."

"I can just imagine, Captain," Hank replied.

The Loc Ninh advisor compound was originally a Special Forces camp and had been improved over the years. On the compound itself were three rifle companies and the regimental headquarters company. The advisor bunker was really a wooden hooch twenty-five feet wide and fifty feet long. It was divided into separate rooms at one end and a common area at the other end. The wooden siding on the outside was lined up to four feet with sandbags. The remaining wall consisted of screens, and the roof was tin.

"There's an empty bed in this room for you, sir," Smith indicated, walking back to the common area. "You want a beer?"

"Sure," Hank said, dropping his gear and following Smith. Entering the common area, he noticed four other men sitting there.

"Let me do the introductions, sir," Smith announced, turning to an older gentleman. "Lieutenant Colonel Schott, this is Major Hank Sabine. He's a—"

"I know, Colonel Miller called me," Schott said, standing and extending his hand. "Glad to have you join us, Major, and if you need anything, just ask."

"Thank you, sir. I'll try not to get in the way."

Richard Schott was the team chief at Loc Ninh and part

of Advisory Team 70. He had previously been stationed in a staff position in Saigon at MACV headquarters and had requested duty with an advisory team. He didn't have the extensive tactical experience that Smith had, deferring to Captain Smith on tactical matters. He also exercised the policy that a senior officer could protect a junior officer, but a junior officer couldn't protect a senior officer when it came to tact. Schott had already discussed this policy with Miller, who agreed that Smith could be the bulldog when it came to dealing with the 9th Regiment's commander.

Captain Smith continued, "Sir, this is Sergeant First Class Lull, Sergeant Wallingford and Captain Wanat." As Smith introduced each, they acknowledged Hank with a nod. "George, I just dropped Major Davidson off at your place."

"Great, Colonel Corley called and said he was coming up until Blair gets back from leave. Just what I want to be doing, wet-nursing him," Captain Wanat said and quickly added, "No offense meant, sir," looking at Schott.

"None taken, Captain," Schott chuckled.

"Hey, sir, did you bring back any mail?" Sergeant First Class Howard Lull asked.

"Got a whole mailbag of stuff. It's in the jeep if you want to dig it out. Got some soda cases there as well. Sergeant Wallingford, why don't you give him a hand?" Schott offered.

"Yes, sir," Wallingford replied and jumped up from where he had been writing a letter home.

Smith walked over to the community refrigerator and grabbed two cold beers handing one to Hank, who dug in his pocket for some money. "It's free, sir. We get a beer ration up here along with Johnnie Walker scotch. One of the benefits of being an advisor," Smith said, taking a long drag on the cold beer.

"Hey, Mike, have you heard the latest?" Schott asked.

Captain Smith's eyebrows rose. "Sir, what now?"

"Remember how Vinh told Hung that he was going to move two companies of the 3rd Battalion out west? Well, he didn't. He moved them just to the south on the hills to cover any withdrawal by the regiment."

"So who's out west, sir?" Smith asked, attempting to control his temper. "Did he notify Hung that he did that?"

"He has the reconnaissance company out there, and, no, he didn't. I let Colonel Miller know this morning of the change." As Hank and Schott discussed Hank's mission in Loc Ninh, Major Davidson walked in with a Vietnamese officer.

"Hey, Hank, let me introduce you to the district chief here," Davidson said, turning to the Vietnamese officer. "This is Major Nguyen Van Thinh. Major Thinh, Major Sabine, the officer I was telling you about." With that, Thinh approached Hank and extended his hand.

"Good to meet. Come see me and we talk," Thinh said.

"I'd like that and will do so," he replied. The rest of the afternoon was spent with Hank taking a tour of the compound with Captain Smith, Major Thinh and Davidson.

# 4

## RUMBLINGS OF EVENTS



**4 APRIL 1972**
  **Advisors' Compound**
  **Loc Ninh**

"Sir, I'm saying the man is an absolute coward and is probably going to surrender as soon as the enemy makes himself known," Smith was telling his boss, Colonel Schott. "Sir, I told him he needed to move the 2nd Battalion minus one company back here. His response was 'we could survive if we provided the enemy a variety of targets.'[1] I told him we needed to blow that scissor bridge over the river by Bu Dop. You know what his response was? He said that would only piss off the enemy commander, and when he surrenders, he could show that he made it easier for the enemy. He's already planning to surrender. He's a frickin' coward."

Smith was losing his temper. He wasn't saying anything that everyone on the advisory team and at team headquarters didn't suspect. Colonel Nguyen Cong Vinh was viewed as a worthless commander and unsuited for command by the advisory team.[2] But so was the division commander, Brigadier General Le Van Hung. Both had been brought up from the Delta, MR-IV, and were totally unsuited for any kind of war above squad level in the opinions of the advisors. The corps commander, General Minh, had surrounded himself with loyal officers—politically loyal regardless of their ability. The day before, Smith had attempted to convince Vinh to move the 2nd Battalion from FSB Alpha back to Loc Ninh. Vinh told him that he had, only for Smith to discover that he had not. Vinh was of the opinion that if the enemy attacked, they would only attack as far as Alpha and not continue on to Loc Ninh.

"Dai'uy Smith, you come quick now," an excited Corporal Hen said, sticking his head through the doorway to the advisor's hooch. "Come quick, come quick."

As Captain Smith walked outside, the young soldier took off at a run for the regimental command bunker across the compound. Smith jogged behind him, wondering what had Hen so fired up. He didn't have long to ponder that question. When he walked into the command bunker, everyone was standing in a semicircle around the radio section. One radio in particular had everyone's attention. The sounds of rifles popping off and the distinct chatter of the M60 machine gun and the Russian PKM could be heard, as well as the earsplitting sound of exploding grenades.

"Dai'uy, you hear?" asked the regimental operations officer. Vinh was standing next to the radio but said nothing.

In his best Vietnamese, Captain Smith responded, "Who is it and where are they?" He and the operations officer moved to a map. It was typical for a US officer to attempt to speak Vietnamese and have the Vietnamese officer respond in English.

"It rifle company and they here," the operations officer said and pointed to a spot on the map west of Loc Ninh.

Smith knew that the recon company was at that location with the rest of the 1st Battalion, 9th Regiment. "Soldier say this is full regiment and has tanks. They come here soon."

As they stood talking, the sounds of gunfire stopped, but a voice very close to the mike said, "We come soon." No more was heard. *This is not good*, Smith was thinking as he walked back to his bunker and filed a report to Colonel Miller. When done, he headed back to the command bunker.

"Dai'uy, we have prisoner," the operations officer announced when Smith entered. "Company ambush captured. He say he part of 272nd NVA Regiment. He say they part of 9th NVA Division and they bypass Loc Ninh and attack An Loc. 7th NVA to block Highway 13 and prevent reinforcements from Lai Khe. 5th VC Division attack here."

With that information, Smith headed back to his bunker and started cranking out another message to Colonel Miller and briefing the other team members. Before he could finish, he was interrupted.

"Dai'uy Smith," a voice called out from outside.

"Yeah, come in," Smith replied. It took him a second to register who'd just walked in. "Chinh Son?" he asked with surprise and relief.[3] "Damn, sir, it's good to see you. How many did you bring in?" Major Son was the battalion commander for the 1st Battalion, which had been in contact to the west. He had left the compound days before with over four hundred soldiers.

"Dai'uy, many NVA, regiment. Have tanks. I see. They come here. My battalion hurt bad. Only one hundred come back with me. Others all dead. They shoot prisoners," Major Son said with tears in his eyes. Smith attempted to console the man, but he also wanted the word out that the NVA didn't take prisoners. Soldiers fought harder knowing that to surrender was to be killed.

"Sir, why don't you go get some sleep? If they're coming

this way, I'm going to need you in this fight," Smith said, guiding the man to the door. After he left, Smith walked back in.

"So with his hundred soldiers, what does that give you to defend this place?" Hank asked.

"Well, between his people, the RF/PF soldiers here, the reconnaissance company and the headquarters people, about two-fifty."

Under his breath, Hank mumbled, "We're screwed."

## 5 April 1972
### 0300 Hours
### Loc Ninh

"Incoming!" Smith yelled as he rolled off his bunk onto the floor, scattering the cockroaches in every direction.

The 9th ARVN Regiment compound had never seen or felt a bombardment like this before. They had received an occasional single round, but now they were on the receiving end of multiple guns and multiple impacting rounds. People didn't dare come out of their bunkers or their foxholes as they would be cut down by the relentless onslaught of shrapnel. This wasn't heavy artillery but a concentration of mortars. But there was also a new sound that no one could identify.

Schott had relieved Smith earlier in the evening. Schott was in the regimental command bunker and had had Smith go to bed. Smith had felt what was going to happen and hadn't bothered to undress. As soon as the incoming let up, Smith and Hank headed for the command bunker.

"Colonel Schott, soldiers report tanks approaching. Must get Task Force 1-5 out of Firebase Alpha and back here. I call now," Colonel Vinh said, reaching for a hand mike.

"Colonel Vinh, not so fast. It's too late for them to get here and it's safer for them at Alpha. They have an antitank ditch and artillery there," Colonel Schott reasoned.

"No, I want here," Vinh insisted and made the call, ordering the cavalry commander to get back to the regimental compound immediately. Task Force 1-5 consisted of the 1st Armored Cav Squadron with two infantry companies and the 74th Border Rangers Battalion.

"What is going on, Colonel?" Captain Smith asked as he and Hank sprinted through the door. Schott explained the situation with the cavalry commander being ordered back to Loc Ninh.

"Hell, sir, Vinh is just trying to protect his ass," Smith said, turning to Vinh and switching to Vietnamese. Smith wanted to be sure Vinh understood what he was saying. "If you would have done what I asked you to do yesterday, you wouldn't be pissing in your boots now. Another dumbass tactical mistake, Colonel." Turning back to Schott, he asked, "What do you want me to do?"

"See if we can get a Spectre gunship up here now and TACAIR at first light."

"Yes, sir, I'm on it." Smith moved over to the radios to start the request for support. As he was filing his report and requests, another radio began communicating. It was the cav commander. Smith listened as Colonel Vinh and the commander spoke. What Smith heard hit him like a lightning bolt.

The TF 1-5 commander, Lieutenant Colonel Duong, had told Vinh that just after they'd left the compound, it had been ambushed and they were now in heavy contact. He couldn't reach Loc Ninh. He was going to surrender. Vinh agreed, and Smith went ballistic.

"You cowardly son of a bitch, Vinh. You have a yellow streak a mile wide up your back and you'll run at the first chance you get," Smith said, his voice rising from a quiet tone to a scream. Vinh just stood there and presented lame excuses, all leading to him probably surrendering too. Smith had had enough.

He grabbed the hand mike out of Vinh's hand. He made sure he was talking to the cav commander. "Duong, do you understand me?" Smith asked. Smith was fairly fluent in Vietnamese but wanted to be sure what he was about to say was understood.

"I do, Dai'uy Smith," came the reply.

"Good, now you understand this. If you surrender, I'm going to drop every air strike I can call up and put them on you. Do you understand me? *Now*, you fight and don't surrender or so help me God..." You could have heard a pin drop in the tactical operations center as everyone was staring at Smith. There was a fire in his eyes, which were fixed on Vinh, who simply stared at the floor.

Hank just took all this in, taking mental notes as fast as he could. He realized that Smith was in charge at the pleasure of Schott, who was seated and taking it all in himself.

"Captain Smith," Hank said, getting the captain's attention. "What can I do?"

"Sir, right now can you go out and check the perimeter? Vinh may have already issued a surrender order to the line dogs, and I need to know if they're standing or running."

"You got it," Hank said and headed out the door.

A few minutes later, the radio came to life again but with a different voice. It was the commander of the 74th Border Rangers, which had been working with the cav.

Again, Smith took the call. "What's your situation?" he asked, hoping the cav commander was dead.

"The cav surrendered. I have Rangers and we have fight through the roadblock. Moving towards you. The cav go

Cambodia driving tanks, armored personnel carriers and towing the artillery."

"Roger, call me if you need air support," Smith said. Then he switched radios and contacted a forward air controller who had arrived on station.

"Sundog, Zippo Three," Smith called.

"Zippo Three, Sundog."

"Sundog, at X-Ray Uniform Seven-Four-One-Five there's a convoy of US tanks and tracks that the NVA have captured. Need someone to take out that convoy. Over."

"Roger, Zippo Three, Spectre is coming on station and I'll send him up there."

An hour later, Sundog was on the radio. "Zippo Three, Sundog, over."

"Go ahead, Sundog."

"Zippo Three, Spectre tells me they came across a convoy of tanks and vehicles moving north towards Cambodia. Couldn't tell if they were the ones you want us to hit, but he assured me that not one of those vehicles will be crossing into Cambodia. How copy?"[4]

Smith acknowledged the report and turned to Colonel Vinh. "No need to worry about those vehicles attacking you, Colonel...they're all dead," Smith said with sarcasm dripping from every word. Vinh said nothing but again looked at the floor, avoiding Captain Smith's fury.

As the Rangers moved south, fortune smiled on them momentarily.

"Zippo Tree," a Vietnamese voice called on the command radio. Smith recognized it as the Vietnamese Ranger commander.

"This is Zippo Three, what is your situation? Over."

"We cross Road One Tree and One Fur. There is one tank and five Alpha Papa Charlies here abandoned. We take and come you, over."

"Roger, I'll have Spectre cover your move to here. Zippo Three out." Grabbing another hand mike, Smith contacted the FAC and requested that the Rangers' move be covered. He was assured it would be. Smith started to breathe a bit easier, for the moment.

"Zippo Tree," came the voice of the Ranger commander, but Smith was tied up on another radio coordinating air support, so Vinh grabbed the handset.

"We three hundred meters north of your position but have major roadblock. Can you assist?"

Smith held his breath to hear what Vinh's response was going to be. Vinh didn't disappoint him.

"You go back to Alpha. Wait there," Vinh ordered.

Smith went ballistic again. "You stupid son of a bitch!" he screamed and ripped the hand mike out of Vinh's hand. "You!" Smith pointed at the communications sergeant. "Disconnect Colonel Vinh's radios. If this son of a bitch wants to talk to anyone, he's going to have to walk outside and see them." The communications sergeant knew at this point not to cross Captain Smith and did as he was told.

"You," Smith said, pointing at Vinh. "Sit in that chair and don't move, don't open your mouth. You're worthless to this command and a danger to all of us. *Now sit down!*"

Smith called the Ranger commander back and told him to disregard Vinh's order and fight through the roadblock.

For the next hour, the FAC worked tactical air support all around the small garrison but the enemy was moving closer. The sensor operator, located in the TOC, monitored an array of sensors and noted the location of every sensor around the compound. When disturbed, the sensor would send a signal to the sensor operator's console. Almost immediately, every sensor sent a signal, which startled the young man. At first, he thought the system had a malfunction; then he realized that they were surrounded and the enemy was just outside the wire.

Before he could issue a warning, the TOC was rocked by an explosion caused by a 75mm recoilless rifle round. Smith was in the middle of a call and didn't get a chance to finish the conversation as the explosion threw him and Schott to the ground. Both were bleeding from neck and head wounds. Two thousand feet above, General Hollingsworth was watching and orbiting the compound. He had been listening to Smith coordinate the air strikes and suddenly cut off.

"Zippo, this is Danger Seven-Nine, over." After a long pause and no response, the voice repeated, "Zippo, Danger Six, over."

"Danger Seven-Nine, please wait one while I get the holes in my head patched." As SFC Lull was putting a dressing on Smith, Hank came back into the TOC.

"Hate to be the bearer of bad news, but I think we're surrounded. The perimeter is holding, but the entire perimeter is in contact. It appears that the district compound and the artillery compound are both in contact as well." Then he noticed the wound on Smith. "Are you okay?" Hank asked. Smith just nodded.

"Zippo, my apology. Get back to me when you can," Hollingsworth said with honest sincerity. After he was patched up, Smith gave Hollingsworth a quick rundown of the situation.

Between the advisor compound and the district compound was a landline connected to two TA-312 field phones. It was ringing.

"Smith here."

"Dammit, Smith, I can't get any air strikes," Davidson was screaming.

"Sir, I run air strikes for this place. You need one, you pass it to me and I'll give it to the FAC. That's the SOP. Haven't you read it, or hasn't Wanat told you?" Smith asked.

"He told me, but I want to control my own air strikes, dammit."

"Well, that ain't happening, so get over it. Pass the request to me and I'll get it for you. Where's George?"

"He's on the perimeter—" And the line went dead.

As noon approached, Smith continued to work air strikes around the perimeter.

* * *

The 5th ARVN Division Headquarters Forward began to move from Lai Khe on morning of 5 April and closed into An Loc on the 6th. The division engineers had built a command post on the eastern side of the city, close to the train station. Although it was well constructed, Colonel Miller told General Hung that the building couldn't withstand a direct hit from a 130mm round and he wouldn't put the division advisors in there. Miller was taking them back to Lai Khe. Before he could depart, Hung offered an alternative location. Within the city, there was an underground bunker. It had been constructed in World War II during the Japanese occupation. The bunker was large enough and built of poured concrete reinforced with steel. Colonel Nhut had used the facility up until 1970, but when US forces had departed, he'd moved to the abandoned US compound on the south side of the city. The retired Japanese bunker was adjacent to the Binh Long Hospital. This location satisfied Colonel Miller, and the US advisor team stayed.[5]

From this new location, the division staff noted the intelligence reports coming in from Loc Ninh provided by FAC aircraft above and reconnaissance teams that were operating in the area. Intel from JCS and MACV was more big-picture material of an informational nature and not intelligence. One of the first disputes on the conduct of the operation occurred before the move to An Loc.

"General, the battle is at Loc Ninh. We need to reinforce there with the entire division. The 9th Regiment is already there. We can bring up the 8th quickly along with the 5th Armored Squadron and TF-52. Those combined with airpower and we can defeat them north of or at Loc Ninh," Miller argued.

"Colonel Miller, I respect your opinion, but that will not be satisfactory," General Hung countered. "We do not have time to move the forces to Loc Ninh and position them to blunt the enemy moving in our direction. Our supply lines will be very long and easily cut if the enemy should get behind us, while the enemy supply line will be very short and he can easily resupply his forces. Lastly, if the enemy can mass a superior-size force and destroy us at Loc Ninh, we would have no one behind us to stop them from rolling to Saigon. I will agree to reinforce An Loc but not Loc Ninh. Loc Ninh must be our screening force and provide us time to prepare An Loc." As General Hung had the final word, Miller could only accept the decision.

As the intelligence picture developed, it proved Hung correct in his assessment.

* * *

The airspace above Loc Ninh was getting crowded. General Hollingsworth was up in his C&C aircraft, orbiting the battle. The FAC was up at around three thousand feet, orbiting and looking for targets. Fast-moving jets were dropping down from ten thousand feet to plaster targets with bombs and napalm as indicated by the diving FAC. Spectre was orbiting at seven thousand, waiting for targets. This was typical when only one major firefight was going on in a unit's sector. It had actually been worse when US divisions were operating because the C&C aircraft alone would stack up to six thousand feet. Now, Colonel Nhut, the Binh Long Province chief, joined the traffic.

The province chief was responsible for all that happened in his province. All air strikes had to be cleared through his headquarters. Ground units had to clear it with his headquarters prior to maneuvering. Nhut was very concerned about the events unfolding below him. His district compound was at the opposite end of the runway from the 9th Regiment's compound. Between the district compound and the 9th Regimental compound were two batteries of artillery. Those guns were firing both in support of the two compounds and defending themselves by lowering the barrels and firing directly into the attacking human wave formations approaching. In these instances, the 105 howitzers were just giant shotguns firing what was called a beehive round of steel balls.

Nhut had monitored a conversation about trucks towing artillery moving south on Highway 13 north of Loc Ninh. He was concerned about the fact that they might be logging trucks as that was a major industry in the area. He told his pilot to fly north. Sure enough, he spotted the trucks towing logs, and from altitude it appeared to be trucks towing artillery. He didn't approve the air strike and explained to Smith why. As he was explaining his reason for stopping the air strike, he noticed something. Far below were the destroyed remnants of TF 1-5, with burned-out tanks and vehicles marking their last position. He was assured that TF 1-5 vehicles hadn't reached the Cambodian border.

## 5 April 1972
### 0500 Hours

. . .

Colonel Ginger, Captain Zumwalt and Sergeant First Class Winland were assigned as advisors to Task Force 52, part of the 18th ARVN Division located at Xuan Loc. Task Force 52 was attached to the 5th ARVN Division. The 5th ARVN Division had positioned them on Route 17, which ran from Tay Ninh in the west to Highway 13. They were on two old firebases that were very close to each other and only five hundred meters from Highway 13. Life had been fairly quiet until 1 April, when artillery or mortars had started to land on their position, and the intensity had only increased in the past couple of days.

Colonel Ginger maintained his position with the task force command post and had Captain Zumwalt maintain his position at the advisor command post. Sergeant Winland moved between the two. Zumwalt was sitting on the beach in Panama City, sipping a cold beer and watching a young lady in a bikini, at least in his dreams.

"Hey, Captain, wake up," Winland said in a soft voice. Zumwalt lay there for a moment with his eyes closed. *Why do people whisper when they're trying to wake you up?* he was thinking, not wanting to open his eyes.

"Okay, I'm awake," he said, opening his eyes finally. "What's up?" Winland was standing over him with two steaming canteen cups.

"I thought you might like some coffee," Winland said, holding out a cup.

Accepting the cup and propping himself up, Zumwalt asked, "I'll take it, but why would I want a cup of coffee at this ungodly hour? What time is it anyway?"

"Sir, it's 0500. The colonel said to get you up. Seems our night ambush made contact a few minutes ago," Winland said, taking a sip of his coffee.

"No shit. How did they do?" Zumwalt asked with some excitement in his voice as he started to stand.

"Sir, they killed fifteen," he replied.

"Fifteen!" Zumwalt exclaimed, nearly choking on his coffee. "Shit, that's half a damn platoon for the Viet Cong."

"Weren't Viet Cong, sir. They were hard-core NVA."

"No shit. I best call that in to Colonel Miller." Zumwalt started asking detailed questions that he knew Sergeant Winland had the answers to.

## 5 April 1972
## 0630 Hours

Captain Causey walked into the briefing room at Long Thanh and surveyed the flight crews before him. They were mostly young men like himself. To be classified as an "old man," one had to be over thirty years old. No one in this room came close to it.

"Alright, here's what we have. There's some activity up around Song Be. They've requested a light team up there. Mr. Windeler, you'll be mission commander, with Captain Spengler as your copilot. Captain Brown, you and Mr. Jackson will be number two with them," Causey said. "Contact information and coordinates are on the mission sheet." Pausing to check his notes, he continued, "Mr. McIntyre, you'll be backup today. Captain Leach will be your wingman."

The officers named all exchanged looks. Windeler was on his second tour in Vietnam and had previously been an AH-1G pilot. Spengler was also on a second tour. His first was as an infantry officer. He'd graduated from West Point and chosen to follow in his father's footsteps. Coming back from Vietnam, he'd decided that an aviation career was superior to being in the infantry. The living conditions in combat were better and the pay was much better, and so he'd requested flight school. A transition to AH-1G awaited him when he graduated.

A moment later, Causey continued, "FYI, Loc Ninh is surrounded and heavily engaged. The Air Force has been up there all night with Spectre, and TACAIR is pounding NVA positions and ground attacks on the perimeters. I wouldn't be surprised if we got a call to get up there, so that's a 'be prepared' mission for today. You'll want to write this down," he said, pausing for the pilots to get out their grease pencils and acetate-covered maps.

"Ground contact at Loc Ninh is Zippo. The FAC is Sundog. The ADA threat is considered high with twelve point seven, twenty-three and reports of thirty-seven mike-mike, so be careful. You'll be loaded with seventeen-pounders on the inboards and flechettes on the outboards. Any questions?" Causey asked. There were none, and everyone departed for their aircraft.

* * *

"Captain Smith, sir," Sergeant Lull said, getting the captain's attention.

"What's up, Sergeant?" Smith responded. *Lull was supposed to be on the perimeter*, he was thinking.

"Sir, we got tanks approaching. There are two on the tree line to the west."

"Shit, let's take a look." Smith headed for the door, grabbing his steel pot helmet and M16 as he did so.

Colonel Schott followed them out. "Major Sabine, can you stay here and work the command net?" he called over his shoulder as he exited the command bunker.

Moving at a low crouch, Smith, Schott and Lull moved outside and climbed to the top of the highest point in the compound, where a 106mm recoilless rifle was positioned. It was the only antitank weapon in the compound aside from some M72 Light Antitank Weapon (LAW) rockets. Smith found the crew hunkered down, however. They weren't engaging targets. In his best Vietnamese, he told them to get up and start shooting. Now it was a case of who they were more afraid of, the enemy or Smith. The ARVN sergeant decided that Smith was the more dangerous of the two, and they got the gun in working order.

Tapping the section sergeant on the shoulder, Smith pointed out the first T-54 tank to engage. It had left the cover and concealment of the trees and was approaching the compound. One shot, one kill. The second tank was still in the trees, and Smith turned to Spectre to take care of that problem, which it quickly did. Throughout the day, artillery continued to fall on the compound with amazing accuracy. There had to be a spotter someplace adjusting the artillery. Captain Wanat found him. In close proximity to the advisor compound was a very nice two-story stone home that housed the rubber tree plantation manager for that area.

"Hey, Smith," Wanat called over the TA-312 field phone.

"What's up?" Smith replied.

"I'm looking at the manager's house. They have a mortar set up in the back and there's a spotter on the roof of the house. Got anything that can take it out?" Wanat asked.

"Yeah, let me call for an air strike," Smith said and reached for the hand mike to call the FAC. "Sundog, Zippo, over."

"Zippo, Sundog, go ahead."

"Roger, Sundog, there's a mortar position in the backyard at the French house and a spotter on the roof. Got something that can take them out?"

"Zippo, I have two Fox Fours inbound and we can deal with that place in a minute or so."[6]

"Sundog, that sounds—" Smith didn't get to finished

before General Hung cut into the conversation. He was safely tucked away in An Loc.

"Zippo, no request. No can do on French home. No can do," General Hung ordered.

Under his breath, Smith was contemplating what physical torture he could place on Hung if he made it out of the engagement alive. Hearing the request canceled, Colonel Schott grabbed the sergeant in charge of the recoilless rifle and pointed to the house. Moments later, the 106mm rifle served as a giant shotgun and fired into the house. The spotter disappeared and the accuracy of the mortar fire deteriorated rapidly.

Schott returned to the TOC and told Smith to inform Colonel Miller that the French home was no longer a problem.

"Tunnel One-Zero Alpha, Zippo, over."

"Zippo, Tunnel One-Zero Alpha," Colonel Miller replied.

"Tunnel One-Zero Alpha, the French house is no longer a problem, over."

"Understand, Zippo. Be advised, elements at Quan Loi are being extracted as we speak. They were hit hard this morning and their position is untenable. The eight advisors there are coming out as well as a large number of defenders. Two elements will remain for as long as possible. How copy? Over."[7]

Smith and Schott exchanged looks at this information. "Understood, Tunnel One-Zero Alpha," Smith said and placed the receiver on the desk. No words were exchanged, but both officers thought the same thing: *This is not good.*

* * *

Six thousand feet above orbited a small Cessna-built jet designated an A-37B. This little aircraft could be referred to as a bastard child at the family reunion. The 604th Squadron was based at the Bien Hoa Air Base and had been flying missions in Cambodia for clandestine operations. The aircraft had seats for two pilots sitting side by side, but one pilot could easily handle the aircraft. Smaller than its big brothers, like the F-4 Phantom jets, it was a fast plane but could also slow down without falling out of the sky. Stall speed, the speed at which an aircraft stops flying, was 113 miles per hour. The ability to fly at a slower speed made the accuracy of bombing runs superior to that of the Phantom jets, much to the joy of the Bird Dog pilots. And it could carry a considerable load of hard bombs, soft bombs and was equipped with a single 7.62mm Gatling gun in the nose. The B-model was introduced in 1967 and had a refueling probe for air-to-air refueling. The Air Force had been interested in the aircraft in 1964 for support to special operations missions but decided to table the little aircraft. In 1966 it had become obvious that the Air Force was losing too many A-1 Skyraiders and needed a replacement. The official name for the aircraft was Dragonfly.

"Hawk One, Sundog, over."

"Sundog, Hawk One, over."

"Hawk One, when you complete this run, return to home base."

"Roger, understood," Lieutenant Wilnich said as he shoved the nose down into a thirty-degree dive at the dense rubber trees outside the wire at Loc Ninh airfield. In that shallow of a dive, the biggest problem the pilot would have was target fixation. The other problem was the amount of green tracers that were passing by his aircraft from the vicinity of the target. Lieutenant Wilnich could observe his target through his dive, which in this case was reported to be tanks in the tree line. Closing in, he was able to see at least one of the tanks. He and his wingman had come home more than once with tree limbs hanging on the bottom of the aircraft. Dropping the five-hundred-pound Mk-82 bombs, Wilnich pulled out of the thirty-degree dive, pulling 4gs and heading back up to six thousand feet and a 180-degree heading for Bien Hoa.

Landing on the huge runway at Bien Hoa, the tiny Dragonfly could be compared to a Cessna 150 landing at O'Hara International airport with its massive passenger jets. The pilot taxied to a parking place and shut down the two General Electric J85-GE-17A turbojet engines, and the ground crew immediately began servicing the aircraft.

"Lieutenant, they told me to tell you to get to the ready room as soon as you shut down. You're going right back out again. We were told to load you with CBU for this trip," the armament NCO said. The cluster bomb unit was a hollow shell with two thousand BLU-3 fragmentation bomblets inside. When dropped at a predesignated altitude, the casing opened, dropping the bomblets. Initially it was designed as an antipersonnel and light vehicle weapon. Walking into the ready room, Wilnich grabbed a cup of coffee and a sandwich. They had been prepared earlier in the day and were constantly replenished.

"Hey, Pete, what you got for me now?" Wilnich asked the operations officer.

"More of the same. As soon as your aircraft is ready, you and McDermott will be going back to Loc Ninh. We're loading him with hard bombs and you with cluster. How's the AA fire up there?"

"It sucks is the only way to describe it. A lot of .51-cal but also at least one 23mm and one 37mm. Didn't hear any radar tracking, however," Wilnich explained.

"Okay, be safe and get back up there as soon as you can."

After a piss break and with something in his stomach, Wilnich went over the mission with McDermott. McDermott would fly wingman and the number two position. Once the decisions were made, they returned to their aircraft. The little A-37B sat so low to the ground that it was easy for a pilot to step into the aircraft. As he did so, the crew chief would hold the two shoulder straps while the pilot eased into the seat. Seldom was the second seat occupied.

Flipping the battery switch on, Wilnich pushed the button to start engine number one. When power was at fifteen percent, he applied the gas and the power began to rapidly climb. At forty-five percent, engine number two came to life and Wilnich began to pull out of the hangar.

"Bien Hoa Ground, Hawk One, scramble two. Over."[8]

"Hawk One clear to taxi."

Wilnich turned to face his crew chief and rendered a smart salute. Rolling down the taxiway, Hawk Two was right behind Wilnich, monitoring the radios. As Wilnich was flight lead, McDermott was relieved of the duties of having to talk to the controllers. His conversations were with artillery control centers for clearance to An Loc.

As they approached the end of the runway, and before taking the active runway, Bien Hoa Tower instructed, "Hawk One, you are cleared for takeoff." The two little birds didn't stop but simply rolled out on the runway and gave full throttle to the engines. In a very short distance, both aircraft were in the air and wheels up.

Cruising at four hundred miles per hour, the flight of two was back over Loc Ninh in about twenty minutes. From the looks of things at that altitude, the situation didn't look good. Wilnich could see movement in the town itself, and it wasn't cars he was looking at. It was tanks, and more than just a few.

* * *

During the day, things quieted down to only an occasional mortar round impacting on the compound. Smith was talking to Sundog and had his attention focused on the map. Colonel Vinh was passing out soda to people in the TOC and speaking with his security detail. *That's about all you're good for, Vinh,* Smith thought.

Suddenly, the security detail broke into a run through the door outside. *I guess the first of the deserters are his security folks,* Schott concluded, only to be surprised when they walked back in. They resumed sitting on the floor, taking up space and oxygen. *Wonder what the hell that was all about.*

A few minutes later, he found out.

"Hey, Captain, who the hell opened the front gates to the compound?" Hank asked, coming in from inspecting the perimeter.

"What the hell are you talking about?" Smith replied, perplexed by the question.

"The front gate to the compound is wide open."

Smith immediately looked around until he spotted Vinh, who quickly avoided eye contact and attempted to slink off.

"Vinh, you piece of shit. Did you have your goons open the gates?" Smith screamed. "Don't bother to answer, you piece of shit, just tell me why," Smith said, almost trembling, ready to beat the senior officer to death.

"Gate open we can leave faster," Vinh said.

"Vinh, if you run, I will put a bullet in your head," Smith said, getting right up to Vinh's face. Vinh knew the American captain was dead serious.

* * *

The flight of two Blue Max aircraft had been working in the Song Be region. Blue Max was the call sign for the 2nd Battalion, 20th Aerial Rocket Artillery Aviation Unit.

"Blue Max Three-Six, change of mission. We've been directed to proceed to Loc Ninh and join up with Blue Max Three-Eight. We will refuel at Song Be and load up on armament. I'll get us clearance into Song Be," Windeler transmitted.

"Understood, Three-Four," Captain Brown responded.

Refueling and topping off on rockets, 40mm grenades and 7.62 ammo at Song Be was uneventful, and the aircraft departed, heading west to Loc Ninh, about thirty miles away. As the aircraft approached Loc Ninh, Windeler gave the call signs and frequency for the ground contact, which Brown quickly dialed in. From the sounds of things, a major fight was in progress. Two other Blue Max aircraft were going to join them. Windeler would be the overall air mission commander and gave the brief.

"Flight, we have an ADA position at..." And he read off the coordinates, which each of the aircraft commanders wrote down with grease pencils on the side of the canopies. "It's suspected to be a 12.7 mike-mike position and there are some .51-cals reported around it. We'll start our run at three thousand. I'll go first. Max Three-Six, follow me."

Looking at the location on the map, it appeared to be a heavily treed area. Arriving over it confirmed that the area was in fact under trees. As the aircraft approached, Windeler contacted elements on the ground.

"Zippo, this is Blue Max Three-Four, over."

"Blue Max Three-Four, this is Zippo, go ahead."

"Zippo, Blue Max is a flight of four approaching your location. Where do you want it?" Windeler asked as he looked down from six thousand feet. At that altitude, he could see smoke at many points around the airfield and compounds but not the fine detail of individuals. He could see the green and red tracers crisscrossing the airfield, however.

"Blue Max, put it on the northeast side of the airfield. Right now that's where our heaviest contact is at. Over."

"Roger, understand the northeast side of the airfield. Where are the nearest friendlies? Over."

"Blue Max, nearest friendlies are on the west side of the airfield in the compounds. Over."

"Roger, we'll be starting our approach in five mikes." Switching frequencies, Windeler contacted his wingmen. "Hey, Three-Six, Three-Eight, Four-Oh, did you monitor?"

"Roger, right behind you. I'll cover you on your first pass. You cover me on mine," Captain Brown transmitted.

"Four-Oh, monitored," Captain Leach transmitted.

"Three-Six, Three-Eight will follow you."

As Brown watched the aircraft move into position to attack the target, he was thinking how nice it was to work with some real professionals. The commander had handpicked each pilot for his unit, accepting only experienced pilots or ones who'd had a previous ground tour in Vietnam.

"You got it. Setting up now." Windeler orbited the northeast end and watched for a minute. Watching and following the green tracers back to their point of origin, he identified a grove of trees. "Hey, Three-Six, you see that grove of trees there?"

"Yeah, is that going to be your target?" Brown asked.

"Roger, I'm concerned with the grove just to the south of that one. That's where I think the ADA is located. There's no fire coming out of it and I can't believe there's no one there. How about you hit that with the guns while I concentrate on the grove?" Windeler ordered.

"You got it," Brown said as Mr. Windeler executed a ninety-degree left turn and dropped the nose of the aircraft into a forty-five-degree dive. The vertical speed indicator immediately dropped to show a rate of descent of fifteen hundred feet per minute.

As the aircraft settled with the target squarely on the nose, Windeler started punching off rockets two at a time and managed to salvo twelve pairs in his dive. Spengler, in the front seat, slaved the nose-mounted minigun and 40mm grenade launcher to his target and placed a stream of 7.62 rounds into the area until Windeler started to raise the nose. The g-force pressed both pilots into their seats. Windeler used a combination of full torque and bleeding airspeed to quickly climb back to altitude while watching Three-Six's dive. As they did so, Spengler engaged the trees with his miniguns to cover Three-Six.

"Three-Six, that looks good. What do you think? I still have fifty-two rockets on board. What say we hit them again?" Windeler queried as he watched the other two Blue Max aircraft strike the target area.

"Three-Four, sounds good. Three-Six right behind you."

Windeler had them in a good position to begin his run and immediately nose over. As they plunged downward, though, something didn't seem right. Suddenly Three-Six witnessed what appeared to be green flaming basketballs rising up and passing his aircraft on one side, slowly at first and then with incredible speed.

"Three-Six, I think I just took a hit," Mr. Windeler said in a calm, almost chuckling voice. Three-Six pulled out of his dive and looked skyward towards Three-Four, who was returning to altitude.

"Windy! You're on fire! Get it down! Get it down!" Three-Six said as he watched the smoke trailing behind Three-Four.[9]

Windeler immediately started descending rapidly, diving for the ground. Flames appeared around the side of the stricken aircraft, streaming back along the bottom. Captain Brown and Mr. Jackson watched in stunned silence as the stricken aircraft's tail boom flexed where it joined the fuselage of the aircraft. At three hundred feet, the aircraft came apart with the tail boom falling from the fuselage, the main rotor spinning off and the fuselage plunging into the rubber trees. The explosion told Brown and Jackson that no one had made it out of that aircraft.[10]

* * *

While Blue Max was taking the fight to the NVA over the district compound, Winland and Hank engaged the attackers. NVA infantry and tanks approached the compound from the west through the trees. Hank was positioned with the 106mm recoilless rifle team attempting to engage two tanks. One of the tanks fired on the TOC, scoring a direct hit. The explosive impact penetrated the walls of the TOC.

Dazed, Smith started to pick himself up off the floor. "Is everyone alright?" he asked, looking around. Corporal Hen was beside him, assisting him to his feet. Through the dust, he could see others moving. What he didn't see moving was Colonel Schott.

"Sir, sir—wake up, sir!" Smith yelled, gently rolling the colonel over onto his back. The gash on the side of the colonel's head told Smith that he was not alright. Finally, Colonel Schott opened his eyes, attempting to grasp what had happened.

"Sir, are you okay? Just lay there for a moment. Let me dress that wound," Smith said, grabbing his field dressing.

As he did so, Major Carlson came through the door, looking around. "Damn, I thought you all would be dead," he exclaimed. "Smith, you're bleeding. Let me take care of that," he added, taking the dressing from Smith and finishing dressing Colonel Schott's wound.

"What happened?" Schott asked, still attempting to process the events.

"We took a direct hit from an artillery round, but the roof held," Smith replied while wrapping the colonel's head. "Sir, you have a nasty head wound. Just lay here for a few minutes. You're probably going to have a hell of a headache, I suspect."

"I'll be alright, Captain," Schott stated as he attempted to sit up. "Well, maybe I will just lay here for a few minutes. Sure glad you're here, Captain."

* * *

"Hung, you have got to face reality here. The main attack is coming to An Loc. We have almost no one here defending this place except the Ruff-Puffs. And the 3rd Ranger Regiment," Miller said, pointing at a map on the table. "The 7th Regiment minus is at FSB 1, six klicks away. Move them back to here now and provide some defense to An Loc. Also move Task Force 52 back to here and the force at the Cam Le Bridge."

"No, the 7th will be in position to stop a force moving from the west against An Loc. And Task Force 52 can move to reinforce either Loc Ninh or the 7th when the time is right," Hung argued.

"General, how the hell do you expect one regiment sitting on FSB 1 to be able to stop probably three regiments with tanks? They can't. All they're going to do is die and grease the wheels on the tanks with their guts. You've got to move the 7th and do it now!" Miller was almost pleading and screaming. Hung just stood there looking at the map. *My God, the man is paralyzed with indecision*, Miller was thinking. After a moment, he asked, "General?"

"Alright, I will issue the order to move the 7th Regiment back to An Loc right away. I will wait, however, on moving Task Force 52 or the force at Cam Le Bridge," Hung said with some resignation.

"Thank you, General," Miller said and followed up with, "Why don't you and I fly back to Lai Khe in the morning so we can consult with your staff and maybe talk with General Minh?"

"Yes, we do that. Now we can get B-52 to bomb around Loc Ninh, yes?" Hung asked.

"No, no B-52 now. We aren't sure where all your people are located. Can't be dropping bombs unless we know where everyone is."

This discussion would last for an hour, with Hung finally realizing that he wasn't getting a B-52 strike.


## 2200 Hours


"Colonel Miller, Zippo is on the horn for you," the RTO said.

"Zippo, Tunnel One-Zero Alpha, how you doing? Over."

"Tunnel One-Zero Alpha, we're hanging in there," Zippo reported and commenced to give Colonel Miller a summation of the day's events.

Miller could tell from just listening to Smith that he was exhausted. Miller was disheartened by the loss of the Blue Max aircraft but glad that the perimeter still held. Smith didn't have to tell him that the town of Loc Ninh was under the control of the enemy and only the compounds along the airfield were still manned. It had been a long day, but they were still in the fight.

**5**

---

# COMMAND DECISIONS

**6 APRIL 1972**
  **Colonel Nhut's Office**
  **An Loc**

Colonel Nhut flew back from Loc Ninh following Highway 13. What he saw disturbed him. The road was crowded with every vehicle, cart, and bike imaginable and they were all moving in one direction, south towards An Loc. *We're going to have to plan for a population of over fifteen thousand at this rate*, he was thinking. Upon landing, he assembled his staff.

"I just flew down Highway 13 and there's a tide of humanity approaching. The refugee flow coming this way is going to overwhelm us if we don't take immediate action. Mr. Tai, I understand you were the last car to come from Lai Khe and you were shot at. Is that correct?" he asked his public works director. He knew the answer but wanted the others to hear it as well.

"That's correct, Colonel," Tai answered.

"That indicates that we're about to be surrounded and cut

off from relief, and supplies. By my estimates, we're going to need thirty tons of rice per day for both the military and civilian population. We're going to need housing for those coming in. Father Huynh, can you set up a refugee collection point at the central train station and plan on housing refugees in the church?" he asked. Father Huynh simply raised his head with a smile in acknowledgment that he understood his mission.

"We need to make sure that any refugees coming into town are in fact refugees and not infiltrators. I will expect the police to be assisting in this effort. Also, I believe we should round up our known and local VC now. They've never been a bother in the past, but this is different. Let's make that a priority and get it done. Also, some of this incoming artillery has been accurate. Let's monitor radio frequencies to see if anyone is transmitting from here with forward observers," Colonel Nhut said, looking at the police chief.

"I already have our radio intercept team working on that one," the police chief said. "I may need help from the Popular Forces in manning checkpoints to screen refugees," he responded.

"I will arrange that. Now," Nhut said as he paused and looked as some notes before him, "let the people know that it is time for them to move to their underground shelters. Loc Ninh has fallen or will shortly and then the enemy will be coming here. They have unmercifully shelled Loc Ninh and we can expect the same here." The local newspaper owner was in the back. He had always been a skeptic of anything the government put out and didn't disappoint Nhut on this occasion.

"Excuse me, Colonel, but aren't you overplaying this? Always in the past when the NVA have launched attacks, Tet of '68 for example, their goal was to win the hearts and minds of the people. They do not do that by simply murdering civilians and destroying their homes. Never before have they shelled towns and villages seriously. Do you really think they will do that here?" he asked.

Several responses passed through Nhut's mind, but now wasn't the time to unload on the press. He was going to need them in the days to come.

"Sir, you are correct. In the past they have spared the civilian population, but this time it is different. This time from what I have seen at Loc Ninh, they are out to punish the people for not supporting them in the past. The deliberate destruction that they are inflicting up there tells me that the civilian population is just in the way of their plans to gain territory and destroy the Army. I pray they will spare us, but I want everyone in their shelters. If I am wrong, all it cost was some nights of uncomfortable sleep," Nhut explained, hoping that his response set the correct tone for the press. Already suspecting the newspaper owner of being a VC sympathizer, Nhut changed the subject before he could ask another question.

"Doctor, how are you set with medical supplies?"

"Colonel, I have a five-day supply of medicine for the civilian population. If we have any military or wounded refugees arrive, I will go through that fairly quick. Bottom line, I do not have enough for what may be coming. The Binh Long Hospital has beds for one hundred and twenty people. I suspect we are going to use all those and then some. I will look at setting up something at the church and the central train station for the less serious wounds," Dr. Khe said.

"I will notify Saigon to be sure and send up more medical supplies. Please give my secretary a list of what you want."

"Communications," Nhut said, looking for the head of the phone company.

"Our communications are good with Saigon, and land-lines are all functioning. We have radio communications as backup if the landlines are cut. That will let us maintain contact with Saigon, but no routine traffic will be allowed. If that time comes, then I will personally decide who can get messages out. We will be operational around the clock," he added.

"Sir," Mr. Bui Huu Tai said, gaining Colonel Nhut's attention.

"Yes."

"Sir, water may be a problem," Tai said.

"Why?"

"Two reasons. First, we need electricity to run the pumps that draw the water from the wells and distribute it. Right now our generators are functioning very well, but if they get hit or if they run out of fuel, then we lose electricity throughout the city. Those pumps for the wells do not have separate generators. Second, our wells can only handle so much capacity. If our population swells, then we will have to start a rationing program. If the population balloons, especially if the military sends in a lot of troops, then we will suck the wells dry," Tai explained.

"What is our fuel situation for the generators?" Nhut asked.

"Right now it is good. We have enough for a thirty-day period as we were just supplied last week. If we have blackout periods, I can double that time," Tai said.

"Good. What do you recommend as the blackout period?" Nhut asked, excited that a solution was already being presented.

"Oh, I think from seven at night until seven in the morning should be sufficient," Tai answered.

Nhut was at a loss for words, but his excitement at the news was visibly absent. Turning to the communications director, he instructed, "Start announcing that everyone needs to start filling every container they have with water and placing them in their bunkers." The town had a centrally managed public address system. These were large speakers spread throughout the town that could address the population in times such as these. The system had proven useful when installed by the Japanese to announce air raids by Allied bombers in World War II. Since then, Nhut's predecessors had maintained and even upgraded the system.

An Loc had been a target for Communist forces since World War II, first by the Viet Minh and then the Viet Cong. Over the years, the RF/PF compound had been attacked by both ground forces and indirect fire, as had the American Special Forces camp. The local population had prepared underground shelters for their own safety, never really expecting to use them to the extent that they were about to. Most of the shelters were basements that had been reinforced and were suitable for hour-long stays or maybe even as an overnight refuge. Few family shelters were designed and equipped for what was about to come.

"Major," Nhut said, addressing the commander of the RF/PF force.

"Sir?"

"Major, we have a good supply of M72 light antitank rockets. I want you to distribute those to every one of your soldiers and give every one of them a training class on how to use the things, and I want that done by close of business tomorrow. Also, I want an announcement broadcast that anyone who wants a weapon to defend their homes can get one, and if they will take an M72, give it to them with a class on how to us it. Understood?" Nhut asked.

"Yes, sir. Understood," the major responded.

"Colonel Thanh," Nhut focusing on his deputy, "let's consolidate all building materials in the city—lumber, concrete, wire to include barbed wire. We may need it to reinforce defensive positions." Thanh acknowledged with a nod.

"Alright, gentlemen, we all have an idea of what we need to do. I want us to meet each morning and evening to go over the events of the day and our situation. I believe we have some trying times ahead, but we will be alright. We just need to remember that we are here for the people. Let's keep them foremost in our actions and thoughts," Nhut concluded and dismissed everyone.

Picking up the phone, he made the call to General Hung, who was in An Loc for the day, monitoring the situation in Loc Ninh.

"General Hung, may I come and see you now?" Nhut asked. Hung was not in Nhut's chain of command, but Nhut knew he needed to show a level of respect to the man.

"Yes, Colonel, I will be expecting you. We need to discuss some things," Hung replied. Five minutes later, Nhut was walking into the 5th Division command post. Colonel Corley accompanied Nhut for this visit. As the two Vietnamese officers spoke, Corley and Miller stayed on the sidelines and listened.

"General Hung, I have been looking at the situation and reevaluating our defenses here at An Loc. Currently, we only have the Regional and Popular Forces here. Based on what I am hearing from Loc Ninh, if the enemy attacks, I do not have the forces to stop them from seizing An Loc," Nhut stated.

"Colonel Miller and I have discussed this, but the priority right now is Loc Ninh," Hung said with some frustration. "Right now, the 7th Regiment minus two companies, which are at Quan Loi, is located only seven kilometers southwest of here. The 8th Regiment is over in Dau Tieng and the 9th Regiment is at Loc Ninh. What do you expect me to do?"

"Sir, I currently have on platoon one kilometer north of the airfield on this hill," Nhut said, pointing at the map on the table in front of them. "From here they can observe about four kilometers to the north, which will give us some warning time. Could you move the 5th Reconnaissance Company there to reinforce that platoon?" Nhut asked. Hung moved closer to the map and studied it for a moment.

"I'll consider that and get back to you, Colonel."

"Thank you, sir. I also have the 254th Regional Force Company operating in the Van Hien village east of the city, which is twelve kilometers to the east. I am going to pull them back to this hill, Hill 169. From here they can monitor any enemy movement from the south or east," Nhut said.

Looking closer at the map and Hill 169, Hung replied, "That hill does offer some strategic importance....yes....I think that would be a wise move, Colonel."

"Thank you, sir, and I will issue the order right away. I have also instructed my deputy, Lieutenant Colonel Nguyen Thong Thanh, to consolidate all construction material in the city, to include lumber and wire of any kind that we could use for obstacles and defensive preparations. We can make this available to your forces as well should they need them," Nhut offered.

"Thank you, Colonel. I will have my logistics officer coordinate with your deputy. Is there anything else?" Hung asked.

"No, sir. I will keep you informed of the situation in the town. Good day," Nhut said, saluting and glancing at Colonel Covey. They both left. Hung stood for a moment and studied the map. As he did so, he could hear the radio traffic from the fighting at Loc Ninh. He could also hear Colonel Miller's words to him about what he needed to do to defend An Loc should the NVA not stop at Loc Ninh. He walked back to his private office and picked up the phone. "Get me General Minh, please," he asked the operator. A few moments later, General Minh answered.

"Hung, what is the situation up there?" Minh asked.

"Sir, Loc Ninh is still in the fight, but I am becoming concerned about An Loc. If the enemy takes Loc Ninh, then right now we do not have much here at An Loc to defend with. I need to move the 8th Regiment back to An Loc and would like reinforcements of the 3rd Ranger Group if possible," Hung requested. Minh did not answer right away.

Finally, he replied, "Hmmm....the 8th is your regiment and you may do as you wish with them. Getting them back to An Loc may be a smart move right now. If we move the 3rd Ranger Group, how soon would you want them?"

"Sir, as soon as you can get them to me. They will need time to establish a defense before the enemy may hit us," Hung said, not wanting to appear anxious, but he was beginning to feel that way. Nhut's comments about the lack of forces in An Loc were beginning to trouble him.

"Let me talk to the staff and I will get back to you on the question of moving the 3rd Ranger Group to you. I will call you back," Minh said and hung up. Hung walked back out into the operations area and continued to monitor activities at Loc Ninh, but not for long.

"General Hung, General Minh is on the phone for you," Major Borstorff, the G-3 advisor, said, handing a receiver to him.

"General Hung, sir."

"Hung, we are sending the 3rd Ranger Group to you. They are moving to the airfield in Tay Ninh and will fly to your location tomorrow," Minh said.

"Sir, would it be possible to get one battalion flown in today? They could begin to survey the position for the group and begin establishing the defense," Hung asked. There was a long pause from Minh as Hung could hear him talking to someone in the background.

Finally, Minh said, "General, the 31st Ranger Battalion will be arriving late this afternoon or early this evening by Chinook helicopters. Be ready to receive them. Anything else?"

"No, sir, and thank you. Good day, sir," Hung said and handed the phone back to Major Borstorff. *That was much easier than I thought it would be*, Hung thought as he returned to looking at the map. He did not know that Hollingsworth and Miller had both talked to Minh about moving forces to An Loc.

**6**

---

# DIFFICULT DAY

**6 APRIL**
**0100 Hours**

"Spectre, Sundog, over."

"Sundog, go ahead."

For the past twenty-four hours, a FAC had been on station above Loc Ninh, providing whatever air support he could. They had been rotating aircraft and pilots from the beginning. After dark, Spectre was one of the best aircraft to have looking over you as he had the loiter time and the equipment to really make life miserable for attacking infantry. At six thousand feet, Hawk One were a couple of A-37Bs from the 604th Squadron. They had ordnance to deliver.

"Spectre, Sundog, we have people in the wire on the west and southwest side of the compound. Zippo wants to know if you can light up the western perimeter. He has tanks moving from the southwest and would like you to deal with them. How copy? Over."

Before Spectre could respond, Hawk One broke in.

"Break, Sundog, Hawk One has good copy. Spectre, can we get illum over the target?"

Interupting the conversation, a new voice joined the conversation.

"Sundog, this is Army Ace Card One-Five. I'm approaching your location with a load of flares. I can drop from two thousand feet and light up the area for the next six-zero minutes. Wind direction and drift will put me dropping north of the town and should be out of the way for Spectre and Hawk. How copy?" Ace Card was a UH-1H helicopter from Alpha Company, 229th Aviation Battalion. They were part of the 3rd Brigade, 1st Cav Division, that had been left when the division had departed and were now operating as an independent brigade north of Saigon.

"Ace Card One-Five, I have good copy. Break, Spectre and Hawk, how does that sound to you?" Sundog asked.

"Spectre is good with that."

"Hawk is good. I'll be making my runs from southeast to northwest, over."

"Ace Card, did you copy?" Sundog asked.

"Roger, I'll be in position in one-zero mikes."

Almost to the minute, the first one-million-candlepower flare ignited at two thousand feet and lit the entire area up. Both Spectre and Hawk could clearly see their targets, as could the ARVN soldiers on the perimeters. For the rest of the night, and until about 0500 hours, the fighting was intense, but the Air Force had broken the attack. As the sun rose, the defenders witnessed the grisly sight of dead NVA soldiers in the wire and the fields beyond. Smith continued to work air strikes west and southwest of the compound.


**0700 Hours**

. . .

The flight from An Loc back to Lai Khe was short. Hung and Miller, especially Miller, wanted to discuss the situation with the 5th ARVN Division staff and get the latest intel update. While there, Hung and Miller met with the commander of the 8th Regiment about his possible move to An Loc. They were about to leave when General Hollingsworth arrived.

"What's the situation up at Loc Ninh?" Holly asked. He had the nickname since he'd commanded tanks under Abrams in World War II.

"Sir, the 9th CP is surrounded, as is the district headquarters. The town is occupied by a possible regimental-size force. Zippo is working air strikes since 0100 this morning," Miller said, giving him a quick rundown.

"Okay, I'm flying up there to get a look. Why don't you two come with me? We can talk on the flight up," Holly offered. His offer was polite and he knew it wouldn't be refused.

Climbing back into Holly's UH-1H aircraft, they took off for An Loc. Flying at four thousand feet, the pilot was dodging scattered low clouds.

"Excuse me, General," the aircraft commander said over the intercom system.

"What's up, Chief?" Hollingsworth responded.

"Sir, are those your vehicles down there on Highway 13 by Chon Thanh?"

Hollingsworth moved forward between the pilots' seats to see where the pilot was looking. He didn't like what he was seeing. "Can you take us down to two thousand feet, Chief?"

"Yes, sir," the pilot replied and immediately commenced a circling descent. The lower he got, the more Hollingsworth's fears were confirmed.

"No, Chief. Those aren't ours—head for An Loc," the general ordered and turned to Hung. "Hung, there's an NVA column across Highway 13. Nothing is going up that road now to An Loc. We're going to have to resupply by air. You best start thinking about the situation and take some action," he pointed out.

He held up his open hand. "One, Loc Ninh is under siege and will probably be overrun tonight or tomorrow," he said, curling one finger down. "Two, Task Force 52 is under attack." Another finger curled. "Three, Quan Loi has contact." Another finger went down. "Four, the 7th Regiment is in contact, attempting to move to An Loc." The thumb was all that was left. "And now, the NVA has cut Highway 13. You have got to reposition your forces *now*," Holly said, bringing his closed fist down into the palm of his other hand.

## 1400 Hours

Once back at An Loc, Hollingsworth dropped off Miller and Hung, expecting Hung to do as he was "advised." But with Hollingsworth having departed, Hung had his own ideas of what should be done and so issued an order through his command channels, which were a bit different from what had been discussed with Hollingsworth.

"Cornish Six-Seven, Tunnel One-Zero Alpha," Colonel Miller transmitted. At first he thought his transmission wasn't received by Lieutenant Colonel Ginger, the senior advisor with TF-52.

"Tunnel One-Zero Alpha, Cornish Six-Seven," was finally heard.

"Tunnel One-Zero Alpha, my counterpart wants your unit to send one battalion to reinforce Zippo's units. What is your opinion? Over," Miller asked.

"Tunnel One-Zero Alpha, I was just discussing that with

my counterpart. Piecemeal commitment, militarily dumber than dirt. Send the entire task force or none, over."

"Cornish Six-Seven, I agree, but there's no dissuading him. Who you sending?"

"It'll be 2nd Bat, and Cornish Five-Seven will travel with them, over."

"Roger, tell him to be careful. Tunnel One-Zero Alpha out." Miller put the hand microphone down and went looking for Hung. *Ginger's right—this piecemeal commitment is dumber than dirt.*

* * *

Hank had been doing what he could to help out Smith, who was in charge even though he was only a captain surrounded by majors. Hank was starting to make an assessment of the Vietnamization Program from where he sat and it was not good—in part because of the quality of the advisors he was witnessing. Lieutenant Colonel Schott was the senior officer but had delegated responsibility to a captain over the majors. The majors were providing little assistance, with one being at the district compound. He didn't appear to be influencing the battle but was constantly on the field phone, berating Smith as he felt Smith wasn't providing air support. The other major was in the inner perimeter and not at the tactical operations center until Smith and Schott were wounded, and then only to administer first aid. He had done little to assist Smith in managing the battle. The captain at the district compound appeared to be a warrior, darting out of the operations center to check the perimeter, encourage the soldiers and provide info to Smith on where air strikes were needed.

As Hank stood surveying the action along the perimeter, his eye caught someone jogging over wearing civilian clothes.

"Hey, Major, how goes it?" the man asked with a French accent.

"Who the hell are you and where did you come from?" Hank asked in surprise.

"The name is Dumond, Michel Dumond. I'm a reporter. I was in the village and could only get out of there this morning, and I have been working my way here. I'm finding some rather good photos here," Michel said, ducking his head a couple of times. "Captain Smith invited me up here a couple of days ago, and when he went down to Lai Khe, I decided to wander over to the village and take some pictures. I was at the police station when this all started and they told me to stay put."

"How are they doing over there?" Hank asked, knowing the six police officers probably hadn't lasted long.

"They were pretty much left alone until last night. They then told me to get out and make my way to you. They were told to surrender or a tank was going to blow their place away. I slipped out the back while they walked out the front. They were shot after they came out."

"That's what we all can expect. You best make your way to the TOC and stay there," Hank said, leading the way.

## 1700 Hours

"Zippo, Spectre, over."

"Go ahead, Spectre," Smith answered.

"Zippo, there's an anti-aircraft gun in the town square on a wheeled vehicle. Over."

"Spectre, if you can take it out without collateral damage, do so. I don't want to hit it with fast movers. Trying to save the town, over."

"Zippo, not a problem. We can take care of it in one mike, over."

"Roger, Spectre, you are cleared to engage."

A few minutes later, Smith heard, "Zippo, target is neutralized. No collateral damage, over."

"Understood, Spectre."

Smith returned to studying the map, assessing the reports of contacts coming in and deciding how he was going to deal with each threat. Vinh continued to sit in the TOC and do nothing. As Smith and Schott and Hank were discussing the situation, another call came in for Zippo.

"Zippo, this is Sundog, over."

"Sundog, this is Zippo, over."

"Zippo, I'm over the north end of the runway. It appears that the NVA have lined up the women and children from the village and are marching them down the road towards your location. There's a body of NVA right behind them, over." Smith, Schott and Hank exchanged looks of shock.

"I heard about the commies doing this in Korea but never here," Hank said.

"Let's get up on the bunker and see this," Schott directed as he headed for the door. Smith and Hank were right behind him, with Corporal Hen bringing up the rear. Reaching the top, Hank couldn't believe what he was seeing. Some women and all the children from the village were slowly walking towards the compound. One of the kids was carrying an American flag. The NVA were right behind them, herding the group towards the compound.

"What are you going to do?" Hank asked, knowing what had happened in Korea. He didn't want to witness that here.

"I'm sure as hell not letting them get to the compound," Smith said as he raised his M16 rifle and fired a long burst. The rounds impacted to the side of the group and over the heads of the children. None appeared to be hit, but all appeared to be more scared of Smith than the NVA. The hostages to include kids and women, scattered like a covey of quail and ran back towards the village, leaving the NVA standing in the road. Immediately the district compound opened fire, as did the ARVN compound, and cut down those standing in the open. Everyone knew this wasn't the last for the day.

"Major, how about giving me a hand placing claymores in the wire?" Smith asked.

"Sure, let's do it," Hank said.

For a couple of hours, Hank, Smith, Corporal Hen and Sergeant Wallingford placed claymore mines and white phosphorus grenades on trip wires around the perimeter just behind the three stands of concertina wire. While they did so, an occasional bullet would pass over them. With each one, Sergeant Wallingford would duck.

"Hey, Wallingford, no need for that," Smith called over after one bullet passed close to them.

"Why's that, sir?" Wallingford asked, gently tying the trip wire to the grenade.

"If you hear it, it's already gone past you and it wasn't addressed to you," Smith responded.

"Yeah, you're right, sir. I'd never thought of it that way before," Wallingford said with a smile.

"Of course, you have to watch out for those ones addressed to 'current occupant' too," Smith chuckled. Wallingford's spirits immediately deflated.

Returning to the command post, Smith and Schott were surprised to see Vinh sitting in the corner in his underwear, a white T-shirt and boxer shorts.

"Vinh, what the hell are you doing?"

Before Vinh could answer, Lull interrupted Smith. "Sir, we got a call," he said as he handed over the microphone.

"Who is it?" Smith asked, accepting the transmitter. Lull just shrugged.

"Zippo, over." At first Smith couldn't understand the sender. The sender spoke Vietnamese, which Smith understood, but was also whispering very softly.

Others watched Smith's facial expressions transition from curiosity to surprise. Then he started jotting notes on a pad of paper. As he listened, he motioned that he wanted the radio for the FAC. Holding both microphones, he called the FAC.

"Sundog, Zippo, over."

"Zippo, Sundog, over."

"Sundog, I have a regiment with tanks at..." And Smith ran off some coordinates.

"Roger, I have a flight of four. And who will adjust? Over."

"I will, over," Smith said.

"Zippo, are you at this location? Over."

"Sundog, negative, but I have eyes on. Over."

After a moment, he heard, "Roger, Sundog rolling hot."

Smith returned to the unidentified sender and spoke to him. A moment later, he called Sundog back.

"Sundog on target, drop, drop, drop. Over."

"Zippo, roger, drop, drop, drop."

Listening on the sender's frequency, Smith held up the hand mike so everyone could hear the sounds of bombs exploding. Then the loud noise stopped completely.

"What just happened?" Schott asked. Hank fielded the question as he understood the conversation that Smith had had with the Vietnamese soldier on the other end.

"Sir, it appears that that young man was the only survivor of the reconnaissance company that Vinh left hanging out there to the west. He just called an air strike in on himself and a regiment of NVA with tanks. Whoever he was, he was a hero," Hank said as Smith placed the receiver on the table and looked at Vinh, who only looked away.

"Zippo, Cornish Six-Seven, over," came over the radio. Smith and Schott exchanged looks.

"Do you know who this is, Colonel?" Smith asked. Schott just shrugged.

"Cornish Six-Seven, Zippo, over."

"Zippo, this is Cornish Six-Seven. Tunnel One-Zero Alpha contacted me earlier. We're attempting to send an element to your location. They've hit an ambush and road-block. They will not be coming. Over."

"Roger, Cornish Six-Seven. Didn't know that you were attempting to join us. Good luck, Zippo out," Smith said, handing the hand mike back to the radio operator and looking at Schott. "It appears we're surrounded in depth if they can't get to us. Dammit."

Throughout the day, Smith and Schott had assessed their manpower. It was not good. Of the original members of the 9th Regiment inside the compound, only fifty or so were left and not wounded. Wounded accounted for another hundred and fifty. Some stragglers from what was left of the 3rd Battalion, most of which had been killed on the hill south of the base on the first day, had made their way into the compound. Some stragglers from FSB Alpha that hadn't surrendered with the cav had arrived as well. Going to the aid station, Hank met the surgeon, who turned to the wounded and told them of the situation on the perimeter. Those that could got up and returned to their positions without a complaint. They all knew what awaited them if the compound was overrun. Fighting was the only alternative at this point.

* * *

Major Davidson and Captain Wanat were weathering the storm at the district compound. They had started the day with two hundred and twenty Regional and Popular soldiers.

Almost all of these soldiers had families living in the town of Loc Ninh. Many had recognized their own children being marched down the road by the NVA.

"Major," Smith said, surprised that the field phone was still connected to the district compound, "I told you, if you have an air strike request, pass it to me and I'll get it for you. Sundog cannot be taking requests from the both of us, and we're not changing procedures now in the middle of a fight."

"Dammit, Captain, when I call for an air strike I expect to get it. You know damn well that air strikes have to be cleared with the district chief, and I'm his advisor," Davidson yelled.

"Sir, you can monitor what I'm calling in and if you have a problem you can cut in, but I'm not wasting time running it all past you before I call it in. And you're not getting any air strikes on the town. Your own troops will mutiny on you if you do that. Hell, they'll turn you over to the NVA if you pull that stunt. That's their families you're calling to hit. I won't do it. Where is Wanat?"

"Wanat is working the perimeter. He's been directing our mortar fire and the artillery, but I need some TACAIR."

"Where do you want the TACAIR? Pass me some coordinates and I'll put it there. I'll pass any attack helicopters we get to you as well when they get here, if you have targets. Fair enough?"

"Alright for now, but this is unsatisfactory in my book. I'll discuss this with Colonel Miller when I see him," Davidson said, and the line went dead.

* * *

Inside the TOC, sporadic shooting had been heard going on all day. Suddenly that sound intensified and the field phone switchboard lit up with calls from the perimeter. Hank grabbed the telephone, although he really didn't need to announce the message, as everyone already suspected.

"The gate's been breached. Appears to be a company," he said and ran out of the TOC to see if he could assist. Smith was on the radio right away, calling Sundog for support. The sounds of incoming artillery could be heard outside. The impacting rounds grew louder, and everyone stared at the ceiling of the TOC. The last round slammed into the roof, which held, but the concussion and blast slammed everyone to the floor.

Spectre gunships destroyed one tank approaching the gate. Napalm destroyed those in the open, along with CBU bomblets. An hour after it had begun, the attack was over, but some NVA were now hiding inside the camp. The gate was open and beyond repair.

As things quieted down, Smith and Hank as well as Schott exited the TOC to assess the damage. Schott insisted on coming with them despite his head wound. The damage was horrific, with hundreds of burnt NVA bodies standing up in the wire. Pieces of human flesh and body parts lay scattered across the ground, both NVA and some ARVN. The ARVN soldiers of the 9th Regiment were mesmerized at that sight.

Then the shooting began again, started by a tank across the airfield. As it fired, it rolled across the airfield and entered the gate. Everyone ran for cover. Smith grabbed an M72 LAW and fired. The round bounced off the front of the tank, which didn't appear to be fazed by the round.

Diving into a foxhole, Smith waited for the tank to roll over him. As he watched, rounds from Spectre bounced off the engine deck of the tank, stopping it immediately. As the crew climbed out of the crippled vehicle, ARVN soldiers shot them.

Returning to the TOC, Smith noticed Vinh continued to sit in his underwear. But he did start to speak.

"It is hopeless. We surrender now. Soon they come and we all die if not surrender," Vinh said in a loud voice, attempting to influence both the Americans and the Vietnamese. "Everyone keep white T-shirt to surrender. We officers are fortunate, we can surrender. All others will be shot. They should run now."

"Vinh, I told you once to shut your mouth. Open it again and I will permanently close it for you," Smith said. He was in no mood to deal with Vinh. At this point he had several injuries—nothing major, but enough to heighten his level of irritation.

"I prisoner before when Viet Minh capture Dien Bien Phu. Prisoner is better than dead. Prisoner not so bad," he said but stopped as Smith approached him with a killer look in his eyes. He didn't reach Vinh before a barrage of artillery hit the compound again.

Hank came back through the door. "The perimeter held on that last attack. They're determined to stop them from getting in," he said, ducking as impacting rounds appeared to be getting closer.

As the artillery barrage lifted, Smith and Hank left the TOC to check the perimeter. Ground assaults usually came right after an artillery barrage. Schott remained in the TOC and took a seat.

"I want to go by the hospital first, sir," Smith indicated to Hank.

When they arrived, Smith took the surgeon aside. The surgeon confirmed what Vinh had said—officers could surrender, soldiers would be shot. Smith and Hank moved to the perimeter and told the soldiers there to strip to their underwear and head for the bridge at Cam Le. Most were Montagnard, Nung or Cambodian and would be shot.[1] Once they departed, there were few remaining on the perimeter. As they moved around the perimeter, lights and movement could be seen across the runway and Smith placed an air strike on it. As it subsided, another ground attack commenced on the east side as well as the west. The gun crew on the 106mm recoilless rifle using flechette rounds stopped one attack and air strikes stopped the second, but each one brought the enemy a bit closer to the compound. Returning to the TOC, they found Colonel Schott walking around like a drunk sailor. He was very unsteady on his feet.

"Sir, why don't you sit down for a bit? Better yet, try to lay down and get some sleep," Smith said.

"Captain, you're as tired as me. I'm so thankful you're here with me. I'm just going to close my eyes for a bit. Did I tell you how thankful I am that you're here with me?" Schott said.

"Just try to get some sleep, sir," Smith encouraged, making eye contact with Hank.

The pair walked off some distance as Hank replied, "His mental acuity is decreasing. I think that head wound may be more serious than we first thought."

"Sir, I'm just glad you're here. You've really been a big help to me on this."

"Hell, what was I supposed to do? Sit in the corner, suck my thumb and watch?" Hank joked.

"No, sir, that's what Carlson is doing over at the advisor bunker," Smith said.

Davidson was occasionally heard complaining about the lack of air support. Even Sergeant Lull was notably depressed. Wallingford was still displaying his Airborne "Go get 'em" attitude.

"Sir, if this place starts to get overrun—and I'm sure it's going to happen—I want you to get out of here any way you can. If a chopper comes in and you can get on it, I want you on it," Smith said.

"Captain, I'm not—" Hank started.

"Sir, I know what you're going to say, and I would say the same, but someone has to get out of here and tell our story. Someone has to be able to get to An Loc and tell them what the tactics of the enemy are. We've never seen this before from them, and An Loc won't be ready for them unless someone gets to them. Please, sir. You're no coward and have shown that, but I need to get the message out, and you're the best person to do that. Please, sir," Smith pleaded.

"I'll tell your story," Hank said with resignation.

All of the advisors and Hank had been at it for almost twenty-four hours straight. Vinh and his staff were doing very little and really only staying in the bunker for fear of either the NVA shooting them or the American advisors doing the same. Suddenly two loud explosions went off, very close to the command bunker.

"What the hell was that?" Schott asked as a third explosion went off, even louder than the first two.

"Sir, let me step outside and take a look," Hank said, slipping out the door into the darkness. It was just after midnight, Smith realized, as he had lost track of time. Shortly Hank came back in and didn't look happy.

"Sir, we lost the aid station with all hands and maybe the doc too," Hank said.

"And the other two...?" Schott asked.

Just then, Lull came running in. "Sir, it appears a rocket hit the artillery ammo dump, and when it blew it took out the guns and the crews. There's no one alive over there." They all understood the seriousness of losing the artillery support. The rest of the night was quiet, the calm before the storm.

* * *

**1700 Hours**

· · ·

"Tunnel One-Zero Alpha, Cornish Six-Seven, over," Ginger radioed, only to initially be met with silence. "Tunnel One-Zero Alpha, Cornish Six-Seven, over."

"Cornish Six-Seven, Tunnel One-Zero Alpha, go ahead."

"Tunnel One-Zero Alpha, we've been requesting a resupply of class one, three and five as well as water. We submitted our first request at 0900 and two subsequent requests since then, and nothing has come in. We're critically low on 155 and 105 ammo, over."

"Cornish Six-Seven, this is the first I've heard about it. Understand you have had no resupply today, over."

"Tunnel One-Zero Alpha, that is affirmative. No resupply today. Over."

"Cornish Six-Seven, let me look into this and get back to you. Over."

"Roger, Tunnel. If we don't get something tonight, we're going to be hurting in the morning, over."

"Understand, Cornish, I will get back to you. Tunnel out."

Captain Zumwalt set the hand mike down and looked over at Sergeant Winland. "Want to share a candy bar? I have one left, along with one cigarette," he asked. That would be dinner for this night.

**7**

---

## LOC NINH FALLS

**7 APRIL 1972**
  **9th Regiment TOC**
  **Loc Ninh**

"What's that noise?" Smith asked, snapping his eyes open. The clock on the wall read 0700.

"Tanks," Hank said, coming through the door, followed by the sounds of a major gunfight going on outside. Hank grabbed an M72 and ran back out with Smith on his heels. As they exited the TOC, a T-54 tank crashed through the perimeter and headed straight towards Smith. Smith saw it coming and dodged behind a bunker. The tank driver saw him and decided to follow. It was apparent that the tank wanted to capture the American. Sitting one hundred feet above this foot race was an OH-6 helicopter.

Captain Dey flew for the 1st Battalion, 9th Cavalry, and had been dispatched early that morning to get up to Loc Ninh. His mission was to find enemy targets for the AH-1G Cobra gunship that accompanied him. As Dey closed on the compound, he realized that the fighting must have been brutal. Both ARVN and NVA bodies were mixed together, indicating that hand-to-hand fighting had transpired over the night. Dropping lower, he was practically landing on the tank chasing Smith. Finally the tank driver noticed the helicopter and lost his focus on Smith. Turning another corner, Smith came up from behind the tank and hit it in the engine compartment with an M72 round. The tank immediately stopped and started to burn.

* * *

"Incoming!" Zumwalt screamed as rounds started impacting all around TF-52. This was not an occasional harassment fire but a barrage of artillery and mortars. Things had been relatively quiet until 0700, but for the last thirty minutes it was one round after another. Many times it was multiple rounds hitting simultaneously. Sergeant Winland was sharing the advisor command post with him when a lull occurred. Peering out the doorway, Winland spotted a young Vietnamese soldier on the ground, wounded and crawling.

"Be right back, sir," Winland said, and he sprinted out the door before Zumwalt could respond. *What the...?* Zumwalt was thinking as he moved to the door position to see what Winland was doing. Sprinting to the Vietnamese soldier, Winland bent to pick him up when a mortar round impacted close by, knocking Winland to the ground. Getting up, and bleeding himself, Winland grabbed the soldier, tossing him over his shoulder and sprinting to the nearest foxhole. When a second lull in the shelling occurred, Winland sprinted back to the advisor command post.

"Way to go, Sergeant. Trying to be a hero? Damn, look at your arm...let me get a field dressing on that and clean it before it gets infected," Zumwalt chastised the sergeant.

"Sir, I just couldn't stand there and watch that kid crawl into the next round," Winland responded.

"How bad is he?"

"Shrapnel cut across his face. I doubt if he'll be able to see ever again," Winland explained.

"Maybe we can get him on a Dustoff," Zumwalt thought out loud.

"Then it best be a Chinook, because there are a lot of wounded out there."

* * *

Smith returned to the TOC, but only momentarily. As he was going in the doorway, Vinh and his bodyguards came running out in their underwear, straight out the main gate. Vinh's XO, Major Nguyen Thanh Lo, paused long enough to start pulling down the South Vietnamese flag. Before Smith could get to him, Lo was running a white flag back up the flagpole. A fight ensued over control of the lanyard. As they fought, soldiers in the TOC began to come out the doorway, pulling off their shirts. Smith realized he had to do more and quickly, or he was going to lose the entire compound. He released the lanyard, drew his pistol, and shot the XO between the eyes. Soldiers from the TOC put their shirts back on and returned to their duties. Smith raised the flag of South Vietnam while Hank covered him with his weapon. Together, they moved back to the TOC.[1]

"Captain, it appears we have another ground attack coming in," Hank said, engaging enemy soldiers from the front door.

"Sundog, Zippo, over," Smith transmitted.

"Zippo, go ahead."

"Sundog, we're being overrun. On my location, drop, drop, drop."

"Zippo, get your people down. I have fast movers inbound now. Good luck."

Smith and Hank along with Schott lay down on the floor of the TOC and prepared for the worst. The concussion wave from the exploding five-hundred-pound bombs lifted everyone off the floor. As the last aircraft streaked over and the bombs exploded, Hank got up and looked out. Bodies and body parts were everywhere. Four large craters were surrounded with dead NVA in a circular pattern.

"Anyone seen Wanat or Davidson? Any word from them?" Schott asked as he picked himself off the floor and took a seat. "Smith, I'm sure glad you're here with me," he repeated as he had done several times before.

"Thank you, sir. I've spoken with Major Davidson," Smith replied.

"Well, how are they doing?" Schott asked.

"Sir, they're hanging in there. It appears that the district compound is holding for right now" was all Smith would say.

"Good call. What about Carlson, Lull and Wallingford?" Schott asked. "I'm sure glad you're here, Smith." Smith and Hank exchanged looks.

"Sir, they're okay and will be here shortly. They're over in our bunker," Smith replied. Schott's eyes were fixated on the opposite wall. Before anything else could be said, the radio came to life.

"Zippo, this is Danger Seven-Nine. Over."

"Danger Seven-Nine, Zippo, over."

"Zippo, I'm bringing in a B-52 strike west of you. The drop will commence in one-five mikes. How copy?" Hollingsworth asked. Smith and Hank glanced at the clock. It was a quarter to ten.

"Danger Seven-Nine, I have good copy, over."

"Roger, Seven-Nine out."

Smith sighed as he placed the receiver on the desk. He

waited. At exactly three minutes after ten, the first bomb exploded. The concussion wave rocked the TOC, and it was quickly followed by one long sound of rolling thunder. Hank sat in a corner, wondering how anyone could possibly live through that hell raining down on them. When the last bomb exploded, a Sabre aircraft was on the radio. Carlson, Lull and Wallingford had heard the conversation with the chopper. Carlson decided that the group should move to the command bunker as Smith was in communications with aircraft.

"Zippo, Sabre One-Eight, over."

"Sabre One-Eight, go ahead, over."

"Zippo, I'm coming in to take out anyone you can get to my aircraft. Over."

"Roger, I have two pax for you, over," Smith said, looking at Hank and Schott. "Sir," he addressed Hank, "please get Colonel Schott on that aircraft. I'll cover you."

Sergeant Lull started to move towards the door.

"Where do you think you're going, Sergeant Lull? Get back on that radio," Smith ordered, blocking the doorway.

"I'll take the colonel to the chopper," Carlson offered.

"Sir, your duties and responsibilities are assigned to this team. Major Sabine is not. I've asked him to take the colonel out. You still have a job to do here," Smith said, turning to Hank. "Sir, time for you to go. Take the colonel."

Hank grabbed Schott and helped move him towards the door, stepping outside. The helicopter was on short final to land fifty feet from the TOC. Smith, carrying an M60 machine gun, took up a position on the TOC roof. Hank was half carrying and half dragging Colonel Schott towards the aircraft, which was now being mobbed by the ARVNs attempting to flee. Hank stopped after moving only ten feet, knowing there was no way he could get both of them on the aircraft. The pilot must have sensed it as well as he began his departure with ARVN soldiers hanging off the skids. The aircraft was designed to carry three and the pilot. Hank was sure he counted eight and the pilot as it left the compound. Smith stood to jump off the roof when something slammed into his shoulder and spun him around. He didn't need a doctor to tell him he had been shot.

## 1830 Hours

Inside, Hank dressed Smith's wound as best he could. It was a clean wound as no internal organs had been hit. Schott was back in his chair, staring off into the distance. Corporal Hen was watching the door to the TOC.

"Sundog, Zippo, over."

"Zippo, Sundog, go ahead."

"Sundog, we're going to E&E. Hit this place with everything you got in thirty minutes. Over."

Sergeant Lull grabbed the handset from Smith and screamed, "*No napalm!*"

"Listen up! We need to E&E, so grab what ammo you can carry, plus water and C rations," Smith directed. "Major Carlson, please notify Major Davidson that we're pulling out and he should now start contacting Sundog directly."

"Captain Smith," Schott called out.

"Yes, sir," replied Smith as he walked over to the colonel.

"Captain, I'm so glad you're here. I can't make it out of here," Schott said.

"Sir, don't you worry. We'll take turns carrying out and down to An Loc. It'll be okay," Smith offered, turning to see if Lull and Wallingford were collecting things they would need. No one was watching Colonel Schott as he removed his .45 pistol from his holster. The blast of the pistol discharging scared everyone, and they turned to see who'd fired. Colonel

Schott, knowing he couldn't make it and knowing they wouldn't leave him behind, had taken his own life.

"*No!*" screamed Smith.

"Sir, he knew he was only going to slow us up. That had to be one of the bravest acts I've ever seen," Sergeant Wallingford said. Smith stood for a moment, breathing heavily.

"Captain, time for us to go," Hank said gently. Smith just nodded and started for the doorway that led out the back of the TOC. Corporal Hen took point, and as they exited, NVA soldiers came through the front doorway before Lull and Carlson could escape. They and the ARVN soldiers in the TOC played dead. Hank and Smith, realizing that their party was already split, lay on top of the TOC along side Hen.

"Zippo, Sabre One-Six, over."

Attempting to be as quiet as possible, Smith answered. "Sabre One-Six, Zippo. We've been overrun. I'm on the roof of the TOC, over."

"Roger, inbound to get you."

Smith sat up, and as he did, a shot rang out and he slumped forward. "Ah shit, that hurts."

"Where did it hit you?" Hank asked, grabbing Smith and helping to take the AN/PRC-77 radio off his back. That was when Hank noticed the bullet hole through the radio. The bloodstain on Smith's back confirmed that the bullet had gone through the radio and lodged in his back. Without the radio, the bullet would have surely killed Smith.

"Let me get a first aid kit out of the TOC," Hank said as he laid Smith down and left. Cautiously going down the stairs, he could hear voices—Vietnamese voices. Peering around a corner, he spotted three NVA soldiers in front of Colonel Schott's body. On the other side of the room lay Sergeant Lull and Major Carlson. They appeared to have been killed along with the Vietnamese that worked in the TOC. One of the NVA had a machete and was hacking

Colonel Schott's body. Hank felt no remorse when he shot all three.

"Let's go!" Sergeant Lull said, jumping up and startling Hank. Carlson was picking himself up as well along with the Vietnamese TOC soldiers.

"Have you been playing possum the whole time those three were in here?" Hank asked, attempting to control his temper. "Where are your weapons?" Lull pointed to where he had been lying. His weapon had been right beside him. "And you couldn't shoot them?" Hank asked as he grabbed the first aid kit and headed out the way he came in. He was too upset to speak to Carlson.

"Captain, sit up and let me get this on you," Hank said as he brought Smith to a sitting position. Pulling Smith's shirt off, Hank placed the field dressing over the hole in Smith's back and tied the bandage around his chest. "It doesn't appear to be a sucking wound. Can you breathe okay?" Hank asked. As he did so, a Sabre OH-6 appeared, coming over the compound.

"Major, you get on that bird."

"I'm not leaving you," Hank said, waving to the pilot, who, identifying the Americans, began an approach.

"Major, I said you're getting on that chopper," Smith said ever so slowly. Hank turned to argue with him. The .45 pistol in Smith's hands told him there would be no argument. "I want you on that chopper. Go tell our story here. Let everyone know what we did. I'm not leaving Wallingford or Lull. They're my responsibility," Smith said.

The chopper was starting to touch the top of the TOC. As it did, the ARVNs that were close clambered to get on board. Hank was having mixed emotions about leaving, but the .45 in Smith's hands convinced him to get on the aircraft. So did the murderous look in Smith's eyes. He knew Smith was serious about him being on that chopper.

Fighting his way through the ARVNs, Hank was able to get his foot on a skid and his hands on the door frame. ARVNs tried to pull him off. The pilot was attempting to pull in power, but the aircraft was going nowhere with all the ARVNs on board. The pilot brought his fist up and punched one ARVN in the face, causing him to drop. The gunner was doing likewise. Hank aided them with a couple of elbows and kicks to get more off. Finally the aircraft began to climb and departed.

* * *

Dragon Seven-Nine was orbiting at five thousand feet. He saw the OH-6 depart but noticed one person lying on the top of the TOC roof. A call from the OH-6 told him they had one advisor on board and one appeared to be shot on the top of the TOC.

"OH-6 departing Loc Ninh, this is Danger Seven-Nine, over," Hollingsworth transmitted, not sure who the Sabre aircraft was.

"Danger Seven-Nine, Tiger One-Six."

"Tiger One-Six, did you pick up an advisor? Over."

"Danger Seven-Nine, affirmative. I got one on board and one's back at the TOC."

"Tiger One-Six, is the one on board Zippo? Over."

There was a pause before the answer was rendered. "Danger Seven-Nine, that's a negative. This guy says Zippo is on the TOC, over."

*Damn,* Hollingsworth was thinking as he watched soldiers climbing on the top of the TOC around the American lying there. The last he'd seen of Captain Smith, he was lying on the ground as Vietnamese soldiers cautiously approached, standing him up. Fortunately, the Vietnamese that helped Smith to his feet were South Vietnamese Rangers, and they took him back to a secured bunker with a radio. Reaching for the radio, he made the call.

"Danger Seven-Nine, Danger Seven-Nine, Zippo, over."

General Hollingsworth was shocked to hear the voice of someone he had seen go down a few minutes before as he orbited the fight at several thousand feet.

"Zippo, Danger Seven-Nine, go ahead, over."

"Danger Seven-Nine, I need air support ASAP, over."

"Zippo, I'm on it. Break, Sundog, Danger Seven-Nine. What have we got?" It had been an hour since the B-52 strike had gone in far enough away that it provided almost no support to the immediate battle. Hollingsworth had determined that General Hung had called the strike without coordinating with anyone. *When I get back there, I'm going to straighten his ass out.*

"Danger Seven-Nine, Sundog here. I have them racked and stacked all the way up. Break, Zippo, where do you want it?"

"Sundog, on me, my authorization. They're all over us," Captain Smith practically yelled. Sundog could hear small-arms fire in the background. He gave the A-37B aircraft from the 604th Squadron the go-ahead to strike the compound. He was also receiving calls from Major Davidson, who was located in another bunker, requesting cluster bombs on the compound and napalm on the wire and exterior. For the next hour, bombs, napalm and machine-gun fire rained down on both compounds while Hollingsworth sat out of the way, wondering if any advisors would be alive after this. What disturbed him as much as the attack was the fact that a white flag was flying from the flagstaff in the compound. Hollingsworth broke station to refuel his aircraft back at Lai Khe. For the rest of the day, TACAIR pounded the area around the compound. When Hollingsworth departed, all communications from ground points ceased.[2]

8

## ESCAPE AND EVADE



**7 APRIL 1972**
**District Command Bunker**
**Loc Ninh**

"Simba Six-Six, what is your situation? Over," Hollingsworth called around 1900 hours when he was able to get back to Loc Ninh.

"Danger Seven-Nine, I have myself, my compadre and maybe twenty ARVNs with me. Over," Major Davidson replied. He didn't want to use Captain Wanat's name.

"Roger. Break, Zippo, what's your status?"

"Danger Seven-Nine, I have myself and three other advisors and about forty ARVNs. My boss is dead, over."

"Roger, what are your intentions? Over."

"Danger Seven-Nine, I'm executing Plan Bravo, over." Danger Seven-Nine knew Plan Bravo was to escape and evade to the south towards An Loc and Quan Loi. This plan had been worked out months in advance and had never been divulged to the South Vietnamese forces.

"Roger, Zippo. You do know that Quan Loi is no longer an option, don't you? I will monitor. Maintain radio contact if possible," Danger Seven-Nine said. What he was really telling Captain Smith was that Smith would have to call him. He wouldn't call Zippo again in case Zippo was in close proximity to the enemy, not wanting to have a radio call alert them to the fact that an American advisor was close at hand.

Captain Smith looked around at the Vietnamese soldiers with him and Sergeant Lull and Major Carlson. "Sergeant, we're getting the hell out of here. Grab your extra ammo and whatever else you can carry and let's go," Smith said.

"Sir, what about them?" Lull asked, nodding towards the Vietnamese soldiers with them.

"They can follow if they want or stay. I don't give a rat's ass at this point," Smith said as he headed for the door carrying the PRC-25 radio in a backpack. Lull was right behind him and so were the Vietnamese soldiers. They were thinking, *Where Smith goes, helicopter goes*, and they weren't about to be separated. As they cleared the bunker, they moved towards a trench line. Zippo made one last call to Danger Seven-Niner.

"Danger Seven-Niner, Zippo. Bad guys have overrun us. I was supposed to meet my wife a couple of days ago in Hawaii on R&R. I obviously didn't make it. Tell my wife that I love her. We're going to E&E. Zippo out."[1]

After a few moments, Danger Seven-Niner came on the air. "This is Danger Seven-Niner. For the record, let it be known the battle is fluid. We did everything we could for Zippo. May God be with him. Seven-Niner out."

* * *

Major Davidson had been lying low in his bunker with a small number of district soldiers. *We can't stay here much longer before the NVA come through the door. Time to leave.*

"Wanat, what say we get out of here?" Davidson asked.

"Sir, at this point I think that's an excellent idea. Not much more we can do here," Wanat added.

Turning to the senior Vietnamese soldier, Davidson communicated in his best Vietnamese his intent to leave and make for other places. "Major Thinh, we *didi mau,*" Davidson said, using the Vietnamese term for "haul ass now." His Vietnamese was good enough as everyone quickly prepared for their departure. When all was ready, he led the small force out and slipped them through a hole in the wire towards town. Thinh was right behind him, followed by Wanat. They didn't get far when the tail-end soldiers were spotted by the NVA and a firefight broke out. Whether the tail end fought a delay action or just to stay alive wasn't clear, but it gave time for the lead elements to sprint towards town and seek some refuge in the buildings there.

"Nguyen, are you okay?" Davidson asked his interpreter, who was the only English-speaking soldier in the bunch, in a panting voice, sucking in air. *Got to stop smoking and start running more,* Davidson confessed to himself. Nguyen gave him a thumbs-up as he was gasping for air as well. As Davidson looked around and assessed his situation, he noticed the soldier with the AN/PRC-25 radio was missing. *Damn, no comms with anyone now. Where the hell is everyone else?*

"Major Thinh, where do we go from here?" Davidson asked, thinking Thinh would have a plan.

"We go south village to village as we move. They friendly and will provide food and water," Thinh said confidently when someone stated shouting in Vietnamese. Nguyen flashed him a look that said it all: *They found us!*

"We go," Nguyen said, and that was an order for Major Davidson, who didn't question it. They bolted for the back door as gunfire broke out in the front of the building, followed by the explosion from what was probably a hand grenade. Davidson didn't stop to look and assess what it was but just ran as fast as he could. Amazingly, Nguyen was running faster with his shorter legs. *Damn, I've got to stop smoking.* Davidson wasn't sure where Nguyen was going, but no one was shooting and no one was yelling at them, so Davidson just followed as they ran into the forest on the south side of town. Finally, Nguyen stopped in a small bomb crater, one of many that covered the landscape around Loc Ninh as the area had been bombed for the past five years. Bomb craters were everywhere except in the rubber tree plantations.

They took a few minutes to catch their breaths, and Davidson pulled out his map and compass. "Nguyen, if we continue south, we might be able to get to An Loc in a day or so. Those are our two closest friendlies," he pointed out.

"I follow" was all Nguyen said. "We go." And he stood. As Davidson got to his feet, he thought, *I wonder how the others are doing...*

* * *

Captain Smith, Sergeant Lull and Major Carlson were still in the compound at 1830 hours. They had moved from bunker to bunker along with some ARVN soldiers. Smith had found another radio and was talking to Sundog. They worked out a plan.

"Spectre, this is Zippo. Whenever you're ready, we're set, over."

"Zippo, Spectre, in one mike, over."

"Spectre, roger."

Smith turned to face the others. "Okay, Sergeant Lull, get ready. He's going to make one pass and hose the place down. We go for the wire right behind that burst," he explained and then repeated the instructions in Vietnamese. Everyone nodded that they understood. Even before the last round impacted, they were out the door and sprinting for the wire. Smith attempted to keep up, but his wound wasn't cooperating and Lull hung back with him. As they moved, they were spotted and began taking fire.

"Aaaah," Smith yelled as the round tore into his groin. Lull grabbed his arm, pulled him to his feet and got him to a covered and concealed position in the jungle beyond the wire. Fortunately, the ARVN battalion surgeon was with him and began examining Smith's wound and doing what he could medically, which was not much.

"Captain, we've got to keep moving," Lull said.

"You're right. Help me up and let's go," Smith said between clenched teeth. The small group continued south in the dark, moving slowly and as silently as possible to avoid NVA patrols. By midnight, however, Smith was drained. He was bleeding out his bowels, which was sapping his strength.

"Sergeant Lull," Smith whispered as he finally lay down.

"Sir?"

"You take these guys and head south. I can't go any further," he said with a tear forming on the edge of his eye.

"Sir, you can make it..."

"No, I know I can't. I'm drained and only holding you guys up. Get going. That's an order," Smith said in a resigned voice. Physically and emotionally, he was exhausted. Lull looked at the officer and nodded.

"Yes, sir, I'll try to get them through to An Loc. Good luck to you, sir," Lull said and quickly turned and departed.

"Hen, you go," Smith said, looking up at his bodyguard, who had been with him since he'd arrived in-country.

"Dai'uy, I stay you," Corporal Hen said with a determined look. The regimental surgeon just nodded, making it obvious he was going nowhere without Smith.

Recognizing that Hen wasn't leaving without him, Smith struggled to his feet and made his way south with the assistance of the regimental surgeon and Hen. As they moved south into a rubber tree plantation, the sun started to crest the horizon. Just then, a bomb strike went in and sprayed them with shrapnel. Attempting to move away, Smith crested a small hill and came face-to-face with an NVA soldier who was eating. The soldier didn't even have a chance to chew what he had in his mouth when Smith fired from his pistol. Then the world turned dark.

Waking sometime later, Smith felt intense pressure on his head as someone had their foot on it. Lying next to him was Hen with a terrified look on his face as the rifle next to his head exploded, along with Hen's head. To the other side of Hen stood the regimental surgeon with his hands tied behind his back. It was obvious that he had been roughed up a bit. The NVA jerked Smith to his feet but let go and Smith collapsed. That didn't make them happy and they expressed their feelings with the toes of their boots in Smith's ribs. The regimental surgeon was screaming something too fast for Smith to understand completely, but it sounded like he was attempting to tell the NVA they had a valuable prisoner and he was badly wounded. Finally they got Smith to his feet and forced him to start walking, back to Loc Ninh. Reaching the town, he was taken to a rather nice home untouched by the fighting as yet. There his wounds were treated as best they could be.

"You are very fortunate to be the guest of Mr. Tra," a senior NVA officer said in rather good English.

"Well, thank Mr. Tra for me. What does he do?" Captain Smith asked, talking through the pain from the multiple shrapnel and bullet wounds.

"You do not know Mr. Tra?" the gentleman asked, a bit surprised.

"Should I?" Smith retorted.

"Mr. Tra is General Tran Van Tra," he replied.

That hit Smith like a sledgehammer. General Tra was the commander of all NVA forces operating in the III Corps region. After Smith was patched up, he was left in a room with a guard. He drifted off to sleep. A tap on his boot woke him up, and he was greeted by the sight of two NVA soldiers standing over him. They motioned for him to get up and pointed to the front door and outside. *They've treated me too good for me to expect a bullet in the head*, Smith was thinking. He was right as a US Army jeep pulled up. Sitting in the back were Major Carlson, Sergeant Wallingford and a French reporter that had been at the compound through the fight.

"How is everyone doing?" Smith asked. He could see that Major Carlson was wounded but looked to be handling it well.

"I think we're better off than you," Carlson said through clenched teeth.

"What happened to Sergeant Lull?" Major Carlson asked. "Or Major Davidson or Captain Wanat?"

"I don't know about Major Davidson, or Wanat. Sergeant Lull took off with some Vietnamese and headed south when I got shot a second time. I ordered him to go as I just couldn't keep up," Smith said.

"Damn, I hope he made it," Major Carlson said as the Vietnamese soldiers motioned for Smith to get in with the others, in the back of the jeep. The US Army M-151 jeep wasn't very big, especially with four Caucasians in the back, and the road to Snoul, Cambodia, wasn't paved. As they rolled north into Cambodia, they suspected that they were heading for a POW compound to wait out the duration of the war.[2]

**9**

---

# COMMAND DECISIONS

**7 April 1972**
**MACV HQ**
**Saigon**


Tension was at an all-time high due to confusion in the events that were happening in MR-I and MR-III. The lack of a clear intelligence picture didn't help either. Until Lieutenant Colonel Turley, USMC, Deputy Commander US Marine Corps Advisory Team, had come to Saigon on 4 April to brief General Abrams, MACV hadn't been aware of how serious the situation was in MR-I. Since then, their focus was on MR-I. Now it appeared that MR-III would be in need of attention. General Abrams had attended a meeting at the Independence Palace earlier in the day that was called by President Thieu.[1] His key general officers were present to explain the situation across the country and what needed to be done to fix the situation. As soon as General Abrams returned to MACV, he called a staff meeting.

"Okay, gentlemen, here's what the Vietnamese high

command is telling the president. There are possibly four NVA divisions attacking in MR-III. General Minh is asking for more troops to stem this assault. The main attack is going to be coming down Highway 13, with a supporting attack from Tay Ninh. The situation in MR-I is bad, with the 3rd ARVN Division hanging on but being pushed hard. The president was reluctant to thin the forces in MR-I but conceded to send an airborne brigade to MR-III. He's also sending the 21st Division, which is operating in the U Minh Forest," Abrams outlined.

"That's good news," General Hollingsworth said, smiling and looking around the room.

"The not-so-good news is that Thieu has notified the commanders at An Loc that they would fight to the death. No retreat. This is going to be the Bastogne of this war. We will give all the support we can to both areas. Holly," Abrams said, getting General Hollingsworth's attention, "you need something, you just ask. Understood?"

"Yes, sir," Hollingsworth replied.

Returning to his headquarters, Hollingsworth had formulated his guidance to all of the advisors and contacted each of the teams. His instructions were simple. Remove all nonessential personnel back to Long Binh. Advisors would remain with their Vietnamese counterparts and not be evacuated.[2] Reports from MR-I indicated that when American advisors were extracted, the morale and fighting spirit of the Vietnamese left behind diminished greatly. American advisors would ensure that all fighting positions were prepared and reinforced to withstand hits from 76mm weapons. All antitank weapons would be manned with trained and assigned crews.

Hollingsworth met with General Minh later in the day, having a heated discussion.

"General Minh, you've been given one airborne brigade as well as 21st Division. The 3rd Ranger Group was brought into An Loc this morning with the 36th and 52nd Battalions, but that still leaves the town lightly defended. Add the fact that when they did land, Lieutenant Colonel Biet and some of his staff were wounded by incoming artillery. Take the airborne brigade and move them into An Loc as well," Hollingsworth explained.

"I think not. I think I move airborne brigade up Highway 13 to clear roadblock and open road to resupply An Loc," Minh responded.

"General Minh, from what we saw and from what intel is telling us, you probably have an NVA division blocking that road. One airborne brigade is not going to break through that. Put them directly into An Loc and ensure that President Thieu's directive to hold to the last man is met," Hollingsworth argued.

"We must ensure the road is open to resupply. 5th Armored Squadron is moving into Chon Thanh today and tomorrow will move up, clearing roadblock. Airborne brigade can quickly move up road behind them. The airborne brigade will open the road," Minh said with some aggravation in his voice.

"General, you can resupply by air. Attempting to use the airborne brigade to open the road is not going to be sufficient, and when they arrive, there may not be anyone left at An Loc to resupply. You've got to put troops in An Loc," Hollingsworth said as forcefully as he could. But he couldn't change Minh's mind.

"I have issued the order and the airborne brigade with the 5th, 6th and 8th Battalions along with the 81st Airborne Ranger Battalion will be moving up to Lai Khe. They will move up Highway 13 to Chon Thanh by truck and then move on foot to open the road."

While Hollingsworth and Minh were discussing the use of the airborne brigade, Colonel Miller and General Hung were having a similar discussion about the remaining forces of the 5th ARVN Division.

"General, we need to reinforce the forces at An Loc. You have two regiments here in Lai Khe that you can push up the road or airmobile into An Loc," Miller said, but Hung wasn't listening. Hung had become demoralized after the loss of Loc Ninh. For a long moment, he just sat and stared at Miller.

"Colonel, I have better idea. Request that the 1st Cav Brigade send two battalions of Americans to An Loc."

At first Miller thought he was kidding, but when he realized he was serious, Miller went ballistic. "It's an ARVN war, General."[3] Pausing briefly, Miller took a more fatherly tone. "General, you really appear to be depressed by all this. Why not let Colonel Nhut take over the command?" Nhut had returned from his trip to Vung Tau and was very active in attempting to locate housing for the refugees streaming in from up north. He had ordered that M72 light antitank weapons be issued to every soldier along with instructions on how to use them. His previous combat experience told him his soldiers were in for a fight.

That evening, Hank Sabine had been sitting in An Loc watching the defense unfold. The 36th and 52nd Ranger Battalions had arrived earlier in the day by helicopter and were preparing their sectors of the perimeter. Hank was sitting in the TOC with Colonel Miller when a messenger handed him a note. Hank was seated next to the door and was the first American that the young Vietnamese soldier saw. As Hank read the note, Colonel Miller kept speaking, but he stopped when he saw Hank look up.

"What is it, Major?" Miller asked.

"Sir, it appears that Quan Loi has fallen. This was their last transmission. The two rifle companies have destroyed their equipment and spiked their guns and are attempting to move to here," Hank explained.

"Damn, they had how many guns up there?" Miller asked.

"Sir, they had two 105 howitzers," another staff officer answered.

Miller looked over at the map, and a frown crept across his brow. "That's going to give them the high ground overlooking this place. Not good" was all he said.

"Colonel Miller," Colonel Nhut spoke up, and Miller immediately acknowledged. "The refugees from the rubber plantation and the villages to the north are reporting seeing tanks moving south. Also, the NVA are confiscating any food they can find. We are going to need to be thinking about how we are going to feed the number of refugees coming into An Loc as well ourselves."

"Handling the refugees is more my problem," Colonel Covey interjected, "but Colonel Nhut is right, we're going to need a joint effort on resupply." Colonel Covey was the senior advisor to the district chief, Colonel Nhut.

"I'll see about getting airdrops by C-123 and helicopters. Helicopters can bring in supplies and fly out wounded," Miller said. *Great, now I not only have to babysit Hung and get his head in the fight but also worry about feeding the refugees. That's not in my job description*, he was thinking.

"Okay, the good news now. An airborne brigade is heading to Lai Khe and will be moving up Highway 13. They'll truck to Chon Thanh and then move towards us and open Highway 13. When they open the road, that should help with the refugee problem as well as the resupply situation," Miller exclaimed. Immediately he could see an increase in the group's motivation. "Be sure you put the word out to the troops. It should raise morale a bit." Pausing for a moment to survey the room, he said, "In addition, Hung has ordered the 8th Regiment with three battalions to redeploy to here. They should be here by the eleventh."

"How are they coming, sir?" Hank asked.

"They're flying up. The 229th will be bringing them." After a momentary pause, he concluded, "If there are no questions, let's call it a night and get some sleep."

* * *

General Hollingsworth was tired, but he still had one more person he wanted to talk to. Turning to his aide, he asked, "Is he here yet?"

"Sir, he just arrived and is coming down the hall now," the aide responded.

"Good, show him right in," Hollingsworth instructed as he quickly scanned a map. He hadn't met the senior Army advisor to the 21st ARVN Infantry Division before but had heard stories about Colonel Ross J. Franklin. Ross stood six foot three with a ramrod-straight posture. He was totally bald and even at his age was solidly built. Although not in his fatigue uniform, when he entered the office, Ross came to attention and rendered a smart military salute. Holly knew of Ross as his reputation had preceded him. Ross was a Distinguished Service Cross recipient for actions while a platoon leader in Korea.

"Sir, Colonel Franklin reporting," Ross said. Holly returned the salute and extended his hand.

"Glad to meet you, Colonel. Heard a lot about you. Sit down."

"Don't believe all that you've heard, sir. Half of it isn't true and the other half is false," Ross said. Holly chuckled at that.

"I wanted to meet with you before we have a sit-down tomorrow with General Minh and General...ah...who's the 21st Division commander?"

"Sir, that'd be Major General Nguyen Vinh Nghi," Ross responded.

"Yeah, him. Minh and the powers in Saigon are worried that the enemy is going to make a push to seize Saigon. The thought process is to move the 21st Division between the enemy and Saigon to block the enemy from doing that. A more serious problem in my view, however, is An Loc and Highway 13. It appears that the 7th NVA Division has interdicted the highway north of Chon Thanh, cutting off all resupply by vehicles to An Loc. Minh's plan right now is to use the one airborne brigade he was given today and have them move up the highway and clear it. I'd rather see that airborne brigade put into An Loc. One airborne brigade isn't going to clear that division off that road," Holly pointed out.

"I agree, sir," Ross confirmed, not sure where Holly was going.

"The 21st is moving up as we speak and the 32nd Regiment, I understand, is moving to Chon Thanh on the eleventh by truck and will be closing in behind the airborne brigade. Let the airborne brigade see what they can do, which in my opinion will be very little even with the armored cav tanks with them. Once the rest of the 21st Division is in place, I'm going to convince Minh to move that airborne brigade up to An Loc and let the 21st have the mission of clearing that road. Any questions?" Holly asked.

"So until the 21st assumes the mission for the road clearance, what's the mission for the 21st?"

"Good question, because the press is going to be asking you that same question and attempting to make it look like you folks aren't doing anything. If they ask, your mission and the mission of the 21st is to find, fix and destroy enemy forces in sector...not clearing that road. At some point that will become your mission, but for right now, it's not. Do we understand each other?"

"Sir, I completely understand and will get General Nghi on board. Coming out of the Delta, it's going to take time to get the 21st up to speed on this kind of a fight. They're good at the squad ambush and small-unit action stuff, but slow and not used to doing things at a company or battalion level. My advisors are going to be busy with this once we take the road-clearing mission. Is there anything else, sir?" Ross asked.

"No, just get them up to speed as quick as you can, because once they're committed, we need that road opened and opened quick."

## 10

### TRAFFIC JAM



**7 APRIL 1972**
**604th Squadron**
**Bien Hoa**

The 604th Squadron had been over Loc Ninh since the start and working closely with Zippo. At times, the 8th Special Operations Squadron would fly An Loc as well when not flying over MR-II. Both were located at Bien Hoa and both part of the 21st Tactical Air Support Squadron. When they went up, they would be talking to the FAC, who were also located at Bien Hoa. Sundog aircraft were the most frequent FACs on station, but Raven aircraft were there as well. Almost twenty-four hours a day, one of the FAC aircraft would be loitering over An Loc. But that was becoming a problem.

The FAC was the traffic manager for aircraft over the battle. Up to this point in time, one FAC could handle the calls for TACAIR as usually it was only one flight of aircraft at a time. Only once before had the code word "Broken Arrow" gone out. That was in 1965, in the Battle of the Ia

Drang Valley, and TACAIR had responded with aircraft of all type stacking up over the target. A single FAC was able to handle the number of aircraft as he was supporting one fight in one location. This was turning into something else. Different aircraft types, with both US and Vietnamese pilots at the controls, attacking in different locations simultaneously with different capabilities. Some were attack helicopters, some were Spectre gunships, some were supersonic jets and some were subsonic A-37s and prop-driven A-1 Skyraiders. All were taxing the FAC pilot's ability, besides the fact that he also had to fly his aircraft. To manage all this activity, the FAC had to talk to at least one person on the ground, each flight leader and the Direct Air Support Center, who received the request for tactical aircraft and launched the aircraft. Something had to be done, and so the 21st Tactical Air Support Squadron headquarters called a meeting. The 21st TASS was responsible for visual reconnaissance and forward air controllers.

"Gentlemen, I believe we have a problem over the battle area and if we don't sort it out, someone is going to get killed. So let's start by identifying the problem. Who wants to go first?" asked Lieutenant Colonel Donald Hogg of the 21st.

"I will, sir," said Major Jamison, a senior FAC pilot. "One of the problems, sir, is that the FAC has too much going on to keep up. He calls for assets and may get one type, say A-37s, and then an AC-130 shows up and the Vietnamese join in with A-1 Skyraiders. Add to the mix attack helicopters—all have different capabilities and different flight parameters. Now toss in a second target and the FAC has got to be a magician to keep up. The problem from where I sit is one of command and control."

"If I may, sir, Captain Abrams, AC-130s. Sir, I was up there the other day. I had a target and was ready to engage when I was called off so higher-priority aircraft could engage the target. I was out of fuel before they were done and had to break station without firing a shot."

"Sir, I can second some of what Captain Abrams says," Captain Baggans interjected. "I was lined up for a shot and had to check fire when, about two thousand feet below me, a pair of Cobra gunships showed up right in my line of fire."

"What did you do?" asked Colonel Hogg.

"Sir, I informed the gunship flight leader that he just entered my line of fire. He apologized and continued engaging the target while I sat and watched."

"So, what I'm hearing is we have an airspace management problem. Is the correct?" he asked. Several present nodded their heads. "What else?"

"Sir, lack of knowledge in capabilities," a major in the back said.

"Please explain."

"Sir, the AC-130 is a relatively new aircraft and has several systems that have been classified since its inception. A lot of the FAC pilots haven't been briefed on the capabilities aside from the guns and cannon. Our PAVE AEGIS system delivers ordnance accurately. They need to be brought up to speed. As an example, the other night, my flare launcher broke. When I told the FAC that, he told me to return to base as he assumed I was inoperative. I had to explain to him that we have other capabilities that would allow me to work the target without flares, a capability that we don't want to discuss over the air. The AC-130 isn't only a weapons platform—we can perform reconnaissance when no one else can, especially at night," Major Hollman concluded.

"So let's add to the list—we have a command and control issue, an airspace management issue and a lack of knowledge about capabilities. Anything else?"

"Sir, you can add cultural differences to your list," a voice in the back said.

"Explain yourself," Colonel Hogg said, looking to see who'd said that.

"Sir, if the Vietnamese Skyraiders enter the battle, they talk to the FAC and take instructions, if, if I say, an American pilot is flying and leading the formation. If not, the Vietnamese pilots just bore in and don't talk to anyone. You're lucky if they even let you know they're in the area. They're almost more of a threat than the SA-7s."

Colonel Hogg wrote "cultural differences" on the butcher paper, along with the three previously listed problem areas. He studied the board for a moment. "Okay, gentlemen, let's start putting solutions to these problems. Command and control first. Suggestions?"

"Sir, if I may. Rather than one FAC being on station to handle everything, how about if we have one FAC that talks to the ground forces? He passes the request to another FAC that forwards it to you folks and does the coordination with you and the TACAIR as it's coming out. When the TACAIR arrives, he hands them off to the requesting FAC. Also, as busy as this fight is with more than one ground unit calling for air support, I would suggest we put two FACs up at a time in addition to the controlling FAC. There are just too many actions on the ground for one FAC to handle," Captain Armstrong recommended.

Hogg thought about that for a minute. "What do the rest of you think about this?" he asked. Most were in agreement that this would make things more manageable for the FACs. An objection was raised by the maintenance folks as this was going to require three aircraft up at a time instead of one. Their objection was duly noted.

"What call sign are we going to use for the coordinating FAC? If it uses a Raven or Sundog call sign, that's going to be confusing," another pilot spoke up.

"Whoever gets the mission will use the call sign King FAC

as that's what he is. He's the king assigning aircraft to the subordinate FACs," Hogg said. "Now, what about airspace management?"

"Sir, it's pretty much situation-dependent. The AC-130 have about six hours on-station time and can cruise and operate well at ten thousand feet. The fighters have a short flight time but burn through fuel quickly and don't have a lot of loiter time. At night, Spectre should have the priority as he has the greatest capability for night support. The fighting usually dies down at night, so in most cases Spectre can handle the situation. In the day, priority should go to the fighters," Captain Abrams said.

"It's a bigger problem than just Spectre and the fighters—it's also the helicopter gunships. They don't normally talk to the FAC. The choppers have VHF and UHF, but I've never heard them come up on the fighter nets. The choppers are working for the ground force directly. The ground force is talking to us. The ground force should control the choppers and keep them out of the area when we're in there," Captain Baggans said.

"Good point, Captain. I will raise that with General Hollingsworth as the ground guys are all his people. The Army advisor with each ARVN unit is who's calling in the air strikes, so they would know best," Hogg said as he jotted down a note. Looking up, he addressed the last issue on the board. "Okay, how do we handle the cultural differences?"

"Sir, I would recommend that the general sit down with his Vietnamese counterparts and explain the situation. Once they understand the problem, we should insist that an American officer leads the flights, or if there are no US FACs in the area, they take responsibility for the entire air operation," Major Jamison said. A hand went up in the back of the room.

"You in the back have a thought on this?" Hogg asked.

"Sir, telling them to stay out of the fight or put an American in charge is just going to piss the Vietnamese off. This is their fight more so than ours. I would recommend that if and when VNAF aircraft show up, the FAC gives them to one unit and takes all other assets out of that area. Assign a specific area just to the VNAF. This would allow the Vietnamese to exercise their system and improve the ground commander's ability to control the air strike. As an example, I was flying support for an ARVN airborne battalion two days ago up along Highway 13. The advisor was on the radio with me and said that the battalion commander for the ARVN airborne battalion wanted to control the air strike. He put the guy on the radio. His English was pretty good, but he couldn't coordinate an air strike to save his soul. They don't get a chance to do it with our advisors down there holding their hands. We never did get the air strike in, and I had to tell the advisor I had to break station to refuel."

Hogg thought about this for a moment. Before he could respond, another hand went up. "You have something, Lieutenant?" Hogg asked the young officer.

"Sir, I know I don't have a lot of experience, but I like things simple. Why not just divide the area up now? Say, all the airspace north of Chon Thanh to the Cambodian border and from the Song Be River west to the Cambodian border is US airspace and VNAF has everywhere else?" the lieutenant said. There was silence.

"I'll consider all three approaches and pass that on to the general. I'll also set up a briefing for the day after tomorrow for all the FACs to get a class on the capabilities of the AC-130. We'll have a morning class and an afternoon class so I'm sure everyone gets it. I'll get out a memo this afternoon, and we'll implement some of these changes first mission tomorrow. King FAC will be in the air first light," Hogg said, taking a pause. "Gentlemen, I believe the bar is open."

## 11

# RANGERS LEAD THE WAY

7 April 1972
**3rd Ranger Group**
**Parrot's Beak**

The 3rd Ranger Group had been operating in the Parrot's Beak region adjacent to the Cambodian border. The region included a portion of Svay Rieng Province in southeast Cambodia and was a panhandle that protruded into Hau Nghia and Kien Tuong Provinces, Vietnam, approximately sixty-five kilometers northwest of Saigon. For many years, it was the terminus of the Ho Chi Minh Trail from Sihanouk, Cambodia. Over the years the NVA had established two major supply caches there, Base Areas 367 and 706. Lieutenant Colonel Nguyen Van Biet commanded the 3rd Ranger Group and was considered by his American advisors to be one of the best.

"Sir, I just spoke with the helicopters and they're about fifteen minutes out. Twelve UH-1Hs and four CH-47s. They'll do multiple turns to get the group into An Loc. I told them how we're postured and they're good with it," said Major Castor, the Ranger group advisor.

"Very good, Major. I want this to go smoothly so we can get into An Loc and get in position fast. I spoke with General Hung and we are to take responsibility for part of the north side and eastern side of the perimeter. That is a large area. The airstrip is on the north side of the town, which means we are going to have to move south and east through the town to get to our positions. That is going to take time, so we need to move off the airstrip very quickly," Colonel Biet explained. "Have you heard how the 31st Ranger Battalion is doing?"

"Sir, they got in just fine yesterday and have moved off to the east. They're occupying some high ground east of the city," Castor replied. "I spoke to Colonel Miller and we should have no problem moving through town. They've had some shelling but no ground probes or attacks yet. He did say they expect to lose Loc Ninh today. Quan Loi is under attack as we speak." In the distance, the familiar sound of helicopters, both UH-1H and CH-47, could be heard. Both men prepared to board a CH-47 aircraft.

The flight to An Loc was thankfully uneventful, until the first of the UH-1H aircraft touched down on the airstrip. As the aircraft approached, small-arms fire rose up to meet them.

"Colonel," Castor yelled over the engine noise of the CH-47 he and Colonel Biet were riding in. "I just was told that the aircraft are taking fire on the approach. The pilots want us out of here as quick as we can when we touch down." Biet just nodded, acknowledging the information. He was confident that his soldiers would do that without being told. After all, they were Rangers, not common ARVN soldiers.

Biet and Castor could feel the aircraft slowing as it came over the landing zone, especially when the tail ramp dropped. As the rear wheels touched, the troops were up and moving to the ramp. Biet led the way with his staff and Castor right behind him. Due to the engine noise, they didn't hear the explosion of the first impacting mortar round, but they certainly saw the explosive impact. This only motivated the soldiers to move faster. Biet turned and stopped to berate the soldiers for taking too long. Since he stopped, his entire staff did likewise. When the next mortar round impacted, Biet and his entire staff were wounded—him not so seriously, but others needed to be medevacked.

Biet was taken to the aid station to have his wound cleaned and dressed. Castor accompanied him. "Major, were you hit as well?" Biet asked.

"No, sir, I'm fine," Castor replied.

"You must live a good life in that case, Major," Biet responded with a smile.

Once Biet was patched up, he and Castor moved to their assigned sector. The 3rd Ranger Group had five companies that had been assigned positions and sectors based on a map reconnaissance they had conducted before they'd boarded the aircraft. Now that they were on the ground in the town, plans might have to be adjusted. First stop for Biet and Castor was the group's command post, located on the eastern side of the town and the southern part of the assigned sector. The group operations officer was also slightly wounded but functioning well, so he updated Biet on the status of the group. It appeared that the only people injured on the landing were the staff. From the command post, Biet and Castor moved along the perimeter of their sector, observing the defensive preparations. What they saw didn't make them happy.

Leaving the command post, they moved to the closest company. It had the responsibility of tying in with the Regional-Popular Forces on the right flank and blocking Route 303. Route 303 was the only road that approached the east side of the town and therefore it would be the best avenue of approach for track vehicles. Route 303 was as good a road as Highway 13 and ran to Dong Xoai in the east. After making some suggestions on the defensive preparations, they moved north and examined the preparations at the next three companies. Reaching the northernmost units, Biet was not happy. Hung had directed that one company be positioned on the northern end of the airstrip. It was sitting about two klicks forward of all the other companies with exposed flanks. The left flank was just short of Highway 13. His left-flank company was covering the south side of Highway 13 but not blocking the road. The boundary between the 8th Regiment and the 3rd Ranger Group was right down the middle of Highway 13 as it came into town.

Biet asked Hung who was responsible for Highway 13 and received no answer. Castor went to see Colonel Miller at the 5th ARVN command post.

"Sir, who is responsible for Highway 13? The 8th or us?" Castor asked.

"Major, I've argued that with Hung from the start. I've told him one of you needs to be responsible, but he feels you both should be and isn't moving the boundary. In truth, we don't have the manpower to cover what we have."

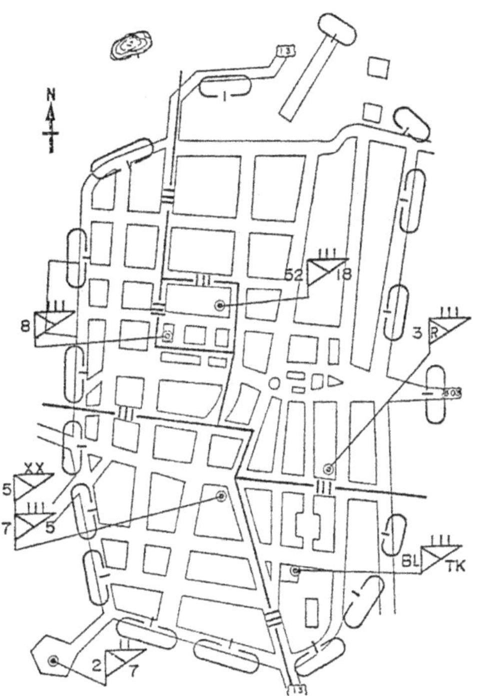

**An Loc Defensive Positions**

"We're stretching things thin. You have the one company on the south side of Highway 13 where it comes into the town. Let him take responsibility for the highway. If the company on the airstrip gets pushed back, have him come back and tie in with that company along the highway," Miller said. "What company is out there?"

"Sir, that's Lieutenant Truong Phuoc's company occupying Highway 13 between Don Long Hill and Be Moi hamlet, which is south of Cam Le Bridge, center of mass X-Ray Tango Seven-Five-Nine-One," Castor said. "There's also an RF platoon on Hill 128 just off the runway on the north side, which is being reinforced by the 5th Recon Company. Colonel Nhut has also recommended to Hung that the 254th RF Company move to Hill 169."

"Did 3rd push anyone out to the east on Hill 169?"

"Yes, sir. One company from the 52nd Battalion pushed out a company to there," Castor said.

"Well, tell Biet that he's sharing responsibility for Highway 13 where it comes into town."

"Okay, sir, I will tell Biet, but he's not going to be happy," Castor said as he departed.

# 12

## PACK UP AIRBORNE



**7 April 1972**
**1st ARVN Airborne Brigade**
**Vung Tau**

A meeting had been called for the advisors of the 1st ARVN Airborne Brigade. Team 162 seldom ever had all the advisors together at the same time. Most of the time, an advisor would only interface with the other advisors in his battalion, which were generally two other Americans, one being a junior officer and the other a noncommissioned officer or NCO. It was equally unusual for all three battalions of the brigade to be operating together. The airborne brigade was considered the strategic reserve for the Vietnamese Army, and as such it only sent out battalion task forces to back up actions being conducted by ARVN divisions in need of assistance. Things had been relatively quiet for the past year and all three battalions of the brigade were at the National Training Center, undergoing training and refreshers. New soldiers had joined the brigade to replace those lost in the Lam Son 719 operation a year ago to the month.

Captain Mike McDermott was the newest member of the advisory team but not new to Vietnam. Mike had been prior service enlisted infantry and had come over to Vietnam with the 101st Airborne Division. He'd returned to the States, attended Officer Candidate School, and been commissioned a second lieutenant, infantry, then returned to Vietnam, serving as an infantry platoon leader. He'd commanded an infantry company in the 101st as well. He knew infantry tactics and could probably have written the book on jungle warfare and counterinsurgency operations. Now he was assigned as the senior advisor to the 5th ARVN Airborne Battalion. Entering the room, he was greeted by his old boss, Major Jack Todd, senior advisor to the 8th ARVN Airborne Battalion. Second Lieutenant Ross Kelly was right behind him as he was the assistant senior advisor to the 6th ARVN Airborne Battalion. Major Morgan, already in the room, was the senior advisor for the 6th Battalion. Lieutenant Winston Cover was beside him along with SFC Ron McCauley. Cover and McCauley were part of Mike's team. In the front of the room stood Lieutenant Colonel Art Taylor, the senior advisor to the 1st ARVN Airborne Brigade. Taylor had served with the 101st during World War II and had seen action in Korea. His entire military career with troops was in airborne units. Seldom did any of the battalion advisors see him, as he generally stayed at the airborne brigade command post at Tan Son Nhat Airport. He was accompanied by another officer that the others hadn't seen before.

"Okay, get seated and we'll get started," Taylor said, pinning a map up on a corkboard. "First, let me introduce Captain Charlie Huggins. Charlie is the senior advisor to the 81st Ranger Battalion, which has been attached to the brigade. Okay, here's the situation. As you're aware, the NVA crossed the DMZ on the thirty-first and are knocking on the door of Quang Tri. Two days ago, the NVA launched a major attack out of Cambodia down Highway 13 and have hit Loc Ninh hard. The 9th ARVN Regiment is holding on by the skin of their teeth. According to General Hollingsworth, Loc Ninh will probably fall tonight or in the morning. They're already getting indications that An Loc is next. What intel they've gathered so far indicates that the 5th NVA Division is hitting Loc Ninh and Quan Loi. The advisors and about a hundred and thirty soldiers were evacuated out of Quan Loi this morning, and the two companies that are there are executing a fighting withdrawal back to An Loc. They're part of the 7th Regiment. Indications are that the 9th VC Division is moving towards An Loc from the northwest, and the 7th NVA Division is moving to block Highway 13 south of An Loc." Taylor pointed out Loc Ninh, Quan Loi and An Loc on the map. The seated advisors exchanged looks of surprise and a bit of concern.

"1st Airborne Brigade is being ordered to move by convoy from here to the village of Chon Thanh, located here, south of An Loc and north of Lai Khe. There we dismount at Chon Thanh and move up Highway 13, clearing the road of any obstacles, into An Loc to reinforce the garrison there. Currently the 43rd Regiment along with the 5th Armored Squadron is in the process of clearing the road. It may be the case that we stay on the trucks and roll all the way to An Loc. Don't count on it. The brigade will move tomorrow morning. Fairly simple and cut-and-dried, wouldn't you say?" Taylor said, sarcasm dripping off every word in his final sentence.

Returning to the 5th Battalion command post, Lieutenant Colonel Nguyen Chi Hieu was issuing the order to his company commanders. Hieu had been cool towards McDermott because McDermott was only a captain and the 6th and 8th Battalions had majors for their senior advisors. Hieu also considered himself an aristocrat as he was married to a movie actress and came from wealthy stock. There were a small number of Vietnamese officers that resented the presence of American advisors and chose to ignore their advice. It was their call. Hieu gave basically the same brief that Taylor had given and indicated that the order of march for the brigade was 5th Battalion, followed by the 6th Battalion, with 8th Battalion bringing up the rear. They would travel all day and spend the night just south of Lai Khe.

The rollout went smoothly and as planned. Traffic on the paved highway up to Saigon and the assembly area south of Lai Khe was heavy, especially southbound from Lai Khe. The movement north wasn't as fast as everyone expected, and they didn't reach Chon Thanh until April 11.[1] McDermott and the other advisors were thankful they rode in M-151 jeeps with their gear. Arriving at Chon Thanh was a bit of a shocker. There, elements of the 5th Armored Squadron and the 43rd Regiment were recuperating and treating their wounded. It quickly became evident that the road north was probably not cleared.

# 13

## TF-52 WITHDRAWAL

**7 APRIL 1972**
**5th ARVN HQ**
**An Loc**
**0530 Hours**

Colonel Miller, Major Borstorff and Major Sabine had finished their morning coffee and C rations breakfast. The humidity wasn't up yet, so the temperature was pleasant, with clear skies. The three had wandered over to the 5th ARVN TOC and checked to see what activity had occurred during the night. Miller was especially worried about the status of the advisors at Loc Ninh. Their last radio transmission was not encouraging. They then returned to their bunker for house-keeping assignments and paperwork. A few hours later, as they were sitting in the bunker, they began to hear gunfire off in the distance to the north. They exchanged looks.

"We have anyone up north of our position?" Miller asked.

"Just Task Force 52, but they're close to Loc Ninh. We shouldn't be hearing any of their gunfire...unless...," Borstorff said, slowly standing. "And 2nd Battalion, 9th Regiment, at the Cam Le Bridge."

"Hung told me the day before yesterday that he told Task Force 52 to pull back to here. That son of a bitch lied to me. He didn't give the order two days ago," Miller finished, grabbing his hat and leading them out the door in a run for the TOC. Lieutenant Colonel Benedit was just coming out of the TOC entrance.

"Did he discuss this with you, pulling Task Force 52 back here?" Benedit asked, looking at Miller.

"Yeah, we discuss it three days ago and he told me two days ago that he had ordered them back here. Oh shit, is that what he did now?" Miller asked.

"He pulled the 7th Regiment on Firebase 1 the day before yesterday, but not the force at the Cam Le Bridge or Task Force 52. He's ordered them all to pull back to here now. Task Force 52 is caught in an ambush and getting their ass kicked," Benedit explained. Task Force 52 was under the command of Lieutenant Colonel Nguyen Ba Thinh, a tough combat commander with a proven record. His unit, Task Force 52, had occupied two supporting firebases ten to twelve kilometers north of An Loc and south of Loc Ninh. His command consisted of two battalions of infantry, an intelligence recon company, a company of engineers and a battery of 105mm and 155mm howitzers. When he had gotten the order from Hung to withdraw, he'd questioned it but hadn't pressed the issue. Now he wished he had pressed harder.

"What about the artillery? Are they...?" Miller started to ask.

"Left it, all of it," Benedit said as Miller pushed past him and entered the command post.

Upon entering, Hung and his staff were standing at the radios, listening to the task force commander. From the sounds of things, the task force was in a fight for its life.

"We get TACAIR, now," Hung ordered before Miller could say anything. *If you had done what you said you were going to do, you wouldn't need TACAIR now to save your ass,* Miller was thinking.

"Where are they?" Borstorff asked, and Hung stabbed the map with his finger. Borstorff wrote down the coordinates and began talking to an airborne FAC.

"General, tell them to mark their position with smoke so the FAC can find them," Borstorff requested. Hung grabbed the hand mike and issued an order for smoke. Borstorff informed the FAC to start looking for the smoke. In a few minutes, the FAC indicated he had smoke...lots of smoke and all different colors in multiple locations. Which one was the friendly forces? The NVA were monitoring the radio frequency, and when the call for smoke had gone out, they'd started popping smoke grenades as well. There was no way to identify friend or foe. Slowly the gunfire died down in the distance. General Hung was paralyzed with indecision. Earlier he had ordered Task Force 52 to dispatch one battalion to relieve Loc Ninh.

"Tunnel One-Zero Alpha, Cornish Six-Seven, over," Lieutenant Colonel Ginger, the senior advisor for Task Force 52, transmitted.

"Cornish Six-Seven, go ahead."

"Tunnel One-Zero Alpha, we're under heavy artillery fire. The 2nd Bat couldn't break through to Loc Ninh and has returned. Understand that your counterpart has ordered us to return to your location, over."

"Roger, Cornish Six-Seven. He told us he issued that order two days ago," Miller transmitted, looking at Hung, who avoided eye contact quickly and walked outside.

"Tunnel One-Zero Alpha, we just got the order this morning to pull out and return to your location."

"Roger, do you need anything?"

"Affirmative, we need class V and water that I asked for two days ago. Have requested medevac, over."

"Roger, I'll see if I can expedite those requests. Over."

Miller went looking for Hung. He found him outside smoking a cigarette. "General, I just spoke with the senior advisor with TF-52. You do know they're surrounded and low on ammo and water, don't you? We've got to get a resupply to them and medevac aircraft as well," Miller explained in a tactful tone. *A pissing contest right now is not going to help anyone*, Miller was thinking.

"I have spoken with my operations officer. He assured me that the situation for Task Force 52 is not as bad as you describe," Hung stated, looking off into the distance. "He has called for a resupply of ammo and water and it should arrive shortly. Let's not meddle in this and confuse the situation, as you American advisors like to do." Miller noticed that Hung's hand was shaking as he attempted to take another drag on his cigarette.

"General, you do realize the seriousness of the situation, don't you? You have what appears to be a major attack coming at you, certainly with the intent to isolate and seize Loc Ninh and maybe, probably, to do the same to An Loc. You've got to take a proactive, aggressive approach to this," Miller said in as gentle of a manner as he could. *Hung is coming unhinged*, he thought.

"I will consult with General Minh and he will order what action I am to take" was all Hung said before he stood and walked off. Miller was beside himself with frustration. After he settled his nerves, he walked into the command post. Hung was just putting down the telephone.

"General Minh understands our situation and will get back to me. We can wait for his guidance," Hung said. Miller moved over to the advisor area and called Cornish Six-Seven.

"Cornish Six-Seven, Tunnel One-Zero Alpha, over," Miller transmitted.

"Tunnel One-Zero Alpha, Cornish Six-Seven."

"Cornish Six-Seven, you should be getting word on a resupply shortly, over," Miller said.

"Roger, I believe it's coming through right now, over."

"Cornish Six-Seven, my counterpart tells me that one has been laid on for you, over." Miller knew that it would take a miracle to get a resupply to them as it would have to be flown by the South Vietnamese Air Force, who never really stuck their necks out for the Army.

"Roger, I'll keep you posted on our progress. Cornish Six-Seven." As Miller laid the hand mike down, he said a small prayer that the resupply would get in.

* * *

Lieutenant Colonel Thinh immediately issued orders for the departure of Task Force 52. He didn't consult Lieutenant Colonel Ginger before issuing the order. When Ginger heard it, he immediately knew it would be trouble. Approaching Thinh, he attempted to get him to change the order.

"Sir, this order of march is for an administrative move. You have the towed artillery and trucks towing the water buffalos in the lead. We need to send out some infantry first to clear the road of any possible ambushes," Ginger attempted to explain.

"The order has been issued. To change now will only create confusion. We go and go fast before they can put in an ambush position," Thinh rationalized. Ginger realized it was pointless arguing with the man. Thirty minutes later, his worst fear was confirmed.

"Cornish Six-Seven, Cornish Five-Seven, over."

"Cornish Five-Seven, Cornish Six-Seven India," Sergeant First Class Winland answered on the advisor net.

"Cornish Six-Seven India, Cornish Five-Seven, we have been hit by an ambush. I say again, ambush, three hundred meters east of your location. Attempting to return, over," Captain Zumwalt transmitted.

"Cornish Five-Seven, are you able to break contact?" Winland asked.

"Affirmative, but we've lost three trucks and three artillery tubes, over."

"Roger, what is the commander's intent? Over."

"Cornish Six-Seven India, he's returning to his original positions, over."

"Roger, Cornish Five-Seven. Anything else? Over."

"Negative, Cornish Five-Seven out." Winland laid the microphone on the radio, wondering what the next piece of cheery news would be.

As he contemplated that, Lieutenant Colonel Ginger entered the advisor command post. Winland informed him of the news, speaking between incoming artillery and mortar rounds. Slowly building in intensity was small-arms fire. The task force was now under ground attack as well. Ginger went to find Thinh and see what he was going to do. Sergeant Winland jogged alongside Ginger until a mortar round impacted, blowing him off his feet. Lying on the ground, he began to check himself over and was happy to find only a small wound. Picking himself up, he looked to see where the colonel was. Ginger was doing the same. With a nod, they resumed their run to the command post. Reaching the TF command post, Ginger bumped into Captain Zumwalt.

"How you doing, Captain?" Ginger asked, quickly scanning the young officer's appearance.

"I'm good, sir. I guess we've been ordered to destroy all equipment and move south to An Loc," Zumwalt said.

"Who ordered that?" Ginger asked with some surprise.

"Thinh just spoke with Hung, who ordered it. Hung said to destroy it all and make our way south."

"Crap! I best see what his plan is or this will be another admin move. Where is he?" Ginger asked, looking around the command post. He couldn't find Thinh but did see the operations officer and approached him.

"Major, what's the plan for our move?" Ginger asked in his broken but understandable Vietnamese.

"We have ordered that everything is to be destroyed, to include trucks and artillery. We will move south and the order of march is 1st Battalion, Headquarters Group, and 2nd Battalion stays behind to cover our departure. 1st Battalion is forming up now. We go now," the major responded, and Ginger noticed that the headquarters element was ready to go as well. When Thinh arrived, Ginger, Zumwalt and Winland moved out as well. What disturbed Ginger was the fact that he didn't hear or see any equipment being destroyed.

"Sergeant Winland," Ginger said quietly.

"Sir?"

"Get on the horn and notify Colonel Miller that they didn't destroy any equipment. We need an air strike on the area to destroy it all. Give him the coordinates," Ginger instructed.

"Roger, sir," and Winland quietly notified Colonel Miller. Forty minutes later, the sound of impacting bombs confirmed that the message had been received. An air strike did what TF-52 had not done. As the column moved, Ginger became concerned. Instead of moving south, they were moving east and in the general direction that the first attempt had moved when it had run into the ambush. Before Ginger could get Thinh's attention and stop the movement, the NVA sprang the ambush on three sides. The column stopped cold and had to fight. In doing so, the 2nd

Battalion that had been fighting a rear guard action closed in on the 1st Battalion. Now the entire task force was surrounded and stopped. Thinh was paralyzed with indecision.

"Sergeant, get on the radio and get me Colonel Miller," Ginger yelled as he attempted to move closer to Thinh. Winland was right behind him, calling for Miller.

"Tunnel One-Zero Alpha, Cornish Six-Seven, over."

"Cornish Six-Seven, Tunnel One-Zero Alpha, go ahead" came an immediate response.

"Sir, Tunnel One-Zero Alpha for you," Winland said, handing the mike to Ginger.

"Tunnel One-Zero Alpha, Cornish Six-Seven, we need immediate TACAIR. We're surrounded and in heavy contact. Our location is..." And Ginger read off the map coordinates, expecting a FAC very soon.

"Cornish Six-Seven, roger."

Ginger had confidence in Colonel Miller and expected that his wait wouldn't be long. However, under intense fire from both small arms and mortars, minutes seemed like hours. He attempted to contact Miller again to find out when a FAC would be overhead, but Miller didn't answer. The situation was not going well for TF-52.

"Cornish Six-Seven, Dynamite Six, over." Ginger and Zumwalt exchanged looks and smiles. The FAC was overhead for sure.

"Dynamite Six, Cornish Six-Seven, damn glad to hear you, over."

"Roger, Cornish Six-Seven, sitrep." Again Ginger and Zumwalt exchanged looks, this time of confusion.

"Dynamite Six, we're in heavy contact and need TACAIR at ..." Ginger read off the coordinates.

"Roger, Cornish Six-Seven, what do you estimate enemy strength and direction of movement? Over."

"Who the hell is this guy?" Ginger said to no one in particular.

"Cornish Six-Seven, Dynamite Six, over."

Finally, Ginger's frustration meter peaked. "Dynamite Six, I'm engaged at this time. If you want to play twenty questions, then I suggest you either call Tunnel One-Zero Alpha or get your ass down here in the fight for a face-to-face brief. Now leave me the fuck alone unless you have TACAIR, medevac or lift ships to get us out of here. Cornish Six-Seven, *out*!"

Turning to Winland, Ginger ordered, "Sergeant, get me General Hollingsworth on the radio." Hollingsworth had told the advisors if they weren't getting the support they deemed necessary, they should contact him directly. Now was the time.

Moments later, Winland said, "Sir, I have General Hollingsworth," handing the mike to Ginger.

"Danger Seven-Nine, Cornish Six-Seven, over," Ginger transmitted.

"Cornish Six-Seven, Danger Seven-Nine, what is your situation? Over," Hollingsworth responded.

"Danger Seven-Nine, Cornish Six-Seven, we're in heavy contact and need air support, over," Ginger said and went on to explain their situation and the lack of air support. Hollingsworth had a few questions that Ginger couldn't answer. All Ginger knew was that somewhere between his request for air support and now, something had gone wrong. While Ginger and Task Force 52 waited for some air support, they attempted to move towards Highway 13. Finally, Ginger received a call from Blue Max.

"Cornish Six-Seven, Blue Max Two-Four, over," Ginger heard.

"Blue Max, Cornish Six-Seven, I need suppressive fires on the tree line to the east of Highway 13, over."

"Roger, Cornish Six-Seven, pop smoke."

Ginger promptly tossed a smoke grenade towards the

eastern tree line.

"Cornish Six-Seven, I have mellow yellow, over."

"Roger, two hundred meters east of the smoke."

"Roger, Blue Max rolling hot."

With that, Ginger and Zumwalt looked up to see two AH-1G gunships enter into steep dives and begin punching off rockets.

Ginger, Winland, Zumwalt and Thinh were moving together with those soldiers of the command group that were still alive. The damage from the bomb strike upon the NVA was evident, with dead and mangled bodies scattered across their path. However, the destruction wasn't total and some NVA were still engaging. The jungle was sparse in this area, and they came upon a large, open depression adjacent to Highway 13 covered in low grass. In the coming monsoon season, this would be a shallow pond. Moving out from the surrounding trees, the group started across. The explosion from the B-40 rocket fired from the tree line knocked them all off their feet. Zumwalt was seriously injured. Winland was wounded as well, for the second time. Ginger's main concern was Zumwalt. His jaw was obviously broken, causing blood to flow down his throat, restricting his airway. Applying a first aid bandage to Zumwalt's head and neck, Ginger noted the pain and blood from his own wound. *This is not good. I've got to get a medevac aircraft in here and get us out*, he thought. Grabbing the radio off Zumwalt's back, he made the call.

"Tunnel One-Zero Alpha, Cornish Six-Seven, over."

"Go ahead, Cornish Six-Seven" came the reply from a voice that Ginger didn't recognize.

"Tunnel One-Zero Alpha, I need a medevac, urgent." Ginger went on to explain their status.

"Cornish Six-Seven, this is Dynamite Six. Send me your nine-line request and I'll forward your request to get you all out. I want all three of you on that medevac, over."

"Roger, Dynamite Six, can we get my counterpart out as well?" Ginger requested.

"Negative, Cornish Six-Seven. He remains with and commands his unit, over." Thinh had been listening to the conversation and said nothing but walked away. Ginger pulled out his codebook and looked up who Dynamite Six was.

"Oh shit," Ginger muttered, looking at the codebook.

"What, sir?" Winland asked as he applied pressure to the side of Zumwalt's neck.

"Dynamite Six is Brigadier General McGiffert, the deputy commander of 3rd Regional Assistance Command," Ginger said as another call came over the radio.

"Cornish Six-Seven, Tunnel One-Zero Alpha, over."

"Tunnel One-Zero Alpha, Cornish Six-Seven, over."

"Cornish Six-Seven, what is your situation? Over."

"Tunnel One-Zero Alpha, Cornish Six-Seven, my deputy is down with a serious facial wound preventing him from breathing without difficulty. My assistant is down with two wounds but walking. I myself am walking with one wound. We'll have to carry my deputy. Without medevac, I don't think he'll make it. Dynamite Six is waiting for my medevac request, over."

After Ginger sent his nine-line medevac request to Dynamite Six, he called Tunnel One-Zero Alpha back and a discussion ensued between Miller and Ginger as to the need for Ginger and Winland to be extracted. Thinh, knowing he wasn't being extracted, gave the order. He was leaving wounded ARVN soldiers with the advisors. He would take the rest of the command that remained and move out towards An Loc. It was midafternoon, and he felt this was the only chance the survivors had of reaching safety.

"Cornish Six-Seven, Raven, over," the FAC called.

"Raven, Cornish Six-Seven, over."

"Cornish Six-Seven, Raven, I have a flight of two Alpha

Three-Sevens at your disposal. Where do you want it?" the FAC in the orbiting OV-10 requested.

Ginger wasted no time in giving him the coordinates where he thought they had the best chance of breaking out towards the south. After he let Thinh know what was being delivered and where, Ginger and the other advisors positioned themselves where they could best observe the strike. The first explosion occurred at 1300 hours, three hours after Ginger had first requested an air strike. If the strike went well, it would blow a hole in the NVA perimeter and allow the force to move southeast towards the Cam Le Bridge and Highway 13. When the last bomb was dropped, the remainder of Task Force 52 began moving, leaving the advisors.

Ginger positioned the remaining soldiers, twenty total, in a tight perimeter behind what deadfall they could secure. Their position was also in a ditch next to Highway 13. The NVA at this point were not aggressive in approaching their position as the FAC was effectively placing ordnance on those targets identified by Ginger. Finally, Ginger heard the familiar sound of a UH-1H helicopter accompanied by two AH-1G gunships. He, along with anyone that had spent time in Vietnam, could tell the difference in the sounds of the various aircraft. Finally, a UH-1H aircraft came into view and was heading right for his position. Coming in rapidly, the aircraft executed a rapid deceleration, only to be met with a hail of bullets from the tree line. The pilot immediately nosed the aircraft over and executed a combat departure, low and fast.

"Cornish Six-Seven, Spade Three-One, over."

"Go ahead, Spade Three-One."

"Cornish Six-Seven, that's just too hot for me. My door gunner is wounded and I need to get him back. I'll see about another aircraft coming for you. Spade Three-One out."

*Damn, this isn't good*, Ginger was thinking as the two Cobra gunships remained behind and engaged the tree line where the fire had come from. In no time, they had expended all their ammo and departed the area.

Ginger sat back and continued to call in air strikes, which kept the NVA at bay. Each time they attempted to come into the open area, the little Dragonfly jets would pounce on them with a variety of ordnance. One variety, however, was not appreciated by Ginger and his team. It seemed the Air Force had a new weapon in its arsenal. It was a bomb that dispensed a CS-type gas. Nonlethal but very much an irritant, especially to those that didn't have a gas mask. Most people in Vietnam never used their gas masks except as a pillow when sleeping. Few carried their gas masks in the field, and those that did most likely didn't have them properly fitted. The introduction of the gas kept the NVA in the jungle, but with the wind blowing right, Ginger and team were being affected too.

"Cornish Six-Seven, Dustoff Triple-One, over." Everyone exchanged looks.

"Dustoff Triple-One, Cornish Six-Seven, go ahead."

"Cornish Six-Seven, inbound to your location, pop smoke."

Winland immediately grabbed a smoke grenade off his web gear and ignited it. Purple smoke streamed out.

"Cornish Six-Seven, I have goofy grape, over."

"Dustoff Triple-One, affirmative."

"Roger, coming in." In the distance, the sound of a Huey rotor could be heard as Dustoff Triple-One made a high spiraling approach, corkscrewing down to one hundred feet, where he executed a deceleration. He was met with a hail of fire from the tree line. Suddenly, the aircraft began to accelerate and departed.

"Cornish Six-Seven, Dustoff Triple-One, my medic has been hit. I can't get in there. I'll try and get another bird out to you. How copy? Over."

"Roger, Dustoff Triple-One, thanks for trying."

TACAIR continued to pound the tree line for the next two hours, but it didn't seem to have any effect on the NVA. Intense ground fire continued to greet each aircraft as it made its bombing run. As Ginger worked the air strikes, he was constantly checking on Zumwalt. Zumwalt's face was swelling up due to the trauma, and he could barely speak with his broken jaw. On the bright side, the bleeding from the cut artery had slowed down. *I need to get him out of here or he isn't going to make it*, Ginger kept thinking. He also noted that the sun was dropping below the horizon, and night came fast in Vietnam.

"Cornish Six-Seven, Dustoff One-Oh-Seven, over."

"Dustoff One-Oh-Seven, Cornish Six-Seven, over."

"Cornish Six-Seven, I understand you have a request for me. Over." Zumwalt and Winland began to stir in hopes of getting out of there.

"Dustoff One-Oh-Seven, affirmative, I have one serious and two walking for you that are US and several locals, over." *I'm not sure he's going to be able to take all the ARVNs out*, Ginger was thinking.

"Roger, Cornish Six-Seven. I'll take as many as I can, but the three advisors should be on the aircraft in this first lift. I'm five minutes out from your location. What's the situation? Over."

"Dustoff One-Oh-Seven, we're surrounded at this time. We're located on the edge of a large open area in a ditch next to Highway 13. Nearest Indians are approximately two hundred meters from my location, over."

"Roger, understood," Dustoff One-Oh-Seven said. Ginger hadn't worked long in the area of operations but had utilized the services of the 283rd Med Detachment on a couple of occasions. They had always managed to get into and out of landing zones and fly the wounded to safety. He was confident that this would be no exception.

## 14

## DUSTOFF ONE-OH-SEVEN

**7 APRIL 1972**
**Dustoff Flight Ops**
**Song Be**

Chief Warrant Officer Robert L. Horst had been flying in Vietnam for over a year. In December of 1971, he had flown a medevac extraction and earned the Silver Star. That was a mission that still gave him sleepless nights. This couldn't possibly be worse than that, he was thinking when he received the call as he approached Song Be with a casualty on board. Shutting the aircraft down, he entered the operations shack to get his pilot briefing.

There were two very different styles of Dustoff pilots, and all helicopter pilots for that matter. There was the very cautious pilot, who put the safety of the aircraft before all else. And then there was the more aggressive style that put the mission before all else. Generally, the aggressive pilots were cav scout pilots and Cobra jockeys. However, the best pilots were the ones that put mission first and the safety of their crew on an equal pedestal. Robert was noted for being in this group. Mission came first, but he considered all aspects for the safety of his aircraft and crew. He had been flying medevac missions his entire time since graduation from flight school and was assigned to the 283rd Medical Detachment out of Long Binh. When he'd first arrived, he had been assigned to the 159th Medical Detachment out of Long Binh. Because of the drawdowns, the 159th had stood down and those remaining had become part of the 283rd Medical Detachment. Robert didn't much care, nor was he affected by the change in unit designation. He still flew the same missions in the same area, Military Region III.

Entering the operations shack, he was greeted by the operations officer. "Bob, I need you for another mission, now!" Captain Morrison indicated, pointing at a wall map. "There's a group of advisors and some ARVNs located in this grid square and they're surrounded. One of the Americans is severely wounded and the other two are priority. Most of the ARVNs there are priority as well. Another aircraft attempted to land there earlier and was shot out of the landing zone with one crew member wounded. Since then, the advisors have had air strikes and attack helicopters pounding the area. The call sign for the advisors is Cornish Six-Seven. How soon can you launch?"

Robert studied the map for a moment before speaking. "Sir, let me refuel and we'll get going. Should be airborne in twenty minutes and it looks to be about forty-three kilometers, so about thirty minutes to get there...fifty minutes and I'll push it so we'll be there in forty minutes if you have nothing else, sir."

"That's it. Your call where to take them, although Lai Khe may be the best place and fastest," Captain Morrison added. "Need any medical supplies?"

"No, sir, we stocked up before we left this morning and

are good. I'll call you when I'm airborne," Robert said, and he departed the operations shack and joined his crew.

The crew consisted of his copilot, WO1 Gerald Beckman, a medic, Specialist Frank Oliver, and a crew chief, Specialist Lovelace. Unlike medevac aircraft, Dustoff aircraft didn't carry any guns. Medevac aircraft performed the same duties as Dustoff but were assigned to combat divisions such as the 101st Airborne Division and the 1st Air Cavalry Division.

Joining the crew, Robert conducted a flight briefing once the aircraft was refueled and in the air.

"Okay, guys, this is pretty straightforward. We have three advisors that are wounded and some ARVNs. They're surrounded and we're going to get them. The PZ is an open area, so we should get in quick and out even faster. Understood?" he asked. They all did, as they had all done this at least twice a day for the past year. Some days were easier than others. The hardest days were those when they used the jungle penetrator, as they had to hold a high hover above the trees while the penetrator was lowered and the patient strapped on and then retrieved. The aircraft was a sitting target in those operations.

Thirty minutes into the flight, Robert could see rising dust dead ahead. Small black dots flicked in and out of the brown dust, which grew into small A-37 jets. Two Cobra gunships could also be seen as he drew closer.

"Cornish Six-Seven, Dustoff One-Oh-Seven, over," Robert called out.

"Dustoff One-Oh-Seven, Cornish Six-Seven, over." Machine-gun fire and explosions could be heard in the background, and they were loud.

"Cornish Six-Seven, inbound to your location."

"Dustoff One-Oh-Seven, roger. Be advised I have no smoke at this time."

"Crap!" Robert exclaimed to his crew. "No smoke. How

the hell are we going to find him down there?" Switching to transmit, he said, "Roger, understand no smoke. Can you mark your location? Over."

"Dustoff One-Oh-Seven, we're on the edge of Highway 13 with a large clearing on the west side of the road, over." From where Robert was sitting, Cornish Six-Seven had just described most of the terrain. "Dustoff One-Oh-Seven, we're south of the 17/13 intersection. Over." *Well, that narrows it down to only half of what I'm looking at now*, Robert thought.

"Okay, Cornish Six-Seven, here's what I'm going to do. I'll make a high-speed pass down Highway 13. When I come past your location, give me mark. I will then come back around and pick you up. How close are you to the road? Over."

"Dustoff One-Oh-Seven, we're in the ditch right on the edge of the road, over."

"Roger. I'll commence my run in five mikes, over."

"Roger, Dustoff One-Oh-Seven."

"Okay, we have a Dustoff aircraft coming to get us. He'll make a high-speed pass down the road, and when he goes past, I'll call mark so he can note our position. Then he'll come back and get us. Everyone, be ready," Ginger said. Reading between the lines, his instructions were for Zumwalt and Winland to be ready to get out of the ditch before the ARVNs and get on that aircraft. With Ginger's instructions, Winland helped position Zumwalt for a quick exit from the ditch without attracting too much attention from the ARVNs. They wanted to get as many ARVNs out as they could—they just wanted to be sure to be on the aircraft themselves before it left.

* * *

"Okay, here we go," Robert said as he rapidly lost altitude north of the 17/13 intersection. The dust was thick, and to facilitate his high-speed pass, his skids were no more than five feet above the ground. Surprisingly to everyone on board, they were taking very little fire compared to what they had thought would happen.

"Hey, sir, they aren't shooting," Gerald said with his hands gripping his knees.

"That's because they've never seen a Huey flying this low and this fast up close before. Keep looking to see these guys," Robert said as he concentrated on his flying. Prior to dropping down, both Oliver and Lovelace had taken up positions on the right side of the aircraft to see the advisors.

* * *

"Here they come," Ginger said, picking up the hand mike. *Wait...wait...wait,* Ginger thought, watching the rapidly approaching aircraft. Just as the aircraft was reaching his position, he transmitted, "*Mark, mark, mark.*"

Immediately, the aircraft pulled up hard and climbed, rapidly corkscrewing back towards his position and reversing into a dive. The maneuver was so quick that it appeared that the aircraft was going to bypass them in the other direction when it started to come to a hover over the road. That was when the NVA stopped watching the air show and opened fire.

"*No!*" screamed Ginger as he watched round after round slam into the aircraft. Suddenly a red stain appeared on the aircraft commander's side window. The aircraft nosed over and accelerated again, running down the road.

"Dustoff One-Oh-Seven, Cornish Six-Seven, over." No response. "Dustoff One-Oh-Seven, Cornish Six-Seven, over." Ginger attempted again to make contact.

"Cornish Six-Seven, Dustoff One-Oh-Seven," a frantic voice responded. "Cornish Six-Seven, we can't get in. Returning to Lai Khe, we have a Kilo India Alpha on board. Will attempt to get someone else out, over and good luck."

All Ginger and the team could do was sit and watch as the aircraft made a turn back to the south and flew on towards Lai Khe.

After thirty minutes or so, a call was received from Hollingsworth's deputy, General McGiffert. He informed Ginger that Chief Warrant Officer Robert L. Horst had been killed in his attempt to rescue them. A plan was now being worked out to get them out, but they would have to sit tight and continue to fight as best they could. It was sizing up to be a long night. A Spectre gunship was en route to protect them through the night.

"Sir, how about we E&E out of here?" Winland suggested.

"We were told to sit tight and that's what we're going to do," Ginger replied, not happy about this conversation.

"Sir, I'm with Sergeant Winland on this one. McGiffert isn't down here and sure doesn't understand our situation. I'm not sure how long I can sit here without some medical attention. I'd rather be moving then just sitting here on my ass," Zumwalt stated.

"Gentlemen, we were ordered to stay put and that's what we're going to do. We go wandering off, they may never find us—or worse, the NVA will find us and shoot us. No. We stay put and no more discussion, understood?" Ginger said with some anger in his voice.

It was a long night. Spectre arrived on station and initially couldn't locate the small group. The solution was for Ginger to turn on his emergency strobe light so the aircraft could spot his location. Of course every NVA soldier also knew the location now. Frequent probes and two assaults stopped only by Spectre happened through the night. Ginger was on the radio all night talking to Major Borstorff, who stayed in the command post coordinating close-air support for Ginger.[1] This gave Colonel Miller an opportunity to get a few hours of needed sleep. As the sun rose, Ginger and the group wondered if this would be the last sunrise for them. The previous night's sunset was the last sunset for the one hundred or so dead NVA that Spectre had killed during the night.

"Tunnel One-Zero Alpha, Cornish Six-Seven, over."

"Cornish Six-Seven, Tunnel One-Zero Alpha."

"Tunnel One-Zero Alpha, what's the plan for our extraction? Over."

"Cornish Six-Seven, Tunnel One-Zero Alpha, I'll have to get back to you on that. Over."

Ginger couldn't believe what he'd just heard. *Get back to me. They've had all night to develop a plan and no one knows the plan.* Ginger went ballistic on the radio, expressing his feelings as to the level of support they were receiving. Only silence was provided from Tunnel One-Zero Alpha at this point.

Colonel Miller hadn't been included in the loop on the rescue plan for the advisors. General McGiffert had contacted Colonel George Casey the previous evening and requested he develop and execute a rescue. Colonel Casey was the deputy commander for the 3rd Brigade, 1st Cavalry Division. All of the division except the 3rd Brigade along with some aviation assets had returned to the States. The 3rd Brigade was located just north of Saigon. All night long, Casey's staff had worked on pulling a plan together. At 0630, the first elements of the plan were executed.

A combination of A-37 jets and Cobra gunships began to engage NVA forces around the advisors at 0630. For the next three hours, the NVA were on the receiving end of bombs, napalm, rockets and machine-gun fire. The firepower being thrown at the NVA was overwhelming and relentless.

"Cornish Six-Seven, Thunder Six, over" came over the radio. *Who the hell is this?* Ginger was thinking.

"Thunder Six, Cornish Six-Seven, over."

"Cornish Six-Seven, Thunder Six, we'll be delivering a little surprise to you shortly. Be ready, over."

Ginger wasn't sure what this message meant but had his suspicions. It was obvious at this point that the NVA were monitoring all transmissions. They had captured enough radios and codebooks in the process of overrunning Loc Ninh that they could monitor almost every frequency.

## 15

## RESCUE OF ADVISORS

**8 April 1972**
 **Delta/229th**
 **Bien Hoa**

"Hey, sir, what we got today?" Sergeant Raymond Waite asked, walking out to his aircraft that morning. Waite was assigned to Delta Company, 229th Assault Helicopter Battalion, which was part of the 3rd Brigade, 1st Cav. He spent his summers with his grandparents in Maine, fishing and watching the lobster fishermen. After one year of college and a year working on a fishing boat, he enlisted in the Army for the infantry.

"We're flying with Whitehead in a two-ship rescue mission. Going to pick up some advisors up north of An Loc. Whitehead is lead and we follow," Lieutenant Dave Ripley replied.

"Sounds like we're not going to get bored today," Waite responded.

"Hey, Sergeant Waite," a voice called out. Turning, Waite

saw Captain John Whitehead waving him over to his OH-6 aircraft.

"Wonder what the captain wants," Waite mumbled under his breath as he walked over. "Sir?"

"I want you to fly with me this morning. Anderson can fly with Ripley," Whitehead said. "Get your stuff and put it in my aircraft. As soon as you're ready, we're going."

"Yes, sir," Waite responded and walked back to his aircraft and past Lieutenant Ripley.

"What did he want?" Ripley asked, a bit confused as Waite began gathering his flight gear and machine gun.

"Sir, he said I'm flying with him and Anderson will fly with you."

"What? Why the switch?"

"Sir, I don't know. I'm just doing what the captain told me to do. You may want to talk to him about the change." Picking up his gear, Waite walked back towards Captain Whitehead's aircraft and passed Captain Whitehead, who was heading towards Ripley's aircraft. As Waite loaded his equipment and put on his flight gear, he noticed Captain Whitehead and Ripley were deep in conversation. Anderson still hadn't appeared on the flight line. A few minutes later, Captain Whitehead returned and began his preflight procedures. Captain Whitehead occupied the right pilot seat and Waite sat on the deck on the right rear with his feet on the skids with his modified M60 machine gun. Waite had modified the weapon so it was shorter and easier to swing in the confined space of the OH-6 helicopter.

Once off Bien Hoa, Whitehead began his mission brief. "Okay, here's what we got. Three advisors have been cut off and are wounded north of An Loc. Yesterday, two Hueys attempted to rescue them. The first was shot out of the LZ on his approach. Couldn't even get in. Crew chief was wounded in the leg. The second aircraft attempted to get in and the pilot was killed. We're going to go get them. First we're going to stop at Lai Khe and pick up some gas masks."

"Gas masks! What the hell for, sir?" Waite asked in surprise.

"Seems the Air Force is going to lay down a gas that puts people to sleep just prior to our arrival. We'll probably fly through the stuff, so the last thing we want is to fall asleep while flying," Whitehead explained. "We'll refuel as well when we get there."

Sitting in the refuel point, a jeep with an ARVN soldier came to a stop. The ARVN handed three gas masks to Waite without saying anything and departed. Waite walked back to Ripley and handed him one and then returned to his aircraft. Removing the gas mask, Waite was appalled.

"Sir, these things are leftover World War Two gas masks. I'll be surprised if they work," Waite said, holding up the mask. Each mask had a two-foot-long hose connecting a canister and the mask itself.

"Well, we'll find out, won't we? Let's go. Is Ripley up yet?" Whitehead asked as he couldn't see Ripley's aircraft behind him.

"Yes, sir, he appears to be ready," Waite said and climbed in, taking the floor right behind Whitehead's seat.

* * *

Ginger and his small band were thankful for the TACAIR and attack helicopters that were constantly overhead and striking the enemy. They knew the only thing keeping the enemy from overrunning their position was the air support they were receiving. Zumwalt was still having breathing problems with blood flowing down his throat, but not as bad as earlier. Ginger noticed, however, that Zumwalt's strength appeared to be decreasing. *With all the blood he's swallowed out of his system, he must be getting weaker. Got to get him out of here and soon*, he was thinking when he received a call.

"Cornish Six-Seven, Tiger One-Five."

"Tiger One-Five, Cornish Six-Seven."

"Cornish Six-Seven, Tiger One-Five, flight of two little birds inbound to your location. Be ready."

Ginger's hopes soared that they might be getting out of this place. "Tiger One-Five, we're standing by. Over."

"Tiger One-Five, Raven. I monitored and have a flight of two Alpha Three-Sevens set to proceed to you, over," the FAC on station radioed. He had been briefed that this operation was going to happen and to have the two A-37 fighters ready to support. They would be followed by four AH-1G gunships that would escort Whitehead and Ripley into the pickup zone.

"Cornish Six-Seven, standing by."

* * *

"Alright, here we go," Whitehead said as he dropped the nose of the OH-6 and bottomed the collective. This put the aircraft into a rate of descent of fifteen hundred feet per minute. The positive G force had Waite almost floating off the deck. Ripley was right behind him. As the two aircraft plunged towards Highway 13, lights began to twinkle on the tree line below them. Slow green lights appeared to be moving towards them. Those green lights accelerated rapidly as they flew past the aircraft. Waite didn't need to be told what to do. He immediately opened fire with his modified M60 machine gun. When he released the trigger, he realized that he had a runaway gun as it didn't stop firing. He had to break the ammo belt to get the gun to stop, then reload the belt once it did. As the OH-6s plunged down, four AH-1G Cobra gunships plunged down, laying suppressive fire along the tree line. They were backed up by four more gunships from Blue Max.

Leveling off at treetop level, it wasn't difficult to see the area of the fight with the dust and explosions caused by the attacking jets. Coming in fast and low, Whitehead executed a high-speed deceleration as intense enemy fire rose from the tree line, directed at the two OH-6 aircraft. Waite managed to reload as the aircraft touched down almost on top of the advisors. Small-arms fire was kicking up dirt around the aircraft and an occasional round could be heard hitting the aircraft. Dust initially provided some concealment, but it settled as Whitehead's aircraft sat waiting for the advisors to get out of the ditch and load. Ripley never did touch down but remained at a hover. Unfortunately, the ARVNs were faster and began to mob the aircraft.

"Waite, get the Americans on board!" Whitehead yelled. Waite stepped off the skid only to face twenty ARVN soldiers attempting to rush the aircraft. He leveled his M60 and they understood that none of them were getting on that aircraft until the Americans were aboard. Waite saw that one of the Americans was having a lot of difficulty, with a large bandage on his face. Waite, still carrying his M60, jogged to the American and half dragged and half carried Captain Zumwalt to the left side of the aircraft, shoving him into the back. Sergeant Winland climbed in on the right side back but broke the ammo belt for the M60. He also grabbed the M60 and wedged it between the two front seats. Waite couldn't get to it now as it was jammed into position. Colonel Ginger was the last to attempt to board, but the ARVNs rushed the aircraft. Waite thought fast how to stop the mob rushing the aircraft, so he started pointing frantically back at Ripley's aircraft. The ARVNs looked at Ripley's aircraft and then just stood there looking at the skids of Whitehead's aircraft.

Dave Ripley didn't have a chance to set down on the ground, so many ARVNs were attempting to mob his aircraft. As Anderson wasn't with him, he realized if he set down, he would have no way of getting some of these people off the aircraft so he could depart. One ARVN managed to climb on the skid and laid on the deck in the back of the aircraft. Another climbed up and was standing next to Dave when the bullet hit him and he dropped. Other ARVNs were clinging to the skids, attempting to get into or on his aircraft. They were receiving the concentration of NVA fire.

As Waite reached the aircraft, Whitehead noticed that the previous small tapping sounds on the aircraft were continuing. He knew each was a bullet hitting the aircraft. With each sound, his eyes flashed to the instruments. Then a sledge-hammer hit the aircraft. Sergeant Winland let out a yell.

"Shit, I'm hit," he screamed. It appeared that a .51-cal round had penetrated the intercom box and then his hand. He looked back over his right shoulder, and there standing on the skid was Ginger.

"Go, go!" Ginger yelled.

"Waite, are we ready?" More tapping sounds. Waite didn't respond.

"Go, go!" Ginger shouted again.

Whitehead started to execute a takeoff, but the aircraft was too overloaded on the starboard side. Waite saw the problem. Too many people on that side of the aircraft. He quickly got the attention of the ARVN standing on the skid next to Whitehead and got him to move to the copilot seat on the port side. Whitehead attempted another departure. It was still overloaded. ARVNs were standing on the skids, resulting in the aircraft being too heavy. The NVA assisted in this problem by shooting several ARVNs off the skids.

The aircraft was at six feet but no higher when it did a 360-degree turn. As the speed increased, the aircraft would lift off and then settle back down but kept increasing its speed. Finally, translational lift kicked in and the helicopter began to fly. As it did so, Whitehead looked down and to his right.

There, dangling below the aircraft, was an ARVN soldier, hanging on to the leg of the American officer for dear life. He could tell that there were other ARVNs hanging on as well until the burst of heavy weapons opened fire as they crossed the tree line. Suddenly the aircraft shuddered and literally jumped in the air. ARVNs on the port skids had been shot and dropped off.

"Shit, what was that? Waite, you okay?" Whitehead exclaimed out loud. He could barely breathe wearing the gas mask. *If this gas was so effective, why weren't the advisors and NVA sleeping?* he contemplated. He didn't receive an answer from Waite. He ripped the mask off.

"Tiger Two-Three, Tiger One-Five," Whitehead transmitted.

"Tiger One-Five, Two-Three," Ripley replied in a strained voice.

"Two-Three, how you doing?" Whitehead asked as he was starting to get in the air.

"One-Five, I'm behind you. I lost three that were hanging on to the skids. I got some holes in my aircraft and a full load inside."

Glancing around, Whitehead was attempting to assess how many people were aboard the aircraft designed to carry four people. As best he could tell, he had four in the aircraft, one standing on the skids, and two hanging under the aircraft; he prayed Waite was somewhere on the aircraft. He kept looking at his gauges to see if any of the aircraft systems were about to fail. All appeared normal.

"Sir, if you could land, I'm sure we all would appreciate it," Waite's voice yelled through his mask.

"Where the hell have you been? Scared the crap out of me. Thought you were left back in the PZ or dead," Whitehead said with a degree of anger but mostly relief.

"Sir, my intercom is out and I've been hanging on to this

lieutenant colonel. He's standing on the skid and has an ARVN hanging on to his legs, and I have one hanging on to mine. I'm holding the colonel's pistol belt to keep him from falling," Waite said.

"Okay, I'm going to land at Chon Thanh. We have a Huey there to take them all to Lai Khe. Is Ripley behind us?"

"Yes, sir, and it appears he has a full load too." Waite was not only having trouble talking, he was having trouble breathing. His hands were full, holding the colonel's pistol belt and holding on to the aircraft himself. The canister for the gas mask was wedged between the aircraft and the colonel and was being crushed. Waite couldn't get any air.

Landing at Chon Thanh, everyone was transferred to a Huey. Waite ripped the gas mask off and took some deep breaths. Having dropped off their passengers with a medevac Huey, the two aircraft flew on to the refuel point at Lai Khe and then back to the staging area, where they shut down the aircraft for the first time. Whitehead, Waite and Ripley started checking over their aircraft to assess the seriousness of the strikes from .30- and .51-cal machine guns. There were some holes, but nothing serious unless they counted the holes in the fuel cells and rotor blades. As Waite stepped off the aircraft, he noticed a stream of fuel coming out of the bottom of the aircraft. *That's not good*, he thought, watching the fuel he had just put in leak out. Once the rotor blades stopped, he noticed the numerous holes through those blades. One blade was almost cut through. Captain Whitehead's aircraft would not be flying under its own power anymore this day. Ripley fared better and was able to fly the remainder of the day.[1]

## 16

---

# PREPARING AN LOC

**8 APRIL 1972**
   **5th ARVN Infantry Division**
   **An Loc**

Colonel Miller met the helicopter that delivered General Hollingsworth to An Loc. As they walked to the advisor's bunker, Hollingsworth filled him in on the general situation in MR-III.

"General Minh was in Saigon the day before yesterday, meeting with the president. He made a case to get additional forces to this area. Of course, I'm sure General Lam from MR-I made the same case as that's where the main threat is perceived. And of course, if Vann was there, he made a case for more forces to MR-II. He's a good man but can be a real pain in the ass at times. Thinks he knows it all," Hollingsworth grumbled. "So anything new happening here today?" He already knew the answer to that question.

"On a good note, the 3rd Ranger Group closed in yesterday and have taken up defensive positions on the east and north side of the town," Miller said. "On the flip side, however, you know about Quan Loi being overrun last night and this morning, don't you?"

"Yeah. I saw that as I was coming up here."

"Sir, it's only four, maybe five miles to the northeast, so I suspect they'll be coming here next. We also captured an NVA soldier, and he reported that they're stripping every store and home of any food they can find. The refugees are confirming this as well. He looked like he hadn't eaten in a few days. He even ate a can of ham and lima beans we gave him. You know he had to be desperate to eat that stuff," Miller stated.

"I suspect that they weren't expecting the border outposts and Loc Ninh to fall so quick. They're probably in a pause until they can move supplies forward. What did we lose at Quan Loi?" Hollingsworth asked.

"There were two rifle companies from the 1st Battalion, 7th Regiment, along with two 105 howitzers."

"Has any of that been recovered?"

"We're getting some stragglers coming in, but the artillery tubes are probably sitting in the enemy's hands right now," Miller explained.

"Well, we have a bigger problem to the south. Yesterday, it appears that the 7th NVA Division cut the road from Lai Khe to here north of Chon Thanh at Tan Khai. The 5th Armored Squadron attempted to move on up to Chon Thanh and only had some artillery hit them. This morning they're getting a bloody nose on the blocking position that the NVA have put in. Appears to have connecting bunkers, all with overhead cover. Minh is going to move the 21st Division when it arrives up the road to break through and reinforce this place. In the meantime, the airborne brigade is heading this way and should close in on Lai Khe by tomorrow evening. When they arrive, Minh is pushing them up to Chon Thanh to start clearing the road," General Hollingsworth explained.

"Any other cheery news, sir?" Miller asked with a chuckle. Holly didn't answer but simply shook his head in the negative.

As they walked into the advisor bunker, Miller continued, "Sir, my biggest problem here right now is getting General Hung to make a decision. I pointed out to him days ago that he had a choice—defend the firebases or withdraw from the firebase and defend the town, but he couldn't do both. Reinforce bunkers, store ammo, reposition soldiers—but, no, he sits on his ass and does nothing. We nicknamed him 'Be No,'" Miller said with a grin.

"Why's that?" asked Hollingsworth, accepting a cup of coffee from Lieutenant Colonel Edward Benedit. Colonel Benedit was the senior advisor for the 8th Regiment and was in the process of coordinating future operations with Miller when Holly arrived.

"We call him Be No because there will be no discussion, be no opinions and be no decisions. Be No," Colonel Benedit said. Hollingsworth chuckled quietly.

"Morning, General," Major Allen Borstorff said as he entered the bunker.

"Morning, Allen, how's the family?" Hollingsworth asked. He knew the family background of every advisor and most of the wives' first names.

"Good, sir. Thank you for the letter you sent to my son explaining why I'm here. My wife read it to him and then they talked about it. It did a world of good," Borstorff said.

"Glad to do it." Hollingsworth always wrote a personal letter to each child of his advisors, explaining why Daddy was there and not home and the importance of Daddy's work.

"Not to change the subject," Hollingsworth said, sipping his coffee, "but has the drawdown hurt you much? We did take your nonessential people out, so what has the impact been?" Despite the known fact that the North was going to launch a major invasion, US policy was to draw down US forces in-country, to include advisor personnel, and that hadn't changed.

"Well, sir, the nonessentials were happy to get out of here, but what about us? Sir, you have to get us out of here today," Miller said

"You sons of bitches will die with your counterparts, Miller. You're staying!" Hollingsworth said with a hard stare at Miller.[1] "Reports from Quang Tri are that when the advisors were pulled out, the ARVNs ran. You are staying."

Hollingsworth's solution was to strip out cooks, bakers and candlestick makers from the advisor teams in order to meet the drawdown goals. It didn't hurt the mission but did hurt morale to some extent. Now the officers were doing their own cooking and vehicle maintenance.

"I have some excellent NCOs and officers that now make up the combat team. I wish we had advisors at the battalion level with the ARVN battalions, but...," Miller said, not wishing to elevate the tension at this point.

"When the airborne brigade arrives, they do have advisors with them at the battalion levels and so does 3rd Ranger Group," Hollingsworth was quick to add as he finished his coffee. Setting the cup down, he stood. "Okay, let's walk over to the TOC and see what Be No has decided."

Arriving at the command bunker, Hollingsworth walked directly over to General Hung, who was sitting in the corner of the TOC. He looked absolutely depressed. Hollingsworth decided to put his best face forward.

"Morning, General. It's a good day today," he said cheerfully.

"No, not good. Enemy come tomorrow. Enemy come soon. I think we should put out white flag," Hung said.

"Now, General, why do that? Your boys put up a good fight at Loc Ninh and they'll make a good fight of it here."

"Will American soldiers come back?" Hung asked.

"No, General, American soldiers are not coming back. We have air support but that's all. Time for ARVN soldiers to carry the fight," Hollingsworth explained.

"ARVN soldier not as good as NVA soldier," Hung said, and Hollingsworth couldn't believe what he'd just heard.

"Now what makes you say that?" he said, attempting to control his temper.

"NVA have Loc Ninh. Better soldier."

"General, that's bullshit. They took Loc Ninh because they had five times the people you had and they had tanks. Man for man, your soldiers are just as good. Your equipment is better. Your logistic supply line is better. You just have to have some faith. I understand you haven't decided where to defend from—the firebases or the town. You've got to make up your mind and get things ready. Where's it going to be?" Hollingsworth asked, knowing he was pushing the issue.

"We use town," Hung reluctantly stated.

"Good. Now that I know that, I'll talk to General Abrams and attempt to get us more B-52 support. How's that?"

For the first time, Hung's face lit up. Anytime an advisor indicated more air support, that meant less work for the ARVN ground commander. "Colonel Miller and Major Borstorff will work up some B-52 strike boxes around here so that we can quickly call strikes on when necessary. Once those are developed, I'll take them to General Abrams and get some additional strikes," Hollingsworth said.

"Yes, yes, we need more air strikes. That good," Hung said enthusiastically.

"Well, then, I need you to run some patrols so we can find where they're hiding. When a patrol comes back in, you get the information to Colonel Miller and we can get a strike right away. Okay?"

The thought of having to send out patrols turned Hung's stomach.

"I will speak to Colonel Nhut. He runs daily patrols with the regional forces. He also has Montagnard spies who provide good information," Hung said.

As Miller and Hollingsworth departed and walked back to the waiting helicopter, Hollingsworth asked, "Do you think he'll send out patrols?"

"Hell no, sir, but Nhut will, you can bet. We're going to have to rely on the FACs giving us intel on troop movements," Miller replied sarcastically.

"Okay, I'll see if I can get some of the aerial scouts out here from the 1st Cav to get some intel for us. Keep me posted." And with that, General Hollingsworth departed back to Lai Khe.

Throughout the day, Hank observed the activities in the town. What disturbed him most was watching groups of refugees moving down Highway 13 from the north. Reaching the outskirts of An Loc, the groups would begin receiving incoming artillery and mortar fire. Children, the elderly and families would run in panic to reach the buildings or seek refuge in the adjacent ditches and bomb craters. Once the shelling stopped, they would run to the town. It was obvious that the shelling was observed and deliberate. Bodies began to litter the highway. As the refugees reached the town, some kept on moving south, only to return later in the day, saying the road south was closed. Others sought food and shelter. Hank realized quickly that this was going to turn into a humanitarian effort as well as a combat effort.

Walking through the town and especially the outskirts, Hank observed the ARVN defenders preparing fighting positions, digging trench lines, reinforcing walls. Antitank ammunition was being pre-positioned on rooftops, and second-story windows were being made into observation posts. ARVN officers with the 3rd Ranger Group were very proactive in supervising the soldiers under their commands. Earlier in the day, he had stopped in the TOC and made a mental note of how the defense was to be laid out. In the north-to-east quadrant, the 3rd Ranger Group had responsibility and was positioning its six companies along the perimeter. To the southeast, the Regional-Popular Forces had three companies positioned. The southwest was occupied by a battalion of the 7th Regiment. The 1st Battalion had been at Quan Loi and there was no word on their fate. The west was occupied by the 8th Regiment, which only had three companies. Leftover remnants of Task Force 52 were located in the center of town as a reserve and collocated with the artillery battery.

For what was expected, Hank knew this wasn't a lot to defend with, but there were some advantages. All the forces were in prepared positions and many with overhead cover. There was also the airpower that the advisors could bring. The enemy, although large in number, was going to have to attack over open ground. Thinking back to his military schoolhouse days at Benning School for Boys, as the US Army Infantry School was referred to by those that had attended, the attacker theoretically needed a three-to-one advantage over a defender at the point of penetration. So in order for the enemy to penetrate this perimeter, the enemy would need to commit one battalion against a company position if it wanted any chance of getting into the town—theoretically. Hank was hoping that theory was wrong and it would take a lot more than a three-to-one ratio.

**9 April**

Gunfire along the entire perimeter woke everyone at 0500 hours. Hung and Miller as well as everyone in the division CP knew the perimeter wasn't strong enough at this point to stop a major attack, which they all expected at any time since Loc Ninh had fallen. The few artillery pieces and the mortars were firing in support of the perimeter and appeared to be sufficient.

Hank was in the CP with Miller. "What do you think, sir?" Hank asked. His modus operandi was to ask questions and listen. It had served him well over the years.

"I suspect this is only a probe to find the weak spots at this point, and we have enough of them on the perimeter right now," Miller said. "The air strikes will keep them at bay for now. As long as they don't send any tanks in, we should be okay. None of the units sound like they're in a panic, which is good, but we've got to get more people in here one way or the other. Hung needs to talk to Minh about sending us some reinforcements." He paused and then continued, "Our problem is going to be the need to resupply as the road is now closed." What supplies had come in were arriving by VNAF C-123 aircraft flying low-level. Things had been quiet the night before, except there appeared to be heavy traffic moving south on Highway 13 to the east, and all of it on foot.

General Hung was talking to a Vietnamese gentleman that was better dressed than most. Miller had met him before and he was some sort of government official that had been in Loc Ninh. Once Hung's conversation ended, he turned to Miller.

"Very bad, very bad," he kept repeating.

"Okay, General, what very bad?" Miller asked.

"NVA tell everyone they will overrun us soon. Kill everyone. Make An Loc new capital of province," Hung said, wringing his hands. *This guy is coming apart and we haven't even gotten into it yet*, Miller was thinking.

"He say last night, all government officials, teachers, and militia officers lined up in Loc Ninh square and shot. He say same to happen here."

"General, that ain't going to happen here. We have two

strong firebases with artillery supporting us. We have B-52 locked in, and with any luck, General Minh got more forces yesterday. Have you heard from him?"

"Yes, he say 21st Infantry Division come from Delta to us in four days. 1st Airborne Brigade on the way too."

"General, that's great news. We get them in here and it'll be very hard for the NVA to root us out. So, what's your plan to use them?" Miller asked.

"We will work on that today," Hung said and walked off towards his operations officer, who was talking with Major Borstorff, the G-3 advisor.

The radio broke squelch as if someone was attempting to call. A lone voice came on the radio.

"We come now. You die." That was all Hung needed to hear and he was ready to strike a white flag. It took the rest of the day to get Hung to coordinate the defensive plan for An Loc now that the firebases had been abandoned along with all the artillery. Talking to Hollingsworth, Miller found out that the 21st ARVN Division was flowing into Lai Khe nine miles south of An Loc and would be coming up Highway 13 to An Loc. In addition, the 1st Airborne Brigade was flowing north and should arrive in a day or two. The morale of the troops in An Loc soared on these reports.

Civilians coming down Highway 13, however, painted a grim account of what was happening between Loc Ninh and An Loc. Executions were common. Those that had been VC sympathizers were now free to come out of the closet, and they started pointing fingers at those that had worked for or supported the government or US forces. Livestock was being seized and butchered, some for food and some just for the sport of shooting a cow. Almost all the civilians were on foot as vehicles, to include bicycles, were confiscated and taken to Cambodia. Each day, the tide of humanity became worse, with the sick, elderly and very young bringing up the tail end. Young women were easy prey for North Vietnamese soldiers.

Despite this display of walking misery, Miller was able to give Hung hope as they mapped out a defensive plan for An Loc and then together supervised the plan going into effect. As they worked together, Miller began to see an increase in Hung confidence and morale. On the morning of the eleventh, plans and coordination were complete. Hung was in great spirits, almost giddy with joy knowing that the 21st Division would be rolling in the next day. Even better, the 1st Airborne Brigade's lead units were moving up to Chon Thanh. Hung expressed his optimism that a linkup with the forces clearing Highway 13 would arrive on the eleventh.

To raise his spirits more, reports came in from the 3rd Ranger Group that soldiers from the 1st Battalion, 7th Regiment that had been at Quan Loi when it fell, were now coming through the lines in large groups. In turn, the Rangers were directing them to continue to move through the town to the south end, where the 7th Regiment was setting up a perimeter.

**17**

---

# 8TH REGIMENT MOVES

**9 APRIL 1972**
  **229th Assault Helicopter Battalion**
  **Lassiter AHP, Bien Hoa**

"Gentlemen, if you'll all take a seat, we'll get this mission brief started," the Killer Spade commander said. Major Hatcher commanded Bravo Company, 229th Assault Helicopter Battalion, part of what remained of the 1st Air Cavalry Division in Vietnam. Once everyone had settled down, a sergeant brought out a map board with a map of the area on it.

"This afternoon we're going to start lifting elements of the 8th Regiment, 5th ARVN Division, up to An Loc. As you all know, Loc Ninh fell, and it appears that An Loc is next. They need two battalions of the 8th Regiment up there and fast. The 32nd Regiment, 21st Division, is at Lai Khe and will start moving up by truck on the twelfth. The 5th Armored Squadron moved out of Chon Thanh but only got six kilometers up Highway 13 before it ran into a roadblock around Tao O and has been stopped. It appears that it may be a regiment from the 7th NVA Division," he explained. Pilots shook their heads.

"We will be joined by the rest of the battalion tomorrow, but we need to get this moving today. The PZ is the airstrip right here at Dau Tieng and the LZ will be the airfield at An Loc. Tigers will fly escort. Flight altitude is three thousand feet with trail formation. We have ten aircraft up for this mission and plan on ten pax per aircraft. Hopefully we can do this today in four turns. Any questions?" There were none as this was old hat to the pilots of the 229th. "PZ time is 1330. We crank at 1300. See you on the flight line."

The flight from Bien Hoa to Dau Tieng was uneventful. Approaching the airfield at Dau Tieng, the aircraft saw the 8th Regiment standing along the edge of the airfield in chalk order with ten men to a chalk, just as briefed. The PZ was the airfield on the north side of town.

When it touched down, the ARVN soldiers quickly loaded the aircraft, with four soldiers moving to the interior of the cargo compartment and three sitting on each side, their legs dangling out the open doorway. The aircraft all departed together.

The terrain from Dau Tieng was fairly flat with some low hills to the east of An Loc and Highway 13. West of Highway 13, there were some gently rolling hills that would mask an aircraft flying low-level. Once heavily covered in jungle trees, the ground had been cleared extensively over the years from logging operations and the use of Rome plows by the 1st Infantry Division.

The 8th Regiment had been left behind at Dau Tieng originally because in early April, Hung had felt that the Saigon River was still a viable avenue for the enemy to move towards Saigon. Over the years, the enemy had used the river at night to move supplies to Bien Hoa and Saigon. Hung had decided to leave the 8th Regiment behind. It was now obvious that the

8th would be needed in order to hold An Loc as it became encircled.

Colonel Truong, 8th Regimental Commander, was flying in a C&C aircraft with his staff and Lieutenant Colonel Benedit, his senior advisor. As they approached An Loc, he was told that the airfield was being shelled. Major Hatcher was the aircraft commander for the C&C aircraft.

"Major Hatcher, the airfield at An Loc is under fire," Colonel Truong announced over the intercom system.

"Yes, sir, I just spoke to the senior advisor in An Loc and he told me. What do you want to do? We can abort and take you take to Dau Tieng, or we can find another place to put you down—it's up to you, Colonel," Major Hatcher said.

Truong pulled out his map and studied it with Benedit. "We land soccer field, yes?"

"No, that's being shelled too, as is the rest of the town. If we're going to land, it's going to have to be outside the town, sir," Hatcher informed Colonel Truong, who resumed his map study.

"Major, can we land here?" Truong said after a few moments, leaning over the radio console with his map, which Hatcher took and studied. After a few moments, Hatcher nodded in the affirmative.

"Sir, let's take a look and see if anyone's there," Hatcher said as he took the controls from the copilot. Switching from intercom to the command VHF, Hatcher notified the flight of the possible change.

"Flight, this is Six. The airfield at An Loc is being shelled, along with the rest of the town. We're going to attempt to put them in three klicks to the south of town. Door gunner and crew chiefs, be on your toes. There are no friendlies on the intended LZ and no prep. Tiger Three-Four, did you monitor?"

"Roger, Spade Six, Tigers monitored." The pucker factor in each aircraft immediately went up.

Maintaining altitude leaving Lai Khe initially made for a quiet flight. The fear of a missile was always on the minds of the crews as rumors abounded that there was a shoulder-fired anti-aircraft weapon in-country.

"Spade Six, Tiger Six."

Tiger Six commanded Delta Company 229th and was equipped with OH-6 aircraft and AH-1G gunships for escort missions. He was transmitting on VHF as they had discussed the possibility that the NVA were monitoring FM frequencies. No VHF radios had been captured as far as everyone knew.

"Tiger Six, go ahead," Hatcher responded.

"Do you want to pass me the location of the new Lima Zulu and we'll get a little bird there to check it out? Over."

"Roger, new location is X-Ray Tango Seven-Six-Seven, Eight-Five-Oh. How copy?"

"Spade, I have a good copy and we'll look at it." With that, Hatcher could see the OH-6 and two AH-1G gunships peel off and move out ahead of the flight towards the new location. Hatcher had the flight go into a circular orbit until they had word back from the reconnaissance team about the landing zone. Finally word came.

"Spade Six, Tiger Six. LZ is cold. I say again, LZ is cold."

"Roger. Break, Flight, this is Six, follow me in."

Hatcher maneuvered to the front of the formation and guided them into the new location. No one engaged them. The troops quickly exited their aircraft and took up defensive positions around the landing zone. As the helicopters departed for the next load, Hatcher silently wished them a peaceful night. He knew he had three more turns to get in before low fuel would cause an hour delay, and by that time it would be too late to complete the mission. They were coming back in the morning to bring in the last battalion. At the time, he wasn't aware that he was also bringing in four hundred individuals that had been released from prison, where they'd been serving time for various offenses such as desertion, insubordination, and a multitude of civilian crimes. All were soldiers and had been given a choice: come fight or stay in prison. Most figured it was better to come fight and take their chances rather than remain in a Vietnamese prison. They were referred to as LCDB personnel. They weren't issued weapons but were assigned duties such as manual labor, to include digging graves, which would become a full-time job over the course of the battle. Before the battle was over, many were given weapons.[1]

The next morning, Major Hatcher picked up the remainder of the 8th Regiment and deposited them back in the previous day's landing zone. The 8th moved unopposed into An Loc that afternoon, 10 April.

## 18

—————

# AIRBORNE INTO THE FIGHT

**II APRIL 1972**
   **1st Airborne Brigade**
   **Chon Thanh**

Up at Chon Thanh, the order of movement was issued. The 5th Battalion would take the lead initially, followed by the 6th Battalion and then the 8th Battalion. Each day, the order of movement would rotate with the follow-on battalion replacing the lead battalion, which would drop back to the third position. McDermott questioned the wisdom of this rotation system.

"Sir," he addressed Hieu, "the brigade is really conducting a movement to contact with one battalion and upon contact is only fighting with one battalion, it appears. That's only one-third of our combat power. Don't you think we should discuss this with Colonel Le Quang Luong, the brigade commander?"

"You are captain, you do not question colonel," Hieu said and walked off.

*No, you may not question this, but I sure as hell am,*

McDermott thought, and he went looking for Colonel Taylor. Finding him, McDermott tactfully approached the subject.

"Hey, sir, what's the intel saying about what's in front of us?"

"Intel says that some roadblocks are up ahead that we should get through fairly easily. Why?" Taylor asked.

"Well, I was just wondering, sir, why are we conducting a movement to contact with just one battalion on point? If it's a serious roadblock, and looking at the remnants of the 5th Armored Squadron, I would think we would be moving against it with two battalions abreast and a third for maneuver."

"Colonel Luong feels that they haven't had time to put in much of a roadblock and one battalion should blow through it fairly quick. We discussed this and I asked the same question," Taylor said almost apologetically.

"Well, sir, we were notified on the seventh to be prepared to move. We moved on the eighth, and it took us three days to get to Chon Thanh and we're starting up the road today. To me, they've had at least four days to put in a roadblock. I hope the colonel is right."

McDermott headed back to his battalion, which had finished unloading the trucks and were moving out with one company on each side of the road. The terrain on the sides of the road was level for the most part and devoid of thick jungle. The area had been the AO for the 1st US Infantry Division, which had departed Vietnam in 1969. Prior to leaving, they had used Rome plows to strip the jungle back from the road for about five hundred yards. What was left now was waist-high grass, scrub brush and some root balls and deadfall trees. Loggers had removed the good trees that had been knocked down by the Rome plows.

The first sign of trouble was sudden and violent. Moving on foot with two companies on line, one on each side of the road, they moved slowly and methodically. Six kilometers up the road, the 5th Battalion hit the enemy trench line and positions. In the early afternoon, 51st Company was engaged from a trench line that was so well camouflaged, it couldn't be seen until one walked right up on it. The NVA allowed the paratroopers to do so before they opened fire. With the first shots, the entire front opened fire into the forward companies, 51st and 52nd.

"Colonel Hieu, I can get you air support to hit them with napalm," McDermott said, coming up close to the colonel.

"The company commander will use artillery first and then smoke to mask his maneuvering. We don't need fighter jets" was Hieu's response. This surprised McDermott, but he stepped back and let the colonel run his show.

The rest of the afternoon was a slugfest, with artillery preceding each attempt to get into the NVA bunker line. Hieu attempted to maneuver to the flanks for the blocking position, only to find more enemy-occupied positions. It was quickly becoming obvious that this was much bigger than a company or even battalion blocking position. Late in the afternoon, the attack was at a standstill.

While 51st Company faced off with the dug-in NVA, the remainder of the battalion moved to a night defensive position that was being prepared just off Highway 13. A bulldozer was brought in and began pushing dirt to create a four-sided position with a five-foot-high berm of dirt. In the center, a trench was dug and a CONEX container with the battalion radios was lowered into the ground to serve as the battalion command post. When it was all completed, 52nd and 53rd Companies settled in for the night. Relief to An Loc would not be by road very soon.

The night was not a peaceful night. After dark, mortar rounds, inaccurately fired, began falling in the vicinity of the unit's location. Eventually some small-arms fire engaged as well. No one was too concerned as this was a typical NVA scenario. Then there was a double explosive so close together it sounded as one to the untrained ear.

"What the hell...?" McDermott said under his breath. But he spoke out of surprise, as he knew exactly what it was. He got up and looked over at his jeep. A telltale column of dust told where the recoilless rifle round had impacted.

"Sir, what do you think it was?" Lieutenant Cover asked.

"Sounded like a fifty-seven. Not enough noise or damage to be a seventy-five. Nonetheless, we need to kill that thing," McDermott indicated as he picked up the radio handset, placing a call to the FAC above.

"Raven One-One, Green Bay Five-Oh, over."

"Green Bay Five-Oh, Raven One-One, over."

McDermott passed the mission to the FAC. Sitting at three thousand feet, the FAC couldn't see where the recoilless rifle was firing from even on this dark night.

"Green Bay Five-Oh, I have no visual. Can you mark the target? Over."

"Roger, Raven One-One. I'm turning on my strobe. Identify. Over." A strobe light at night very much appeared as a muzzle flash, so it was always best to coordinate before turning the light on.

"Green Bay Five-Oh, I have your strobe, over."

"Raven One-One, from my strobe on a two-nine-oh heading approximately two hundred meters is the target," McDermott indicated.

"Roger, Green Bay. Negative sighting, but keep your strobe on and I'll bring them in. North–south run west of Red Ball."

McDermott understood. The fighters would come from the north on their run and keep the highway between them and the friendly forces. He waited.

The first indication that things were about to happen was

when in the night sky a rocket was launched from an unseen aircraft and streaked to earth. The impact caused a white phosphorous cloud. The recoilless rifle continued to fire. As the A-1 Skyraiders roared past, their engine noise was suppressed by the sound of the string of Mk 81 Snake Eye bombs that exploded parallel to the highway from the first aircraft. That got everyone's attention. When the napalm hit from the second aircraft, even Colonel Hieu paid attention.

"Stop! Stop!" Hieu started screaming. McDermott just looked at him as he danced about.

"Raven One-One, put the next pass just west of that last pass," McDermott requested. Again, a missile plunged to earth, leaving a shower of sparks in its wake. And as before, for a minute or two nothing happened, until the next string of bombs detonated, followed by the fires of napalm. Colonel Hieu just stood there in amazement with his mouth open. The recoilless rifle didn't fire again that night. As the air strike was rolling in, lights from many vehicles could be seen moving up the road from Lai Khe.

"Colonel," McDermott said, gaining the colonel's attention. "What are all those vehicles doing?" McDermott pointed back towards Lai Khe.

"That is lead elements of 21st Division...their 32nd Regiment. They will take up position behind us and begin securing the area to our rear and back to Lai Khe," Hieu responded. McDermott didn't think much of it after that.

Two days later, on 13 April, the 8th Battalion moved past the 5th and 6th Battalions to take the lead and replaced the 6th on the line. From the sounds of the battle to the north, it didn't appear that much movement had occurred the previous day. The 5th Battalion didn't get any orders to move north either. When the mortar rounds started dropping around the 5th, McDermott knew that things weren't going well up north. He took a seat in the shade of his jeep to monitor the ground battle, the fire support net and communications with the FAC. His attention was interrupted by a UH-1H landing and covering everyone and everything in dust. *Who the hell is this now?* he was thinking when a Vietnamese colonel jumped out and approached the TOC.

He was short in stature even for a Vietnamese officer, and it was obvious the heat didn't bother him. His steel pot was fastened under his chin, his flak jacket was zipped up right to the top and the neck collars were pushed all the way up. His appearance from the waist up reminded McDermott of a standing turtle. His Ray-Ban sunglasses topped off the ensemble. Colonel Truong Huu Duc, commander of the 5th Armored Squadron, was not a happy camper. He had been up the road earlier and had his lunch handed to him. He didn't relish the idea of taking his squadron back up the road. He was getting a situation update from Hieu and then was going up for a recon of the battle area, something he hadn't done before.

Departing the 5th Battalion CP, he raised his arm in a circular motion and the VNAF helicopter started. He seated himself in the cargo door and strapped in. Kicking up the usual amount of dust, the aircraft executed his takeoff and began climbing as he turned north. The pilot was flying IFR, evidently—"I Follow Roads."[1] In this case it was a mistake. Approximately one hundred meters north of the 5th Battalion's location, a heavy anti-aircraft weapon opened fire. The enemy gun crew had slipped close to the berm in the tall grass and had remained hidden until just too good of a target came by. The aircraft twisted and turned, attempting to avoid the fire, but it was evident when the smoke started coming out of the engine that he had been hit. Crash-landing from where he'd departed confirmed the fact. The other confirming detail was the limp body of Colonel Duc slumped over with the top of his head missing. Hieu ordered 53rd Company to find and kill the anti-aircraft crew, which they did in short order.

McDermott returned to monitoring the radios. From the sounds he was hearing and the conversations on the radios, things weren't going well up north. As night closed in, even the FAC was becoming more excited as increased anti-aircraft fire was noted, not only in quantity but in caliber as well. The 23mm twin-barrel gun had a much different sound than the .51-caliber machine gun, and the 37mm anti-aircraft gun was even more distinct in its sound and muzzle flash. At first light, things began to heat up when six M48 tanks and two M113 command tracks came from the south and stopped on the shoulder of Highway 13. After a short conference with Hieu, four of the tanks started up the road. Standing on the berm, a small group gathered to watch what was about to happen. The tanks spread out and charged forward, passing 8th Battalion soldiers and plunging into the enemy's trenches. Emboldened, 8th Battalion soldiers charged forward and mopped up the trenches. Everyone was confident that they had found the solution to punching through to An Loc. Ammunition and fuel resupply vehicles moved past McDermott en route to refuel the tanks and resupply the infantry. Just after dark, they were ready to continue the attack.

The tanks assumed a single-file formation and moved up the road. Every other vehicle had the main gun pointing to the opposite side of the road. The tanks were driving in blackout and moving cautiously. A half mile down the road, they ran into an ambush of sorts. It surprised the enemy as much as it surprised the tankers. Hundreds of NVA troops were along the road, waiting to assemble for a move. The tanks rolled into the middle, not realizing where they were or what they had gotten into. The NVA swarmed the tanks, who had all their hatches open. It became a melee, with NVA climbing on tanks and tanks firing beehive rounds at other tanks to clear the

NVA off. Ammo trucks began to explode as the NVA moved down the convoy. In no time, the victory was turned into a rout back down Highway 13 with the NVA in pursuit. Seeing the tanks or what was left of them started a panic in the 8th Battalion as it broke and ran past the 6th Battalion, which held as the NVA didn't press the attack. The next day, the units were notified to withdraw and be prepared for the next operation.

# 19

## SECOND PROBE



**11 April 1972**
  **36th Ranger Battalion**
  **An Loc**

The 3rd Ranger Group, under the command of Lieutenant Colonel Nguyen Van Biet, had arrived in An Loc four days prior. They were the first reinforcements to arrive as only the RF/PF had been stationed in An Loc. Hung had Colonel Biet move up and occupy a position by the airfield and Highway 13. With the arrival of the 8th Regiment the day before, Biet was able to shift his forces more to the east and south on the perimeter of the city. He already had one company pushed out one kilometer to the east. That was the first of his units to engage the NVA.

Major Hank Sabine had spent the night with the 36th. He and Captain Khue, the assistant operations officer for the 3rd Ranger Group, were concerned that An Loc was only lightly defended and the 36th was covering a large area. It couldn't really be called a defense but more of a screening force to prevent the NVA from identifying weak points in the defense. Hank thought that was almost comical as the entire defense of An Loc at this point was weak, with only the RF/PF forces in the southeast, the 8th Regiment in the north and west now and the 3rd Ranger in the north and east. Hank knew a serious attack would overrun the town. The sounds coming from the company positioned forward told him it might be starting.

"Dai'uy," Hank said, getting Captain Khue's attention, "is 1st Company in contract?"

"He is reporting sporadic fire at this time, but he can hear what he believes to be tanks," Captain Khue responded with concern.

"Have you been talking to the FAC?" Hank asked.

"We were about to do that, sir," Captain Moffett, the advisor for the 36th Ranger Battalion, said as he walked into the CP with a PRC-77 radio in one hand and a map in the other. The tempo around the 1st Company sounded like it was picking up. Khue was on the radio talking to the company commander and he was describing the fight that was building.

Khue turned to Captain Moffett. "He say he sees tank," he said with a look of concern.

"Okay, I'm going up on the roof where I can see his position and the FAC. You want to join me, Major?" Moffett asked as finished plotting the company's position and potential assembly areas for the enemy.

"Right behind you, Captain," Hank replied, wanting to observe the action. Climbing on the rooftop of the building that the CP occupied gave them a clear view of what was happening. The company position was on a small rise surrounded by open fields. Their position was covered with trees, which offered some concealment. From where Hank stood, it appeared that the position was being attacked from the west, north and east. Moffett couldn't see any tanks, but from the sounds, he figured they were coming from the north, and the company commander confirmed that.

"Raven Five-Oh, Broadside Three-Six, over," Moffett transmitted. High above, barely audible, Raven Five-Oh orbited like a chicken hawk.

"Broadside Three-Six, Raven Five-Oh, have you got something for me or is someone just celebrating the Chinese New Year down there?" Raven asked, noting the red and green tracer rounds being exchanged.

"Raven Five-Oh, we have tanks reported north of the unit's location," Moffett said and gave the coordinates for the unit, which Raven plotted on his map. Raven was on his second tour in Vietnam as a FAC. In his first tour, he had been flying the O-1 Bird Dog airplane, which was a rather cramped cockpit and a holdover from World War II. The O-2 that he was flying now was luxury, with two pilot seats side by side. He had plenty of room to spread his map out on the adjacent seat as he was flying today without a copilot. The O-2 was a military version of the Cessna 337 Super Skymaster airplane with two engines, one in the front and one in the rear. This airplane had come into service in 1967 and was already being replaced by the OV-10 Bronco, also a twin-engine aircraft.

"Broadside Three-Six, I got it and am coming down for a look."

"Roger," Moffett replied and looked up to see the small aircraft. In the early-morning light, it was difficult to spot the small plane sitting at six thousand feet. Hank and Moffett could hear the aircraft as it approached and clearly saw it when Raven fired a rocket. The impact was obscured from their line of sight, but the white cloud of smoke was easily identified rising above the trees. Moments later there was a flash of movement above the trees and then an eruption of trees, dirt and some people as the Mk 81 bombs from the two jets impacted in the vicinity of the reported tanks. Surprisingly, the tempo of small-arms fire increased dramatically.

"What the hell," Hank mumbled as Captain Khue came up on the roof.

"First Company commander say infantry is trying to close on his position to avoid the bombs from jets," Khue said.

"Makes sense. They figure if they can get in close enough, we won't bomb for fear of hitting our own people. We don't have any attack helicopters yet that could get in close and won't for another hour or so. They're on their own, I'm afraid," Moffett said.

Hank, Moffett and Khue stood on the rooftop and watched the green and red tracers cross the knoll. At times, the green tracers were originating from points very close to the red tracers' point of origin. After an hour, however, it was becoming clear that the red tracers were pushing the green points of origin back and eliminating them. Two hours later, things had quieted down considerably to sporadic shooting. Other events that morning were going to become center stage events.

As the three observers were about to depart the rooftop, Khue got a call from his company that was overwatching Route 303 coming from the east. Looking through his field glasses, he could see a large group of civilians being led by a Buddhist monk coming towards An Loc from Xa Tan Loi, a village three klicks east of An Loc. They were waving a white flag and walking with women, children and some men.

"Colonel Nhut will have more mouths to feed and shelter tonight," Khue said. Before anyone could respond, the first artillery or mortar round impacted in the head of the column. Before anyone could run far, several other rounds impacted in the middle of the group. No one was spared as the mortars continued to rain down on the defenseless civilians. Khue could only stand there with tears streaming down his cheeks. Hank's eyes were watering as well.

When it was over, Hank walked back to the 3rd Ranger Group CP with Khue. Khue explained to Colonel Biet what he had seen. As they talked, 52nd Battalion called to say they had an American officer that claimed he had been at Loc Ninh and had evaded to An Loc. His name was Major Davidson. He was with the survivors of the 7th Regiment that had fled from Quan Loi, all four hundred of them. Davidson was allowed to proceed to the RF/PF compound and the men from the 7th Regiment were directed to the southwest to join their unit, bringing the strength of the 7th Regiment up to eight hundred and fifty now. They would be needed in the days ahead.

# 20

## IT BEGINS

**12 April 1972**
**5th ARVN CP**
**An Loc**

Over at the 8th Regimental area, Hank watched as a CH-47 helicopter approached the airfield. All night, the town had been on the receiving end of intense mortar and artillery fire. Payback was a B-52 strike that went in at 0500 due west of the town. The B-52 strike was awesome in itself, but this one hit something big, as the fireball that rose above the jungle instantly was noticed by everyone and the secondary explosions hadn't stopped for the past three hours. Earlier, he had walked with a company commander from the 8th Regiment. The young Vietnamese captain wasn't the model of confidence that was needed at this point. In fact, Hank was noticing a major lack of confidence in the entire Vietnamese chain of command. Being under artillery fire for the past seven days, with no reports of relief coming, didn't enhance one's confidence.

"Morning, Captain," Hank said, walking up to two advisors from the 3rd Ranger Group who were sitting on some rubble and making coffee. "Mind if I join you?" The two advisors stood.

"No, sir, please do. Coffee?" Captain Mulford offered.

"How are your people holding up?" Hank asked, taking his helmet off and finding a seat. "And, yes, I would take a cup if you have some left." Sergeant Lael had a coffeepot perking just off the edge of the fire.

"Give me your canteen cup, sir. Now this is cowboy coffee, sir. Hope you like it." Lael said.

"Cowboy coffee?" Hank responded with a quizzical look.

"Yes, sir. You get the water boiling—and in this place, I would recommend that for all the water. Once it's boiling good, you put your coffee grounds straight in the water. No basket. Let it perk and when the color's right, crack an egg and drop it in. Voilà, cowboy coffee."

"Why drop in an egg?" Hank asked, curious now and accepting the cup.

"The egg sinks to the bottom as it cooks and drags down all the coffee grounds. We can always find eggs, can't always find coffee," Lael added.

"Sir, what have they got you doing, may I ask? I've seen you around," Captain Mulford said.

"I'm assigned to the Pentagon and here as an observer. I just didn't think I would get to observe this firsthand. Now the senior advisor is using me as a troubleshooter. If he needs an advisor someplace or needs something taken care of, he asks me to do it," Hank explained. As the three sat and enjoyed their coffee, a second CH-47 approached the airfield. As it passed over the tree line on the west side, the sound of heavy weapons could be heard. The aircraft started to smoke. All three advisors stood, watching the final approach. The aircraft landed hard, smoke curling out of one engine. The crew almost immediately began coming out when the mortar round landed on top of the fuselage. The aircraft exploded in a massive fireball that engulfed the crew members.

"Shit!" Mulford said in disgust. "They nailed that aircraft. I'll bet that'll be the last we see of anyone coming into this airfield." While they watched the burning wreckage, movement caught Lael's attention.

"Sir, we have people moving down the east side of the airfield," Lael pointed out. Hank and Mulford directed their attention towards the group. Mulford pulled out a pair of binoculars that he carried and commenced to scan them.

"Sir, it appears they're positioning forces in that tree line. Let me see if I can get an air strike in on that location," Mulford said as he grabbed another radio tuned to the FAC frequency.

"In that case, I best make my way back to the CP. I want to hear how that went down. Thanks for the coffee. I'll try to find you a cold beer in exchange," Hank joked.

"You do that, sir," Lael responded, almost laughing. Hank put his canteen cup away and started jogging towards the 5th Division CP. As he moved along, he could see the looks on the faces of the civilian population. Doom and gloom was everywhere. The civilians that had crawled out of the shelters during the brief lull in the shelling never drifted far, knowing that they would have to get back quick. Everyone's hearing was tuned to the distant booms of mortars and the sounds of artillery shooting. Even the local dogs weren't wandering the streets.

Ducking inside the CP, Hank spotted Colonel Miller and approached him. "Sir, I see we got part of 7th Regiment back."

"Yeah, and they're moving down to take responsibility for the southeast sector with 1st Battalion," Miller said, pointing at the map.

"Well, that's some good news," Hank replied.

"Yeah, but now we're running into a refugee problem. Seems the good padre, Father Dieu Huynh, went out east and rounded up about five hundred Montagnards and have brought them back here. Nhut is having them all checked at the railroad station before he lets the padre take them to the church. We also have a report from the RF/PF that there was a group of civilians moving towards the east gate and they were being herded by the NVA, which were moving right behind them."

"How did you handle that one?" Hank asked.

"I didn't. That was Nhut and Cowley's problem. I think Nhut ordered the troops to fire over the civilians' heads and they scattered. I guess the ones in the front were more afraid of being shot by friendly forces rather than the enemy behind them. The NVA pulled this same trick up at Loc Ninh with the kids," Miller grumbled.

"You know, sir, if you're out to win the hearts and minds of the people, force-marching them in front of you with a rifle in their backs isn't the way to do it," Hank observed.

"Forget that hearts and minds crap. In Tet '68 they were trying to win the hearts and minds. This time it's different. This time it's payback for not supporting them in Tet. This time it's about gaining ground. Screw the hearts and minds. Look outside on Highway 13. There are civilian bodies everywhere. Every time the civilians cluster together, the bastards hit them with artillery. Women, kids, old, sick, lame and lazy—makes no difference, the NVA are going to kill them." The more Miller spoke, the angrier he became.

As Hank and Miller talked, two US officers walked in.

"Excuse me, sir, Colonel Miller?" one of them asked. Miller didn't have his fatigue jacket on, only his green T-shirt.

"Yeah, who are you, Major, and where did you come from?" Miller asked.

"Sir, I'm Major Haney and this is Captain Willbanks.

We're from the 18th Division and came over to replace Colonel Ginger and Captain Zumwalt with Task Force 52," Haney explained.

"How the hell did you get here?" Hank asked.

"We came in on a medevac bird that just picked up some folks," Haney explained.

"Well, glad to have you. Let me give you a rundown on where we are and what to expect," Miller said. As he did so, the sound of incoming rounds could be heard as they impacted along the streets of An Loc.

"We've been getting shelled for about a week now. You can see the results of that outside. We have the 8th Regiment sector on the west-to-north side; the 3rd Ranger Regiment on the north-to-east side; the RF/PF on the east-to-south; and the 7th Regiment on the south-to-west side. We've positioned the remnants of Task Force 52 here in the center around the artillery position. We don't have a lot of artillery here and it's a favorite target of the NVA, so if we get a penetration, defending those guns for as long as we have them is key. Understood?" Miller asked.

"Understood, sir. We'll head over and find the task force CP if you have nothing else, sir," Haney said.

"No, good luck," Miller said and then added, "Tell Colonel Thinh I thought he did a hell of a job getting his people back here. He lost half of his task force but probably could have saved a lot more if someone had gotten his head out of his ass and ordered them back here early in the first place. Check and see how he's doing. I understand he was wounded and still came through it all."

With that, Haney and Willbanks departed, moving from covered position to covered position through the incoming artillery and mortars. As they departed, a Vietnamese soldier handed Miller a note, which he attempted to read.

Looking at Hank, he asked, "Can you read Vietnamese?" he asked.

"I'll take a stab at it, sir," Hank responded, taking the note and scanning it. As he did so, a smile crept across his face.

"Good news?" Miller asked.

"It appears that the 21st ARVN Division is arriving at Lai Khe and will be heading this way," Hank said, which placed a smile on Miller's face too.

# 21

## SIEGE OF AN LOC

**13 April 1972**
**5th ARVN HQ FWD**
**An Loc**

"Incoming!" screamed Major Borstorff as the first artillery round slammed into the town and very close to his bunker. As he rolled out of bed and landed on the floor, he glanced at his travel clock. It was 0400 hours. In the command bunker, reports of tanks or heavy equipment had been flowing in since midnight. The 7th Regiment had been hearing the noise all night. With the first reports, Spectre gunship was requested and arrived, finding some trucks to the west and quickly dispatching them into the eternal life. That must have made someone angry, and the artillery started pounding the town. It would continue for the next couple of hours. The small dirt airfield on the north side of the town was particularly hard hit as the ammo dump and fuel depot were located there. Soon, however, both were lighting up the morning sky as they took direct hits. While attention was focused on the exploding north side of the town, five hundred meters to the east side, trip flares and claymore mines began igniting and exploding as infantry and tanks approached. The ARVN defenders did as expected —they ran.

Colonel Miller had been in the TOC since midnight, reading the intelligence reports coming in. He fully expected that this was the day that they had been preparing for. Spectre gunships pretty much confirmed what he'd suspected was coming at them. Hung had left the CP earlier in the evening after going over the defensive plan with Miller.

"Okay, now we have the 3rd Ranger Battalion along the east and northeast side, and the 8th Regiment across the north and west side, blocking Highway 13. Those elements of Task Force 52 that could get back are on the north in a very narrow sector between the 3rd and the 8th Regiment. The 7th ARVN Regiment is on the west and southwest of our defense with the Ruff-Puffs filling in the gap between the 7th and the 3rd," Colonel Miller explained to Lieutenant Colonel Robert Corley. Colonel Corley commanded Advisor Team 47, which consisted of advisors to the Binh Long Province chief and his Ruff-Puffs. Team 47's mission had previously been to focus on the economic development of the province and not so much on the military aspects of defense. That was all about to change. "We should be sitting okay for the time being," Miller said.

As Borstorff barreled into the TOC, the incoming artillery was increasing in volume and intensity. "Damn, I think someone's serious about kicking us out of here," he said, hoping to inject some humor into the situation as the ARVN staff was looking as if they were ready to panic.

"Have you heard from the trenches?" Borstorff asked, looking at Colonel Miller.

"No, nothing yet, just reports of the shelling. Captain

Moffett with the 3rd Rangers checked in when this shelling started, but no word since."

Suddenly there was a series of explosions, closer and louder than the others. "Sounds like he just shifted his fires. Could he be probing to find us?" Corley asked.

"Could be, but I would think he'd concentrate his fires on the perimeter," Miller said, looking up from the map overlay of the city and friendly positions. Looking back down, he quietly whispered, "Oh shit. Major."

"Sir," responded Borstorff.

"Look outside and see what the condition of the hospital is. That incoming sounds like it's damn close to it, and I bet they didn't take the medical flag down."

"Yes, sir." Borstorff slipped out the doorway. A few moments later, he was back.

"Sir, the hospital is gone," he said with a shocked look. "I think they deliberately targeted the place as it's flattened. I doubt if anyone got out."[1] As the advisors discussed the situation, an ARVN radio operator became very excited.

"Tanks come, tanks come!" he screamed, getting everyone's attention. Miller moved over next to General Hung, who was showing panic on his face.

"General, what is he screaming about? Did he get a report of tanks?"

"Yes, tanks are attacking on the western perimeter. Also from north against 3rd Ranger. They will break through," Hung said. Immediately Miller grabbed the advisor radio handset and called Moffett.

"What is your situation?" he asked.

"We have tanks in the wire. A couple have broken through and these guys are panicking and running. I've got to stop this or the whole line will collapse. I'll get back to you," Moffett said. As he departed his fighting position to stem the flow of retreating, panic-stricken ARVN Rangers, he grabbed Colonel

Biet. "Colonel, we have got to stop them," he said in his best Vietnamese.

"How? They scared" was the colonel's response.

Moffett thought about that for a minute before he acted. *To stop this, they have to be more afraid of me than the damn tanks.* Grabbing his radio, he sprinted to the street down which the soldiers were starting to flee. As his position had been behind the front line with good observation, he was able to see what was happening. Reaching the street, he fired his weapon in the air in front of the mob. The panicked leaders stopped, with the remainder of the soldiers behind them. His interpreter stood next to him. Although his Vietnamese was understandable, he wanted there to be no mistake as to what he was about to say.

"Stop. Stop running or I will call an air strike on you." His interpreter translated, and immediately the looks told him his threat was effective.

"Get back in your positions and use your weapons to stop them. If the tanks get by, then let them. Stop the infantry. Now get back." Almost immediately, the ARVN Rangers began running back to their positions, skirting around buildings to avoid the first of the tanks that had breached the wire. Returning to his overwatch position, Moffett notified Miller of the situation.

"Sir, I got them going back to the original positions, but a tank got through and is heading down Highway 13 through the town."

"What about his infantry?" Miller asked.

"His tanks had almost no infantry support as it appears the tanks outran the infantry. His infantry is hitting the line now and it looks to be an entire regiment if not two."

"Can you hold?"

"For now, yes, but not sure how long," Moffett said.

·  ·  ·

## ARVN Disposition, 13 April 72[2]

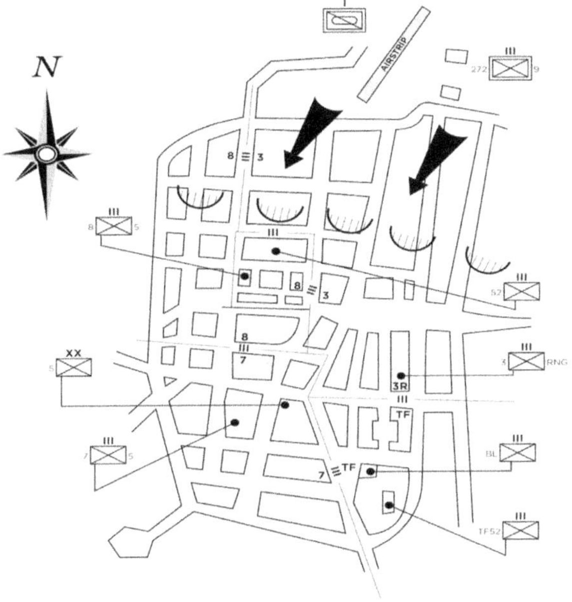


As the sun rose, so did the flight of three AH-1G Cobra gunships from F Battery, 79th Aerial Rocket Artillery Battalion, call sign Blue Max. Major McKay was flight lead on this morning flight and had discussed with General Hollingsworth the day before what he thought of the intelligence picture. His assessment: the enemy was going to hit An Loc hard this morning. McKay was on target. Arriving over the city, he could clearly see the lines for friendlies and enemy from the exchanges of green and red tracers.

"Tunnel One-Zero Alpha, Blue Max Six, over."

"Blue Max Six, Tunnel One-Zero Alpha, over." Miller sounded very anxious, McKay thought.

"Tunnel One-Zero Alpha, Blue Max is a flight of two.

Where do you want us?" McKay asked as he looked down and saw the tanks coming towards the town as well as entering the streets.

"Blue Max Six, we have tanks in the town. You can't help us as the collateral damage will be too great."

"Tunnel One-Zero Alpha, Blue Max Six, I have HEAT rockets. Minimal explosion and perfect for knocking out tanks. Let me take a shot," McKay asked.

"Blue Max Six, roger, but minimize the collateral damage. Let's see what you can do."

With that, McKay picked out the tank that was furthest into the town. He rolled over and pointed down, punching off a rocket. With the steep dive, low altitude, the probability of a miss was minimal, McKay thought. He was right. The rocket hit the very top of the turret. As McKay pulled out of his dive, he looked back over his shoulder. Suddenly the turret blew off the tank and flames shot out of the top hatch on the turret. Miller was on the radio.

"Blue Max Six, that tank was five hundred meters from my location. Take out any you can find. Nice shooting."

* * *

Major Hank Sabine had moved up to the forward position of the 8th Regiment. The company was located on a small but steep hill just northwest of the airfield and overlooking Highway 13 as it approached from the north. It had been designated as Hill 129. The company was well dug in with good fields of fire and long-range observation. What they saw was not good. Fifteen tanks were moving down Highway 13 right towards them. The infantry was about a klick behind the tanks, which by all appearances were outrunning the infantry. Hank thought this pretty odd as tanks in an urban environment needed supporting infantry or else they were subject to easy ambush by infantry in the buildings. An O-2 FAC was above and darting down to fire a white phosphorus rocket, marking targets for the jets that were loitering above, waiting for a target. Today they would not be disappointed. It was going to be a target-rich environment.

Suddenly, Hank saw the troops climbing out of their foxholes, slowly at first, and moving back towards the town. Grabbing the company commander, he asked, "Dai'uy, what are you doing?"

"We go, we no fight tanks, we go," the young officer said with terror in his eyes, pulling away from Hank's grip. "We go now!" And then he was leading his men off the hill.

*Son of a bitch*, Hank thought as he started moving back with them. *First time they see tanks and they run…oh crap! This is probably the first time they've ever fought against a tank and they've only used the M72 against bunkers. Shit, got to show them that the M72 will stop a tank.*

As Hank moved south, headed for the 8th Regiment CP, he noticed that the RF/PF unit that was defending the airstrip was also pulling back, with NVA soldiers moving right behind them. The NVA pursuit was curtailed when the ripping sound of a Spectre gunship was heard.

Hank paused long enough to get a picture of the NVA attack. It appeared that they were coming right down Highway 13, with one infantry battalion on each side of the road and the tanks on the road. The tanks moved right through the first line of defense but stayed on Highway 13. As the infantry reached the first line, the ARVN artillery that was available opened fire with final protective fires. This broke the back of the northern ground assault, temporarily. Hank took one last look and decided to get to the division command post and relate to them what he had seen.

In the CP, Hung was standing in front of the map board. A city map was on the board with an acetate cover. The unit's friendly positions were marked on the acetate in blue. In red grease pencil, an ARVN staff officer was marking where the enemy was hitting the perimeter. It appeared that the entire north half of the perimeter was under siege, with the bulk of the enemy coming right down Highway 13. Outside, the sounds of small-arms fire were intense, more so than should be expected if the perimeter was holding.

"Borstorff, get the FAC on the horn and get some air strikes on the north. His call sign is King FAC. I'm going to have a look at the perimeter," Miller said as he headed out the door with his M16 and helmet. Lieutenant Colonel Corley was right on his tail. As they moved from building to building, it became obvious that the perimeter in the north wasn't holding well but being pushed back into town. As they went into a one-story building, they bumped into Sergeant First Class John Hutchinson, who had an ARVN sergeant with him, Sergeant Ta. Ta was always with Hutchinson who was considerable older and more of a father figure to the young Vietnamese. Both were carrying an armload of M72 rockets.

"Where you heading with those?" Corley asked as Hutchinson technically worked for him as part of Advisor Team 47.

"Sir, there's a tank that got through and is rolling down Highway 13 through the camp. There are no LAWs with our people, so we came and are taking these down there. Hope to stop the bastard," Hutchinson said.

"Go get 'em" was all Corley said as he and Miller resumed their trip north.

SFC Hutchinson and Sergeant Ta moved as rapidly as possible between direct fire from the few NVA that had managed to infiltrate the town and the incoming artillery rounds to get back to the Ruff-Puffs located in the southern part of the town. As they did so, they would catch a glimpse of the tanks moving on Highway 13. The tanks were just creeping along and appeared to be confused as to where they were and where they were going. Most of the tank commanders were standing in open hatches and looking around. Hutchinson made a mental note that these were T-55 tanks, World War II vintage. What Hutchinson didn't witness was what was transpiring deeper in the tank formation.

The fifteen tanks were in a trail formation, one tank behind the other as they moved. The first two tanks were buttoned up with all hatches closed. This greatly restricted the visibility for those track commanders. When the third tank in the formation was hit by a direct-fired 105 howitzer round, the tanks behind him stopped, but the two in front didn't, continuing on down Highway 13. As those behind the third tank sat, soldiers of the 8th Regiment closed in and began hitting them with M72 antitank weapons. Quickly tanks four, five and six were destroyed. The remaining tanks found the reverse gear and began backing out of town. The infantry, however, managed to get a foothold at this point on the northern part of the town, having pushed the 8th Regiment and 3rd Ranger Group back.

"Sergeant Ta, start passing those LAWs out, but be sure whoever you give one to knows how to use the damn thing," Hutchinson instructed. He had given the soldiers a class on how to operate the M72 LAW, but some of these soldiers weren't the brightest he had ever served with. The LAW was a simple fire-and-throw-away weapon to put into operation; knock off the end caps, grasp each end in one hand and extend the weapon. This opened the weapon up and caused the front and rear sights to pop up as well as arming the weapon. Fired from the shoulder, the M72 launched a 66mm antitank rocket with a range of two hundred meters. As Sergeant Ta passed out the weapons, most soldiers were exchanging looks that asked, *Are you going after a tank?* The corresponding answer was *No!* But one soldier didn't return the look as the sounds of a tank coming down the road through the middle of town could be heard.

The young private, new to the ranks of the Ruff-Puffs, released the end caps on the launcher and extended the tube. Placing the lightweight weapon on his shoulder, he entered a building and moved to the open doorway. His comrades watched from their positions. As the tank slowly passed his position, the private stepped out of the doorway, took slow aim at the lumbering metal beast that was now only one hundred feet away, and fired. The 66mm round slammed into the side of the tank just below the turret. Immediately there was an explosion and smoke began to pour out of the top hatch, followed by NVA tankers attempting to get out. That was when the ammunition in the tank began to explode. Within minutes the tank was just a burning hulk, but the morale of every soldier had soared. Now that they'd realized they could destroy tanks, everyone wanted in.

Private Pham Cuong Tuan was new to the RF/PF program. Sixteen years old, he had just completed his basic training when he'd come home to his parents' house in An Loc. The day before, he had seen that house destroyed by a direct hit from an artillery round. He was thankful that his father had built a strong underground shelter a couple of years before. They were in the shelter when the house was hit.

"Binh, Giang, come with me, and bring some of those weapons," Pham said, soliciting the aid of his two school-mates. Binh and Giang weren't in the RF/PF but certainly realized they were in this fight. Grabbing two M72s each, the trio started up the stairs to a rooftop overlooking Highway 13. The lumbering metal beast was slowly approaching as Pham carefully peeked over the edge of the roof. Binh and Giang watched as he squatted down and began to put the M72 into operation. They each picked up a weapon and imitated his actions. For a moment, they sat and listened. Slowly, Pham lifted his hand and extended one finger, then he paused and raised a second. Shifting his position, he then raised the third finger and stood up to look over the edge of the roof. Binh and Giang followed suit. Directly below was the tank. All three fired together at the top of the tank. The resulting explosion blew all three soldiers onto their backs and gave them mild concussions. Looking around and shaking their heads, they realized what they had done and began laughing.

"Pham, let's go get some more," Binh said with a broad smile.

Major Borstorff had been out of the TOC, checking on advisors as well as the forward positions. He had an opportunity to observe the enemy firsthand, up close and personal. Moving back to the TOC, he found Colonel Miller and Lieutenant Colonel Corley hunched over a map, looking for known and suspected enemy locations.

"What's the situation out there, Major?" Miller asked.

"Sir, they took the top half of the town, but the line has been stabilized. The west, south and east are holding their own. The saving grace is the fact that the enemy isn't sending his infantry in with tank support or his tanks with infantry support. The TACAIR is hitting them hard whenever they start to come together. They're attempting to get in close to negate our use of TACAIR," Borstorff explained.

"Well, glad you could find a shining light in this mess," Miller quipped.

"There is one thing...we need to get a medevac bird in. Captain Mike Evergram with the 3rd Rangers was wounded."

"Okay, I'll get on the horn and call for a medevac bird. Hospital was pretty much destroyed?" Corley asked.

"Yes, sir, and most of the staff with it, along with our medical supplies," Borstorff said.

"No need to cry about it now...we'll need to come up with an alternate medical station close to the soccer field. Corley, have you got someone that can take care of that for us?" Miller asked as Corley was more familiar with the locals than Miller's team.

"Yeah, I'll get someone right on it," Corley responded. He headed for the door but paused as the next flight of incoming artillery could be heard before it impacted. Since first light, the shelling on the town had been constant. Anytime a helicopter approached, the shelling would increase in intensity. When he started out again, he was shocked to see an NVA soldier coming through the door. He started to draw his .45 pistol when an ARVN officer shoved the NVA soldier to the floor.

"What the—" Corley yelled, looking first at the NVA soldier and then the ARVN officer.

"He prisoner, Colonel. He have good story," the ARVN office explained as Corley bent over and helped the NVA soldier up. This was the first time Corley had been up close and personal with an enemy soldier who was alive. The soldier was young and looked terrified. Corley guided him to a chair and sat him down, then handed him a warm Coke. Almost immediately he could see the kid start to relax. Turning back to the ARVN officer, Corley asked, "Okay, what's his story?" Words were exchanged between the officer and the prisoner, who started talking rapidly.

"He say he in Hanoi last month and come down Ho Chi Minh Trail for one month. He get here two days ago. He told that this would be easy and defenders would run away, not fight. Political officer say people would welcome them and have big parade for them. He brought new uniform that was in his tank just for the parade. He say fellow soldiers not happy about fighting and bombing. Not happy with big bombers," the ARVN officer translated. While the fight was raging in An Loc, decisions had been made about reinforcing the garrison.

* * *

Later in the morning, General Minh met with General Nghi, the 21st Division commander. General Hollingsworth was in attendance, as was Colonel Ross J. Franklin, the senior advisor to the 21st Division.

"General Nghi, your mission is to destroy enemy forces between Chon Thanh and Lai Khe. The airborne is responsible for opening the road north of Lai Khe. We're going to move the 1st Airborne Brigade to An Loc, and the 3rd Airborne Brigade will conduct missions north of Chon Thanh," Minh directed.

"Sir, I can move the advance element of the 31st Regiment today with air support to this clearing at the Soi Tre Hamlet just north of Chon Thanh and the 32nd Regiment advance element to Chon Thanh by truck as well," Nghi indicated. Glancing at Hollingsworth, Ross nodded his head, indicating that he thought the division could execute this properly.

"Then proceed with our mission, General," Minh ordered.

22

# 1ST AIRBORNE BRIGADE AIRMOBILE

**14 APRIL 1972**
**1st Airborne Brigade CP**
**Chon Thanh**

The soldiers of the 1st Airborne Brigade were slugging it out on Highway 13 as the airborne brigade commander, Colonel Luong, was meeting with General Minh and General Duong Quoc Dong, the Airborne Division commander in Lai Khe.

"Here is the situation, gentlemen," General Minh began. "The enemy is tightening the noose around An Loc. The road is closed, but we must get reinforcements into An Loc. I am considering an airmobile insertion by the 1st Airborne Brigade into An Loc. What are your thoughts?" Minh asked.

"Can the choppers get into An Loc? What is the air-defense threat?" Luong asked.

"I was thinking," Dong interjected as he looked at the map, "that we could land outside of An Loc and move in rather than attempt to land right in An Loc. I understand the enemy artillery is pounding the place. They see the first helicopter and they will start shooting airfields or anyplace else big enough to handle the aircraft."

"There are considerations for landing on or off the objective in an airmobile operation," Colonel Luong stated. "One consideration is the availability of landing zones for the size force. With the airfield being overrun and the soccer field in no-man's-land between the enemy and our forces, that is not good. Besides, if we started landing on the soccer field, they have it registered with artillery. I think it would be best to land outside of town and move into the town."

His words didn't fall on deaf ears. Minh pulled out a map and spread it across a conference table. "Where do you propose to land the brigade?" Minh asked. This question brought all three to move over the map. "It appears that the enemy is the strongest in the north and the west. I would not recommend a landing zone in that area."

Luong continued to look at the map.

"Sir, there is a small force on this Hill 169, is there not?" General Dong asked.

"Yes, Hung had pushed out an element of the 3rd Ranger Group when they arrived, and I understand there is a listening element up there monitoring NVA radio traffic."

"Sir, I recommend we land at the base of Hill 169 and move from there into An Loc," Luong said. "This high ground overlooks An Loc, and if I could get my artillery up on this hill, call it Windy Hill, then I could support the fight in An Loc. I could put the artillery up there with one battalion and maneuver with my two other battalions and the 81st Ranger Battalion into An Loc."

"Where exactly would you want to land?" Minh asked.

Luong took a closer look at the map. "Right here, sir. X-Ray Tango Seven-Nine-Eight, Eight-Five-Eight. It is big enough, it is covered from anyone watching An Loc on the east side, and it appears to be open enough for the whole force to land at once if you have that many helicopters," Luong said.

"You will get all the helicopters we can get, but it may take a couple of lifts to get you in there," Minh said.

"I think we can improve our chances of getting the force in there unopposed," General Dong said.

"How is that?" Minh wanted to know.

"You have a press briefing later today, do you not?" Dong asked.

"Yes, but—"

"In the press brief, you let it slip that we will be taking back the airfield at Quan Loi and maneuvering behind the forces attacking An Loc. We will be doing that tomorrow afternoon. The enemy spies will see the helicopters massing and know an airmobile insertion is about to take place. They will report it. Without a cover story, the enemy will assume that force is going to An Loc, but—"

"But if we say we are going to take back Quan Loi," Minh interrupted, "he will shift forces back to that area and away from An Loc. Might even take any forces he has on the east side and run them back up to Quan Loi. It is worth a try. Let's do it. Colonel Luong, I will have the 21st take over on Highway 13 from you. Move your brigade back to Chon Thanh and be prepared to airmobile to take Hill 169 and Windy Hill. Upon closing, move your brigade minus into An Loc. I will notify General Hung that you are coming. Good luck."

Later that morning, Colonel Luong had assembled the battalion commanders and advisors for a quick brief on what was going to happen once 21st Division conducted the linkup and assumed responsibility for Highway 13. Conducting an airmobile insertion was pretty much by standard operating procedures as it had been done so many times over the years. The discussion would focus on the landing and movement into An Loc.

"Gentlemen, we will be landing here, X-Ray Tango Seven-Nine-Eight, Eight-Five-Eight," Luong said as he pointed at the map that was spread out across the hood of his jeep. "The order of insertion will be 6th Battalion, 5th Battalion, and then 8th Battalion. Upon landing, 6th Battalion will move to this hilltop, X-Ray Tango Seven-Niner-Five, Eight-Seven-Four, and establish a secure fire support base. When ready, eight howitzers will be flown in to support An Loc. We will call this hilltop Doi Gio.[1] This will commence at 1400 hours today. Any questions, Colonel Dinh?" Luong asked.

"No, sir," Dinh replied, jotting down some notes.

"Currently there are elements of the RF/PF on Hill 169, securing a radio listening station there. They are reporting no enemy activity at this time. That could certainly change quickly. In the morning, the 5th and 8th Battalions will land and move to An Loc along two routes. 5th Battalion will take this northern route and 8th Battalion the southern route," Luong instructed as he pointed at the map that had the two routes marked. "The brigade CP will initially move to Hill 169 and from there follow 8th Battalion into An Loc. A jump CP will remain on Hill 169 for the time being. More details will be available to the 5th and 6th Battalions after I speak with General Hung. Gentlemen, if there are no questions, I will see you on the PZ," Luong concluded.

Major Morgan, Lieutenant Kelly and Colonel Dinh moved back to Morgan's vehicle and rode over to where the battalion was assembling for the upcoming airmobile insertion. Dinh's main concern was the insertion with no artillery prep of the landing zone. Morgan assured him that they would have close-air support standing by if needed. He was also concerned about the possibility of tanks coming down Route 245 from the north.

"We need to be sure that we have someone to block this road from Srok Ton Cui," Dinh indicated.

"Sir, we have those new XM-202 FLASH weapons and everyone has been trained on them. They, along with the M72 LAWs, will put fear in any tanker's mind. They can stop a tank, and they can sure as hell scare them," Morgan assured him as they pulled up in front of the company commanders.

Dinh motioned for them to gather around as he spread his map out on the hood of the jeep. "This afternoon, we will conduct an airmobile insertion to this landing zone," he indicated with his finger on the map. "We will then move to this hilltop, which we call Doi Gio, and secure for a firebase. Once it is secured, eight howitzers will be brought in and we will provide fire support for An Loc. The order of movement will be 60th Company to secure the landing zone for the rest of the battalion. The command post will come next with 61st Company. Once 64th and 63rd Companies arrive, they, under the command of Major Bang, will attack a small enemy outpost on Doi Gio. There is a unit from the 52nd Ranger Battalion here on Hill 169. It is 3rd Company. They have reported a small VC unit on Doi Gio. Any questions?" Dinh asked.

"Sir, does 60th Company stay securing the landing zone or join you on Doi Gio?" the 60th Company commander asked.

"You will remain securing the landing zone until tomorrow, when the remainder of the brigade will be inserted. Then you will move up and join the rest of the battalion. If there are no more questions, let's get ready to board the aircraft."

In Bien Hoa, Major Nguyen Van Uc was responsible for the aviation support to the 1st Airborne Brigade. The 43rd Helicopter Squadron, 3rd Air Division, had no problem with the troop lift. Soldiers were proficient in airmobile operations and all went well.

The troop insertions went smoothly. The battalion XO, Major Bang, quickly got the 63rd and 64th Company commanders together and set out for the top of Doi Gio. Major Morgan thought it best that he go with Bang.

"Ross, I'll move up with 63rd Company. Why don't you stay here with Colonel Dinh and move up when he comes up later? That way we have everyone covered if need be," Morgan directed.

"Yes, sir. Just be careful, sir. See you on the top," Ross replied and picked up his rucksack, heading out to find Colonel Dinh. The landings had been as desired, unopposed and quiet. This allowed the battalion to get organized quickly and the two rifle companies to move out in the direction of Doi Gio. The terrain was not very restrictive, so the paratroopers moved fairly quickly and in an orderly fashion. They became more cautious as they approached the crest of the hill. They didn't see the hidden bunker until it opened fire. A small firefight ensued, with the VC being quickly killed—but not before damage was done.

"Shit, that hurts," yelled Major Morgan, sitting on the ground and holding his leg. A young Vietnamese soldier was getting a tourniquet on the leg and applying a field dressing. Bang came over.

"Major, you no go on. We medevac you. I call Ross," Bang said, picking up Morgan's radio. "Condor Two-Six, Panther Five, over."

"Panther Five, Condor Two-Six, over," Lieutenant Ross Kelly answered.

"Condor Two-Six, Condor One-Six need medevac. He no walk no more."

*Shit, how bad is he and can I get a medevac up there?* Ross wondered. "Roger, Panther Five, I take it that he's not critical, over."

"No, he not critical, but he no walk."

That news made Ross feel a lot better, and he submitted a medevac request, giving the LZ as the pickup point. Colonel Dinh wanted to get on the top as quickly as possible, so Ross set out with him. On the way up, they met Morgan, who was being carried down, his leg bleeding and bandaged. After some brief words, each continued on his way. As soon as the hilltop was secured, the first CH-47 arrived with a small bulldozer that began pushing dirt to create a berm and a cleared area for the artillery. VNAF Squadron 237 was responsible for moving the eight 105 howitzer artillery pieces. They flew CH-47 aircraft as the UH-1H wasn't capable of lifting the 105 howitzer. Picking up the howitzers at Lai Khe, the flight of eight CH-47s took a trail formation, with one-minute separation between aircraft. One minute should allow sufficient time for an aircraft to approach the intended touchdown point and set the load down.

As they approached the top of Doi Gio however, the last two aircraft came under fire and were badly damaged. Both aircraft pickled their loads into the jungle from several hundred feet. Only six howitzers would be located on Doi Gio.

As the work progressed around him, Ross looked off to the west towards An Loc. The hill had good observation of the town. Ross noticed the rubbled buildings and the rising smoke from burning buildings. Nothing looked in order, with smashed cars in the streets, broken windows, and collapsed roofs. As the 61st Company moved up from the landing zone, enemy mortar rounds began to drop on the landing zone. Only 60th Company remained there, and they did take some casualties. The night was relatively quiet.

The remainder of the 1st Airborne Brigade arrived early in

the morning of 15 April. Luong wanted to get the brigade minus 6th Battalion into the town before dark. Both 8th and 5th Battalions, once organized on the landing zone, moved out as well. During the night, Luong had worked out with Hung where the 5th and the 8th Battalions would be situated as well as the 81st Ranger Battalion, which would be the last unit arriving. As 5th Battalion was the first to arrive, they were the first to move out and took a path through rubber trees towards the railroad running north on the east side of An Loc. Captain Mike McDermott was pleased at how well the paratroopers moved with speed and caution through the rubber tree plantation.

About halfway to An Loc, the forward movement stopped. McDermott felt a need to move forward and see what the hold-up was. When he found the lead company commander, it was quickly evident what the problem was.

"Dai'uy, why are we stopping?" Hieu asked as he moved with McDermott. The company commander only pointed. Following his finger, Hieu and McDermott first noticed a body wearing a maroon beret, then another and another. They quickly lost count of the number of bodies that were lying amongst scattered equipment. These were Rangers from 3rd Ranger Group that had struck out for Doi Goi and had been ambushed on the 7th when the group had arrived. The more the McDermott looked about, the more it became evident that the Rangers had become surrounded and fought to the last man. They normally wore steel helmets, but during the course of the fight they'd realized that they weren't going to break out and were going to die, so they'd removed their helmets and put on the maroon berets that they were so proud of. The NVA had gone through their pockets and backpacks, taking anything that might be useful and leaving the rest scattered about. The scene sickened McDermott but also enlightened him as to the fact that they were going up against a very determined and deadly enemy. An enemy that was giving no quarter.

Hieu ordered the battalion to press on to An Loc. Burial of the Rangers would have to wait. As they moved, they came across a fresh graveyard of NVA soldiers. The Rangers had taken many with them across the Rubicon. Before they reached An Loc, the 5th Battalion would be taking many across the Rubicon as well.

## 23

---

# MOVEMENT TO CONTACT

**16 APRIL 1972**
**5th Battalion, 1st ARVN Airborne**
**Soc Gon Hamlet**

The 5th Battalion was halfway to An Loc when it moved up on the tiny hamlet of Soc Gon. Thatched huts for the plantation workers were about all that existed in the deserted village. The usual occupants of chickens and pigs were absent, as were the people. Seeing such a deserted community made for uneasy feelings in the battalion as it usually foretold that the enemy was present. The battalion had been moving through the rubber tree plantation with its neatly laid-out rows of trees, evenly spaced apart as if a survey had been done on each tree before it was planted. The vegetation between the trees was minimal as the workers kept the vegetation low and the lack of sunlight was not conducive to growth on the plantation floor. However, the neatly laid-out trees and lack of vegetation made for very clear fields of fire for a defender.

"Dai'uy McDermott, we have prisoner," Hieu said,

approaching McDermott. "Come, we talk him." The unit had found this young man wandering through the plantation and stopped to question him. They were located in a small saddle between Soc Gon (XT 780, 881) and another hamlet, Phu Hoa. Before they could begin to question him, small-arms fire was heard coming from the direction of Soc Gon. The intensity quickly picked up, and Hieu was on the radio, talking with the 51st Company commander.

Turning to McDermott, Hieu said, "He say battalion-strength unit attacking his position."

"Sir, I'll move up and get an air strike to support if he needs it," McDermott said, motioning for his assistant to follow him. Hieu waited at the battalion CP location, well behind the units in contact.

McDermott's progress was slow as in the open plantation lanes, one had to be cautious about movement. The closer he got, the more intense he could tell the shooting was becoming. In addition, from the sounds, it appeared that the enemy was maneuvering to the flanks of the 51st Company. Reaching the company commander confirmed that the enemy was indeed maneuvering to encircle him, and it now appeared that it might be a full NVA regiment. McDermott pulled out his map and confirmed the forward positions for the company. He then reached for the handheld transmitter/receiver.

"King FAC, King FAC, Falcon Five-Oh, over," McDermott transmitted.

"Falcon Five-Oh, King FAC, over."

"King FAC, Falcon Five-Oh, stand by for nine-line. Over," McDermott said, looking up to see King FAC.

"Falcon Five-Oh, ready to receive nine-line."

"India Papa X-Ray Tango Seven-Seven-Seven, Eight-Seven-Seven," McDermott said, providing his location on the ground. "Heading, three-five-five degrees," he continued as he looked at his compass. "Distance, three hundred meters," he went on, again looking at his map. "Elevation, in a draw. Target description, troops in open under canopy maneuvering," he noted, looking towards the enemy fire. "Target location, Seven-Seven-Five Eight-Eight-One." McDermott was estimating the location of the main body of enemy troops. "Target mark, white smoke. Friendly location, danger close. Egress. Recommend back to India Papa, over." McDermott waited for King FAC to come back.

"Falcon Five-Oh, I have a solid. Raven Two-One will be over you shortly." McDermott waited. Almost immediately, he heard, "Falcon Five-Oh, Raven Two-One, over."

"Raven Two-One, Falcon Five-Oh."

"Falcon Five-Oh, I'm over your location, I believe. Pop smoke."

McDermott pulled out one of the three smoke grenades he was carrying and tossed it on the ground. Green smoke began to drift up to the canopy of trees.

"Falcon Five-Oh, I have goofy grape and green, which are you?"

"Raven Two-One, hit the goofy grape, I'm green. I say again, hit the goofy grape."

"Roger, Falcon Five-Oh. They were good enough to mark the target for you."

Now McDermott had known the NVA were monitoring his transmissions, but it seemed they were also stupid enough in this case to mark their own location. They were rewarded with a string of Mk 81 Snake Eye bombs delivered by two F-4 Phantom jets.

Second Lieutenant Vu Van Hoi was a platoon leader in 51st Company in the thick of the fight. He thought the F-4 jet was going to crash on his position, it passed so low over his head. He was convinced that it did when the trees in front of his position were uprooted and the blast wave swept over him, rendering him momentarily unconscious. Regaining his composure, he immediately noticed no one was shooting. He looked to the front where the enemy had been, only to see not a rubber tree plantation but an open area the size of a soccer field. Lying in front of his unit's position were forty to fifty dead NVA soldiers. He immediately assessed the situation and sent a request for a medevac.

It took Hieu a few moments to get the other companies to move up and join the 51st. Hieu ordered them to assume a defensive position so the wounded could be evacuated and resupplies be brought in for what they had expended. His plan was for them to resume their movement when this was completed, hopefully reaching An Loc before dark. It was not to be. At 1200 hours, 52nd Company on the right flank reported the sounds of tanks.

"Dai'uy, we have tanks by 52nd Company, you go look," Hieu directed.

McDermott picked up his rucksack and his assistant and headed out. Before he reached the 52nd Company, the firefight started and the sound of the main gun of a tank could be heard.

"Falcon Five-Oh, Raven Two-One, over."

"Raven, Falcon over," McDermott said through inhaled breaths as he was jogging to 52nd Company's location.

"Falcon, Raven, I have tanks on the route just north of your last location. Am I cleared?"

"Raven, you are cleared. We're still at my last location."

"Roger, coming down." McDermott couldn't see the FAC through the trees, but he could hear the sound of the O-2 and the release of a rocket. Moments later, the sounds of explosions were heard close by. The main guns of the tanks weren't heard again. Just to the north, the sound of thunder could be heard. On such a beautiful cloudless day, McDermott knew that the thunder was from a B-52 strike. He hoped it was killing something besides monkeys. When the smoke cleared and the NVA retreated, 52nd Company policed the battlefield, collecting enemy weapons and examining the two tanks. Inside the tanks, they found the crew. All three crew members had been chained to the inside of the vehicle.[1] Again, medevac aircraft had to be called in to extract the thirteen wounded paratroopers and withdraw the bodies of the three soldiers killed. NVA bodies were left to rot in the heat. Due to the delays, Hieu decided that they would hold their current position for the night.

"Incoming!" someone shouted as the first of the incoming rounds hit the trees over the battalion's location at 0530 hours. The exploding treetops showered the soldiers with wood shrapnel that was as deadly as the rounds themselves. The paratroopers knew what was following the artillery and prepared for it. The NVA tactic was a heavy artillery barrage followed by a human wave assault. There was no fire and maneuver in the assaults as US and Vietnamese forces exercised. The NVA had for years simply lined everyone up shoulder to shoulder and rushed forward. Lives were of little concern to the NVA leadership, thus the human wave tactics. The result was generally the same—massive numbers of NVA dead, yet few NVA wounded. The attack was over in less than two hours. The 5th Battalion again policed up the battlefield, evacuated their wounded and began the final leg of their march to An Loc.

Approaching An Loc and their assigned position, they came across a small NVA force that was dug in along the railroad tracks. Before the 5th could settle in for the night, that force had to be illuminated, which was done quickly. By 1000 hours, the battalion closed on its assigned position and began preparing defensive positions. Later that morning, the 81st Airborne Ranger Battalion passed through them to assume its assigned position between 8th Regiment and 3rd Ranger Group, both having been badly pushed back the day before.

Captain Charles Huggins, senior advisor for the 81st Airborne Ranger Battalion, and McDermott spoke briefly as the 81st passed through the 5th to its assigned position in the northern part of An Loc. They would close after dark and took a position between the 3rd Ranger Group and the 8th Regiment.

Colonel Luong and the brigade staff remained on Doi Goi with the 6th Battalion for the night. Colonel Taylor remained as well, talking with Lieutenant Kelly about the situation and the movement of the regiment into An Loc. They monitored the forward progress in anticipation of having to call in air strikes for the 5th and 8th Battalions.

The 8th Battalion on the southern route met no resistance and moved easily into its assigned position overlooking Highway 13 on the southern side of An Loc and forward of the RF/PF sector. Colonel Luong and the command group had traveled with the 8th Battalion and upon reaching the outskirts took up residence in a building on the southeast side of the town.

Colonel Luong was anxious to get to the 5th ARVN CP and meet with General Hung.

## 24

---

# RESUPPLY

**16 April 1972**
   **374th Tactical Airlift Wing**
   **Tan Son Nhut**

Colonel Andrew P. Iosue was the commander of the 374th Tactical Airlift Wing home-based in Ching Chuan Kang Air Force Base, Taichung, Taiwan. He and his crews were ordered to Vietnam on a temporary duty basis so they could not be counted against the drawdown strength. Elements of two of his subordinate squadrons, the 36th and 61st Tactical Airlift Squadrons, were with him. He had called a meeting with some of the pilots to discuss the mission of resupplying An Loc.

"All I'm saying is, there's got to be a better way of resupplying An Loc than what we're doing," Major Ed Brya said. Ed was one of the C-130 pilots.

"For three days now, we've tried to come in north to south low-level and pop up to six hundred to drop the load. The first aircraft using the CARP got in just fine, but those of us who followed got the crap shot out of us," Major Robert Highley added.[1]

"That's why I've invited Major Preacher to join us. Major Preacher and I flew FAC together back in '68. For some crazy reason he's still doing that," Iosue said and turned to Preacher. "You know our problem now. Any suggestions how we can get in better and be more effective? Half our loads are going to supply the NVA right now."

"Well, sir, one suggestion might be to stop following Highway 13 into and out of An Loc. They have spotters all along that road, and as soon as they see you, they're alerting the ADA units around An Loc. They're waiting for you when you arrive at that two-minute pop-up point. They have a good idea of where that point is and are just waiting for you," Preacher said.

"Okay, but without the road, it'll be a bitch to navigate and pinpoint the drop zone as we approach An Loc," Highly injected.

"A solution for that might be to contact whatever FAC is up that day, King FAC, and have them determine what appears to be the safest route in and out. That way you have three hundred and sixty different approaches into the place," Preacher offered.

"Let me see if I understand this right," Iosue said. "We approach at low-level altitude, call King FAC inbound, who would give us the best approach heading into the drop zone. Two minutes out, we pop up to six hundred feet, the minimal altitude for parachute opening, drop the load and dive to the deck to egress. Is that about it?"

"Sounds about right to me, sir," Brya said.

"Okay, let's give it a shot. Ed, you're flying with me to see how this works out. We take off at 1600 hours. I'll notify the folks at An Loc to expect us."

At 1500, Ed and Colonel Iosue were strapping in and

doing their run-up. The cargo was loaded and the loadmaster had checked each load to see if it was secured for what was undoubtably going to be a twisting and exciting flight at treetop level. An ARVN parachute rigger was double-checking the parachute attachments and the security of the loads. The flight engineer was in the cockpit, sitting between and behind the pilots. Clearance from the tower was received and the aircraft rolled out to the active runway. Short of the active, Colonel Iosue ran the engines up to full RPM and checked the gauges. All appeared to be good. This trip was going to be exciting enough without self-inflicted engine troubles. When everyone was satisfied, the aircraft rolled on to the active runway and departed.

Seldom had C-130 aircraft in Vietnam gotten the chance to fly treetop-level. Low-level to C-130 pilots was around five hundred to six hundred feet. Flying at 250 knots and being eyeball to eyeball with monkeys was a new experience for these pilots. As Iosue piloted, Ed navigated.

"You know, sir, I'm rapidly developing a new respect for the Army helicopter pilots that generally fly at this altitude every day," Ed said as a monkey flashed him a look from the top of a tree they'd just passed. Ed was more afraid of hitting a bird at this point than enemy fire.

As they approached their contact point, Ed called King FAC. "King FAC, Boxcar Oh-Six, over."

"Boxcar Oh-Six, this is King FAC. Best approach will be one-two-oh degrees with an oh-four-five departure, over."

"King FAC, roger, good copy. Five minutes, out," Ed transmitted and looked at his map. He gave Iosue a final correction, which was immediately made. He then notified the loadmaster that they were four and a half minutes from the pop-up point. A C-130 aircraft flying at 250 knots and treetop level created a lot of negative Gs on individuals as suddenly the aircraft rose and slowed down to a drop speed of 130 knots.

Without warning, those forces would drive someone standing almost to the floor. The loadmaster and the ARVN braced themselves for the pop-up.

At the two-minute mark, Iosue pulled back on the yoke, causing the nose to rapidly come up while Ed chopped the throttles to help kill the airspeed. The aircraft was at six hundred feet almost immediately, and the loadmaster lowered the rear ramp. Although not as intense nor as accurate as previous missions, anti-aircraft fire greeted the aircraft. Suddenly the green light in the cargo area came on and the loadmaster released the load. As the last pallet departed the plane, he notified the pilots and braced as the aircraft went into a steep nosedive, filling the windshield with trees. Pulling out just before impacting with the wide-eyed monkey, Iosue turned for a heading back to Ton San Nhut.

On the ground, Miller, Hank and Corley watched as the aircraft popped up.

"Where's he going?" Miller asked.

"Maybe it's a divergent course before he turns final," Hank said, curious as to what the aircraft was doing.

"Maybe he has the wrong fucking location," Corley said as the first pallet exited the aircraft. "Son of a bitch! He's resupplying the NVA!" The three stood in disbelief as the aircraft dropped his load someplace other than the designated drop zone and right into the arms of the NVA.

* * *

**21st ARVN Division**
   **Lai Khe**

The 21st ARVN Division had been alerted on 7 April that it would be leaving the Delta and coming to help with the actions in III Corps. Colonel Ross J. Franklin, along with the division commander and staff, had arrived at Lai Khe on 12 April and established their command post adjacent to the III Corps forward command post. Advance elements of the 31st Regiment arrived with the headquarters and almost immediately flew by helicopter to the hamlet of Suoi Tre, two klicks north of Chon Thanh. The 32nd Regiment arrived as well and immediately loaded trucks and headed up Highway 13 to link up with the elements of the 1st Airborne Brigade at Chon Thanh. Ross had no illusions about the 21st Division as it had had a pretty easy time in the Delta, not having to coordinate combined-arms operations on a large scale. Actions in the Delta were generally small-unit contacts that were over very quickly. He had extensive experience with combined-arms operations, having served in Korea and now on his third tour In Vietnam. As a recent 1950 West Point graduate, Lieutenant Franklin had earned the Distinguished Service Cross for his actions in Korea. Throughout his Army career, he had commanded at the platoon, company, and battalion level and had been the deputy brigade commander for the 173rd Airborne Brigade prior to coming back to Vietnam to serve in the capacity of advisory team chief.

Ross had gathered his advisors for a meeting to go over what would be the mission for the 21st Division. Seated in the room were all the advisors for the units of the division that had advisors, which were the regiments. Lieutenant Colonel Edward J. Stein, Lieutenant Colonel Burr McBride Willey, and Lieutenant Colonel Charles L. Butler were the senior officers for the 31st, 32nd, and 33rd Regiments. Captain Harold J. Fridermeyer was with Colonel Willey. Both would be flying up to Chon Thanh after this meeting.

"Not sure when we'll all be together again, so I wanted to go over the plan for now. We've been assigned the mission of hunting down and killing the forces south of Chon Thanh at this point. We haven't been given a mission of clearing Highway 13, which is the mission of the 1st Airborne Brigade and one mission we don't want," Ross said, pausing.

"Why's that, sir?" Captain Fridermeyer asked.

"Good question, Captain. First, there's an entire North Vietnamese division between Lai Khe and An Loc, intel tells us. That's a combat ratio of one to one. If you're the attacker, you want a three-to-one advantage at a minimum. If he's in battalion-size defensive positions, that means we need to commit a full regiment against that position and it has to be coordinated. Second, the 21st has never done a coordinated attack of that size. If they do, it's going to fall on us to coordinate the artillery with the maneuver, and if it gets dicked up, we get the blame," Ross said. "I want—"

"*Incoming!*" someone screamed as a 122mm rocket came screaming into the compound, followed by the sound of the explosions of several others. Lai Khe was always noted for being the rocket capital of the NVA.[2] Suddenly a huge explosion was heard, followed by several others. Strange sounds could be heard as well, followed by more explosions.

Lying on the floor, the advisors decided it was safer to stay in place than attempt to run to some distant bunker. "Ross, what the hell?" Colonel Butler said. "I think they hit the ammo dump." Butler was a classmate of Ross from the Academy. He had also received a Distinguished Service Cross for his actions in Korea.

"Shit, if they did, the petroleum storage area is right next to it," a voice in the darkness spoke up.

"If that goes, we can forget about getting up to Chon Thanh," Ross said, standing up and moving rapidly to the door. Outside, he watched the fireworks at the ammo dump, which was tossing artillery shells in the air with each explosion, and those shells were exploding when they hit the ground. He took off at a sprint, heading for the base of the airfield tower.

The fire department was operated by a civilian contractor company. Those contractors were nowhere to be found as their trucks sat idle. Reaching the first truck, Ross looked in the cab. The keys were in the ignition. Jumping in, he started the vehicle and accelerated down the runway. *I hope one of those damn shells doesn't land on me*, he prayed as he did so.

The main road, Highway 13, went right through the middle of the Lai Khe base camp. On the west side was the ammo dump. On the east side, across from the ammo dump, was the petroleum storage area with one hundred thousand gallons of various fuels. Ross immediately came to a screeching halt, attempting to decide where the limited water he had should go. *Well, the petroleum isn't burning, so it goes on the ammo closest to the road*, he decided. After he pulled hoses off the truck, it was pretty easy to figure out how to get the pump going and start a flow of water. As he started to put everything into operation, two of the civilian contractors arrived and joined him in getting water on the ammo. For the next five hours, Ross and the contractors remained in place, keeping water on the ammo and praying that an artillery round didn't land in the petroleum storage area.

## 25

# AIRBORNE LINKUP



**17 April 1972**
**5th ARVN Division CP**
**An Loc**

Colonel Luong wasted no time getting to the division CP once he got into An Loc. It was 1300 hours and a day later than when he'd thought he would arrive. Colonel Taylor accompanied Luong. While Luong and Hung talked, Miller took Taylor aside.

"You look worse for wear," Miller said as he handed Taylor a cup of coffee. "Wish I could offer you something a bit stronger, but we're out. Resupply has been sketchy at best since the twelfth."

"How are you getting resupplied?" Taylor asked.

"Right now it's by C-123 from the VNAF, but they've been taking a lot of ground fire. They come in low-level and kick out as they pass over at a thousand feet. About half of the loads are recovered by us and half by them. We did have a couple of C-130 from the US Air Force make runs on the fifteenth. They came in using the computerized aerial drop system at six hundred feet, and the first one nailed it on the soccer field. The second aircraft approached thirty seconds behind the first and got the shit shot out of it. I understand the flight engineer was killed and three other crew members were wounded, to include the copilot. Two of the pallets were on fire when they came out of the aircraft and exploded in midair. The aircraft was smoking, with only two engines functioning the last that I saw of it. Was told it got back to Saigon and landed. The third aircraft supposedly had ramp problems and couldn't drop, so he aborted. I guess the Air Force is working on a new plan to resupply us. We'll find out the day after tomorrow when the next drops are scheduled," Miller said.

"Okay, what does Hung want us to do?" Taylor asked, pulling out his map and spreading it out.

"For right now, he wants you to keep one battalion on Hill 169 and Windy Hill. He—"

"Windy Hill? Where is that?" Taylor interrupted.

"Oh, that's what we've been calling Doi Gio," Miller said, surprised that Taylor hadn't heard it called that before.

"Okay," Taylor acknowledged.

"So keep one battalion on Windy Hill, one battalion here on the railroad tracks using the railroad berm for protection, and one battalion to the south blocking Highway 13." Miller pointed out each location as he spoke.

"Good, that's where we are right now. What about the 81st Airborne Ranger Battalion?"

"We want to move them up between the 8th Regiment and 3rd Ranger. The last major attack, they managed to penetrate right between those two and gained a quarter of the town in the north. Who's the advisor for them?"

"That'd be Captain Charlie Huggins. Pretty damn good officer. He has a very capable NCO, too, from what I've seen.

I'll have him report to you once the 81st gets going," Taylor said.

"How is the 81st? They're more commando than conventional, aren't they?" Miller asked.

"Yeah, and they scare the crap out of the NVA once the NVA find out they're in the area. They do almost everything at night and do it with knives and quiet. Don't be surprised if Colonel Huan asks that no illumination be fired tonight."

"That the battalion commander?" Miller asked.

"Yup, Lieutenant Colonel Pham Van Huan, and he hates the NVA. Has some sort of personal vendetta with them. He don't take prisoners."

Miller had Major Sabine move with the 81st and guide them to where the 5th wanted them to be. As he moved forward with Colonel Huan and Captain Huggins, he realized that this was a no-nonsense professional unit. As they moved into their assigned sector, NCOs immediately went about the business of positioning soldiers and weapon systems, assigning sectors of fire, issuing ammo and grenades—a lot of grenades, Hank was thinking. He also noted that at some point everyone had taken out a large knife and was sharpening them. The standard-issue military bayonet was ever present, but each soldier also carried a personal knife, usually the US Ka-Bar knife made famous by the USMC in World War II. After Huggins and Hank walked the line, noting especially the NVA positions across the street in the buildings that lined the street, they returned to the battalion CP.

"Ah, Dai'uy Huggins. I have asked and it was approved that no illumination tonight. We leave after dark. Let's work out our plan," Huan said. He spread out a handmade map of the area in front of their sector, with each building numbered accordingly.

Hank was impressed that someone had been developing the map since they had moved into the sector and had one for each of the company commanders. With everyone assembled, Huan assigned certain buildings to each unity and designated just how far they would go. It appeared that their final objective would be four hundred meters north of the current front lines. When the briefing was concluded, Hank moved with Huggins to a company CP. Huggins was going to move out with one company and his assistant with another. 3rd Company was staying back and filling in where the other companies had been. As Hank observed, he noted that anything that could make a sound was removed or taped. Face paint was applied to assist the soldiers in blending into the landscape. Steel pots were discarded for soft caps or berets.

Just after dark, the soldiers began departing, slipping out across the street in small groups. Stealth was foremost in their minds. Soon it became evident that the NVA didn't know the paratroopers were inside their positions, and the silent killing was happening. At first light, the members of the 81st Airborne Rangers were sitting on their objective and hunkered down four hundred meters behind the NVA front lines.

**26**

---

# WINDY HILL HEATS UP

18 April 1972
**6th Airborne Battalion**
**Windy Hill**

The artillery battery had been providing fire support for three days to the defenders at An Loc. Small probes had been made during the hours of darkness, but nothing serious. This morning, things started out differently, with mortars and an occasional artillery round impacting in close proximity to the defenders. The enemy was having difficulty especially with the artillery hitting the firebase, but the mortars were fairly close and Ross could hear a mortar when it fired. As the day wore on, it became evident that more than one mortar was engaging them. Movement in the surrounding rubber trees indicated that sappers were present and small probes began. What troubled Kelly the most, however, was the sounds of track vehicles.

"Kelly," Colonel Dinh announced, getting Kelly's attention, "you call for TACAIR. Hit north for possible tanks."

"Roger, sir," Kelly replied and grabbed his hand mike,

examining his map for possible hide positions for the tanks. The thick overhead cover offered by the rubber trees made observation of the tanks difficult, but the equal spacing of the rubber trees also made it difficult for the tanks to maneuver through. Due east of his location, Kelly noted the hamlet of Srok Ton Cui. The 61st Company was located there, blocking Route 245. They had reported sporadic contacts and hearing tanks north of their position. There was a trail that came from Srok Ton Cui and passed on the north side of Windy Hill, but that was the steepest side of the hill as well. There was another group of hooches north of Srok Ton Cui along Route 245. To the west was another hamlet that connected with that trail. There was some open ground between Windy Hill and that hamlet. Kelly decided that the hamlet north of Srok Ton Cui to the east was the most likely and dangerous at the moment.

Contacting King FAC, Kelly requested an air strike on the small northern hamlet. Kelly's heart sank when King FAC told him no TACAIR support was available and quickly followed up with an offer of a Spectre gunship. Kelly readily accepted and put the gunship to work. Throughout the night, a Spectre gunship loitered above Kelly and provided the protection he needed as the ground probes turned into outright assaults. Repeatedly, the firebase was receiving tank fire from the north. This pattern continued into the next day. Kelly was becoming increasingly concerned with the amount of pressure the battalion on Windy Hill and the brigade TAC CP on Hill 169 was receiving.

"Condor One-Six, Danger Seven-Niner, over." *Who the hell is this?* Kelly was thinking when he picked up his hand mike.

"Danger Seven-Niner, Condor One-Six, over," Kelly responded while he dug out his codebook to look up the call sign.

"Condor One-Six, Danger Seven-Niner, I'm above you at

eight thousand. How you doing down there?" Kelly looked skyward immediately and caught a glimpse of a UH-1H helicopter passing over a cloud.

"Danger Seven-Niner, things are a bit warm down here. We didn't get much sleep last night and the day has started out a bit frosty if you know what I mean. Over."

"Roger, Condor One-Six, I do know what you mean," Hollingsworth responded. "Now, Condor One-Six, I want you to tell your people to get down in five mikes as I'm about to deliver the mail to you. Do you copy? Over." Kelly understood very clearly what was about to happen.

"Roger, Danger Seven-Niner, in five mikes. Roger," Kelly replied and began to look around. Currently, no probes were pushing up the hill.

"Affirmative, Condor One-Six. Danger Seven-Niner out."

Kelly immediately left his radio and jogged over to Colonel Dinh. "Colonel, get them all down, get them down now!" Kelly yelled as he approached. At first, Dinh didn't comprehend what Kelly was yelling about, but then it sank in and Dinh was on the radio giving the order.

Unlike in Hollywood, falling bombs make no noise. There is no whistling sound or announcement that they're coming. The first indication is when the first bomb explodes. Kelly looked skyward from where he lay in a foxhole that he had dug two days before. Before the first bomb went off, he could see the glint of sunlight off one of the three B-52 bombers that were passing over his position thirty thousand feet above him. *Lucky bastards will be in Guam or Thailand tonight, sipping cold suds after they've sat on a real toilet and had a hot shower. Probably complain because their hamburger was overcooked,* Kelly was thinking when the first bomb exploded six hundred meters away. The explosion shook the ground and physically lifted him a few inches. He was thankful he wasn't above ground as the shock wave rolled over the firebase. Depending on how close you were, that wave alone could render you incapacitated. There was no separation between bomb blasts but one long rolling blast sound.

Moments after the noise stopped, paratroopers left the protection of their foxholes and looked over the protective dirt berm that separated them from the enemy. Dust and smoke covered the area where the bomb strike had landed. Between that area and the paratroopers, however, wandered dazed and confused enemy soldiers. Some were just in a trance; others were more seriously wounded. The shock wave had blown eyes from their sockets and ruptured eardrums. The paratroopers felt no remorse and opened fire immediately. For the rest of the day, things remained relatively quiet, but the intensity slowly returned as nightfall approached.

During the day, Kelly was moving across the firebase when he heard the sounds of anti-aircraft fire. Stopping, he looked towards An Loc to see a C-130 passing over the town. It was being held in the grip of anti-aircraft fire as the aircraft discharged its cargo of supplies, which drifted down over the town. However, what held his interest was the aircraft approaching his location and diving for the trees. As it did so, one engine burst into flames, which spread along the right wing. One engine on the left wing wasn't working at all. Kelly watched until the aircraft was out of sight, heading south and leaving a trail of black smoke behind. *I guess those guys won't be drinking at the club tonight*, he thought as he turned away.[1] Throughout the night, the probes of the perimeter continued.

With sunrise on 20 April, the expected ground assault commenced. Typical of NVA tactics, human waves came through the rubber trees, only to be cut down by the defending paratroopers sitting on higher ground. Artillery tubes were lowered and fired point-blank beehive rounds into the charging waves. Gaping holes appeared in the NVA formations each time a 105 howitzer fired. Unfortunately, the NVA indirect fire was targeting the six artillery howitzers on the firebase, and soon they were out of commission.

"Colonel Dinh," Kelly said over the sounds of gunfire. "Sir, we're getting low on ammo, and at this rate, I'm not sure we're going to be able to hold out much longer. I think they really want this hilltop," he said, attempting to inject some humor into the grim situation.

"Kelly, you may be right. I call Colonel Ngoc," Dinh responded and informed Ngoc at the brigade TAC CP of the situation. The situation at the TAC CP wasn't much better. A few minutes later, Dinh was getting a call. Kelly was working another air strike and didn't pay much attention.

"Kelly, we go," Dinh said, surprising Kelly.

"We go? Where?" Kelly asked.

"Colonel Ngoc say 6th Battalion Headquarters and 62 Company move to reinforce 61 Company in Srok Ton Cui. The 63 Company and 64 Company stay and defend Doi Gio. Major Bang command here. We go," Dinh said, more forcefully than ever before. Leaving two companies on the hill with the battalion executive officer in command didn't sit well with Kelly.

The movement down the hill to Srok Ton Cui went quickly. What Dinh had failed to tell Kelly was that the 63rd and 64th Companies were moving off Doi Gio to reinforce Hill 169. Once everyone had linked up with Colonel Ngoc at the brigade forward CP, Ngoc issued new orders for the force now to move over the same path as the 8th Battalion had followed days earlier. The morning of April 21 witnessed elements of the 6th Battalion, 3rd Reconnaissance Company, the engineer company, and the brigade TAC CP closing in on 8th Battalion.

Colonel Dinh and the elements at Srok Ton Cui were under pressure as NVA forces crested Doi Gio. The battalion was down to less than one hundred soldiers. Dinh gave the order and the survivors began moving to the southeast, towards Song Be. The last anyone saw of Colonel Dinh was when he jumped into a foxhole and refused to leave.[2] Kelly and the operations officer weren't about to follow Dinh's example. Kelly got on his radio and made a call to the deputy senior advisor, Major Jack Todd.

"Condor Three, Condor One-Six, over," Kelly transmitted.

"Condor One-Six, Condor Three. I understand your situation, and we have plotted a series of boxes supporting your plan. How copy?" Major Todd replied. Todd was under the impression that Kelly was heading for An Loc, but Kelly and the battalion operations officer had decided it would be more advantageous to head for Song Be.

"Condor Three, Condor One-Six. Change in plan. I can't wait here. We're heading southeast towards Song Be. Condor One-Six, out."

Movement was difficult as they were out of food and ammo and were carrying sixty wounded soldiers. During the night, Hollingsworth contacted Kelly three times to confirm the battalion's location, and each time a B-52 strike went in to the west of the battalion's movement, attempting to reinforce the idea that the battalion was moving to An Loc. The next morning, 20 April, Kelly took a head count. They now numbered sixty soldiers, in various states of health. Occasionally, they would bump into a small NVA patrol and short, violent firefights would occur. Hope reigned eternal at 1745 hours.

"Condor One-Six, Danger Seven-Nine, over." *Oh God, that's Hollingsworth*, Kelly thought as he grabbed the mike.

"Danger Seven-Nine, Condor One-Six, over," Kelly transmitted.

"Condor One-Six, there's a clearing one hundred meters

to your front. Move into PZ posture as quick as you can. Aircraft inbound, over."

This was music to Kelly's ears. Grabbing the operations officer, Kelly repeated the instructions, which were carried out immediately at a dead run by everyone. As they broke into the clearing, these tired, wounded paratroopers didn't forget their discipline but quickly positioned themselves in chalk order for the sound that they heard, which was getting louder. Over the tree line, a flight of Vietnamese UH-1H helicopters appeared in trail formation and approached. As the aircraft came to a stop, they maintained a five-foot hover and would not land. Exhausted soldiers were jumping to grab the skids and climb into the aircraft. The pickup zone was a muddy bog but suitable to land the aircraft, but the Vietnamese pilots refused to do so. As stronger soldiers got in the aircraft, they in turn attempted to pull up those that were too weak to get up by themselves. Kelly jumped and grabbed a skid that was at chest height for him. He turned and reached to grab his radio operator but watched in horror as the aircraft suddenly began to rise up and depart, only half-full and with many soldiers still in the pickup zone.

Kelly was livid at the cowardice of the Vietnamese pilot's actions. He grabbed the pilot and told him to go back. Fear was all Kelly could see on the captain's face, and they hadn't taken any fire in the pickup zone. In a rage, Kelly drew his .45 pistol and put it to the pilot's head. The pilot called Kelly's bluff and maintained a beeline for Lai Khe. All Kelly could do was sit down and cry, but he was too exhausted himself and passed out. He awoke on a stretcher in Lai Khe.[3]

## 27

—————

# CONDITIONS IN AN LOC

**18 April 1972**
  **5th ARVN HQ**
  **An Loc**

The artillery impacting around town was a constant factor. When it wasn't impacting, then and only then did one take a chance and move outside of a bunker or building. Bets were you had a fifty-fifty chance of being killed if you left the protection of the bunker. But some had to leave the bunker. The 81st Airborne Rangers were receiving good air support but needed mortars. Mortars weren't organic to their unit, but they needed one. Sergeant Yerta, advisor to the 81st Airborne Rangers, had pleaded his case to Colonel Miller and Colonel Taylor. Taylor had found a mortar but no sight for the mortar. Miller had acquired a sight—a sight that was new to the system. Sergeant Yerta and Captain Huggins had never used one before but could read the instructions. Miller asked Hank to get the new sight over to Captain Huggins.

Leaving the protection of the 5th ARVN command post,

Hank jogged or, as required, sprinted from building to building. As he did so, he began to notice the city. Captain Moffett had come in earlier in the day and said the city looked like Berlin at the end of World War II. Hank couldn't argue with him about that. There were no standing buildings that weren't heavily damaged. Rubble clogged every street, some to the point of not being passable. The stench was the first thing to assault one's senses. A mixture of rotting garbage, sewage, dead animals and the pungent smell of dead human bodies permeated the air. Add in the smell of spent powder from small arms and exploding rounds and the stench was overwhelming. Breathing through one's mouth was the best way to approach the air.

Moving along, Hank came to what had been a cemetery— it still was, but few were buried there now. Most of the buried bodies were now above ground, the result of impacting artillery unburying the dead. Bodies were scattered across the ground, lying on rooftops, hanging in the few trees still standing and impaled on broken tree limbs. The landscape was like the surface of the moon, with every inch being a portion of a crater.

Hank passed the Catholic church with its front doors blown open. A destroyed tank stood on the street with its main gun pointed at the doors. The bodies of its crew lay about the tank, where they had been killed once they'd surrendered. They'd only surrendered once they'd had expended their ammunition against the congregation of worshippers that were inside the church. The ARVNs that had witnessed the slaughter had not been in a forgiving mood and had executed the prisoners. Hank wondered, looking at the tall statue of Jesus in the church courtyard. It didn't have a mark on it despite all the shelling.

Continuing on his walk, Hank came across the Quoc Hoan School. Many of the schoolchildren's bodies were still there. The school building was a favorite target for the incoming artillery, it appeared, as the first rounds would impact there before fire was adjusted to new targets. Parents had attempted to retrieve the children, but each attempt was met with incoming rounds. Finally it got to the point that parents were fearful of attempting to move towards the school.

Reaching the CP for the 81st Airborne Rangers, Hank found Captain Huggins.

"Hey, Captain, you want a mortar sight?" Hank asked, approaching Charlie.

"Sure do, sir, have you got one?" Charlie asked, moving to grab what he saw in the major's hand.

"Here you go, but you're going to need to read the instructions. Personally, I've never seen a sight like this before. The instructions are in the carrying box," Hank indicated as he relinquished the sight to Charlie.

"Let's take it over to the tube and rig it," Charlie said with a grin like a kid with a new bike. Both officers moved out the back of the command post and sprinted across the street. There was a bombed-out pharmacy there that had an enclosed backyard. Surrounded by a brick-and-mortar wall, it was the perfect place to conceal the mortar position. When they arrived, Sergeant Yerta had a gun crew sitting around, explaining to them how to operate the mortar, to include fire direction center actions with a plotting board. All that was lacking in the instruction was a sight. A Vietnamese officer was present. Charlie would read the instructions and Major Lan would translate them for the soldiers. The soldier manning the radio contacted one of their forward units when told to do so and requested a fire mission. Charlie, Yerta and Hank stood back and watched as the mortar crew went into action. When the command to fire was given, the soldier dropped the mortar round down the tube and swung away from the muzzle. Almost instantly, the round was on its way. They were anxious to see what adjustments had to be made to the mortar to put the round on target. Finally the answer to the question came over the radio. "End of mission, target destroyed." Smiling faces were seen all around.

"Sergeant Thinh, you take over as mortar squad leader. You have it now," Sergeant Yerta said. He had already cleared the position with the battalion commander. Thinh couldn't have been happier to be given such an important position in the battalion. His was the only mortar supporting the front-line soldiers.

"I have one problem that I must solve quickly," Thinh said. Charlie and Yerta both exchanged looks. *Now what is he going to ask for?* Charlie was thinking.

"What's that?" Yerta asked.

"You see. I take care of," Thinh responded and quickly departed the courtyard. Moments later, the sound of a Lambretta could be heard as it started and departed. Before Charlie and Yerta could leave, the Lambretta returned and Thinh walked in. He said something to the gun crew and they scampered out of the courtyard.

"So where did you go?" Charlie asked.

"Dai'uy, I solve problem," Thinh said as his mortar crew returned, carrying full 81mm mortar ammo boxes. "I, how you say, *nguoi chi huy...*"

"Commandeer," Yerta responded.

"I commandeer transport," Thinh said proudly. Thinh and the squad had used the three-wheeled vehicle until an incoming artillery round had destroyed it. Then they'd used a wheelbarrow to move ammo. Getting the ammo was another problem in itself.

Besides the unsuccessful resupply drops, what resupply was being recovered was being hoarded. Whatever unit or individuals were closest to a pallet when it landed, they would lay claim to it whether they needed those supplies or not. The problem was becoming acute, as units furthest from the designated drop zone were the least likely to get anything. Those units were the airborne units. Colonel Luong had had enough when he and Taylor approached General Hung.

"General, we need a resupply. Yesterday when we arrived, I told you I needed a resupply of ammo and food. We haven't received a thing. If you expect me to hold the southeast side, I need a resupply," Luong said forcefully. Miller could easily tell that Luong was pissed. One look from Taylor confirmed it.

"I understand your situation, Colonel, but we have a problem. First, the airdrops are not very successful. Second, no one is in charge of the drop zone and soldiers are seizing the loads and carrying them off. Third, with the civilians, which we must resupply as well now, we need about two hundred tons a day and we are not getting half of that," Hung answered.

"General Hung, you have got to put someone in charge of recovery and control of the parachute drops. Otherwise we're going to have hoarding, black-marketeering and internal gunfights over those loads," Miller explained to Hung.

"Colonel, everyone is desperate for supplies. Let them just take what lands in their sector," Hung responded. Miller could not believe his ears. Colonel Nhut had entered the command post as he also had legitimate concerns.

"General, right now soldiers are seizing loads and not allowing any of the civilians to have anything. You are responsible here for the support not only to the military but also to the civilian refugees," Colonel Nhut said, looking to Miller for support on this issue. Corley nodded his head in agreement.

"Well, what do you recommend?" Hung asked.

"I would recommend that you place one of the colonels in charge of recovery and all the supplies be brought to your S-4 for redistribution. Set up a couple of locations with guards and have all the supplies distributed from those locations.

That way if one location is hit by artillery and destroyed, we have other locations that can distribute supplies. Each location should have some food, some ammo, and some water. The S-4 can keep track of who needs what for the number of people and where it gets distributed," Miller said.

"I agree. I will set up a distribution point in my compound for the civilians. From there we will take the supplies out to substations in the neighborhoods that people can reach," Colonel Nhut said, again looking at Miller for confirmation of his plan. Miller just nodded his head.

"Alright, I will have the commanders come and we will discuss the plan," Hung said. "You can brief them on what we will do," he said, looking at Miller. Miller responded by turning his back and walking out of the room. *Son of a bitch can't even brief his own commanders. Worthless!* he was thinking.

Luong said nothing for a moment, then responded. "General, I cannot do anything about loads missing the drop zone, but I can do something about the drop zone. Put me in charge of the drop zone recovery effort. I will make sure all the loads that can be recovered are recovered and turned over to your supply people for distribution, equal distribution between the units. I am not doing this if the distribution is going to be 5th ARVN Division regiments first and what is left over goes to us. Equal distribution based on number of people per unit, to include whatever Colonel Nhut says he needs for the civilians."

Hung looked to Miller, who just returned his stare. Finally, Miller advised, "General, I believe Colonel Luong's offer makes sense and will greatly improve things for everyone."

"Colonel Luong, you are in charge of drop zone recovery. I will have Major Nguyen Kin Diem coordinate with you. He is our supply officer," Hung said and walked off. He was embarrassed that he had not addressed the issue sooner. He didn't go far as the intensity of the artillery fire hadn't diminished much.

Miller and Taylor were studying a map, waiting for the artillery to stop so Luong and Taylor could move back to their own command post.

"Does he ever stop shooting?" Taylor said in a bit of frustration.

"I've noticed there are times when he does," Miller said, not looking up from the map.

"Really? When's that?" Taylor asked.

"I've noticed that if a FAC is up, he will stop shooting, especially if the FAC is close to his gun position. They know we have no counterbattery fire now that he's knocked out all the guns except maybe one or two that we have here, and he's destroyed the guns on Doi Gio," Miller pointed out.

"I've noticed, too, that the sound of the fire seems to be moving around. Either he has a lot of tubes surrounding us or he's moving his tubes after firing just a few rounds," Taylor said.

"How about both? He'll shoot from one location, stop, start from another location, and while the second location is shooting, he's moving the tubes in the first location," Miller explained.

"He's using our own artillery on us too," Taylor said. "The 105s he captured at Quan Loi have been firing on us, but evidently he's out of fuses for them. I saw a couple of rounds the other day that he fired and impacted but they didn't explode. I went to look at them and sure enough, they still had the shipping plugs inserted. Either he's not familiar with our artillery ammo or he doesn't have any fuses for them."

"They can still kill you if they hit you with one of those big bullets," Miller replied. "We have plenty of 105 ammo and fuses, just no tubes to fire them."

"Well, let's use them for mines, then," Taylor said, piquing Miller's interest.

"How so?" Miller asked.

"We take a round, pack the fuse hole with C-4, and run a wire to it. Bury it and command-detonate. Hell of a land mine. Could probably mess up a tank with that," Taylor explained.

"Damn, let's go get the Rangers on this," Miller said. He headed out the door now that the incoming had stopped.

## 28

### RESUPPLY PROBLEMS



**19 April 1972**
**5th ARVN Command Post**
**Lai Khe**

"Sir," Colonel Miller said as General Hollingsworth picked up the phone on his end.

"How's it going this morning?" Holly asked.

"Sir, we need some help on resupply. Since that VNAF CH-47 was hit back on the twelfth, they're not flying any more resupply to An Loc. The VNAF C-123s and C-119s have been air-dropping since then, but they're doing it during daylight hours, initially at five hundred feet, but the anti-aircraft fire was so intense they pulled up to five thousand feet. Now the accuracy of the drops has gone to hell in a handbasket. Thirty-four tons of supplies were recovered in a twenty-four-hour period out of one hundred and thirty-five tons. We're resupplying the enemy better than our own troops, sir. Something has to be done," Miller concluded.

"Yeah, I know. I heard from the Air Force guys up at

MACV that they're not happy about the VNAF performance," Holly said.

"Sir, you know we lost another C-123 this morning. He exploded in midair while commencing his run. He was full of ammo. I doubt if we'll get any more VNAF resupply birds in here. That makes, what, one CH-47 and two C-123 VNAF aircraft in less than a week," Miller pointed out.

"How were the drops on the fifteenth by the 374th Tactical Airlift Wing?" Hollingsworth asked.

"The first aircraft got in fine and put his load right on the soccer field. The second aircraft got the shit shot out of it, wounding the copilot and navigator and killing the flight engineer. The ammo cargo had to be jettisoned as part of it was on fire from incendiary rounds and two of those pallets exploded in midair. The plane limped back to Ton Son Nhut. The third aircraft had mechanical problems and couldn't get the ramp down," Miller explained to Hollingsworth.

"Okay, let me talk to the Air Force folks and see if something can be worked out," Hollingsworth responded. "I'll get back to you."

Hanging up the phone, General Hollingsworth notified his helicopter crew to get ready for a trip over to Ton Son Nhut airport, where the 374th Tactical Airlift Wing was located. Arriving at the headquarters for the 374th TAW, he was met by the wing commander Colonel Iosue and the commander of the 345th Tactical Airlift Squadron, Lieutenant Colonel Phillip J Riede.

"General Hollingsworth, welcome to the 374th Tactical Airlift Wing." Colonel Iosue said, extending his hand, which Hollingsworth accepted. Continuing, Iosue turned slightly to the officer next to him. "May I introduce Lieutenant Colonel Riede, commander of the 345th Tactical Airlift Squadron?"

"How do you do, sir?" Riede said.

Hollingsworth acknowledged Riede with a nod and a simple, "Colonel."

"Glad to be here, as we've got to come to a conclusion as to how we get An Loc resupplied," Hollingsworth said, wasting no time.

"General, let's go into the conference room. I have some of the pilots that flew the last mission there and we can pick their brains a bit," Riede said, leading the way down the hall and opening the door to the conference room. Seated along one side of a conference table were several Air Force officers. They all stood when the brass walked into the room.

"Let me introduce these gentlemen. First is Major Ed Brya, and next to him are Major Bob Highley, Major Bob Wallace, Major Brown, and lastly Captain Bill Caldwell and Captain Don Jensen." As Riede introduced them, each officer acknowledged the introduction with a nod. Riede continued, "Captain Caldwell's aircraft was shot up pretty bad on that last mission. He lost his flight engineer and had his copilot as well as the navigator wounded. The bird was in such bad shape that the loadmasters have both been put in for the Air Force Cross. Captain Jensen and Major Brown made an attempt yesterday, and their aircraft is now sitting in a rice paddy outside of Lai Khe it was shot up so bad. We're thankful to the guys from the 229th for picking them up."

After a short pause, Hollingsworth said, "I want to thank you gentlemen for your actions on behalf of the guys at An Loc. Please sit." Once everyone was settled, Iosue asked Major Brya to cover the last mission that he had flown on 15 April.

"Sir, we were at seven hundred feet and following Highway 13. We had about a minute separation between aircraft over the drop zone and I was lead. I got in almost unscathed and dropped my load. However, when Captain Caldwell came over, they were ready for him. Bill, you tell your story," Major Brya directed.

"Well, sir, as Major Brya said, I was a minute behind him and I watched him drop his load. My ramp was down, thank God, when we started taking fire. They raked the cockpit on the right side, wounding Lieutenant Hering and Lieutenant Lenz. Tech Sergeant Sanders was standing behind Hering's seat and he was killed right away. Over the intercom, my loadmasters, Sergeants McAleece and Shaub, started screaming that we were taking fire. Then they started yelling that one of the loads was on fire. They jettisoned the loads, and good thing they did as one pallet blew up. It was on fire and all ammunition. We had one engine out and limped back to Tan Son Nhut only to find that we couldn't get the landing gear down. McAleece had to hand-crank the gear down. That's about it, sir."

"And how did you fare, Major Highley?" Hollingsworth asked.

"Sir, I guess I could say I fared very well, because on the run in, my ramp wouldn't come down, so knowing that I wasn't going to be able to drop, I aborted as I approached An Loc and didn't make the final run in," Highley said.

"Captain Jensen, how about your mission?" Hollingsworth asked.

"Sir, pretty much as Major Brya explained. Flew it the same way and got the same results."

"Okay, so how do you think we need to go at this to get them resupplied? Because without you, they aren't going to last long," Hollingsworth indicated.

"Sir, we've been discussing that since that last mission. We were talking to the FAC pilots. They're out there all day and have a good idea of where the heaviest concentrations of antiaircraft fire are at. We think if we came in low-level, actually treetop-level, and talked to the FAC on the approach, he could tell us which heading to approach the town on. It may mean we won't hit the soccer field, but we will hit the town someplace. We would come in at two hundred and fifty knots, pop up to six hundred feet, jettison the load and back on the deck for the exit. The pop-up would be executed two minutes to drop," Brya explained.

"Why pop up? Why not just stay on the deck?" Hollingsworth asked.

"Sir, six hundred feet is minimum drop altitude if we want the chute to open. Lower than that and the load will just crash into the drop zone."

"Okay, you guys are flying the missions, so whatever you think will work is fine by me, but we've got to get resupply to An Loc. They're getting desperate for ammo and food as well as medical supplies. Besides the soldiers we have there, there are about fifteen thousand civilian refugees trapped in the town that the NVA aren't allowing to leave. When they try, the NVA call artillery in on the group, killing them," Hollingsworth exclaimed. This had the pilots all looking at each other in disgust.

"There's another technique we can try. We have GRADS capability," Iosue said.

"GRADS—what's that?" was Hollingsworth's response.

"GRADS stands for Ground Radar Aerial Delivery System. We would fly in at eight thousand feet and on the GRADS signal drop the load using a high-altitude, low-opening mechanism on the parachutes. The loads would drop and open at about six hundred to nine hundred feet," Major Brya explained.

"That sounds to me like the safest way to go. Protects you guys and put the loads on target. Please give it a shot," Hollingsworth pleaded. All agreed that this would be the technique for the next attempts.

**29**

---

# 5TH AIRBORNE

**20 April 1972**
**5th Airborne Battalion**
**An Loc**

Once Windy Hill was overrun, the NVA turned their attention to the 5th Battalion, and McDermott suspected they would be next. The NVA didn't disappoint him. As the survivors from Hill 169 were moving rapidly towards 8th Battalion, mortars began dropping on 5th Battalion with increasing intensity. Finally, in traditional NVA tactics, the human wave burst from the rubber trees and was cut down by the defenders as the sun set in the west. Throughout the night, the mortar and eventually artillery fire continued to impact on the 5th Battalion's position.

As the earth completed its rotation and the sun rose in the east, so did the ground assault. McDermott was back on his radio at first light, calling for air support.

"King FAC, Falcon Five-Oh, over."

"Falcon Five-Oh, this is King FAC, send it, over." King

FAC had been over An Loc so many days now that he could recognize the voices of the different advisors that were calling him for air strikes. He knew if he received a call, it was going to be for an air strike and not a social call. As soon as he heard the call coming, his pen was in his hand and he was ready to copy. The O-2 was normally flown by one pilot, although there was a second seat. The workload had become so great, however, that two pilots were now in the aircraft, one flying and the other taking down and forwarding requests to higher. When the attack aircraft arrived on station, the pilot manning the controls would receive their call and pass them off to the advisor on the ground. The only aircraft in the fight that King FAC wasn't controlling were the attack helicopters, who reported directly to the advisor on the ground, and the B-52s. General Hollingsworth controlled the B-52 strikes if the strike location needed to be changed from what was planned. Fifteen minutes before a B-52 strike would go in, everyone monitoring the Guard channel would be notified of the location and knew to get out of that box.

Although McDermott was processing one air strike after another on known and suspected enemy locations, they just kept coming. Early in the afternoon, reports of tanks were starting to come in. McDermott knew the tanks would have difficulty coming through the rubber trees, so he directed air strikes on likely avenues for the tanks. The enemy troops didn't seem to care that their own mortars were firing as the NVA soldiers pressed the attack through the barrage. The close-in fight was starting to become hand-to-hand as NVA soldiers were getting into the trench line or overrunning a bunker. Something had to be done.

Others in positions of authority were thinking the same thing when the order was given for the 5th Battalion to pull back. The order didn't have to be given twice. While others pulled back, 51st Company was ordered to stay and provide time for the others to withdraw.

"Colonel," McDermott said as he and Sergeant McCauley were grabbing their stuff, preparing to move out. "Sergeant McCauley will move out with you and I'll pull back with 51st Company once I get these next air strikes in."

Hieu turned and looked at McDermott with as serious a look as McDermott had ever seen. At first, Hieu pointed in the direction that the battalion was going without taking his eyes off McDermott. "We go that way!" He then reached over, grabbed McDermott's shirt, and pulled him in close. "Do not stay here long; 51 Company will die today."[1] Hieu departed immediately, along with the remainder of the staff, falling in step with another rifle company.

McDermott was in shock that a commander was abandoning one of his units. But he also recognized that an orderly withdrawal was necessary at this point. If the futility of defending at this point had been recognized sooner, then an entire rifle company wouldn't have to be sacrificed. McDermott knew that, throughout history, units had been wiped out defending a position so that others could get away to fight another day. He'd just never realized he was going to be involved in such an action. This was Vietnam. This was supposed to be low-intensity conflict, not a conventional midintensity battle. The explosion of napalm in front of the forward trench line brought him back to reality. The reality was that the napalm strike gave the frontline soldiers a few more moments of life and they knew it. Many began to remove their steel pot helmets and put on their maroon berets. Their airborne pride was all that was carrying them at this point. They wanted the enemy to recognize who they were. McDermott called one more air strike and turned to join Hieu. His movement to catch up was slowed by the equipment he was carrying and his own physical weakness from days of no sleep and a lack of food and water. Each time he stopped and rested, he would call another air strike. The last air strike he placed on what had been the 51st Company's position as the small-arms firing had ceased at that location. There were no friendly forces there.

## 30

**ENGAGE AND REINFORCE**

General Hollingsworth had flown up to Lai Khe to meet with Colonel Franklin, Major General Nghi, General Minh and Colonel Ho Trung Hau, operations officer for the Airborne Division. When General Minh entered the room, the meeting got started.

"Yesterday, the 101st Regiment of the 7th NVA Division ambushed a bus ten miles north of here. This has got to be rooted out and destroyed," Minh said, staring daggers at General Nghi.

"Sir," Nghi said, "I have ordered the 32nd Regiment to begin clearing Highway 13 to the south, with 33rd Regiment supported by the 5th Armored Squadron to begin moving north from Lai Khe. This action will catch the 101st Regiment between the two regiments and allow for that unit to be quickly destroyed." Ross exchanged a sideways look with Hollingsworth.

"The 101st Regiment should never have gotten that far in the first place. We need this road opened and quick," Minh said, turning to Colonel Hau. "Colonel Hau, the airborne division has the mission of clearing the road from Tao O Creek to Xa Cam just south of An Loc. What is your plan?"

"Sir, 3rd Brigade will finish closing on Lai Khe tomorrow. On the twenty-fifth, the 2nd Airborne Battalion will conduct an airmobile insertion into this location northeast of Tao O and this location one kilometer east of Tan Khai," he explained, pointing at the map. "Once on the ground and having secured their position, a battery of 105-millimeter artillery will be airlifted into their position to provide fire support," Hau said, pausing briefly for Minh to look at the map. "The next day, the twenty-sixth, the 1st Airborne Battalion will conduct an airmobile insertion into the Duc Vinh area, which is four kilometers north of the Tan Khai location. I will retain the 3rd Airborne Battalion in reserve to exploit the success of 1st and 2nd Battalions or to reinforce if necessary," Hau stated. Silence held in the room for several moments as everyone waited for General Minh to say something. Finally Hollingsworth broke the silence.

"Excuse me, General Minh, but this is just not feasible. We're pretty sure that the 7th Division has three regiments. We've identified one, the 101st Regiment north of Lai Khe and south of Chon Thanh. That leaves two regiments north of Chon Thanh, and the plan is to put two light airborne battalions in to open the road. Good tactical sense says an attacker should have a three-to-one advantage, and that's clearly not the case here. We're committing a light battalion against each of his regiments with three battalions each supported by artillery and tanks. Sir, the two battalions are not going to be able to open that road," Hollingsworth explained.

"So what would you have us do, General?" Minh said, almost spitting the words out.

"Sir, move the 3rd Airborne Brigade into An Loc to reinforce that place. Move the 21st Division up Highway 13 to clear it and open the way to An Loc. Once the situation in An Loc stabilizes, then 3rd Airborne Brigade can move south along Highway 13 to link up with the 21st Division. This way you ensure the defense of An Loc and maintain pressure on the 7th NVA Division, and you'll open the road at about the same time if not sooner to resupply An Loc," Holly pointed out. Again silence fell on the room, with everyone waiting on Minh to make a decision.

"The 21st Division was given to me for the express mission of preventing the enemy from launching attacks on Saigon. If I have committed them to opening Highway 13, they cannot do that. No, we will stick with the plan as briefed," Minh ordered. Holly just shook his head.

"We will move the remainder of the 1st Airborne Brigade into An Loc as soon as possible to reinforce. That is all, gentlemen, good night," Minh said as he stood and moved to the door.

## 31

## RESUPPLY PROBLEMS CONTINUE

**24 April 1972**
**5th ARVN TOC**
**An Loc**

Colonel Miller was on the radio talking to Hollingsworth, who was in his helicopter at eight thousand feet above An Loc. Colonel Iosue from the 374th TAW and Colonel Riede from the 345th TAS were with him. All three wore headphones so they could monitor the conversation.

"Danger Seven-Niner, these past four days have been a mixed bag of success with this high-altitude, low-opening technique," Miller indicated.

"How so? Over," Hollingsworth responded.

"Danger Seven-Niner, some loads are landing in town and setting down nicely. Some loads are breaking apart before the chutes open. Some loads are drifting over the enemy and resupplying them. And some loads, the chutes aren't opening at all and they're coming in like a bomb. The other night one landed on the district chief's command bunker and injured six guys. One of yesterday's loads became a target for the enemy gunners while coming down under the chute and it exploded," Miller explained.

"So what's the success rate, you think? Sixty percent, seventy percent?" Riede asked.

"Right now it's about thirty percent," Miller transmitted. Riede and Iosue exchanged looks of disgust.

"Okay, let's go back to the drawing board and see if we can come up with something better. Danger Seven-Niner out."

As the UH-1H aircraft flew back to Ton Son Nhut, the three officers discussed the problems.

"First is the loads themselves. You guys have no control over the chutes not opening or the loads coming apart in the drop. I need to get with the riggers and work that one out. As for loads drifting off course, that's on you," Hollingsworth said.

"Yes, sir. We need to get some better winds aloft data from Air Force Weather to adjust the drop point. Let me see if we can get a weather team up at Lai Khe and send up a balloon an hour before the drop to get better winds aloft data. Right now that data is coming from the team in Saigon, but there are some local differences that we need to know about. Those hills around An Loc may be influencing wind patterns in that area to a small degree, just enough to affect a load under a chute. We'll look into this one," Iosue said.

"Okay, but for the immediate future, what can we do to get a resupply to them?" Hollingsworth pressed them.

"Tonight we're going to attempt a mass drop with seven aircraft. We'll use the container delivery system. We have an AC-130 Spectre gunship covering us on the approach and departure to suppress any fire we take. We may just have the element of surprise on our side as they won't expect us at night, and the gunship should keep them off our backs," Iosue explained.

"Well, I wish you luck on this one. When we land, give me the details and I'll be sure Miller and company are standing by," Hollingsworth responded. He was not optimistic but said nothing about it.

## 25 April 1972
### 0300

"So how did the drop go?" Hollingsworth asked Miller over the radio.

"One of the best drops we've had. Every load landed in the town if not on the designated drop zone. If they can continue this, we'll be in great shape," Miller exclaimed.

"How bad was the anti-aircraft fire?"

"From what I could see it wasn't bad. The first four aircraft came in and received almost none except some AK-47 stuff. The last three aircraft had some shooting, but as soon as it started, Spectre was all over it and pretty much cut it off. I'll be surprised if any of the aircraft were hit," Miller said with some enthusiasm in his voice. "Have you spoken to the pilots?"

"No, they should be landing about now and will go into a debrief. I'll talk to their boss in the morning or this afternoon. If this went well, we'll see about the same thing for tomorrow night. Don't get your hopes up, but we may have broken the code on your resupply problem."

That afternoon, Hollingsworth met with Colonel Iosue to get an idea of how things had gone from the pilots' perspective.

"Sir, we took some fire going in on the drop run, but nothing compared to what we were receiving on daylight runs. The Spectre gunship was able to take out anything that started shooting at us before they could be effective. We have a couple of holes in a couple of aircraft, but nothing that can't be fixed with a patch. We'll make another run tonight again with seven aircraft. Change up the time and approach path so we don't establish a pattern, but it should go okay. If Miller could mark the drop zone with more lights, that would help. Maybe some cans of sand and burning diesel fuel," Iosue requested.

"Yeah, they can do that. I'll get with him and have them standing by...and thanks," the general said.

That evening at the Tan Son Nhut airport, seven C-130 aircraft taxied to the end of the runway. Major Harry A. Amesbury was making his second run at An Loc, having participated in the drop the previous evening. Harry's aircraft were home-based in Taiwan and would come down to Vietnam for a three-week period before returning to Taiwan. Harry had sixteen years in the Air Force and planned on returning to his home in Idaho when he hit the twenty-year mark. His crew for this trip were all fairly young men. His copilot, First Lieutenant Richard L. Russell, and his navigator, First Lieutenant Kurt F. Weisman, were both on their first extended temporary duty assignment, and both thought it was a bit exciting. Until the previous evening, neither had ever been shot at before. Tech Sergeant Don Hoskins was on his second tour over in Vietnam as a flight engineer and the loadmasters, Sergeants Calvin Cooke and Richard Dunn, were also experiencing their first trip to Vietnam. Everyone had flown to bases in Korea, Borneo and Japan, but this was a first for most.

"Everyone set? Here we go," Harry said over the intercom system as the C-130E took the active runway and increased speed on his takeoff roll. Harry knew the six other aircraft behind him were doing the same as he broke ground and started climbing into the night sky. As they turned northbound for An Loc, they watched all artificial light disappear as there were few villages with electricity the further north one traveled.

"Sir, it's sixty-seven miles to An Loc and sixty-two miles to the release point. There we drop to six hundred feet for a two-minute run to the drop point at one hundred and fifty knots," Lieutenant Weisman said.

"Roger, same as last night. Right?" Harry questioned. "Okay, Rich, you have the aircraft."

"I have the aircraft," Lieutenant Russell said, taking the controls.

"Maintain two thousand feet. No need to climb to ten thousand on this short run," Harry directed. "Sergeant Cooke, how do the loads look?"

"Sir, they're fine. We're just checking them over again to make sure we have a clean drop," Sergeant Cooke responded.

As the flight of seven aircraft raced northward, Harry contacted the Spectre gunship that would be supporting the night's mission.

"Spectre Two-One, Golden Eagle, over."

"Golden Eagle, Spectre Two-One, go ahead."

"Spectre, we're about fifteen minutes from RP at two thousand. What's the situation up there? Over."

"Golden Eagle, it appears to be quiet at this time. Occasional incoming artillery on the town, but otherwise nothing. Understand your inbound heading will be two-double-oh degrees, over."

"Spectre, that is correct. Once drop is completed, we will turn to a new heading of one-four-oh degrees and climb out, over."

"Roger, will position to cover approach." It gave Harry a warm feeling just talking to Spectre, knowing someone with some firepower was watching over him.

Harry was lost in thought when Rich interrupted his daydreaming.

"Sir, we're two minutes from RP," Rich indicated.

"Okay, Kurt, I have the aircraft," Harry indicated, placing his hands on the yoke and feet on the pedals. "Cooke, Dunn, we're two minutes from RP. Be ready to lower the ramp," he instructed. Without a response, Harry knew that they were getting everything ready if it wasn't already set.

"RP," Rich said, and Harry lowered the nose for the descent to six hundred feet. Hoskins, sitting in the jump seat, reached up and reduced the throttles for the engines to slow the aircraft down. Harry saw the light flash on the console indicating that the rear ramp was coming down. In the darkness, tiny lights began appearing in a circular pattern indicating the drop zone.

"One minute," Rich indicated. Kurt reached up to hit the green light signal when they reached the appropriate release point. That was his last act as a 23mm shell ripped through the nose of the aircraft and hit him. It was followed by several others that tore through the cockpit of the aircraft. The burst of gunfire shorted out the electrical systems, and therefore the green light to release the loads never came on. In the back, the three crew members realized something was wrong when the aircraft bucked violently, throwing all three to the floor. As rounds ripped through the interior of the aircraft, all doubt as to what was about to happen was dispelled. At the low altitude, there was no time to grab a parachute and jump. A short prayer escaped Dunn's lips before the aircraft hit the ground and exploded.[1]

**32**

---

# OPEN THE ROAD

**23 APRIL 1972**
  **21st Division CP**
  **Chon Thanh**

Ten days earlier, General Nghi had stood on the road, watching the 32nd Regiment preparing to move out. They were the lead of the division and had arrived before any of the other regiments. The 5th Armored Regiment, consisting of M48 tanks and M113 armored personnel carriers, met them at Lai Khe and preceded them up Highway 13 to Chon Thanh. Now the picture had changed. Yesterday, the 101st NVA Regiment had cut the road between Chon Thanh and Lai Khe. The 33rd Regiment was beginning to move north to meet this threat and open the road. Colonel Ross Franklin stood with the general outside of Lai Khe, watching the 33rd Regiment move north on Highway 13. Reports were coming in indicating that elements of the 3rd Airborne Brigade that had been inserted north of Chon Thanh almost a week earlier were in a major battle.

"Colonel, with the 32nd Regiment coming down from the north and the 33rd Regiment coming up from the south, this enemy regiment, the 101st Regiment, will be quickly destroyed. I expect to see the 32nd Regiment in Lai Khe tonight," Nghi said with some confidence.

"General, the enemy is in a prepared position that he's had at least two days to prepare. As a defender, he has the advantage as he knows the ground and the fields of fire and has had time to emplace obstacles that complement his fields of fire. You can bet he's laid in his indirect fire, probably just mortars but they're laid in. The only advantage you have is you'll have him fighting in two directions. You don't even have overwhelming combat power, with just two regiments against his one regiment. This is not going to be an easy-won battle that your units are moving into," Ross predicted.

General Nghi considered all that Ross had said. He looked displeased and even a bit confused as he walked back to his awaiting jeep. Standing with Ross was Lieutenant Colonel Charles Butler, senior advisor for the 33rd Regiment. Charles was a West Point graduate like Ross and a classmate of Ross's at the Academy. Also like Ross, he had received the Distinguished Service Cross for actions in Korea.

"Charlie, I want you to be careful on this one. Nghi thinks this is going to be a piece of cake operation, but I don't. This is the first time this division has run up against hard-core NVA soldiers instead of the wimp-ass VC of the Delta. I don't think he has a clue as to what they're in for," Ross said with some concern.

"Hey, Ross, no need to worry about me. My hero days are over with. I'm a double-digit midget with less than ninety days before I rotate home. I have a son I need to make up some lost time with," Charlie said, watching the vehicles roll out. "Any guidance for me before I get down the road?"

"No, you have this. Just be careful. Tell Burr I said hello when you two link up and I'll have a cold case of beer waiting for you," Ross said, turning and walking back towards his vehicle. Ross was referring to Lieutenant Colonel Burr McBride Willey, senior advisor for the 32nd Regiment. Willey wasn't a West Point graduate but a mustang as he had served in World War II as an enlisted soldier and received his commission afterwards. He was Special Forces–qualified and had served on multiple tours in Vietnam as well as in the Korean War. Willey was easy to spot, as the mangiest, ugliest dog that Ross had ever seen faithfully followed Willey everywhere, even into a firefight.

As Ross drove back into the compound at Lai Khe, he noticed C-130 aircraft arriving with soldiers wearing the red beret of the Vietnamese airborne. The 3rd Airborne Brigade was joining the 21st in opening the road. The lead elements had arrived and set up their CP in Chon Thanh in preparation for airmobile assaults north of the town.

Almost from the start, both the regiments ran into strong resistance. The 101st Regiment had prepared the battlefield well, taking advantage of the slow pace that the 21st Division displayed on arriving at Lai Khe. The 21st and the regiments of the division were not accustomed to a fast-paced battlefield and a fight bigger than squad- or platoon-level. Both regiments were in a steep learning curve, and the 101st Regiment was a demanding taskmaster.

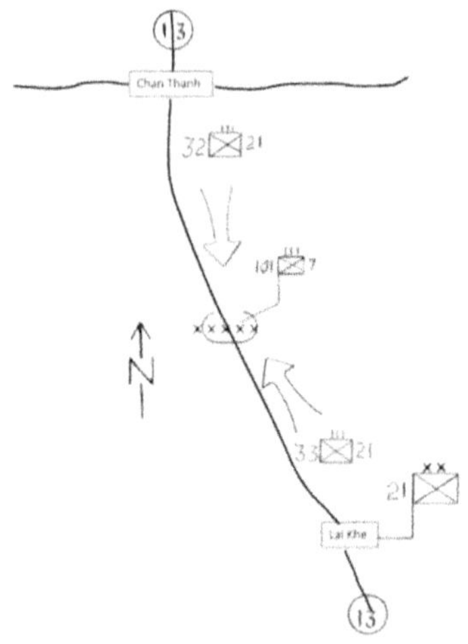



*21st Division Initial Operations to Clear Highway 13*

For the next five days, the 101st Regiment delayed the opening of Highway 13 south of Chon Thanh. In the end, the survivors of the 101st Regiment slipped away after exacting a heavy toll on the 21st ARVN Division.

## 33

———

# COMMIT THE STRATEGIC RESERVE

**24 APRIL 1972**
**1st ARVN Abn Div Fwd**
**Chon Thanh**

The decision had been made that the situation north of Saigon was becoming critical. The ARVN Airborne Division had always been considered the Vietnamese strategic reserve and had been committed as brigades on an as-needed basis. The 3rd Airborne Brigade, which had been in Saigon, was uncommitted at the time as the 1st Brigade was already in An Loc and the 2nd Brigade was committed in the Central Highlands around Kontum. Colonel Ho Tung Hau of the Light Headquarters of the Airborne Division was notified to move immediately to Chon Thanh to coordinate with General Nghi. Colonel Hau would coordinate activities between the 3rd Airborne Brigade and the 1st Airborne Brigade in An Loc.[1]

"Colonel Hau, we are very glad to have the assistance of the airborne force. Your brigade will be the force to open Highway 13," General Nghi said when he first met the colonel. Ross had his doubts about this as he had been with General Nghi and the 21st for some time and knew that nothing got done in a well-coordinated manner.

"Sir, we look forward to the opportunity to do this. Can you give me an update on the situation up the road?" Hua asked.

"Of course. Right now An Loc is surrounded with the 5th NVA Division in the north and east and the 9th VC Division on the west, and the 7th NVA Division has come south of An Loc and established several blocking positions across Highway 13. Our 32nd Regiment arrived in Chon Thanh by truck initially, but then the 101st Regiment of the 7th NVA Division slipped between Chon Thanh and Lai Khe. We now have the 32nd Regiment moving south and the 33rd Regiments moving north to clean out that resistance, which is the 101st NVA Regiment. This engagement started yesterday, and heaviest fighting is fifteen kilometers north of Lai Khe. The 5th Armored Squadron has also joined in this engagement. Frankly, I thought the road would be open today, but the fighting has been very difficult. There is an enemy position in the vicinity of the Tao O Creek and others north along Highway 13 to the Xa Cam gate just south of An Loc," Nghi said.

"How big are those forces and positions?" Colonel Hau asked.

"We believe that they are battalion and smaller-size positions. We have not had a great deal of intelligence coming from that area, and the aerial reconnaissance have not provided a clearer picture. We suspect the enemy have dug in and are well camouflaged," Nghi added. "Your mission, Colonel Hau, is to coordinate the actions of the 1st Airborne Brigade and the 3rd Airborne Brigade and open the road from Tao O Creek north to An Loc. Understood?"

"I expect helicopter support...," Colonel Hau said, not

finishing his sentence.

"Colonel Hau, both the Vietnamese Air Force and the American 229th Assault Helicopter Battalion will provide aviation support to you," Colonel Franklin said. "Your advisors will have TACAIR support as well as attack helicopter support."

"I have faith in the American helicopters but not so much in the Vietnamese Air Force. I will speak with your operations officer and prepare my plan," Colonel Hau said and departed.

While Ross and Nghi observed the ground forces moving out, Colonel Hau was laying out his plan for the clearing of Highway 13 north of Chon Thanh. He was joined by the three airborne battalion commanders and Colonel Rumgay, the senior advisor for the 3rd Airborne Brigade, as well as the airborne battalion advisors.

"Gentlemen, we are responsible for clearing the road from Chon Thanh north to An Loc. We will accomplish this with the following actions. On the twenty-fifth, the day after tomorrow, the 2nd Battalion will conduct an air move to seize this area northeast of Tao O as well as place a company on this location one klick east of Tan Khai. When the first location is secured, we will establish Firebase Anh Dung and bring in a battery of 105 howitzers to provide fire support to our operations and the garrison at An Loc. Any questions?" Colonel Hau asked, addressing the 2nd Battalion commander. There were none.

"The following day, the twenty-sixth, the 1st Battalion will conduct an airmobile assault to seize this ground four kilometers north of Tan Khai and destroy enemy forces. There will be no artillery coming into your location. Any questions?" Hau asked and again was met with silence.

"On order, the 3rd Battalion will conduct an airmobile move to a location between Tao O and Tan Khai and link up with 1st and 2nd Battalions. The brigade will then move north to complete the opening of Highway 13. Initially 3rd Battalion will be in reserve. I anticipate when the 3rd Battalion does arrive that there will be few enemy forces remaining in the area. Look over the plan and see me if you have questions or concerns. I look forward to entering An Loc with the lead elements of the 21st Division if not before them," Colonel Hau said. The speechless advisors looked at each other in shock, as they had not been informed of this planned operation. Two days later, the 2nd Battalion was in PZ posture. Captain Pannachia had been the advisor with the unit for three months and was confident in its ability to hold its own.

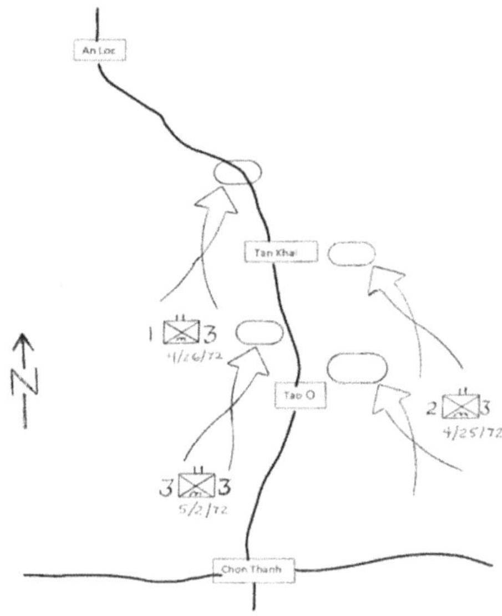


*3ʳᵈ Airborne Brigade Airmobile Operations*

He had a good working relationship with the battalion commander, Major Nguyen Van Xuan. The battalion had been in Saigon with the rest of the brigade and was anxious to get into the fight as the 2nd Brigade was in Kontum and the 1st Brigade in An Loc. Xuan's nickname for Pannachia was "Captain Hooah" as he was a proud Ranger and used the term "Hooah" frequently.

"Captain Hooah, you ride with me. We have comms with FAC, yes?" Xuan asked.

"Yes, sir. I've been talking to the FAC and he's ready for our calls," Captain Hooah responded. As he answered, he looked skyward and could barely see the FAC above circling.

Dropping his eyes slightly, he could see a flight of UH-1H helicopters in the distance approaching. *Now the butterflies will start*, he thought. Captain Hooah hated flying in the choppers. He would gladly jump out of an airplane with a parachute, but he hated the helicopters flying low with no parachute. He'd first served in the 82nd Airborne on his first tour in Vietnam as a platoon leader after Ranger school. Some said Ranger school had brainwashed the young lieutenant, as he constantly attempted to emulate the Ranger image. His second tour was as a company commander in the 101st Airborne Division after he'd spent one year back in the States attending the U.S. Army Infantry Officers Advance Course, he was now back as an advisor. He wore his red beret with a good deal of pride as the airborne advisors all wore the red beret of the Vietnamese Airborne Division. Lost in his thoughts, he didn't notice Major Nguyen move to the touchdown point being marked by a young soldier until Nguyen yelled at him to get his attention.

The aircraft were American helicopters, which made everyone happy. The Vietnamese Air Force controlled all the helicopters for the Vietnamese Armed Forces, and frequently they would cancel with some phony excuse why they couldn't fly. They were also noted for their corruption and cowardice under fire. The pilots and crews of the 229th Assault Helicopter Battalion were noted for just the opposite, courage and dedication. Lifting off, Captain Hooah noted that the flight altitude was going to be low-level. *Great, I'll puke before we get there*, he was thinking. *Good thing I didn't eat this morning.*

Initially the flight followed Highway 13 until it approached the last ARVN position, then it swung east of the highway by a wide margin to hopefully avoid any enemy positions. The tactic worked as the first lift landed without enemy fire, but shortly after, they came under artillery fire. This lift was quickly followed by two CH-47 helicopters, one slingloading a backhoe and one a small bulldozer. Captain Hooah knew that if these CH-47s were being flown by the South Vietnamese Air Force, the artillery tubes would never be delivered. As the troops secured the perimeter of the clearing that they landed in, the bulldozer went to work creating a defensive berm. The backhoe began digging a hole to place the battalion command post within when it arrived as it was contained in a CONEX container. The second lift arrived on time as well and unopposed. Nguyen was feeling pretty good when that lift was completed and still no contact had been made except the incoming artillery.

"Major Nguyen," Captain Hooah called out, gaining the commander's attention. "I have a FAC on station if we need him. Have you heard from the company that landed in the LZ to the east of us?"

"Hooah, they all good. No contact," Nguyen replied. "Can FAC get artillery?" he asked as another round slammed into the landing zone.

"I'm on it," Hooah replied, calling King FAC. Shortly, the

artillery stopped, but no one was sure if that was because the FAC had killed it or it had just shifted fire into An Loc.

* * *

"Our mission is to find, fix and kill the 7th NVA Division and not to be fixated on opening Highway 13," Ross said as the reporters were gathered around them. They wanted to get to An Loc but couldn't due to the roadblocks. For two days, the 21st Division and specifically the 32nd and 33rd Regiments had been engaging the 101st Regiment, part of the 7th Division, south of Chon Thanh. Ross wasn't enamored with the press but knew that he had to use them to present the right picture to the world.

"Colonel Franklin, there are a lot of helicopters picking up troops at Lai Khe and flying north. Are you reinforcing the garrison at An Loc?" a reporter asked.

*I just explained to this dumbass what our mission is and they ask another stupid question*, Ross was thinking. "Sir, those helicopters are supporting another unit, not part of the 21st Division, so I cannot speak with any authority as to what they're doing. You should find someone from that unit and pose that question to them," Ross tactfully replied.

"Colonel, when do you expect to have Highway 13 open?" another reporter shouted out.

"Our mission is to find, fix and kill the 7th NVA Division, and right now that's the 101st Regiment. Some other unit is responsible for opening Highway 13, not the 21st Division," Ross stated with some frustration. *How many times do I have to say the same damn thing?*

General Nghi motioned for Ross to join him. Nghi didn't speak to the press but faked that he spoke no English. Moving off away from the reporters, Nghi looked troubled.

"What's wrong, sir?" Ross asked.

"The 2nd Battalion, 3rd Brigade, landed but was immediately hit with artillery fire," Nghi said.

"Are they asking to be extracted?" Ross asked with some surprise and concern.

"No, they call TACAIR and bring in artillery. They fight."

"Well, that's good, sir, but what's troubling you?"

"How long can they hold out? We need to move faster opening road to Chon Thanh," Nghi said as he watched elements of the armored squadron roll past, heading north. Ross knew that this action was not going to be over fast. It wasn't in the nature of the 21st Division, as fighting in the Mekong Delta where the 21st came from was never done in a hurried fashion. Small-unit actions would generally occur in the early-morning hours and be over before noon. The afternoons would be spent with both sides resupplying and moving casualties, then they'd settle in for the night to run patrols. Seldom did the units fight as a company size, so this warfare was new to them and they were in a learning curve.

## 34

### RELIEF FOR AN LOC

**26 April 1972**
  **1st Battalion, 3rd Airborne Brigade**
  **Duc Vinh**

Nguyen Bao Dai had worked in the plantation forest his whole life, and for his whole life he had had war raging around him. As a child, it was the Japanese that had trampled through his mother's gardens and demanded their rice. As an adolescent, it was the French soldiers who'd made comments to his sister that he hadn't quite understood but had infuriated his father. As a teenager, it was the Viet Minh and then the Viet Cong that had made them pay a tax—for what, he didn't understand, but he knew that the family had to pay. At least the Americans had pretty much left them alone, venturing into the plantation only on occasion and traveling along Highway 13. Now the Americans were almost gone. His hope that peace was finally at hand had been shattered when Vietnamese soldiers from the north had swept through the area and demanded any food that his family had. They'd made him and other plantation workers dig trenches and bunkers adjacent to Highway 13 while the sounds of a battle could be heard to the north. Then the world around him had exploded one night when without warning it seemed that the earth erupted. The B-52 bomb strike hit only one thousand meters north of the position that they were digging. He never heard the planes, as he sometimes did when they swooped down from above. Hours later, he saw North Vietnamese soldiers coming towards them. Some were walking as if in a trance. Some were bleeding from their noses and ears. Some had their eyeballs partially out of their eye sockets. He said a silent prayer that he would get out of this before those bombs started to fall on his location.

High above him, a lone UH-1H helicopter orbited. Colonel Hau and Colonel Rumgay were aboard, watching the first lift being inserted. Rumgay was confident that the lift would be successful as it was being flown by US forces. He knew if the VNAF was flying, they would have either never shown up for the mission, canceled at the last minute or turned tail and run as the first sign of trouble. Down below by about eight thousand feet, he knew the battalion advisor, his best advisor, was aboard the first aircraft.

Captain Joe Grubich rode in the door of the UH-1H, which was the first aircraft in a flight of twelve aircraft. He had been an advisor with the 1st Airborne Battalion for over six months. Joe was considered an old captain and was on the promotion list for major. That promotion would bring added pay and time back in the States in a relaxing atmosphere for a time, he hoped. He was waiting to see how soon he would be pinning on those major leaves, which depended on his sequence number. Each month, the sequence number range was published, indicating who would be promoted. It seemed the range was getting smaller each month, with fewer and fewer of those on the list being promoted. Officers commissioned in 1965 spent one year as a second lieutenant, one year as a first lieutenant, and three years as a captain before pinning on major. Joe had been commissioned in 1966 and thought that the same speed of advancement would apply to his year group. He'd made the major's list for promotion on that same time schedule, but fewer majors were needed now with the drawdown in Vietnam and therefore the Army wasn't promoting as fast as it had been. Joe had been a captain promotable for the past year.[1]

The sound of the door gunner's machine gun snapped Joe back to the moment. A few feet off the ground, Joe exited the aircraft and immediately took up a prone position on the ground, expecting ground fire. However, the only ground fire was coming from the soldiers of the 1st Battalion as they fanned out across the landing zone. In less than three seconds, the aircraft were departing the landing zone and heading back to get another load of soldiers.

"Dai'uy Joe," Major Tran Lanh called out, getting Joe's attention. Lanh was pointing at a small rise to the northwest of the landing zone. Joe didn't have to ask. Major Tran wanted an air strike on that hill as he knew there was probably an observer up there. Before Joe could get an aircraft, the incoming artillery confirmed that an observer was in fact on the hill. The incoming artillery was actually mortars, which meant that the enemy was very close. As the second lift approached, more mortar rounds impacted on the landing zone, but the choppers landed and off-loaded the soldiers. Actually, the soldiers didn't wait for the aircraft to land but exited as soon as they thought they could jump and not break a leg. No one wanted to be inside a helicopter with mortar rounds landing around them. Joe moved over close to Major Tran and began comparing notes.

"Major Tran, I have us plotted right here," Joe said as he

pointed at his map, "and Tan Khai is south of us by four kilometers. Looking at the craters from this incoming, I'd say the mortar positions are down there and not north of us."

"Dai'uy, you correct. Can you put TACAIR on those positions?"

"I'll see if we can. We could also call for artillery support from the battery that's with the 2nd Battalion at Anh Dung firebase," Joe suggested.

"Okay, Joe, you put TACAIR on hilltop and I will put artillery on mortars, Okay?"

"Roger, sir. I'm on it," Joe said and moved to make the call on his radio to the FAC orbiting above.

Colonel Rumgay monitored Joe's TACAIR request to King FAC. He also monitored the negative reply. Rumgay was not a happy camper at this point.

"King FAC, this is Talon Six, over," Rumgay transmitted.

"Talon Six, King FAC over."

"King FAC, why is our request for TACAIR support not approved? Over."

"Talon Six, the priority for TACAIR is to the units in An Loc, over."

"King FAC, we're tying up units that could be committed against An Loc. We need some TACAIR and now," Rumgay explained.

"Talon Six, I understand, but to get a higher priority, someone above my pay grade is going to need to tell me to change the priorities. Like everyone else, I have my orders. Over," King FAC said. King FAC was reaching his frustration limits. He was just doing what he was told to do, and yet everyone was raising hell with him as if he determined the priority for close-air support. The last sentence wasn't needed but he decided in his frustration he was going to hook the barb in someone else. He was successful.

"King FAC, Talon Six. You'll be hearing from someone with a higher pay grade. Talon Six out!" Colonel Rumgay said in anger. He began looking through the CEOI.[2] Finding what he was looking for, he changed the radio frequency and made the call.

"Danger Seven-Niner, Talon Six," Colonel Rumgay transmitted.

"Talon Six, Danger Seven-Niner, over," General Hollingsworth replied.

"Danger Seven-Niner, Talon Six. I know the situation at An Loc is tense, but I need some priority on TACAIR support. King FAC is telling me I'm low man on the totem pole and can expect nothing. We're keeping a lot of folks from An Loc and I need some support, over," Rumgay stated. He waited and didn't hear anything. Becoming impatient, he transmitted, "Danger Seven-Niner, Talon Six, did you monitor my last? Over."

"Talon Six, I did, and give me a minute," Hollingsworth calmly responded. Rumgay silently chastised himself for his impatience.

"Talon Six, Danger Seven-Niner," Hollingsworth transmitted.

"Danger Seven-Niner, Talon Six, go ahead."

"Talon Six, contact King FAC for close-air support. Danger Seven-Niner out." This was music to Colonel Rumgay's ears, and he switched frequencies immediately to King FAC.

"King FAC, Talon Six, understand we are now a priority. Over."

"Talon Six, you are as long as nothing major heads to An Loc, over," King FAC responded.

"Roger, I'll have my element contact you immediately. Talon Six out."

As soon as Colonel Rumgay contacted Joe, he was on the radio talking to King FAC. Joe passed him the coordinates where he wanted the air strike, having a good idea of where this observer might be. Joe requested napalm but would take whatever they delivered. This may have seemed like overkill, but the hillside was out of range for artillery support at this point and something had to be done. Joe also believed in using up someone else's ordnance before you expended your own, which was why he wanted close-air support instead of using his own mortar ammunition. Moments later, he got a call from an airborne FAC.

"Sundog, Raven Two-Two," Grubich heard.

"Raven, this is Sundog," Joe transmitted immediately.

"Sundog, Raven, understand you have a target for me?"

"Raven, Sundog, affirmative." And Joe began his request for close-air support, occasionally looking skyward to see if he could spot the small O-2 aircraft. When he was done, he asked, "How copy?"

"I have a good copy, Sundog. We will be delivering shortly." Moments later, Joe could see an O-2 aircraft in a steep dive, and a single rocket departed from under the wing and impacted on the side of the hill that Joe wanted destroyed.

Nguyen Bao Dai heard the strange sound of an airplane. This was not the droning sound but almost a silent sound followed by the increasing sound of a rocket motor. The impact of the rocket wasn't an explosion but a burst of white smoke that seemed to blanket everything. Dai had been around long enough to know immediately what this meant. He dropped his shovel and began running down the hill that he had been forced to dig on. He didn't care at this point if someone shot at him. As he sprinted, he noticed that the NVA soldiers around him, which were not many, were doing the same thing or getting into the prepared bunkers. *I run, run fast, might escape*, he was thinking as his lungs were screaming for air. He didn't see the jets as they passed by, but he heard their noise as he ran headlong into a deep ditch that he hadn't seen. The intense heat that crossed his back was only momentary as he dropped below ground level. The fireball passed over him, but no burning napalm dropped into the ditch with him. He didn't move but lay as still as he could and thanked his maker for keeping him alive. As he did so, his world turned dark and he drifted off to sleep.

It was dark when he opened his eyes. The night sounds could be heard as he lay wondering if he was alive in this world or if he had passed over into the next. Slowly, he started to move, first his hands and fingers, feeling the soil under his fingers. Moving slowly into a crouch, he peered over the top of the ditch. He saw nothing in the blackness of the jungle except small fires around his hiding place. He was afraid to move, fearing he might be shot by ARVN soldiers or captured again by NVA soldiers. Listening intensely, he finally heard some voices higher up on the hill but couldn't understand what they were saying. That convinced him to crawl ever so slowly down the hill. He began to slither across the jungle floor but determined that moving on two feet was a better mode of travel. He decided he would just keep moving south until he came to someone friendly, whoever that might be.

The night sky was giving way to the creeping light from the east. Joe and Major Tran were sipping coffee and reviewing the day's planned activities when one of the soldiers approached them. He was accompanied by a civilian gentleman who was obviously in despair. Major Tran began speaking with the man, and the more they talked, the bigger the smile on Tran's face became.

Finally Tran turned to Joe. "This is Nguyen Bao Dai. He on hill yesterday. He say air strike do much damage. Kill many soldiers. He say you do good," Tran said.

For a moment, Joe said nothing but looked up at Nguyen

with no change in his facial expression. Finally, a wide grin broke out on Joe's face and he extended his coffee to Nguyen, "How about some coffee and a cigarette?" Joe asked. Nguyen gladly accepted both.

## 35

## 229TH DOES IT ALL

**1 MAY 1972**
**RF/PF Command Post**
**An Loc**

Dr. Tran Van Doan was exhausted. He had been the local doctor for years and knew most village residents on sight. He had delivered a good number of the babies in the village as well, supplementing the three or four local midwives. The hospital was small, as it would normally be for a community of ten thousand. Now, however, the civilian population had swollen to twenty thousand and that didn't include the four to six thousand soldiers fighting and dying on the perimeter. He was thankful that the military had brought in some medical staff, but it wasn't nearly enough for the number of casualties. He could treat some, but many had medical conditions that taxed the ability of the local hospital. The best he could do was make them comfortable until death removed them from this hellhole.

Colonel Nhut and Colonel Corley were in the RF/PF compound command post when Dr. Doan entered.

"Colonel, may I speak with you?" Doan asked humbly.

"Doctor, please come in. You are always welcome here. Please sit. Can I get you some coffee? It is about all we have," Nhut offered as Corley grabbed an empty chair and set it down for Doan to sit on. Doan was in his sixties but pretty sprightly for a man his age. Once Doan was seated and had a sip of his coffee, he began to explain the purpose of his visit.

"Colonel, the hospital bunker is full, as you know. Both the church and the rail station are as well with the refugees and the lightly wounded. Colonel, we have many that we can save if we can get them to a major hospital," Doan said.

"Doctor, the International Red Cross has requested a cease-fire so we could get wounded out, but the NVA delegation in Paris refused to consider the request," Nhut said.

"Then we must get medevac helicopters in here to get them out. I'm losing young men that we could save with proper medical attention, but I don't have the facilities, the staff or the supplies to do that since the NVA blew up the hospital last week. A simple wound now requires drastic measures to save a life," the doctor explained. "And the civilians. They are the second priority and get almost no treatment or medicine. Children!" he yelled.

"Okay, Doc. I get the point. Let me get on the radio and see what we can do," Corley said.

"Where are the medevac helicopters? Why aren't they flying in here to get the wounded out?" Dr. Doan asked.

"The enemy has a tight anti-aircraft ring around here. The helicopters are having a hard time of getting into this place," Nhut answered.

"I think it is more like the medevac pilots have a yellow streak. American helicopters seem to get in here—with difficulty, but they get in. Why no Vietnamese medevac aircraft?" Doan asked.

"Good question, Doctor. Let me look into this and I'll get back to you. Okay?" Corley asked.

"That would be satisfactory, Colonel. We have got to do something. Soon we will have no place to bury the dead and dying," Doan said, finishing off his coffee and standing. After he left, Corley went to the advisor radio net and made a call.

"Danger Seven-Niner, Beagle Six, over."

As usual, Hollingsworth was orbiting over An Loc at eight thousand feet, coordinating B-52 bomb strikes and giving words of encouragement to his advisors down in An Loc.

"Beagle Six, Danger Seven-Niner, over."

Colonel Corley went into a detailed explanation of the situation with medevac and how desperate they were to get something in to extract the wounded. He didn't need to exaggerate the situation as it was as dire as he stated, and Hollingsworth had an idea that it might be bad. After a few minutes, Hollingsworth said he would get into the problem with General Minh when he got back to Lai Khe.

"General Minh, we have a problem and it needs to be fixed now," Hollingsworth started off. He and Minh had a pretty good working relationship and could be frank with each other. "The problem is that Vietnamese medevac pilots won't go into An Loc and the wounded are stacking up."

"Holly," Minh said, using Hollingsworth's nickname, "I have no control over the medevac aircraft. Helicopters all belong to Vietnamese Air Force. Unlike American Army has control of all helicopters, here Vietnamese Air Force has all the helicopters. We must speak with Air Force commander," Minh explained.

"Well, let's get him on the horn, because they need medical evacuation and supplies up there." After a lengthy discussion and a power play on the part of Minh, a meeting was set for the next day at Lai Khe.

Colonel John Richardson commanded the 12th Combat Aviation Group and had arrived with his personal aircraft, a UH-1H. When he landed at Lai Khe, he noticed four Vietnamese UH-1H helicopters sitting at the base of the control tower. Some of the crews were lounging about the aircraft, but he didn't see the pilots. When he entered the command post, he found the pilots were in the designated meeting room and none looked especially happy. When the purpose of the meeting was explained, he understood why. This was a surprise to them.

General Minh chaired the meeting. "You have been directed here to support this mission. Colonel Richardson will be flight leader and you will follow him. Each of your aircraft will carry medical supplies into An Loc and bring out wounded. Do you understand?" Minh was coming down hard on the pilots, but he knew if he didn't, then there was a high probability that they would balk at going into An Loc. "You will do exactly what Colonel Richardson tells you to do and fly exactly as he does. No questions. Now go!"

Reaching the flight line, Colonel Richardson explained to the Vietnamese pilots how he intended to fly the mission. The Vietnamese pilots all spoke English as they'd all attended flight school at Fort Rucker, Alabama, and Fort Wolters, Texas. When he was done, each went to their respective aircraft and started them up. The designated formation was trail, and Richardson didn't intend to change that in the flight. "Keep it simple, stupid" was the principle for the day. Taking off, the aircraft came up in a loose trail formation and flew low-level, barely above the trees, all the way to An Loc.

* * *

The 5th Battalion was in renewed contact with NVA forces. Pressure on the frontline soldiers was constant, and the only respite was the support and engagement by TACAIR that Captain McDermott was employing. Mike McDermott had been notified that a flight of aircraft, Vietnamese, would be passing over the 5th Battalion's position on a medevac mission. That news raised morale but also concerned Mike. Passing over his positions would first have those aircraft passing over NVA positions, which would engage the helicopters. They would return fire and probably not stop shooting until they landed in An Loc. In his opinion, the Vietnamese Air Force helicopter crews were trigger-happy. Mike sought out Hieu.

"The Vietnamese Air Force is going to have a flight of five aircraft passing over our position at low level on a medevac run to An Loc. I think we should have everyone get under some overhead cover. These guys are trigger-happy and will probably be shooting when they pass over us," Mike said.

"Dai'uy, that is good idea. We put word out. We get everyone down," Hieu said, moving back to his own covered command post.

Approaching An Loc, the usual intensity of small-arms fire was inflicted on the flight. Richardson had talked to a FAC and received intel on what the FAC thought would be the best approach into An Loc. Flying low-level, the heavy anti-aircraft weapons didn't have an opportunity to engage the aircraft. Small arms such as AK-47 and PKM machine guns did engage. Immediately, the VNAF helicopters opened fire and continued to fire until they were on final approach over the town. The landings had been prearranged, so Richardson and his flight of four behind him had patients waiting for them when they approached. Richardson was the first to land, quickly kicking off medical supplies and loading litter patients and walking wounded. His aircraft clearly had

US markings and was equipped with machine guns, which his crew chief and door gunner sat behind and pointed at the mob of Vietnamese standing on the side of the landing zone. The next three aircraft to land were clearly marked Vietnamese and were mobbed by those standing on the side of the landing zone. Litter patients were dumped on the ground or stepped over as the people, to include Vietnamese soldiers, fought to get on the aircraft. The fourth Vietnamese aircraft never touched down but kicked out his medical supplies and departed.

* * *

"Son of a bitch," McDermott uttered as the increasing sound of automatic weapons firing and the distinctive popping noise of rotor blades announced the approach of the five UH-1H helicopters. Mike crawled into his one-man bunker and waited. He didn't have long to wait before the first aircraft passed over, but it wasn't shooting. However, the next four laid down steady streams of M60 machine-gun fire all across the 5th Battalion's positions. When the last aircraft passed, Captain McDermott was on the radio, expressing his opinion of the Vietnamese Air Force to Colonel Taylor.

* * *

Back at Lai Khe, Richardson went over how to get in and out of An Loc with the Vietnamese pilots as well as with their commander, who was not on the flight.[1] As he did so, he heard the sound of the flight of UH-1H aircraft first, and looking outside, he saw the remainder of his battalion landing at Lai Khe refuel point. *What the hell is this?* he thought, watching them land. His question was soon answered when a jeep pulled up and a sergeant stepped out.

"Sir, are you Lieutenant Colonel Richardson?" the young man asked.

"Yes, why?"

"Sir, your presence is requested in the 21st Division Command post. I'm to run you over there. You may want to bring a map with you," the sergeant instructed.

"Sergeant, do you want to give me a hint as to why it appears my entire company is here and I'm being asked to come to the TOC?" Richardson asked.

"Sir, I think it best to let Colonel Franklin explain that to you," the sergeant said, returning to the jeep. Richardson was smart enough to know that if his whole company was here, that could only mean one thing—a combat assault was in the works and they would be flying them in. Walking into the command post, Richardson was taken to where Ross was studying a map.

"Colonel Franklin, you wanted to see me," Richardson said, approaching.

"Yes. General Hollingsworth cleared this mission and I need your unit to execute and support it. We're going to insert the 31st Regiment north of Chon Thanh at this point here," Ross said, pointing at a spot on the map six kilometers north of Chon Thanh and south of Tao O. "The landing zone will be prepped fifteen minutes in advance by a B-52 strike and you'll have artillery prep from H minus six to H minus two," Ross explained.

"Sir, we're looking at two lifts and then I'll have to refuel," Richardson stated, hoping that this would kill his unit's participation in this exercise.

"We understand that. After you refuel, you will be able to get two more lifts in before dark and that should be enough. In the morning, we have some CH-47 support that can bring in any remainder as well as heavy equipment. Your PZ is Chon Thanh for the first two lifts, and the last two will be from here at Lai Khe. The units in Chon Thanh are in PZ posture at this time. H-hour is scheduled for 1100 hours, which gives you an hour from now. Any questions?" Ross asked.

"Yes, sir, just one. What the hell is the Vietnamese Air Force doing with all the helicopters we've given them? Aside from the ones I just showed how to get in on medevac missions, I don't see any others," Richardson said with some frustration.

"What they're doing, Colonel, is not your concern. You have your mission. I know you'll execute it well. Have a good day. The sergeant will provide you with call signs and frequencies to contact. You'll be talking to the advisors with the 31st Regiment," Ross said and nodded to the sergeant, indicating that the conversation was over.

Arriving back at the flight line, Richardson gathered his aircraft commanders and gave a quick flight brief. He was mildly surprised at how well the news was received, with very little complaining about the Vietnamese Air Force or lack thereof. When he was done, the aircraft began cranking. As they did so, Blue Max aircraft and Smiling Tigers, which were part of Richardson's unit, completed rearming and moved into position around the flight as it completed the first pickup. In the distance, the dust was settling from the B-52 strike that had just gone in. Richardson had planned a flight route that took fifteen minutes to reach the landing zone. He didn't want to give the reception party that he was sure to be there any time to set back up. At H-6, the first of the artillery began impacting on the landing zone. When the flight was two minutes out, a white phosphorous round went off in the middle of the landing zone, indicating that the artillery was done shooting and tubes were cleared. Immediately the Cobra gunships of Blue Max began punching off 2.75-inch rockets with a combination of high-explosive and flechette. Door gunners began shooting as well as the aircraft slowed to land, and so did the tree line.

"Two taking fire!" was heard on the radio at first and then everyone reported taking fire.

*How the hell could anyone be alive here, let alone fighting with the B-52 strike hitting them?* Richardson was thinking as the ARVN soldiers quickly dismounted even before his skids were on the ground.

"Lead coming out," Richardson transmitted as Lieutenant Colonel Willey began moving forward and firing his weapon from his hip. His dog, Moose, was right behind him.

## 36

## TARGET IDENTIFICATION

**1 May 1972**
  **D/229th**
  **An Loc**

Smiling Tiger Three-Six, Captain Mike Henry, was cruising at eight thousand feet with a full load of rockets. There were three aircraft in the flight, all AH-1G Cobra gunships. Henry was flight lead and his immediate wingman was Captain Roger Fox, Smiling Tiger Three-Seven. Both were on their second tours in Vietnam flying the AH-1G. Today's mission was the same as almost every day for the past thirty days—get to An Loc and provide support.

"Cobras flying in the vicinity, this is Danger Seven-Niner, on Guard, come up two-four-six, over." Everyone knew who Danger Seven-Niner was. General Hollingsworth had been over An Loc and Loc Ninh since the start of this NVA campaign back on 1 April. Henry quickly flipped his UHF radio to Guard.

"Roger, Danger Seven-Niner, this is Tiger Three-Six, on

Guard, coming up two-four-six." He switched to UHF radio to the designated frequency. "Danger Seven-Niner, this is Tiger Three-Six with a flight of three snakes in the vicinity of An Loc, on two-four-six, over."

Hollingsworth responded almost immediately. "Roger, Tiger Three-Six, I'm pulling you off your attack mission. An Air Force C-130 pilot reported trucks in the open close to the Cambodian border. I want you to go to the area and check it out. Are you ready to copy grid coordinates? Over."

Henry had anticipated that some coordinates would be coming and had given the flight controls to his front-seat copilot/gunner. The canopy made for a suitable note-taking pad.

"Roger, Danger Seven-Niner, understand trucks in the open. I'm ready to copy, over."

Hollingsworth passed Henry the grid coordinates, which he wrote down. Pulling out his map, he checked the location, then tapped his intercom button. "Hey, Brad, come to a heading of two-four-zero degrees."

Brad immediately executed the turn and Henry looked back to see that Fox made the turn with him, as did the other two aircraft.

"Danger Seven-Niner, this is Tiger Three-Six. We're turning southwest at about eight thousand and heading to the target area, over."

Danger Seven-Niner wasted no time in responding to Henry. "Tiger Three-Six, this is Seven-Niner. I've checked with ARVN forces, US military advisors and other points of contact that may have trucks in the area. No friendly forces are in that area. Consider this a free-fire zone and engage at your discretion, over."

"Engage at your discretion" was always music to a Cobra pilot's ears. It meant he didn't have to clear anything with anyone but was totally free to engage the target or targets as he saw fit.

"Roger, Seven-Niner, understand free-fire zone. I will advise when over the target, over."

"Roger, Three-Six, Seven-Niner out." With that, Henry took the flight controls back from Brad and flipped his communications control switch to the VHF radio to contact the flight.

"Flight, did you all copy info from Danger Seven-Niner?"

"Three-Six," Fox responded, as did the other two aircraft.

As they cruised along over the Michelin rubber plantation, Henry's mind drifted to what was below his aircraft. The rubber plantation had always been an NVA sanctuary of sorts. The US forces were restricted from employing artillery or air strikes in there as the US government had to reimburse Michelin Tire for each damaged tree. The NVA weren't subject to such restrictions, so they established base camps in the plantations. Plantation managers knew where they were and ignored them. Flying low over the plantation was an excellent way to draw anti-aircraft fire from .51-caliber machine guns or even 23mm and 37mm guns. Now the SA-7 anti-aircraft missile had been introduced and the threat of flying over the plantation was even greater. Eight thousand feet was a nice height to stay out of the range of the missile.

Prior to these missiles entering the battlefield, helicopters had generally flown between one and two thousand feet above the ground until reaching the target and/or landing areas. The fast movers and cargo aircraft used the higher levels (five thousand feet and above) so that all types of aircraft had their respective operating environments in which to function.

Those heat seekers were nasty weapons. The exhaust gas temperatures of the Cobra was six hundred degrees Celsius and higher. Once that heat seeker locked on, there was no escaping and no maneuvering that would make it miss. The tail boom attaching point, which was only four bolts for the Cobra, was directly below the exhaust stack. When the missile struck, it exploded when hitting this section of the aircraft, severing the tail boom, resulting in a catastrophic event from which recovery was granted only by the grace of God. Only one Cobra helicopter crew had survived a missile strike, and that was the day before. How they had done it was on everyone's mind. Most guys flying in this environment were a bit concerned, maybe frightened, maybe scared, certainly cautious and very aware of the tactical situation. As the gun platoon leader, Henry was normally flight lead, which just added to his level of stress. Attacking trucks in the open was every gun pilot's dream—such excitement accompanied by high levels of adrenaline! Viewing the terrain from eight thousand feet and above was not always the best vantage point.

After about a fifteen-minute flight to the southwest and remaining at about eight thousand AG, the flight of three arrived over the target area.

"Danger Seven-Niner, this is Tiger Three-Six, over."

"Tiger Three-Six, go ahead, over."

"Roger, Seven-Niner, we're over the target area at about eight thousand feet and observe what appear to be trucks in the open, generally running from a south-to-north direction. We'll be setting up a gun run running from east to west with right breaks. I understand that this is a free-fire zone, over." Henry wanted to confirm his information one more time.

"Roger, Tiger Three-Six, I copy. You are cleared to engage the trucks."

"Flight, this is Three-Six. We will fly out to the east and begin a shallow descent. I will engage with rockets and then have the front seater engage with twin miniguns in the turret. I intend to overfly the target at a low level. Number two, cover me on my break and break short of the target. Number three, cover number two. We will form up to the north for further engagement. How copy? Over."

"Three-Six, Three-Seven, roger."

"Three-Eight copies."

The flight of three flew out to the east, ten miles or so while in a shallow descent. Executing a 180-degree turn to a westerly heading, Henry ensured that the master arm switch was on and called, "Tiger Three-Six, inbound, hot!" By this time the flight was below two thousand feet, about 160 knots airspeed, and quickly approaching the target. Henry's eyes locked on the target as his finger tightened on the trigger. "Cease fire! Cease fire!"

Passing over the target, Henry shared his thoughts with Brad. Shortly, Danger Seven-Niner was on the radio. "Tiger Three-Six, what's up? Over."

"Danger Seven-Niner, this is Three-Six. I made a pass over the target. Those trucks are rocks or boulders stacked on what appears to be a road under construction. From altitude, these rocks certainly looked like vehicles!"

"Roger, Tiger Three-Six, return to station, refuel and await further missions, over."

"Roger, Danger Seven-Niner. Three-Six out."

"Flying high" didn't always provide the best picture of what was happening on the ground. Air Cavalry, with its "low and slow" style, provided the accurate picture of what was happening on the ground that day.

## 37

## PILE ON

**2 MAY 1972**
  **3rd Battalion, 3rd Airborne Brigade**
  **Chon Thanh**

The day before, the decision had been made that the 3rd Battalion was needed to assist the 1st and 2nd Battalions in their fights between Tan Khai and Tao O. Colonel Hau had assigned the mission for the battalion to push out west of Highway 13 and link up with the other two battalions already in fights with a stronger than expected NVA force. Again, the 229th Aviation Battalion was called upon for the lift ships. Captain Mike Kelly stood as the aircraft approached, appreciating the fact that it was American aircraft that were supporting the insertion.

Like most advisors, Mike was on his second tour and first as an advisor. His language skills were minimal, but between his bad Vietnamese and Major Le Hong's passable English, they were able to communicate adequately. There was a high level of respect between the two officers, which made the working relationship a good one.

"Dai'uy, we go first aircraft," Hong said and began to approach the ground guide, who was holding his weapon over his head to mark the touchdown point for the first aircraft. The other twelve aircraft were in a trail formation behind the lead. Loading the aircraft went swiftly as these soldiers had done it many times before. Loading didn't concern the crews of the 229th at this point. Unloading the aircraft was on their minds, however. Vietnamese troops under fire in a combat assault were often reluctant to depart the aircraft, and some only did so when a crew chief or door gunner literally grabbed them and tossed them.

Mike wanted to be sure the flight leader was on the same sheet of music as to where they were going, so he tapped the left-seat pilot on the shoulder. "Hey, can I see your map and where we're going?" Mike asked.

The flight leader passed his map to Mike, who scanned it and passed it back to him. The pilot had a curious look on his face. As Mike passed the map back to him, he said, "Damn, I was hoping I was wrong and you were taking us to Bien Hoa."

That got a chuckle from the flight leader. "I'll be back there tonight and have a steak and beer with you in mind, Cap'n," he said with a smile and a chuckle.

A few choice words of profanity passed through Mike's mind, but he said nothing. As Mike sat down, the aircraft began to depart. The flight maintained a low-level flight altitude, skimming over the jungle canopy. At times, Mike was eyeball to eyeball with the gibbon monkeys that lived in every tree in Vietnam and traveled in packs. A pack could be a few or several hundred. When threatened, especially at night, the packs were noted for throwing rocks and sticks in the direction of the perceived threat. They could be a dead giveaway for a night ambush site, many a GI had discovered.

Looking out the forward windshield, Mike could see an air strike being inserted in the vicinity of where he thought the landing zone would be. *Well, if they didn't know where we were going to land, they probably have a good idea now*, Mike was thinking when the flight leader held up two fingers. The crew chief and door gunner immediately opened fire with their M60 machine guns. As the aircraft came to a low hover prior to touchdown, most of the Vietnamese were already off the aircraft. For the flight crews, this was better then they had hoped for. Within three seconds, the aircraft were departing the landing zone, returning to pick up the next load. Immediately the soldiers began fanning out, securing the perimeter of the landing zone. Mike and Hong moved to the location of the 1st Company and began conducting a map reconnaissance. They were on the west side of Highway 13. As they studied the map, they realized that they were south of the 1st and 2nd Battalions, as 2nd Battalion, since being inserted, had moved north to the location of its 1st Company and was now due east of Tan Khai. Word was that 1st and 2nd Battalions had been in heavy contact since they'd been inserted.

"When rest of battalion come, we move out and go north to link up with 1st Battalion," Hong said, dragging his finger across the map. As Mike studied the map, he had two concerns. The route to move north to link up with 1st Battalion that was south of An Loc was through a combination of rice paddies, rubber tree plantation and dense forest. Numerous places for the enemy to be hiding. The other concern was the lack of priority for close-air support, as most of it was going to the forces in An Loc. Mike started plotting suspected locations where he thought the enemy might be hiding.

* * *

## 31st Regiment

The 31st Regiment, 21st Division, had been inserted the day before seven kilometers north of Chon Tanh. Almost immediately upon landing, the 165th Regiment of the 7th NVA Division pounced upon them. For the past twenty-four hours it had been pitched engagement. The 2nd Battalion, 3rd Airborne Brigade, had been inserted on 25 April in two locations and now was consolidated at a firebase outside the village of Tan Khai. The firebase was equipped with 105 howitzers, providing fire support not only for the 3rd Brigade but also for An Loc defenders. The 31st was supposed to move north and link up with the 2nd of the 3rd Airborne at the firebase named Anh Dung.

Lieutenant Colonel Ed Stein surveyed what lay before the 31st Regiment. *Shit*, he thought as he scanned the area that the enemy fire was coming from. He was looking at an abandoned railroad line on the west side of Highway 13 with prepared fighting positions on the eastern side. The enemy had dug communication trenches on the west side and was moving people and supplies to the fighting positions almost with impunity. Direct-fire weapons were having little impact on the enemy.

The enemy position was well laid out. It dominated Highway 13 from the west, engaging anything that attempted to move up the road with RPGs and heavy machine guns. His mortars were all registered on the road as well as some artillery support that Stein noted. The enemy position was parallel to Highway 13, so normally a flank approach could roll the enemy position up. In this case, however, the southern flank of the enemy was protected by a major swamp that was difficult to traverse and easy to defend with a small force. Stein's best bet was to hit the deep, narrow communications trench that was supplying the covered positions. Easier said than done with artillery. His repeated requests for close-air support were denied as the priority was still to the forces fighting for their lives at An Loc.

It had been mutually agreed in the start that Vietnamese Air Force aircraft would support the fight south of An Loc with US aircraft over An Loc. All Stein could expect would be A-1E Skyraiders, which were good aircraft in the close-air support role, just not enough, however, and they couldn't be turned as fast as the US jets. Helicopter gunship support from the Vietnamese Air Force was dismal at best. The Vietnamese Air Force had no AH-1G Cobra gunships. No one expected the VNAF helicopters to provide and support as they were considered to be cowards in Stein's mind and the minds of almost every US advisor and most of the Vietnamese soldiers as well. Early in the war, it had been decided by some bureaucrat that since all the helicopters were in the Vietnamese Air Force, all the advisors would be Air Force pilots qualified in helicopters. They were good pilots, but US Air Force helicopter pilots didn't fly in combat assaults or gunship missions. They were rescue pilots or VIP pilots. They couldn't adequately advise the Vietnamese helicopter force in formation flying or tactics. The result was a very poor opinion of the Vietnamese helicopter force.

* * *

General Nghi opened the envelope that had just been handed to him at the 21st Division CP. Ross was seated in the room as they had been discussing the events. Nghi was expressing his disappointment that they had not made more progress in opening Highway 13 by 2 May as directed by President Thieu when General Minh and Brigadier General Ho Trung Hau, the recently promoted assistant division commander for the

3rd Airborne Brigade, walked in unannounced. Minh had handed the envelope to Nghi and directed that he should read it. As Nghi read the contents, Ross noted that his hand began to shake. Slowly Nghi looked up. "I have been relieved of my command." It was more of a statement than a question.

"Yes, General Nghi, you are relieved. General Hau will assume command immediately. Once you have packed, he will arrange transportation to take you to Saigon, where you will report to my headquarters for further assignments," Minh said in a cold and detached tone.

"But—" Nghi started to say before Minh cut him off.

"You were directed to have Highway 13 open by May second. You failed. You are relieved," Minh said and turned to General Hau. "General Hau, you have your orders. Do you understand your orders?"

"Sir, I understand completely," Hau replied.

"Good" was all that Minh said before he turned and walked out the door. For a moment no one said anything as Nghi reread the letter from the president relieving him of his command. Hau stood uneasily, looking at Nghi and then at Ross.

Ross finally broke the silence. "General Hau, what are your orders and how can I help?"

"My orders are simple, Colonel Franklin. They are the same as General Nghi's orders were. I am to clear Highway 13," Hau said.

## 38

# INTELLIGENCE PICTURE

**6 May 1972**
  **5th ARVN HQ**
  **Lai Khe**

The 5th ARVN Division forward command post was located at An Loc. Division main was and had always remained at Lai Khe, where there was a more robust support operation for the division as well as better communications. Getting timely intelligence was always a problem during a major campaign. This was proving no different.

Hollingsworth was meeting with members of his staff as well as the US advisors from Advisor Team 70 that weren't located in An Loc and those from Advisor Team 51 that weren't up at Chon Thanh. Everyone was focused on what were the enemy forces going to do and when. The NVA delegation in Paris had sworn in early April that they would control An Loc by 20 April. It was now obvious that was not going to happen on their timeline. The conclusion was that a major push was coming, and it would be big.

"Sir, we've been able to glean through radio intercepts that the 9th Division commander, Colonel Nguyen Thoi Bang, was publicly reprimanded for not taking An Loc by the twentieth of April. The mission has been turned over to the 5th Division. On the first of May, the 5th Division moved their command post to south of Hill 169. They, in turn, have the 21st Tank Regiment and have moved the 165th Regiments north along Highway 13 to an area west of Tao O," the briefing officer, a major, said before he was interrupted by Hollingsworth.

"Is the 7th NVA still blocking Highway 13?" Hollingsworth asked.

"Unfortunately, yes, sir," the major responded. "The 21st Division got the area south of Chon Thanh cleared, but the 3rd Airborne Brigade hasn't cleared the area north of Chon Thanh. The 2nd Airborne Battalion landed and met some resistance, as did the 1st Battalion the next day. A battery of 105s was moved in with the 2nd Airborne Battalion but was only on the ground one day when it was hit with recoilless rifle fire and we had three tubes badly damaged. They're in heavy contact now against well-prepared fortified positions with interlocking fires. Yesterday the battalion commander for the 2nd Battalion was wounded by indirect fire and Lieutenant Colonel Ngo Le Tinh, the deputy brigade commander, has assumed command. That battalion has been reinforced with the 21st Division Reconnaissance Company. The 3rd Battalion is in a running gun battle as we speak," the major outlined, pausing momentarily. "The 31st Regiment of the 21st conducted an insertion on May first, six kilometers north of Chon Thanh, and has been in heavy engagement since with the 165th NVA Regiment."

"Keep me posted on what the 3rd Airborne Brigade is doing. Okay, what does the rest of the intel look like?" Holly inquired.

"Sir, the 271st and 272nd Regiments have moved to the northeast of the city," the briefing officer said, pointing at the map. "The E-6 Regiment and the 174th Regiment have taken up positions around Windy Hill close to the 275th Regiment, which has occupied Windy Hill since the 1st Airborne were forced off."

"How do we know that?" Hollingsworth asked, always suspicious of the information.

"Sir, Colonel Nhut has a large Montagnard population within the city now. Some have left and returned to their homes. The NVA evidently don't think much of them and allow them to freely move about, returning to the city. They've been providing the information to Nhut," the major said. "In addition, sir, we have a prisoner, a lieutenant, that confirmed the information that Nhut's people reported."

Hollingsworth's skepticism disappeared. "How did you get him to talk?" he asked.

"Sir, he asked if he could have a can of fruit cocktail. Seems they've been enjoying our C rations that have been dropped into their laps so often," the major said.

Turning to his aide, Hollingsworth said, "Make a note for me to talk to the air forces about the airdrops. This has got to stop. Alright, what else have you got?"

"Right now, sir, it appears that there are about ten thousand enemy soldiers surrounding An Loc versus our four thousand, of which probably one thousand are walking wounded. They control all the high ground around An Loc."

"What else did this POW lieutenant tell you?"

"Sir, he said that a major attack is in the works but didn't know when. He guessed it would be a week or so as they have to reposition some forces, he was saying. The plan is for the 5th to attack from the south and from the north with some assistance from the 9th Division. In addition, it will be coordinated with the 7th to launch an attack down Highway 13," the major stated.

"Saving the good news for last, Major?" Hollingsworth asked in a joking manner, relieving the tension in the room. He turned to his aide again. "Make a note, we need to relook B-52 boxes."

"What about his artillery?" Hollingsworth inquired.

"Sir, it appears he's relying more on his heavy mortars than his long-range artillery. This could be from a shortage of ammo or our finding his artillery and destroying it with air strikes. The mortars are much easier to hide in the rubber tree plantation," the major concluded.

"Good rundown," Hollingsworth said. Turning in his chair to Miller, who he had extracted just for this intel brief along with Corley, he asked, "What's the morale of the defenders? Are they holding up okay?"

Miller and Corley exchanged looks. Miller fielded the question. "To be truthful, sir, morale is pretty low. The soldiers have been in the fight for a month now. They're living on half to quarter rations; they're constantly being shelled, and that's been going on for a month now. The water, what there is, has to be boiled. The stench is intolerable and the dead are everywhere. Every day they're beating back another ground probe. Morale is damn low, starting with General Hung," Miller said, pausing for a moment. "Sir, we doubt that the Vietnamese can withstand another major attack. I tried to get General Hung to go over on the offensive two weeks ago to push the perimeter back out a couple of blocks. His comment was, 'What's the use?' We've had two C-130 aircraft shot down attempting to resupply us, one on the twenty-fifth of April and one on the third of May. The soldiers saw both those aircraft go down and morale went down just as fast. I requested no more C-130 resupply runs as we're resupplying the enemy more than our own soldiers," Miller explained.

"I'm aware of the resupply situation and I've talked to the Air Force about it. We may have a solution. The 549th Quartermaster Company stationed in Okinawa is sending over seventy-six riggers to look at the situation and make a recommendation. Part of the problem, we think, is the Vietnamese riggers haven't rigged enough heavy loads to know what they're doing. Let your people know we recognize the problem and are working on a solution," Hollingsworth announced. *And we better have a damn solution damn quick*, he thought.

**39**

---

# SUCCESS AT LAST

**8 May 1972**
**345th TAS**
**Tan Son Nhut**

"Gentlemen...if I can have your attention, we will get this briefing started," Lieutenant Colonel Riede said, placing some notes on the podium. His audience was the aircraft commanders and navigators for seven C-130 aircraft. Once everyone settled down, he continued, "We have a mission for tonight, dropping loads over An Loc." Moans and groans along with a few words of profanity were murmured in the group. "I know, but this will be different and I believe a lot more successful."

Before he could continue, a voice spoke up. "How so, sir?"

Riede could hear the negativity in the voice and saw the expression of doubt on all the faces.

"A couple of reasons, actually. First, drop altitude will be ten thousand feet—"

"Oh, good, so we drop from ten thousand and nothing

hits the drop zone. Resupply the enemy again," a young captain voiced. They were trying Riede's patience.

"If you'd let me finish before your next snide remark, Captain, you might better understand," Riede said, glaring daggers at the offending captain. *I really can't blame them for their attitude after what we've been seeing*, he thought.

"Sorry, sir," the frustrated captain commented, knowing he was in the wrong.

"Second, we're going to use the high-altitude, low-open drop technique, and before you raise objections that we've done that before and it didn't work, we've solved the problem. Two days ago, an Army rigger unit from Okinawa was brought in and found that the Vietnamese riggers were rigging the loads wrong. The American riggers are now rigging the loads and supervising the Vietnamese riggers. They'll also be flying aboard our aircraft to make sure all is well. This should improve our accuracy and the supply situation in An Loc. We will fly with seven aircraft tonight. If there are no other questions for me—or snide remarks," Riede said, looking at the vocal captain, "Major Brya will give the mission brief. I'll be flying last aircraft. Major Brya."

* * *

Sleep was always a welcome feeling and a welcome exercise. Being disturbed just after falling asleep, however, was never welcomed. General Hollingsworth was and had been in a deep sleep for three hours when his aide woke him up. "Sir, sir, sir, wake up, sir."

"Dammit, I'm awake," Hollingsworth said, not wanting to open his eyes to the light in the room.

"Sir, Colonel Miller is on the phone and wants to talk to you."

"Did you tell Miller I was asleep?"

"Yes, sir. He said to, and I quote, 'wake his ass up, Captain.'"

"Alright, I'll be there in a minute," Hollingsworth said, reaching for some slippers. He already had his pants on as he seldom ever got fully undressed for bed, knowing this would and did happen frequently.

Arriving at the command center, which was down the hall from his quarters, he headed straight to the radios.

"Danger Seven-Nine here."

"Danger Seven-Niner, good morning."

"What's so damn good about it. You woke me up."

"The resupply drop was just finished."

"Well, how did it go?"

"Over ninety percent of the loads landed on target. The other loads broke up in the descent and one streamered in as the chutes didn't open. One pallet of mortar ammo exploded when it landed. One load hit the top of the command post, killing an ARVN lieutenant. Overall I think we've broken the code on this one. Please pass my congratulations and appreciation on to the flyboys," Miller transmitted.

"Great news—now can I go back to bed?" Hollingsworth asked with a smile.

As daylight showed the dropped loads, a new problem arose for the defenders. Seems that wherever the load landed, those closest were claiming that load for their own. Colonel Luong and the airborne soldiers were not having any of that. The airborne forces were positioned outside the town and would be the last to get anything. On 18 April, it was decided that Colonel Luong would be responsible for airdrop recovery. Gathering his remaining two battalion commanders the day before, as well as the commander of the 81st Rangers, he laid out his plan.

"Tonight there will be an airdrop. You will each from provide a ten-man recovery detail. They will act as a security force around the designated drop zone. They are there to secure the pallets and turn them over to Major Nguyen Kim Diem, division S-4, who will have a detail to collect and move the supplies to distribution points. You are to prevent anyone from interfering with the collection. You may exercise deadly force if necessary. I want an officer in charge of each detail. Any questions?" Luong asked. There were none.

During the early-evening hours, the airborne details moving to the intended drop zone and positioned buckets of dirt soaked with diesel fuel around the perimeter. Thirty minutes prior to the drop, they ignited the pots. This wasn't so much for the aircraft but more for them to see anyone attempting to steal the supplies. Captain Huggins was present and supervised the detail. As each pallet landed, two airborne soldiers would move to the pallet and remain with it until the division S-4 arrived and had his detail break the pallets down and move the supplies to distribution points. After the first night, hoarding and looting of the pallets ceased.

## 40

***

# MAJOR PUSH

**10 MAY 1972**
**MACV HQ**
**Saigon**

General Hollingsworth felt it in his bones—the NVA would hit and hit hard at An Loc in the morning. Too many battle-field indicators of a major attack were telling him it was coming. Holly felt that too often MACV headquarters over-looked or ignored the tactical intelligence in favor of strategic intelligence resulting in wrong intelligence estimates for the field commanders. To make his case, he asked for a face-to-face with General Abrams. A long discussion ensued.

"Holly, what makes you so sure you're going to get hit with another major attack?" Abrams asked.

"Sir, we know that the corps commander was told to take An Loc by the twentieth of April. He failed. We know that Colonel Nguyen Thoi Bung was reprimanded because the 9th VC Division failed to take the town. We know that responsibility for taking it has shifted now to the 5th VC Division and they've moved their command post to better control the operation. The 5th VC commander has publicly proclaimed that he will show the 9th VC how to do it. They know our supplies have run low, but they also know that we had a successful delivery the other night and for the past two nights. We know their morale is low right now," Holly said.

"Excuse me, sir, but a lot of that is speculation," Abrams's intelligence officer interrupted.

"Oh, really? Well, how about the intel reports we've been sending you on the sightings by the air cav of tanks and vehicle movements? What about the intel reports we've been sending you on what our Montagnard scouts have been reporting? What about the intel report we've sent you about Warrant Officer Nguyen The Hoa, the sapper we captured on the perimeter who confirmed an attack was coming soon? Is all that speculation?" Holly asked with some venom in his voice. The intelligence officer had nothing to say.

"Okay, say all this points to a major attack—what can we do?" Abrams asked.

"Sir, I want priority on B-52 strikes and I want one strike every hour for a twenty-four-hour period," Holly replied.

"Sir, that's going to task the Air Force to the maximum. It'll also pull aircraft from both Military Region I and Military Region II. John Paul Vann and General Kroesen, or maybe General Cooksey, depending when this goes down, are not going to be happy with that," General Carley, the J3 Operations officer, pointed out.

"If they don't have a major attack coming at them, then how can they really complain?" Holly replied, not waiting for a response. "They can't. We've already plotted out and designated boxes around An Loc that we suspect are assembly areas, logistic points, attack positions and avenues of approach. Each is a designated target box. Fifteen minutes before a strike package arrives, we will notify them of which box to hit if it's different than the designated box for the strike. We need to be able to change the designated box at the last minute depending on the situation on the ground," Holly concluded.

"And when do you think they'll launch this major attack?" Carley asked.

"I think they'll launch their offense tomorrow morning," Holly responded without batting an eyelash.

"That soon?" Carley asked in surprise.

"Yes, that soon," Holly replied.

"What are your concerns if they do launch that soon?" Abrams asked.

"I have two major concerns. The first is if they make this attack a coordinated attack with the forces pushing on the My Chanh line up north. That would divert some B-52 support. The second is the level of combat fatigue among the defenders of An Loc. The defenders and their American advisors had been in the fight now for over a month. An intense month of ground attacks and constant artillery and mortar shelling. Resupply had been nil for over a month and was only beginning to start again. The defenders were on meager rations and low on ammunition. They have no supporting artillery and very little in mortars. They had no tanks or heavy antitank weapons. I wonder how much longer they can hold out. How much more can they take? How much more can they give?" Holly responded.

Abrams looked at his J3 and the other staff officers in the room. No one said anything for a long moment. Then Abrams spoke up. "Okay, Holly, you got what you want. Let's get a new air tasking order out and put a plan in operation. I'll deal with Kroesen and John Paul Vann. Anything else, Holly?" he asked.

"No, sir," Holly said and excused himself to get back to Lai Khe.

That afternoon at Lai Khe, as Colonel Ulmer, accompanied by Majors Ron Skarupa and Ken Ingram, climbed into Holly's UH-1H aircraft, Holly asked him, "Colonel Ulmer, you do understand the situation up there, don't you?"

"Yes, sir, I believe I have a clear picture of the situation. The NVA have the town surrounded and are now right where we want them," Ulmer said, attempting to repeat an old airborne joke.

"Damn paratroopers always play that tune when things are bad. Okay, let's go," Hollingsworth directed his pilot.

The flight up to An Loc was made at eight thousand feet. Arriving over the town, the pilot put the aircraft into a steep spiraling descent, bottoming the collective and showing a rate of descent of fifteen hundred feet per minute. At the last two hundred feet, the pilot came in with full power to check the descent and land quickly. As Major Borstorff climbed in, Colonel Miller and Colonel Ulmer shook hands and exchanged a few brief words. *This has to be one the fastest change-of-command ceremonies ever*, thought Colonel Ulmer. No one wanted to be standing on the landing site knowing that NVA artillery was being loaded and aimed at them. Ulmer was quickly led to the command post and the aircraft departed before the first round impacted.[1]

Entering the command bunker, Ulmer was immediately introduced to General Hung. He had been briefed by Hollingsworth on the relationship between Miller and Hung. Ulmer was hoping for a different relationship. Ulmer wasn't new to the advisor role as he had been with the 40th Regiment in the 22nd Division in the Central Highlands in previous years. Introductions to Colonel Nhut, Colonel Corley, Colonel Taylor and the regimental commanders were made and briefings commenced. Hung had arranged it for him, and although he pretty much knew the situation, he listened intensely to gain their perspective on the situation. Their perspectives were pretty much in line with his. While the briefing was being conducted, artillery and mortar rounds were landing outside.

"Let me ask, what's the latest intel on the location of his forces and how do you think they're going to come at us?" Ulmer asked.

"Sir, we believe the 174th Regiment of the 5th Division is to the north," Major Boarman said, pointing at general locations on the map. "The E-6 Regiment of the 5th is in the northeast, towards Quan Loi, the 271st Regiment of the 9th Division is in the south, and the 272nd Regiment of the 9th Division is in the west. Our intel says they'll hit us with all four simultaneously."

"Do we think he has a reserve to exploit a breakthrough with?" Ulmer asked.

"Sir, he has the 275th Regiment of the 5th positioned in the north."

"What about tanks?"

"We believe he has six to eight tanks with each of the regiments. He does, however, have a command-and-control problem with them. The tanks aren't under the command of the division but under a tank regiment that gives them their orders. Typically, what we've seen is the tanks initially move up with the infantry and at some point break from the infantry and rush to get into the city, leaving the infantry behind. This allows us to get in with our LAWs and take out the tanks. Let's hope they don't learn a lesson from their past mistakes," General Hung said.

"Sir, right now we have a situation in the in the 52nd Ranger sector. All day we've had probes on the perimeter, but in the 52nd we've had the Rangers forced back from their forward positions. They've dropped back and reestablished a new defensive line two blocks back from the old line," Lieutenant Colonel McManus said. McManus was the senior advisor to the 3rd Ranger Group.

"The Rangers are generally the best of the South Vietnamese forces. What do you attribute this fallback to?" Ulmer asked, concerned.

"One factor, sir. Piss-poor leadership. The battalion commander, Major Dau, reacted too late and issued the wrong orders despite all the indications. When it went to hell in a handbasket, his deputy took over and got things turned around," McManus answered. "I'll stay with him from now on."

"From the sounds of things, he has plenty of artillery ammunition. How long has this been going on?" Ulmer asked, referring to the bombardment that the town was taking.

"Sir, this most recent bombardment started yesterday. He'll back off a bit tonight but start up again around 0500 tomorrow," Major Boarman responded as a particularly close exploding round made him duck slightly.

"What's the strength here?" Ulmer asked. Hung just shrugged his shoulders.

"Sir, we estimate that there are about four thousand soldiers between the ARVNs and territorials. Of those, about a thousand are walking wounded."

"Okay, let me get a look at the lay of the land. Can someone show me around?" Ulmer asked.

"Sir, I will," Hank said.

"And you are Major...?" Ulmer asked, not sure who this major was.

"Sir, I'm sorry. I should have introduced you to Hank. Major Sabine is out here on an inspection tour from the DoD IG office and sort of got stuck here. Since he's been here, he's filled in wherever we need filling in. He was up at Loc Ninh until it fell and was one of the last to get out of there," Major Boarman stated.

Ulmer eyed the newly introduced major, noting a MACV

combat patch as well as a Pentagon Warrior Patch, Ranger tab, Senior Airborne wings, and Combat Infantry badge.

"I noticed the Pentagon assignment patch and thought that was a bit odd. Only one tour as an advisor?" Ulmer asked.

"Yes, sir. I had two tours with the 101st as a platoon leader and a company commander. My S-3 time was with the 82nd at Fort Bragg," Hank replied. "After CGSC I got pushed into the Pentagon."

"Well, Major, we all must bear our crosses. Let's get started on the tour."

As they walked between incoming rounds from one position to another, the sound of a helicopter dropping in and quickly departing caught Ulmer's attention.

"Is that General Hollingsworth?" Ulmer asked.

"No, sir. That's General Hung running back to Lai Khe. He doesn't spend the night here," Hank replied.

Ulmer spent the rest of the day cautiously moving about the town, observing the positions and conditions of the defenders. He had an opportunity to meet with all the senior commanders and discussed with them how things might go the following day.

# 41

## STRELLA

**10 May 1972**
**F Battery, 79th Artillery**
**Bien Hoa**

"I'm telling you there are Strella heat-seeking anti-aircraft missiles up there," Chief Warrant Officer Hosaka said. A group of pilots were sitting through an intelligence brief on the air defense systems that had been appearing around An Loc. The briefing was being conducted by a major from TRAC headquarters.

"Chief, you can say that until you're blue in the face, but that doesn't make it so. We haven't had any confirmed reports of a heat-seeking missile in the III Corps area of operations," the major argued.

"Sir, I can tell you for a fact, my wingman was knocked out of the sky on 27 June 1970 by one right here north of Song Be.[1] We reported it to the chain of command and we got the same bullshit answer. Not confirmed, so it didn't exist." Mr. Hosaka looked around the room. "I'm telling you guys, they're here or will be shortly and you best be thinking through how you're going to deal with them."

"I heard that a cav aircraft flying up at Loc Ninh when that fight started had one fired at him. He was low-level and it missed," Captain Strobridge said.

"I repeat, gentlemen, reported but not confirmed," the major said.

"Tell you what, Major. You come fly with us and then if you see one, you can confirm it. How does that sound?" asked one of the younger warrant officers. It was becoming clear that the major was briefing a hostile group, and he sought to extricate himself from the crowd.

"I heard a transmit on Guard the day before yesterday that an F of the 9th bird took fire from one, and last night a FAC reported taking fire from one. How much more do you people need to say that there are Strellas in the AO?" Captain Williams asked.

"We need a confirmed sighting. Two or more pilots sighting the same missile launch at the same time in the same location, or the ground forces actually capture one that hasn't been fired. Aside from that, it's all just speculation," the major explained. His answer didn't sit well with the audience. He cut his presentation short as he realized that this group was done listening.

Once the major departed, Captain Brown stood and moved to a refrigerator that was in the conference room doubling as the unit bar. "Who wants a beer?" he asked. All hands were raised. Brown scooped up a handful and started passing them out. "So what do we do if one of these things hits us? Does anyone know anything about the damn things?" he asked.

"I don't know about these, but I do know something about anti-aircraft missiles," Captain Northrup said. "First, when the missile is fired, it needs time to acquire a heat signature or target. So it stands to reason that once it's launched, there's a time lapse before it locks on to the target. I suspect if you're low, like treetop low and fast, they don't have time to lock on to you."

"That may be the case with the guy up north. I understand he was low and fast," Mr. Williams said.

"The shooter is going to need a clear field of fire. He's not going to be able to launch it through the trees," Captain Brown said, taking a pull on his beer.

"I wonder if they can lock on you if the sun is behind you," said Mr. Hern.

"Good question," Lieutenant Shields asked, looking at Captain Northrup for the answer.

"Don't look at me. I suspect if the sun was a greater heat source, it would lock on, but I doubt it. Our exhaust is six hundred degrees, and I doubt if the sun is that hot to the tracker on the missile," Northrup replied.

"I wonder if you're hugging a tree line or a ridgeline if it could lock on?" Mr. Hern said.

"I can tell you back in '70, they were on a ridgeline, and rather than shoot down at the slicks, they fired up at us gunships. I'll bet they can't fire at an aircraft that has a tree line or a ridgeline behind it," Mr. Hosaka said.

"If it's locking on our exhaust, then I would think we would want to turn into the missile if we saw it and had time," Brown said. "Present the smallest picture to the missile and mask our exhaust."

"That makes sense. What if we fired off a rocket when we saw one coming at us? Would it lock on the rocket's exhaust?" Lieutenant Shields asked.

"Good point. That just may be the answer," Mr. Hern said. "Fire a pair of rockets to break the lock the Strella has."

"Not so sure it would. What's the velocity of our rockets?" Lieutenant Shields asked.

"About twenty-three hundred feet per second. I'll bet that's way too fast for a missile to lock on to. It would just continue to track towards us," Captain Williams said. "Gents, in my opinion the best thing to do is stay low and fast and if you're at altitude and one is fired, get to the ground as fast as you can. If you're at altitude but as high as you can get, eight thousand, even ten."

"Ohhh, I hate being at ten. The controls are just too damn sloppy at that altitude."

"The slicks can fire off a flare if they see one, but not us. We need a modification on the aircraft to fire off some flares if we see a missile. Need to write that up and take it to the CO. Maybe they can make a modification on the aircraft right here in-country for a flare dispenser," Mister Hern said.

"Might work, but not going to solve our problem right now. We all need to think on this some more and see if we can come up with a tactic or procedure to combat this thing," Captain Brown said as he stood. "Right now, my gut is telling me it's time for chow. Think about this and let's get back together."[2]

That evening, Mike attempted to write a letter home, but his mind kept wandering back to the questions about the Strella. The more he thought about it, the more his mind twisted the problem with questions. *What's the maximum altitude for these things? What's the range of the missile? What's the minimum distance from launch to lock-on? What's the speed? Can a Cobra outrun the missile?* He answered that question right away—*No!* Lastly, *What technique can I employ if I'm hit to maybe survive?* The air-defense threat was bad enough already, causing attack aircraft to either fly right down on the deck or climb. Blue Max pilots were used to flying at three thousand feet and firing their rockets at targets three thousand meters away. Now as the anti-aircraft threat increased, they were being forced higher, which reduced the accuracy of the rockets if the same flight attitude was maintained. To compensate for the higher altitudes, the dives became steeper in order to maintain accuracy. Steeper dives caused a faster increase in airspeed, which presented a shorter engagement window as the aircraft couldn't exceed 190 knots. It was becoming a new world for Blue Max pilots.

# 42

## ON ALL SIDES

11 May 1972
**5th ARVN Command Post**
**An Loc**

The shelling by the North Vietnamese artillery was a bit earlier than usual and certainly more intense. Just after midnight, the artillery began at a high tempo and lasted for four nerve-racking hours. To those hiding in basements and bunkers, it seemed like there was no break in the rounds coming in, when actually it was only one round every five seconds by some accounts. The defensive perimeter had been shrunk over the past month to an area of only about twelve hundred by twelve hundred meters. Suddenly, the artillery stopped as if a switch had been turned to the off position. The sudden silence was at first welcomed, but then suspicions arose as to why and soldiers began to move back to their fighting positions.

At 0430 hours, the switch was turned to the on position and the intense artillery fire commenced immediately.

"Sir, the units are all reporting heavy probes on the

perimeters. Tanks are being reported on the road north of here. It appears that his main attack may be going against the boundary between the 8th Regiment and the 81st Airborne Rangers," Lieutenant Colonel Benedit said as Ulmer entered the command post. "The 8th is reporting that their 3rd and 4th companies are being hit hard and falling back. They've retained a pocket on the top floor of a two-story building."

"Who is the advisor up there?" Ulmer asked.

"Sir, that's Captain Huggins," Benedit replied. "He's connected to us with a landline."

"Call him. I want to know what his situation is right now," Ulmer said. Benedit went over to a TA-312 field telephone and cranked the handle. Finally he handed the receiver to Ulmer.

"Captain Huggins, Colonel Ulmer here. What's your situation?"

"Sir, we have a full regimental attack on our perimeter in typical human wave fashion with tanks. The tanks broke through, but our small reserve is dealing with them with LAWs as the tanks have no infantry with them," Huggins explained.

"Can you hold is the question, Captain?"

"Sir, in honesty, I suspect we're going to be falling back shortly. There are just too many of them."

"Roger, Captain, give me as much time as you can." Ulmer put the receiver back in the cradle and turned to Boarman. "Is the FAC up yet?"

"Yes, sir, he just reported in," Benedit replied.

As he did so, Ulmer moved over to a table that had a map of the area laid out. On the map were B-52 strike boxes. The FAC had the same map in his aircraft with the same boxes. "Tell the FAC that I want the first B-52 strike to hit this box," Ulmer said, jabbing his finger into a box located right in front of the 81st Airborne Ranger Battalion's locations. Fifteen minutes later, the earsplitting sound of rolling thunder created by three B-52 bombers unloading eight hundred meters from the command post was overwhelming and reassuring.

"Get Huggins on the line," Ulmer directed. Benedit did so and handed the receiver to him.

"Captain, did the strike help any?"

"Sir, we were fixing to fall back when it hit and it gave us the time to do so and establish a new defensive line. He's doing nothing right now," Huggins reported. "The concussion wave injured some of the civilians as we have some bleeding from eyes and ears, but they'll be okay. Major Khanh, the battalion commander, didn't get the word and it scared the crap out of him."

"Good, just keep me posted," Ulmer said before he hung up. Reports were being received from all the units, but as the morning wore on, it was evident that the main attack was from the north and a supporting attack was coming in from the west against the 7th Regiment. As the situation unfolded, Ulmer responded by repositioning the B-52 strikes while the FACs were directing tactical air strikes against concentrations of soldiers that they could observe. Attack helicopters were expending their ordnance and returning to Lai Khe as fast as they could for refueling and reaming.

On the south side of the perimeter sat the 5th and 8th Airborne Battalions. As they were located on both sides of Highway 13 and about a thousand meters outside of the town, they hadn't been subjected to the intense artillery bombardment that those in town had experienced. The battalions had been alerted the night before that the attack might come in the morning. The sounds heard in the morning left no doubt in soldiers' minds that the attack was coming. Soldiers began stacking hand grenades and full magazines on the edge of their foxholes. They were ready at 0600 hours when the mortar barrage began. Soldiers hunkered down in their foxholes, knowing full well that as soon as it stopped, the enemy would be in or close to being in the wire. They were not disappointed. Ten seconds after the last mortar round exploded, the airborne soldiers emerged from their foxholes and engaged the massed enemy with accurate and sustained final protective fires. Hand grenades effectively cut down anyone that managed to get within range. Claymore mines ripped swaths through the human waves of attackers.

Captain McDermott was on his radio, talking with the airborne FAC and requesting air strikes, to no avail. Every request was denied due to higher priority in the north or west.

"King FAC, Falcon Five-Oh, request close-air support," McDermott transmitted.

"Falcon Five-Oh, King FAC, all strike packages are committed at this time. Over."

"King FAC, can I get something? Anything? Over."

"Falcon Five-Oh, wait one." *Where the hell does he think I'm going?* McDermott was thinking.

Moments later, King FAC was back on the radio. "Falcon Five-Oh, King FAC, over."

"King FAC, Falcon Five-Oh, go ahead."

"Falcon Five-Oh, I have a flight of two AH-1 gunships five minutes from your location. Best I can do right now. Over."

"King FAC, I'll take them. Over."

"Roger. They had been supporting operations south along Highway 13 but are just coming out of refueling and rearming. Contact Tiger Three-Seven. He'll be coming to your push, over."

"Roger and thanks, King FAC."

McDermott had a good idea where the mortars that had been pounding the perimeter for the past four hours were located. That was what he wanted the gunships to silence. The paratroopers of the battalion were handling the attacking NVA, but the mortars were becoming a problem.

"Falcon Five-Oh, Tiger Three-Seven, over."

"Tiger Three-Seven, Falcon Five-Oh," McDermott answered, looking to the sky in hopes of seeing the gunships.

"Falcon Five-Oh, Tiger Three-Seven is a flight of two fully loaded. Understand you have targets for me. Over."

"Tiger Three-Seven, that is affirmative. Enemy mortar position located approximately three hundred meters south of my position. I need you to take it out. Over."

"Roger, can you mark your forward positions? Over."

"Tiger Three-Seven, roger. Will mark with smoke, but it's going to take a few minutes. Over."

"Roger, Falcon Five-Oh, I have one hour of fuel on board, so take your time."

McDermott got the message clearly despite the words. *Take your sweet-ass time there, Falcon, but in one hour I'm out of here* was how it translated.

"Roger, Tiger Three-Seven" was all McDermott could respond with. He switched his radio and contacted Colonel Hieu to get a marker out. After what seemed like an eternity, a soldier threw out a colored smoke grenade.

"Tiger Three-Seven, Falcon Five-Oh, smoke out." Mike watched the red smoke drift lazily up.

"Roger, Falcon Five-Oh, I have the smoke—all three smokes. I have the purple, the yellow and the red. Which one are you?"

McDermott rose up higher in his position and started to see the other color smokes much closer to his lines drifting up as well. He now had confirmation that the NVA were listening to his transmissions.

"Tiger Three-Seven, Rosie Red is ours. The mortar position should be about three hundred meters south from the smoke. Over." McDermott still couldn't see the gunships because of the overhead cover offered by the rubber trees. Then the all-too-familiar sound of rockets being fired from the gunship was heard and the impacting explosions of the rockets. Then he heard rockets being fired but no sounds of explosions. *Must be firing flechette rounds*, McDermott thought. *Against troops with no overhead cover, the flechette round is a better weapon to use*, he concluded.

"Falcon Five-Oh, Tiger Three-Seven, over."

"Tiger Three-Seven, Falcon Five-Oh, over."

"Falcon, I don't think that mortar is going to bother you anymore. Little bird confirms we got it. Still have ordnance on board. Have you got another target for us? Over."

"Roger. The purple and yellow smoke are his positions, over."

"Falcon Five-Oh, that was mighty nice of you to get them to mark their own positions for me. Tiger Three-Seven rolling hot." And McDermott continued to supply Tiger Three-Seven with targets until Tiger had to break station as his ordnance was expended.

## 43

---

## # 68-15009 GOES DOWN

**11 May 1972**
**F/79 Artillery**
**Long Thanh North**

"Captain Strobridge, sir, time to wake up," the night operations clerk said, gently kicking the base of Rodney's bed. He knew better than to actually touch a sleeping person.

"Yeah, I'm awake. What time is it?" Rodney asked, wishing to just roll over and go back to sleep, but he knew better.

"Sir, it's 0600 and you have an 0730 mission brief," the clerk responded as he moved on to wake the other pilots.

"Hey, before you disappear, Specialist, who am I flying with today?" Rodney asked. He was a fairly new pilot to the Blue Max family and hadn't attained aircraft commander status, so he was a copilot/gunner. This was his second tour in Vietnam; his first had been as a fixed-wing pilot in the Central Highlands. He was an air-defense officer by branch but only had served briefly in an air-defense unit before flight school. As

353

such, he bounced around with different aircraft commanders, learning new techniques from each. Due to the drawdowns, Blue Max was overstrength in captains and pilots, so just to be getting into an aircraft was a stroke of luck.

"Sir, you're flying with Captain Williams. He's up and told me to tell you he would be over at the mess hall if you wanted to link up before the briefing. Two other aircraft will be going out with you," the clerk responded. "Anything else, sir?"

"No, thanks," Rodney said as he swung his legs out of bed and stood. After the usual morning routine of a piss, a shave and emptying one's bowels, Rodney headed over to the mess hall and linked up with Robert "Bob" Williams.

Rodney enjoyed flying with Bob. Bob was on his second tour in Vietnam. He was an infantry officer but had flown the AH-1G Cobra gunship on his first tour. When he'd arrived in-country on this tour, he was first assigned to the Cobra transition training team in Vung Tau as an instructor pilot. When that organization had stood down, he'd been transferred to the Blue Max family.

"Grab something to eat. It's going to be a long day from what I saw on the board," Bob said as Rodney approached him. "They managed not to burn the scrambled eggs this morning but did a number on the toast. Coffee's okay." Rodney changed course and moved to the chow line. As usual, the bacon was undercooked as it was baked on large cookie sheets and never got crisp. He didn't think it was possible to burn powdered eggs, but the mess hall was full of surprises. The bread was a combination of sawdust and flour, so it burned rather easily. He poured a full cup of coffee.

"Okay, what we got today?" Rodney asked, taking a seat across from Bob.

"It appears that we're part of a flight of three today and will be over An Loc. They got hit hard yesterday, and I suspect it'll be raging up there today. This looks like it might be the enemy's second major wave to overrun the place. Reports are he's tightened up his ADA ring around the city. We should get a full update in this morning's briefing. We'll fly up to Lai Khe and refuel there, so when we get over An Loc we'll be almost full fuel," Bob explained.

"Sounds good. How's the family?" Rodney asked, and the conversation drifted to families back in California and Daleville, Alabama, where Bob was from. After the coffee was drained and the bladders emptied, both pilots grabbed their flight gear and headed over to flight operations for the morning brief along with the other crews.

"Good morning, gentlemen," the operations officer started.

"What's so good about it? You're not flying up there today?" Mr. Causey asked in a snarling tone. Mr. Causey was the aircraft commander on the second AH-1G in this morning's mission.

"No, I'm not, Chief, and that's why it's a good morning. Now...weather today is cloudy with low overcast. Ceiling is four thousand feet and possible rain," the ops officer reported. Low moans could be heard. "No change in the air-defense threat."

"Any report of SA-7s?" someone asked.

"Nope, none that we've received," Ops answered. "If there is no more questions, Captain Williams, you're flight leader. Be safe."

Bob turned to the other aircraft crews. "Okay, let's launch in thirty minutes and come up battery VHF. We'll head up to Lai Khe and refuel and then head to An Loc if we don't get a mission en route for something else. Staggered left formation going up. Any questions?" There were none, and everyone walked together to the flight line.

The flight up to Lai Khe was uneventful as usual and refueling went effortlessly. Being that the Cobra gunship didn't carry a crew chief, the refueling duties generally fell to the copilot/gunner, although many times pilots would switch off so that every two hours a different pilot got to get out and stretch his legs and massage his aching ass. Williams was in his seat when the call came.

"Blue Max Three-Two, Danger Seven-Niner, over."

"Danger Seven-Niner, Blue Max Three-Two, over." Bob had been up here enough to know who Danger Seven-Niner was.

"Blue Max Three-Two, Tunnel One-Oh Alpha has requested a medevac. Contact Dustoff Two-Five on two-four-five Uniform and provide escort. He's coming out of Bien Hoa and proceeding to An Loc over."

"Roger, Danger Seven-Niner. Wilco." Changing frequencies to his UHF radio, he transmitted, "Dustoff Two-Five, Blue Max Three-Two, over."

"Blue Max Three-Two, Dustoff Two-Five. We're off Bien Hoa and approaching Lai Khe. Understand you're escorting me, over."

"Dustoff Two-Five, affirmative. We're just topping off at Lai Khe and will be airborne in five mikes, over."

"Three-Two, perfect. I should be abreast of Lai Khe in five minutes. See you in the air."

"Roger, we're a flight of three and will take up positions on each side and above," Bob announced and switched to VHF battery frequency. "Flight, give me an up when you're ready. We're providing escort for a medevac mission going into An Loc. I'll take the right side position, Three-Four, you take left side, and Three-Three, you go high and trail. Any questions?"

"Three-Four is good."

"Three-Three is good."

"Flight Three-Two coming out," Bob transmitted and

hovered out for his takeoff once Captain Strobridge was back in the aircraft and ready. The other aircraft fell right in behind him as he obtained clearance from the tower at Lai Khe and departed, turning right, coming out of POL and flying down the middle of the runway. As they climbed to altitude, Bob spotted the Dustoff aircraft and took up a position providing security for the medevac aircraft.

Flying north, it wasn't hard to spot An Loc from a long ways off. Highway 13 ran straight north from Lai Khe to An Loc. The smoke and explosions in the distance clearly marked the location of the besieged town. Lumbering AC-130 aircraft flew in orbits, spewing streams of molten lead down on the rubber trees, destroying artillery, tanks and anything else that could be pointed out to them. Small A-37 jets darted down and up, releasing bombs that tore up the countryside. Larger F-4 Phantom jets came in low-level and left a trail of burning black napalm in their wake. To Bob and the pilots, it must have been hell down there.

As they approached the town from the south, Bob spotted a couple of locations that anti-aircraft fire was coming from.

"Dustoff Two-Five, what's your plan to get in there?" Bob asked.

"Blue Max Three-Two, I'm going to approach from the south to the north just west of the highway and attempt to get into the center of town."

"Roger, we're going to gain a bit of altitude and lay down suppressive fire on both sides of you as you approach. Once in, we'll orbit until you say you're coming out and we'll come low and suppress your exit path. Over."

"Blue Max, sounds good. Dropping down now." And the Dustoff bird started a rapid descent. Two kilometers south of An Loc, the Cobras were in position to cover Dustoff.

"Flight, let's clear a path for him," Bob called out and began punching off rockets into the rubber tree plantation on the south-southwest side. Three-Three and Three-Four did likewise with both miniguns and rockets.

"Oh my God!" suddenly came over the battery VHF radio. Causey looked over to his right. Three-Two was gone. An explosion in the rubber trees caught his attention slightly behind and to the right of his aircraft, where Three-Two should have been.

"Three-Two is down, Three-Two is down," yelled Three-Three over the battery net.

"Three-Three, Three-Four, what happened?"

"I don't know. Did you see what hit him?"

"No, we were watching the medevac bird. Shit, taking hits." Intense ground fire was reaching skyward to the AH-1G Cobras as the medevac aircraft had a clear path to the landing zone. The enemy was more intent on engaging the Cobra gunships than the medevac chopper. The two Cobras continued to unleash every rocket and minigun round they had, covering the medevac chopper out. They did it because it was their job to cover the medevac aircraft. They did it because they were pissed that two of their family members had died before their eyes.[1]

# 44

## CRITICAL DECISIONS



**II MAY 1971**
   **5th Division CP**
   **An Loc**

Colonel Ulmer and General Hung were studying a map of the city. Reports coming in from the units were not encouraging. The 81st Airborne Ranger Battalion was barely holding and had given up considerable ground. The situation on the west was equally dire, with the 7th Regiment under pressure from infantry and tank assaults. The 8th Group had been reduced to one battalion holding a position on the north side of a salient, pushing on the 7th Regiment from the west. In the south, the 5th and 8th Airborne Battalions were under pressure but holding their own with no withdrawals. They were not being subjected to the intense artillery strikes that those in the town were under.

"General, I think what he's attempting to do is link the penetration from the north and the west together and thus split our forces," Colonel Ulmer said, pointing at the map.

"I concur, Colonel. Only our air strikes were keeping him at bay at this point. The B-52 strikes are preventing him from reinforcing his forward elements," General Hung said. "I do no understand the lack of coordination between his tanks and infantry, however. In almost every case the tanks rush in ahead of the infantry and then seem to wander around lost as to where to go or what to do," Hung questioned.

"Let's just be thankful that he doesn't have them working close together. We've been able to knock out most of the tanks with LAWs because his tanks have no infantry protection. I heard that yesterday a tank stopped next to a building that was occupied on the second floor by an old man. The gentleman simply walked over to his window, pulled the pin on a grenade and dropped it right in the turret hatch of the tank. Blew the tank to hell. If infantry had been with the tank, then the old man would be dead," Ulmer explained. As he did so, a soldier handed General Hung a note.

"It is from the 7th. Seems the enemy has seized the public works building," Hung said with some disappointment in his voice.

"Hell, that's only three hundred meters from here," Ulmer pointed out and glanced at the map. "Sir, we've got to reinforce the forces inside the town."

Hung looked at the map. "We have no reinforcements, Colonel," he concluded.

"Sir, then we accept risk and pull someone into the two from the outside. We have the 5th and the 8th Battalions holding on the south. The enemy has made no progress against them. I would recommend we pull one of those battalions back into town to reinforce the 7th or the 81st Battalion," Ulmer stated.

For a few moments, Hung said nothing. Finally, he stated, "I will order Colonel Luong to send one battalion to reinforce

7th." He moved to locate his operations officer. *Thank God, the man is making a decision*, Ulmer thought.

* * *

"Colonel Taylor," Luong said, gaining Taylor's attention.

"Sir?" Taylor said, getting up from his chair, where he had been talking to Colonel Corley, and walking over to a map that Luong was looking over.

"We have order from Hung. He want one battalion to move to reinforce 7th in town," Luong said. He didn't ask for a recommendation per se, but it was understood that was what he was seeking. Taylor studied the map for a moment and looked at Corley, who had stood and joined them.

"These two battalions are in front of your positions. Both have been in contact. If we pull one out, which will have the least impact on your forces?" Taylor asked. After a moment, Corley tapped the map.

"The 8th Battalion is more of a blocking force across Highway 13 than the 5th Battalion. If you have to pull one out, I ask that it be the 5th," Corley replied, visibly upset with having anything pulled out between the RF/PF forces and the NVA.

"Thank you, Colonel," Luong said, acknowledging that it was not an easy decision. "We will notify the 5th to move. The 8th will just have to spread out a bit and cover a portion of that sector as well," he indicated.

"Colonel Luong, if you will excuse me, I'll get on the radio and inform the advisors of this change coming their way," Taylor said as he stepped away.

"Yeah, I best let Colonel Nhut know about this change. He may want to shift some forces," Corley said as he grabbed his helmet and headed for the door to run over to the RF/PF command post. *Colonel Nhut had best hear it from me rather than get a surprise*, Corley was thinking when he cleared the door and began to run the gauntlet of incoming artillery.

$$45$$

# TAO O

11 May 1972
## 32nd Regiment
## Tao O

The 31st Regiment had been beating its head on the enemy positions six kilometers north of Chon Thanh since 1 May. The decision was made to deploy the 32nd Regiment five kilometers further up Highway 13. The airmobile went smoothly until the forces landed, and then all hell broke loose. The 3rd Airborne Brigade was in a meat grinder north of Tao O and Tan Khai. The enemy had no intention of pulling out at the sight of so many helicopters preceded by close-air support strikes and a B-52 bomb run. Captain Harold Fridermeyer was an advisor with the 2nd Battalion of the 32nd Regiment. He was branch-qualified in field artillery in 1967 through the Officer Candidate program and had served in a battery at Fort Bragg with the 82nd Airborne Division prior to his first tour in Vietnam. As with all advisors, his duties with the 2nd

Battalion were mostly adjusting artillery and close-air support. Today was no different. Prior to the insertion, the senior regimental advisor, Lieutenant Colonel Willey, pulled all the advisors from the battalions together.

"Okay, they're inserting us five kilometers up Highway 13. I suspect that we can't expect an easy time of this. Intel says that the NVA have dug in positions along the abandoned railroad bed to the west of the highway. The B-52s went in earlier this morning and plastered the area, but I still expect we're going to get into it. TACAIR is on standby—use it. He'll be employing his mortars and artillery and I doubt we have any artillery that can reach his, so we have to rely on the FAC to locate and destroy that."

Colonel Willey continued, "The 31st Regiment has been point on this clearing operation, but two days ago the regimental commander was seriously wounded, so the job is being shifted to us. Also the 165th Regiment is pretty well beat up and they've been reinforced with the 209th Regiment, so I'm told. Further up north are elements of the 3rd Airborne Brigade, and they've been in a fight north of Tan Khai. You should be happy, we're keeping two regiments from going against An Loc. Any questions? If not, be safe, stay in touch," he concluded.

An hour later, the regiment boarded the helicopters. They were aircraft from the 229th Assault Helicopter Company, so everyone was feeling assured that they would get into the landing zones.

Harold assumed his usual position next to the battalion commander and in a door position. Besides him and the battalion commander, six other ARVN soldiers were aboard. Harold considered them to be the battalion commander's bodyguards because wherever the battalion commander traveled, these same six were with him. Since Harold had been with the battalion, he had made friends with this small band and felt secure with them. In the past, Harold had shared some of the contents in his "care packages" that he received from home, which always brought smiles and laughter from the group. As the flight continued down the flight path to the landing zone, Harold looked up and saw the FAC orbiting high above. It reminded him of a chicken hawk or vulture looking for a meal. He just prayed they weren't the meal for this day.

He was brought back to the moment when the pilot yelled, "Two minutes," and the crew opened fire with the aircraft's M60 machine guns. He was mesmerized watching the Cobra gunships nosing over and punching off rockets into the tree line on both sides of the landing zone. It didn't appear that the gunships were receiving any return fire, which was a good sign. Maybe the B-52s had done the job?

That positive thought evaporated as soon as the aircraft touched down. The tree line on the west side of the road was spewing streams of green tracers across the landing zone as the aircraft quickly departed. A small ditch on the west side next to the road was providing some concealment for the attacking ARVN soldiers, who weren't holding back on their own fire. Harold knew it was coming, and he wasn't disappointed when the first enemy mortar round slammed into the highway. *At least it didn't hit the ditch*, he was thinking as he called for artillery support. His own battalion mortars were getting into action and he was using them to hit the tree line.

"Dai'uy," Major Xuan shouted over the roar of gunfire, getting Harold's attention. "Can you hit their mortar?" Xuan asked, pressing his face closer to the ground as the next round impacted just outside the ditch.

"Let me see if I can get a better position to observe," Harold said. Lying in the ditch with everyone else, he couldn't get a good fix on where the enemy mortar was hiding. He could hear rounds leaving the tube, so he knew it was close and a general azimuth to the mortar, but he couldn't pinpoint the enemy position. Looking around, he noted the highway was a bit higher than the bottom of the ditch and there was a small rise on the eastern side of the highway. *That has got to be a better position than this*, he thought, and with that he jumped up with his weapon in one hand and the radio in the other. The sprint across the road at a low crouch didn't attract too much enemy fire, thankfully, he thought as he positioned himself on the top of the low rise. As he took up a position, small-arms rounds began to impact around him as he was exposed to the enemy now. *Damn, I guess I can't have everything*, he thought as he formulated his request for close-air support on the enemy mortar position, which was very visible now.

"King FAC, King FAC, Gopher Six-Two, over," Harold transmitted.

"Gopher Six-Two, King FAC, over."

"King FAC, Gopher Six-Two, I have targets for you, over."

"Roger, Gopher Six-Two, send them." And Harold passed the coordinates for the enemy mortar position that he could observe. Moments later, he saw an O-2 FAC aircraft in a steep dive and releasing a single rocket that impacted in close proximity to the enemy mortar. It was followed by two A-37 jets dropping two canisters each of napalm. The problems created by the enemy mortar went up in smoke and flames.

"Dai'uy, Dai'uy," Harold heard along with the sound of someone running up from behind him. Spinning around, ready to engage, he recognized the battalion executive officer, approaching almost out of breath. "Good shoot, good shoot. Major Xuan very happy," the executive officer stated between breaths.

"Glad he approves," Harold said, being cut short by the

sound of distant artillery, which was replaced with the sound of a freight train getting louder until the round impacted, causing a massive crater in the road. Harold and the executive officer pressed themselves into the ground. Harold heard the next round momentarily until it impacted, on his position.[1]

**46**

---

# RAPID RESPONSE

**11 May 1972**
  **5th Airborne Battalion**
  **An Loc**

Contact along the line had quieted down by 1200 hours. A B-52 strike earlier in the morning south of their position appeared to have taken the steam out of the NVA assault on the perimeter. McDermott was enjoying a minute of peace when Colonel Hieu came trotting over.

"Dai'uy...we go. We move into town with new orders. North side and northwest side of town been pushed. We go plug hole. We go now," Colonel Hieu said. Mike acknowledged the change of plans and started packing his stuff. Wasn't much to pack, and in five minutes he was ready to move out. *Surprised Colonel Taylor didn't let me know about this*, Mike was thinking as he stuffed his rucksack.

The trek north into town was quiet with the only noise being small-arms fire in the distance and artillery impacting in the town. Soldiers were almost oblivious to the noise around them, only reacting when a particularly close round impacted or was heard. The first friendly forces they encountered coming north were the RF/PF forces defending the southeast perimeter. They were expressionless as the battered paratroopers proudly maneuvered past them. Words were not exchanged. As the paratroopers moved past the RF/PF compound, they began to get their first look at the town, or what was left of it. No building was left untouched by artillery rounds impacting. Gaping holes and blackened walls were visible on every building. Windows were missing and furniture was scattered across the streets. Some burned-out tanks that had entered the town in earlier attacks were present with their decaying burnt crews still inside. The stench of decomposing bodies, human waste, and garbage mixed with the smell of burning oil and buildings was putrid. Animal as well as human remains littered the streets and no one made an effort to move them. Open graves were everywhere, opened by impacting artillery rounds. The flies were sharing with the rats the dinner feast that had been laid before them. As they moved along, hugging the sides of buildings for some protection, McDermott noted the absence of emotions among the paratroopers. They were numb to the death and destruction they were passing through. A block after the 5th Division command post, Colonel Hieu gave the signal for everyone to stop.

The company commanders converged on Hieu along with McDermott. Hieu was studying his map.

"We attack enemy one block north of 5th Division command post, but where is block? All buildings are destroyed. Just rubble in street. No can tell what is street and what is building," Hieu said, addressing McDermott. Mike looked around and had to agree with the commander. The maps looked nothing like the landscape before them.

"Sir, I would recommend that you assign a pile of rubble

to each company commander as their objective and we move forward. I believe that that pile might be the old public works building and it's probably occupied. The other is the Montagnard elementary school. I'm sure the enemy will let us know where they are," McDermott indicated. After a brief discussion, it appeared that was exactly what Hieu ordered as the companies began to move forward. Quickly, the enemy did reveal their positions as they were hiding in the rubble. Hand grenades and light antitank weapons were used extensively to quiet enemy positions. Surprising to Hieu was the fact that the defense didn't consist of a linear defense but strong points established by both sides throughout the town. Night didn't hinder the paratroopers as they continued the attack. Close-air support was planned and used to isolate the enemy forces as the paratroopers moved and seized their assigned final objectives, which were about five blocks or what was thought to be five blocks north of the 5th ARVN Division command post. Once the objectives were seized, the paratroopers dug in for the remainder of the night.

The battalion command post took up residence in an abandoned bunker left over from the days of French occupation. The night would not be quiet, however.

"Incoming," McDermott yelled as two rounds came screaming and impacting across the street, or what was thought to be a street. *Damn, those were big rounds,* he was thinking as he started to stand up. It appeared that everyone was okay as people resumed what they had been doing. Then he heard the familiar sound again. This time one of the Vietnamese announced the incoming round, which impacted a short distance past the command post. That was when everyone realized who the target was, as these weren't random rounds. Two rounds fired at the same time. The first two rounds were short of the bunker. The next two rounds were over the bunker. The bunker was bracketed. It became obvious very quickly that this was adjusted artillery fire. There had to be an observer someplace close adjusting it.

"King FAC, Falcon Five-Oh, over."

"Falcon Five-Oh, King FAC, go ahead."

"King FAC, we're under bombardment from what appears to be two big artillery pieces. The azimuth to the guns, I believe, is three-four-two degrees. We believe they have a spotter adjusting. Can you find them? Over."

"Falcon Five-Oh, roger. We'll head over that way and take a look."

King FAC went in search of the artillery tubes. The shelling didn't stop, but it wasn't as frequent as it had been, which led McDermott to conclude that King FAC was in the vicinity of the guns and they were shooting only when they could see that he was out of position to see the guns fire. Then the guns stopped shooting entirely.

"King FAC, Falcon Five-Oh, over."

"Go ahead, Falcon Five-Oh."

"Roger, King FAC, did you get those guns? Over."

"Falcon Five-Oh, that's a negative."

"Roger, understood. They've stopped. Over."

"Roger, keep me posted."

Hieu and McDermott couldn't figure out why the guns had stopped completely if King FAC had not destroyed them.

* * *

Adjacent to the 5th Airborne Battalion was the 81st Airborne Rangers. Captain Huggins had been observing the incoming rounds from a rooftop. He didn't realize that those rounds were targeted against the 5th Battalion command post. As he watched, he became more convinced that they were being adjusted for some reason at that specific location. A movement caught his eye. It was two young ladies running from a pile of rubble to a burned-out building. At first, the advisor thought they were simply seeking better protection than what a pile of rubble offered. *This shelling has been going on almost all day and night, so when did they get to the pile of rubble, and how long were they there? Hell, that burned-out building is no better*, he was thinking, fearing for their safety.

"Hey, Sergeant Yerta, did you see those two girls duck into that burned-out building over there?" Captain Huggins asked.

"Sure did, sir. Why?" Yerta answered.

"Hell, that building is no safer than the pile of rubble they came out of. Let's go get them and bring them back here. Hasn't been any enemy noted in the vicinity of the building. You and I can police them up," Huggins said, picking up his weapon and moving towards the stairs to the ground level.

"Right behind you, Captain," Yerta said. Reaching the ground floor, both paused for a moment to observe the area. When satisfied, both sprinted across the garbage-covered street to the building that the girls had run into. Cautiously, they began to move towards the door when Huggins heard a voice, coming from a radio transmission. He quickly raised his hand to stop Yerta and listened. One of the girls was speaking and then the squelch on the radio resumed, a clear indication that no one was now talking. *What the hell?* Huggins thought. Turning to Yerta, Huggins gave the hand signal for "on three we go" and began curling fingers. As the third finger closed, Yerta plunged through the doorway, ready to open fire. Huggins was right behind him.

The two girls turned around quickly, surprise clearly visible on their faces. They weren't teenagers or children but young women in their twenties or early thirties. One held a map and the other a radio transmitter that could be purchased in any civilian store. As they stood there frozen, looking down the barrel of Yerta's M16, the radio squelch broke and a Vietnamese male voice was heard loud and clear. Yerta and

Huggins spoke enough Vietnamese to understand the male was asking for the next coordinates. The women said nothing as Yerta approached and took the map and radio. Their hands were quickly tied and they were taken back to the 81st Airborne Ranger command post. Their days of adjusting artillery rounds on the town were over. They were turned over to Colonel Nhut's forces and not seen again.[1]

As first light appeared, a new sound was heard that chilled the nerves of the paratroopers. The clanking sound of tanks was always unnerving to infantry soldiers.

"King FAC, King FAC, Falcon Five-Oh, over."

"Falcon Five-Oh, go ahead, over."

"King FAC, Falcon Five-Oh, we have tanks approaching our position from the north. Over."

"Roger, I'll get something on it shortly, out." All McDermott could do was wait and hope they got the tanks before they reached his positions.

Captain Huggins heard the call to King FAC and began scanning the northern perimeter. He noticed two tanks break off from the main column and begin moving directly towards his positions and no others.

"Sergeant Yerta, we need some LAWs up here, I think," Huggins said, looking over the wall that surrounded the perimeter of the roof. Yerta rose up and took a quick look before he headed to the stairs to retrieve some of the light anti-tank weapons. Huggins continued to watch as the tanks maneuvered towards his and the 5th Airborne Battalion's positions. Four thousand feet above, Raven Five-Oh also watched the tanks.

"Falcon Five-Oh, King FAC, over."

"King FAC, Falcon Five-Oh, go ahead," McDermott answered anxiously.

"Contact Raven Five-Oh on four-five-four-five, over."

"Roger, King FAC, Falcon Five-Oh out." And McDermott quickly changed the frequency on his FM radio. "Raven Five-Oh, Falcon Five-Oh, over."

"Falcon Five-Oh, Raven Five-Oh, understand you have a tank problem, over."

"Raven Five-Oh, Falcon, that's affirmative and it's getting closer. Over."

"Roger, Falcon. We're going to solve that problem shortly. I have your problem in sight."

McDermott watched as Raven Five-Oh made a second orbit before rolling over on his back and plunging towards the ground in a steep dive. At about what looked like two thousand feet, a single rocket left Raven's wing and exploded in a puff of white smoke next to the lead tank.

"Hawk One, Raven Five-Oh. Target is marked. Tanks in the town or what's left of a town. How copy? over."

"Raven Five-Oh, Hawk One, I have good copy and have the target in sight. King gave me an update on enemy threat. We're coming in low-level south to north with a right break. How copy?" Hawk One reported.

The little A-37 jet affectionately called Dragonfly was small, agile and almost perfect for close-air support. The pilot, Lieutenant Colonel Weed, commander of the 8th Special Operations Squadron, was on the controls. Today he flew solo. Approaching An Loc from the south at treetop level, he was almost too fast for enemy gunners on larger weapons to lock on to him. He fixated on the white phosphorous round and the tank that was moving past it. At what he considered the exact moment, he pickled the two-hundred-and-fifty-pound bomb and immediately pulled back into a climbing right turn to watch the destructive power of the bomb. A small smile crept across his face, only to be replaced with disbelief as the bomb crashed into the front of the tank but didn't detonate. The tank stopped.

*Son of a bitch*, he was thinking as he dove the aircraft in a tight turn towards the same tank. "Not this time, mother...," he muttered to himself as he released the second bomb at five hundred feet and continued in low-level flight mode to escape the hornet's nest of anti-aircraft guns. He didn't need to look back to see if the bomb had detonated as the shock wave of the explosion told him he had detonation this time.

"Hawk One, Raven Five-Oh, scratch one tank" was heard over Weed's headphones.

From where McDermott sat, the tank became pieces of flying metal as the bomb, like the first, was a direct hit. In addition to taking out the tank, it took out a good number of enemy infantry soldiers that were around the tank. Follow-on tanks began to back up.

Huggins watched the Dragonfly neutralize the tank, but he still had two tanks heading in his direction. As they approached, they traversed their turrets, looking for targets such as ARVN machine-gun positions and mortars. Finding either, they would fire their main guns to destroy the position and everything in the position. As Huggins and Yerta watched from the rooftop, the lead tank slowly rolled next to the building with the second tank close behind. Words didn't need to be exchanged. Both advisors prepared a LAW and together stood and peered over the roof, looking down at the tanks. Both fired simultaneously and both tanks exploded simultaneously.[2]

* * *

"Things seem to be quieting down," Hank said as he sat with Colonel Nhut in the Ruff-Puff compound. Rifle fire was sporadic across the town, and even the artillery barrages had decreased significantly. Friendly air support still roamed the sky above with no absence of targets provided by the advisors and the FAC, and the air-defense threat remained high. There was also an absence of the sounds of tanks as the ones that had reached the town were either destroyed or abandoned by their crews. Some still had the engines running. Adjacent to the compound, the remains of the 271st Regiment along with six tanks cluttered the streets with burning vehicles and bodies. The wounded could be heard, but when medical assistance attempted to reach them, they were fired upon, so the wounded NVA soldiers were just left where they had fallen, at least for the time being.

"There is not much left of my village to fight over, is there? The commies have pretty much destroyed the entire village, and for what? So they can say they have liberated us from the corrupt government in Saigon," Nhut said. It surprised Hank that the colonel would talk this freely.

Noticing the expression on Hank's face, Nhut said, "My comments surprise you, Major? I know how politics works. In my country we are a bit more open about the corruption than in your country, but it exists with all governments. Men of power will always attempt to accumulate wealth any way they can. Same in Hanoi as here. This campaign has not been about winning the hearts of the people. Do you think any of these people will welcome the Communists after this? This is about seizing ground and punishing the people for not supporting the Popular Front since 1954. After you Americans leave, they will come again, and the next time they will probably win and overthrow the government of South Vietnam," Colonel Nhut said, not looking at Hank.

"Why do you say that, sir? Your troops have taken everything that has been thrown at them and have shown courage against overwhelming odds," Hank responded with some surprise.

"Look up and tell me what you see," Ninh said, pointing his finger skyward.

"Sir, I see some B-52 contrails, a FAC and a couple of fast

movers making bomb runs. There's a couple of Cobras over the town as well."

"Yes, but we have no B-52s in the Vietnamese Air Force and no Cobra gunships. We have close-air support, but have you seen much of them here? No. What is making the difference in this fight is the air support that you bring. The Vietnamese Air Force does not bring anything to the fight, and because of that we will not stop the NVA on the next major campaign. Once you leave, your government will not have the Air Force return to help us. We will be on our own," Ninh explained as he gazed over the killing fields.

"What will you do, sir?" Hank asked.

"I have made arrangements for my family to leave Vietnam. They are going to Tampa Bay, Florida. Do you know Tampa Bay?" Nhut asked.

"No, sir. Never been there."

"I have relative there and he is going to bring them over very soon. I will follow sometime after that when I think it wise to leave, but I will wait until absolutely the last moment. I no coward, but I no martyr either," Colonel Nhut said with a smile. "Best we check the perimeter. It will be dark soon and I suspect we will have probes all night," he added as he stood and picked up his weapon.

"Right behind you, sir," Hank said and followed the colonel around the camp.

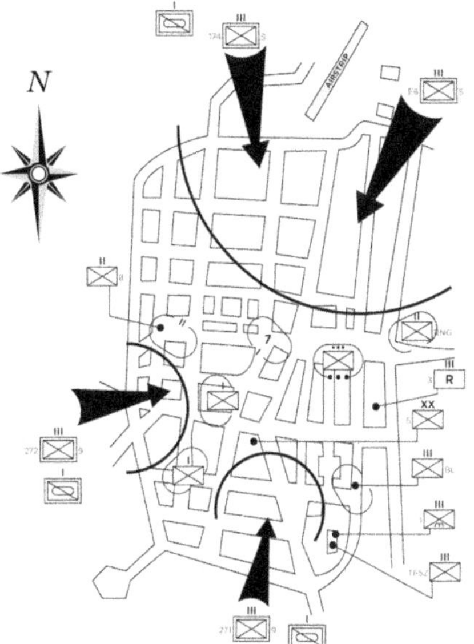


*Enemy Assault, May 11–12, 1972*

## 47

**SMALL REPRIEVE**

**13 MAY 1972**
  **Ruff-Puff Compound**
  **An Loc**

The evening of May 11 and all day on May 12, enemy forces were probing the perimeter or exfiltrating out of town. Throughout May 12, ARVN forces conducted patrols to root out the pockets of NVA soldiers that were still in the town and attempt to push the perimeter back. Hank was drinking coffee with Colonel Nhut when they were approached by a Catholic priest and Buddhist monk.

"Colonel Nhut, may we speak with you?" the priest asked.

"Certainly, Father," Nhut replied.

"We would like to take our congregations out of town and move them to Lai Khe if you will permit it," the priest said. Nhut and Hank exchanged looks of surprise.

"Father, you do understand that this fight is not over yet. There are still NVA forces surrounding us, and the road to Lai Khe is closed. I am not at all sure that the NVA will allow you to pass through," Nhut said. "Right now with you all here, we are using our supplies to feed and care for you and the NVA know that. They would rather see you remain here, adding to our supply difficulties. We have heard that the last group that went down the road last month were seized and made to dig fortifications subject to bombing. The children were all lost, either killed or wandering in the forest. I will not hold you here, but I warn you it is not exactly safe for you to travel that road."

The monk and priest exchanged looks for a moment. "We have considered the dangers of moving our congregations and have discussed it with them. They would rather take their chances on the road rather than to live here under the threat of artillery and with the stench of death all around them," the priest said.

Nhut turned to Hank. "What do you think, Major?"

"Sir, I think they're taking a hell of a chance but understand their need to get out of this place. I would recommend that no one who was a government official, teacher or vocal anticommunist make the trip. If they do, there's a good chance that someone in that group will point them out to the NVA, resulting in a bullet in the back of the head. Also, any of the very old shouldn't go as that's a long walk."

Nhut thought about what Hank had said for a few moments. "Father, see Captain Kia for some food supplies to take with you. You will also want to be sure to take some water with you as well. If you get to any ARVN forces, please tell them what we have done and the conditions here."

"I will, Colonel, and thank you. We will leave in about an hour," the priest said and departed with the monk.

"Do you think they'll get through?" Hank asked as the two walked away.

"They might. Some will, some will not. Any able-bodied men will be pressed into preparing fortifications. Young women will probably be raped. The old will be allowed to continue or shot. This is not about winning hearts and minds. This is about retribution," Colonel Nhut said, watching the group forming up and distributing food and water. When they were ready, the priest and monk led the party of over one hundred people out the gate and down Highway 13.[1]

As they watched the group move down the road, a voice called out, "Major Sabine." Hank turned to see SFC Yerta approaching.

"Over here, Sergeant Yerta," Hank responded, recognizing the NCO from the 81st Airborne Rangers. Yerta saw Hank and approached without saluting. No officer wanted to get shot returning a salute if a sniper was watching.

"Sir, Colonel Ulmer asked me to grab you and bring you back to the 5th Division Command post."

"Any idea what he wants?" Hank asked, his curiosity raised.

"No, sir. He just asked that I get you and your gear and have you come up to the CP. Captain McDermott and Captain Huggins are both there as well. Things between Captain McDermott and Colonel Ulmer are a bit heated. Captain Huggins is sort of supporting Captain McDermott's opinion right now," Yerta said.

"And what's that all about?" Hank asked.

"They're attempting to impress on Colonel Ulmer that we need some close-air support in our sector and we're not getting any. Seems General Hung wants it all for his regiments and none for the airborne units," Yerta said.

"And how am I involved in that discussion?"

"I don't think you are. I think there's a chopper inbound to get you. If you do leave, can you take this letter out for me to my wife if you get someplace to drop mail?" Yerta asked as he pulled a crumpled envelope out of his shirt pocket. "Kind of like to let her know I'm okay."

"Sure, I'll drop it at the first post office I come to," Hank replied, taking the letter and placing it in his shirt pocket. "Tell Colonel Ulmer I'll be along as soon as I get my stuff together."

Reaching the 5th Division CP, Hank found a vigorous conversation between Captain McDermott, Captain Huggins and Colonel Taylor. The captains were attempting to explain that every time they called for an air strike, someone in Hung's staff was shortchanging the request to one of the ARVN units. Taylor was taking it all in and jotting down notes in a small green notebook that Army officers have carried since World War II.

"Okay, I hear you and I will discuss this with Colonel Ulmer. He's walking softly right now, getting to know Hung, so let's give him a chance to rock the boat gently. I'll see that you two get priority on the attack helicopters in the meantime. Okay?" Taylor offered.

McDermott and Huggins exchanged looks and nodded in agreement, but Taylor could tell they weren't happy with this arrangement.

When the discussion died down, Hank asked, "Sir, I was told to come up here and see Colonel Ulmer. Can you tell me where he is?"

"He's meeting with Hung right now and you best not bother them. There's a chopper inbound with Hollingsworth aboard. Ulmer was told to have you standing by to get on that chopper. Seems someone wants you out of here. Hollingsworth wants to take you down to the 21st Division so you can spend some quality time with them," Taylor said with a sarcastic tone to his comment. Reaching in his pocket, he added, "Can I ask you to drop this letter off for me if you get to a mail drop? Maybe the pilot will take it out for you." Taylor handed a soiled envelope to Hank. Instead of a postage stamp, the word "Free" was written in its place. Service members in a combat zone didn't have to put a postage stamp on a letter to send it back to the United States.

"Yes, sir, I'll be glad to do that. Have another one right here to go with it," Hank responded, taking Sergeant Yerta's letter out of this pocket and placing it next to Taylor's. He looked at Huggins and McDermott before he made the offer. "You guys want to write something short and sweet for me to take out too?" he asked. Both came back a few minutes later with an envelope for Hank.

## 48

# BATTLE OF TAO O BRIDGE

**14 May 1972**
 **21st Div Hq**
 **Chon Thanh**

Colonel Ross Franklin was frustrated at the slow pace of the operation. He had really expected the division to be more aggressive against the enemy but had to remind himself that down in the Mekong Delta where they had been, combat operations were small-scale guerrilla operations and not conventional combat operations with combined-arms assets as they were experiencing here. The previous contacts with the enemy at the battle of Bench Mark 75 had lasted for twelve days. What they were running into here was much more significant than what they had found at Bench Mark 75.

"Ross, what do you think you're going to run up against this time?" Hollingsworth asked as he departed his helicopter at the division headquarters in Chon Thanh. Major Hank Sabine was lagging behind him with all of this worldly possessions in one rucksack.

"Sir, I'm afraid we are going to see more of the same. Let me bring you up to speed on the events that have unfolded so far this month. As you know, on the first of May, the 31st Regiment got into it with the 165th NVA Regiment seven kilometers north of Chon Thanh at Bench Mark 75. That was a three-day hold-up when we saw Sagger missiles for the first time. They took out three tanks and it shook up the tankers pretty good. The 165th was reinforced by elements of the 209th NVA Regiment," Ross said.

"How do you know the 209th was involved?" Hollingsworth asked.

"We captured a couple of officers from the 209th. Rather talkative folks."

"Well, if the 209th is down here, that means they aren't around An Loc, so I guess that's good news."

"Yes, sir. On the sixth of May, the 32nd Regiment began an envelopment around the NVA positions, and two days later the 3rd of the 31st Regiment conducted an airmobile assault north of that position to cut off any reinforcements. Unfortunately, on the 9th, the commander of the 31st Regiment, Colonel Nguyen Huu Kiem, was wounded and evacuated, causing the unit to pause. Two of the battalion commanders were killed also, Captain Hoi and Captain Nhuong. Two days after that, the 2nd Battalion, 32nd Regiment, was overrun in a two-day firefight. Captain Fridermeyer was killed in that action," Ross explained, "and so was the battalion executive officer who was with Fridermeyer."

"I heard about that. What exactly happened?" Hollingsworth asked.

"Well, sir, the battalion was in a close-in fight and being shelled by mortars and artillery, 130mm. Harry was on the east side of Highway 13 adjusting artillery fire but thought that if he moved to the west side of the road he would have better observation. Before anyone could stop him, he up and sprinted across the road and moved to a small knoll. From there he started adjusting some accurate fire on the NVA positions. It also exposed him on three sides. They quickly figured out where he was and called in indirect fire on his position. You'll have the recommendation for a Distinguished Service Cross on your desk within a couple of days," Ross said.

"I'll sign off on that," Hollingsworth said and paused. "So what is the plan now?"

"On the eleventh, the 32nd Regiment with elements of the 5th Armored Squadron and the 6th, 73rd and 84th Ranger Battalions attacked enemy positions. It was a tough fight, but yesterday the enemy began withdrawing and pulled back to a new defensive line south of the Tao O Bridge on the south side of the creek. Today, the 9th Armored Cavalry Regiment with a battalion from the 15th Regiment and a battery of artillery have been ordered to move east of Highway 13 and will establish firebase vicinity Tan Khai. We attempted to fly in one company of the 2nd Battalion into An Loc, but the ADA was just too much for the Vietnamese flight crews. Tomorrow we're hoping to move eight 105 howitzers and two 155 guns to the firebase that will be established for support of the clearing of Highway 13 and some fire support of An Loc. General Hau is redesignating the 15th as Task Force 15 with the 1st, 2nd and 3rd Battalions, 15th Recon Company, 9th Armored Squadron, and one battery of 105 howitzers and a platoon of 155 howitzers," Ross outlined.

"I spoke with General Minh about setting up a firebase at Tan Khai to support both the 21st and the forces at An Loc. Is there an advisor with the task force?" Hollingsworth asked.

"Yes, sir, Major Mandela Craig is the advisor and has a good working relationship with the task force commander, Lieutenant Colonel Ho Ngoc Can. He's an aggressive commander," Ross pointed out.

"Good. Hopefully we can get his road open,"

Hollingsworth said, pausing for a moment. "Ross, this is Major Hank Sabine. He's on a special assignment from the Pentagon as an observer of the ARVN forces." As Hollingsworth continued to talk, Ross acknowledged Hank with a nod. "The major has been good enough to let us abuse him into any and every combat role we had at Loc Ninh and An Loc. We're going to abuse him some more. He's yours for the time being to assist you in any way he can. Major Sabine has extensive combat experience and is fluent in Vietnamese. Don't abuse him too much, but use him where you can. Any questions?"

"No, sir," Ross said and then turned to Hank. "Drop your gear over at the CP, Major, and I'll be over shortly to talk with you."

"Yes, sir," Hank responded and began to move towards the CP. He had heard about Ross J. Franklin as he had made a name for himself in Korea. Hank didn't have long to wait before Ross appeared.

"So, Major, what's this special assignment that the general spoke of?" Ross asked.

"Sir, I'm assigned to the Pentagon and have been directed to make an assessment of the ARVNs and Vietnamization Program. My report will be sent directly back to Washington," Hank said with all the respect he could muster.

"I understand that I don't get a shot at reviewing the report," Ross stated.

"You do not, sir. That order was made very clear to me. I'm not to discuss it with you or anyone here in Vietnam," Hank replied, expecting a tirade.

"Okay, how can we help each other?" was all Ross asked.

"Well, sir, I would like to get in with the troops and observe them in action. I've seen how the Airborne and Rangers operate, so being with the regular forces would be good," Hank said.

"I can put you right up close and personal with their ground forces. I need an advisor up with the 2nd of the 32nd Regiment since Captain Fridermeyer was killed. Can you take on that assignment?" Ross asked.

"Yes, sir, that would be good," Hank responded.

"You understand that the unit was overrun a couple of days ago and is in need of a strong advisor and some help. I'll give you all the support I can," Ross pledged.

"Sounds good, sir. How do I get up with the unit?"

"I'll have a vehicle take you up there on today's resupply run," Ross said before adding, "Let's get some chow and then we'll get you up on your way."

## 49

---

# MOVE TO TAN KHAI

**14 MAY 1972**
   **TF 15**
   **Tao O Bridge**

"Colonel Ho Ngoc Can," Major Craig said, approaching the colonel behind his command vehicle. Colonel Can commanded Task Force 15.

"Yes, Major," Can responded. Can spoke passable English, so the two were able to communicate very well as Craig's Vietnamese language ability was equally passable.

"Sir, I understand that the 1st Battalion reinforced by the 9th Armored Squadron and a battery of artillery are going to be the lead units moving to seize Ngo Lau to bypass the Tao O Bridge and move up to Tan Khai," Craig said.

"That is correct. 2nd Battalion and us will fly to Tan Khai and await their arrival. VNAF helicopters will pick us up in the morning and insert us on the outskirts of Tan Khai. You fly with me. Okay?" Can ordered.

"Okay, sir. I'll coordinate with the FAC and see if we can

have air support overhead when we land," Craig said. He knew that his major role as an advisor was to coordinate and direct close-air support. The problem for him and the other advisors for the 21st was the type of close-air support they could get. It had been decided early in the operation that US close-air support would remain in the vicinity of An Loc and VNAF aircraft would support the forces attempting to clear Highway 13. This meant that Craig and the others could expect only Cobra gunships and Skyraider aircraft flown by Vietnamese pilots. It was a case of who would best respond to calls. Generally the Cobra gunships were more responsive and accurate.

The morning sun rose with a clear sky, surprisingly low humidity and a pleasant temperature. The 2nd Battalion and TF-15 regimental command post moved into PZ posture and awaited the arrival of the lift helicopters from the VNAF. At one end of the PZ, 155 and 105 howitzers were prepared for sling-loading by CH-47 and CH-53 Skycrane helicopters. The CH-47 aircraft were being flown by VNAF pilots as well, but the Skycrane helicopters were flown by US pilots. At the appointed time, it came as a bit of a surprise to everyone when the UH-1H aircraft appeared to pick up the 2nd Battalion. The flight route was well east of Highway 13 and the Tao O Bridge, so it was almost uneventful. Although the landing zone was treated as a hostile landing zone, very little resistance was met and the 2nd Battalion had quickly established itself. The CH-47s and CH-53s were punctual in delivering the artillery. Craig was able to breathe easy as there was no need to call in close-air support—yet. For the remainder of the day, the 2nd Battalion continued to improve their position. Late that afternoon, 1st Battalion linked up with the 2nd Battalion, adding their artillery to the already present artillery.[1]

## 50

# STANDING SALUTE

**15 MAY 1972**
 **D/229th**
 **Highway 13**

The day was clear with scattered clouds at eight thousand. The 21st ARVN Division was still attempting to push through the 7th NVA Division blocking Highway 13. Forward progress was slow at best and more of a stalemate. Aggressive ARVN actions were lacking at this point, with heavy reliance on close-air support to pave the way up the road. Early in the campaign, it was decided that VNAF aircraft would support the 21st ARVN Division. As far as attack helicopters went, Delta Troop 229th was about the only unit left in the area with a cavalry reconnaissance mission.

Captain Roger Fox, Tiger Three-Seven, was the flight leader for the day. His wingman, Captain Mike Henry, was flying the second AH-1G gunship, and the OH-6 scout bird was piloted by Captain Whitehead. Cruising at twenty-five hundred feet, Henry and Fox maintained visual contact with Whitehead, who was down low. Earlier that day they had returned to Lai Khe after their first mission to refuel and rearm. In the rearm area, the aircraft shut down and all the pilots started loading rockets.

"Hey, put those rockets back. You can't have those," a pudgy major in stateside fatigues yelled as he came out of a hooch adjacent to the rearm point.

"Excuse me, sir," Fox said with some surprise.

"I said put those HEAT rockets back unless you're going after tanks. Those are only for tanks. If you're not, then put them back," the major explained. The four Cobra pilots exchanged looks of surprise.

"Sir, we aren't really choosy as to who we're shooting at. If we see a tank, we shoot; if we see troops in the open, we shoot; and if we see a bunker, we shoot. Aside from the choice between explosive rounds and nails, we select the nails for troops in the open and the HE rounds for everything else. So if you have a problem with what rounds we're taking, I suggest you call Danger Seven-Niner and he'll order us to put them back. Here's his frequency," Fox said, giving the major General Hollingsworth's radio frequency.

"Who is this Danger Seven-Niner?" the major asked.

"Oh, he's our boss. He's in the air right now, so you should be able to get a hold of him. We'll wait," Fox said as he continued to load the rockets in his outboard pods, which held seven rockets.

"Well, we'll see about this," the major said as he stormed off to his hooch. He never returned and the aircraft departed.

Once airborne, Fox briefed the flight. "Flight, this is Lead. We'll head up Highway 13 to the vicinity of Tao O Bridge and conduct a recon to the west of the highway. That puts us about three kilometers south of An Loc. Tiger Three-Six, how about you and I drop to fifteen hundred feet? Keep your eyes peeled for the damn SAMs."

"Roger, Three-Seven, right behind you," Henry responded as the two aircraft started to descend to the lower altitude. Whitehead was already at treetop level with his door gunner, Sergeant Waite, in the rear. They fully expected to find the enemy, and they were not disappointed.

"Tallyho, truck with dual 23mm in the bed," Whitehead yelled, cutting back across a trail through the jungle. Immediately a white phosphorous grenade exploded that Waite had dropped to mark the truck's location as Whitehead turned the aircraft to get away from the anti-aircraft gun on the back.

"Tiger One-Five, I have the location and coming down," Fox said, nosing his aircraft around and diving towards the target, which he couldn't make out in the forest. Two 2.75-inch rockets leaped from his rocket tubes, then two more before he pulled out of his dive and watched four more rockets streak past, punched off by Tiger Three-Six. The secondary explosion told everyone that the truck and anti-aircraft gun were destroyed.

"Hey, Tiger Three-Seven."

Fox recognized the voice of Captain Whitehead. "Yeah, Tiger One-Five."

"Three-Seven, I have a tank track about three hundred yards in front of that truck and a tank making those tracks. Over."

"Alright, mark it and we're coming," Fox replied, chasing after Whitehead's aircraft. As they approached Whitehead, they could clearly see the tank. Whitehead's door gunner was shooting at it with his M60 machine gun. The only result was that he was pissing off the tank crew, who were standing in the open top hatch, attempting to engage the fleeting helicopter with the 12.7mm machine gun on the turret.

"Tiger One-Five, call off your dog and let us finish this," Fox transmitted. Whitehead acknowledged not with words but action as he pulled out of the way and Waite stopped shooting. Once clear of the tank, Fox nosed over and punched off one rocket of flechettes. The nails weren't capable of hurting the tank but killed the soldier in the turret hatch and forced the tank to close all its hatches. Buttoned up, the tank had very limited visibility.

"Tiger Three-Six, let's take him out," Roger said as he again nosed his aircraft over and started firing his rockets. Several hit the tank, as did a couple from Tiger Three-Six, but none were HEAT and the tank kept on rolling.

"Tiger Three-Six, have you any HEAT rockets left?" Roger asked.

"No, I expended mine. How 'bout you?" Mike asked.

"No, I'm out too," Roger responded. "Let's just watch him and see where he goes. Might be an assembly area we can hit. Did you copy, Tiger One-Five?"

"Three-Seven, I copied. I'll hang back and just watch him lead us to home," Whitehead transmitted. For the next five minutes, the two Cobra gunships orbited above the tank at twenty-five hundred feet. As Roger was looking down at the tank, he suddenly saw a shadow pass over the tank. *What the...?* was all he had time to think when the tank blew up. Roger quickly looked up. The shadow was an AC-130 Spectre gunship that had been tracking the tank and hadn't seen the two Cobras or the LOH.

Switching to Guard, Roger transmitted, "Spectre gunship 3K southwest of An Loc, this is Tiger Three-Seven. Nice kill on my tank."

"Tiger Three-Seven, ah, sorry about that, we didn't see you down there." Spectre had destroyed the tank with one shot from the 105mm howitzer that was mounted in the left-side door.

"No harm, no foul, Spectre, have a good day. Smiling Tiger Three-Seven out," Roger transmitted, switching back to the company VHF. "Flight, let's head for refuel and rearm," Roger commanded, and all three aircraft turned south towards Lai Khe. As they turned south, Roger noticed the two A-1E Skyraiders at four thousand feet. They were in a trail formation. Suddenly, the lead aircraft exploded in a black-and-orange ball. The engine and propeller separated from the fireball, as did the wings and tail. *My God! That guy didn't have a chance*, Roger instantly thought as he watched the pieces fall to earth.

The call from Three-Six snapped him to attention. "Three-Seven, Three-Six, do you see the parachute?" Drifting down and out from behind the black cloud that once was an airplane came a parachute.

"Flight Three-Seven, follow him down. Tiger One-Five, do you have eyes on?"

"Three-Seven, I do not but will shortly," Roger heard as Whitehead was below and ahead of them and had to turn back. Finally, Whitehead spotted the chute before it hit the ground and headed for it.

"Three-Seven, I'm seeing a lot of signs that this guy may be in trouble," Whitehead reported.

"Whatcha seeing, One-Five?"

"Where he landed is a field with a large tree in the center. Across the field at about two hundred meters is a tree line with bad guys dug in. They're keeping low and watching the chute. I don't see our man in the chute, though."

"Small aircraft circling chute, I'm in the tree" was announced on Guard. Whitehead quickly looked towards the large tree but couldn't see who had transmitted the message. He didn't want to be too obvious about looking the tree over in case the down pilot was in the tree. Whitehead made a wide circle and took some small-arms fire.

"Three-Seven, if you and Three-Six will hit that tree line, I'll move in to extract," One-Five reported. Immediately Roger and Mike rolled their aircraft into dives and began unloading their rockets. Roger's aircraft was equipped with a 20mm gun, which he was proficient with and could fire as a single shot. Once the rockets were expended, the 20mm began to sing.

While the two Cobras kept the enemy engaged, Whitehead swooped in and landed next to the big tree. Sure enough, a man in a gray flight suit dropped out of the tree and sprinted to the LOH, diving into the back. His entrance was so forceful that he would have slid right out the opposite side if Sergeant Waite hadn't grabbed him. Whitehead immediately executed a combat departure as best he could with the Air Force pilot hanging on to him and hugging him. Waite stopped him when the grateful pilot attempted to kiss him. The second A-1E Skyraider had been orbiting the rescue mission the entire time. The LOH with Whitehead, Waite and the Air Force pilot climbed to altitude and joined the two Cobras.

"Flight, let's head to Lassiter and drop this guy off. It's about end of mission for us anyway," Roger transmitted. He got a positive response from everyone. The flight took a staggered left formation with the LOH in the lead and Henry to the rear and right of Fox. Flipping to intercom, Roger asked his copilot, "Hey, you want to take it?" The copilot gladly took it for the stick time. Cruising at three thousand, it was almost peaceful.

"Hey, Three-Seven, Three-Six," Henry called.

"Three-Six, go ahead."

"Three-Seven, move just your head and look to your left rear. Just your head, slowly!"

Roger did as commanded, very slowly. There with its right wing under the rotor blade of Roger's aircraft was the other A1-E Skyraider. To Roger at that moment it looked huge. What really got his attention wasn't the close proximity of the fighter to his helicopter but the fact that the pilot had moved his canopy back. He was standing in the front seat at the position of attention and saluting Roger and Mike. That night at the Officer's Club at Bien Hoa, drinks flowed courtesy of the Air Force.[1]

## 51

# JOIN THE 32ND



**16 May 1972**

   **32nd Regiment Command Post**
   **Tao O Bridge**

Lieutenant Colonel Burr Willey had spoken with Ross about a replacement. Major Sabine had arrived the evening before and Burr was almost ecstatic. He had a combat-experienced officer of equal rank to the Vietnamese battalion commanders and almost fluent in the Vietnamese language. Burr didn't care that Hank was on a fact-finding mission from Washington. He was here now and could find all the facts he wanted firsthand.

"Major, I'm very glad to have you with us. We've been stuck here for the past five days. You're replacing a fine young captain that we lost to artillery a few days ago. Please don't expose yourself as he did. I don't want to lose anyone else," Burr said, scratching behind Moose's ear. As Willey talked, Moose sat beside him. Looking down, Willey noted that Moose was chewing on something. "Moose, what the hell do you have there?" Willey asked. Moose looked up at the sound of his name. When he did, he exposed the leg bone he was chewing on—the human leg bone.

"I promise, sir. I'm not out medal hunting," Hank replied.

"Good, I'd like you to go down to the 2nd Battalion for now. That's the unit that Captain Fridermeyer was with when we lost him and the battalion executive officer. They've been at the front for the whole time, but we have no one to replace them with. And they have a tough nut to crack," Burr said, taking out a pencil and paper. "Let me show you how the enemy has arrayed his defensive positions." And Burr began to draw. "They've dug into the railroad bank a series of V-shaped positions with the point of the V connecting to a trench line that connects to all the positions. The open ends of the V are gun positions that are mutually supporting the positions of the adjacent V. This whole system is laid out in a horseshoe pattern, so there really is no assailable flank. This flank," he indicated, tapping his pencil on the map, "is protected by this swamp that we can't get through without coming under fire. In addition, they have a trench system to the rear that's allowing them to resupply almost with impunity. To make matters worse, about every three days they bring in fresh troops, relieving those that had been there," Burr explained.

"What about TACAIR support? Can't they root them out?" Sabine asked.

"TACAIR has been pounding them, but they have about two to three feet of overhead cover on those positions and plenty of camouflage. At eight thousand feet, the FAC can barely see the target. We've been using the FAC to try and keep the enemy artillery off our backs. Appears we have nothing that can range far enough to reach his artillery, so we have to rely on TACAIR and attack helicopters to find the artillery and kill it before it kills us. Yesterday, TF-15 conducted an air move to Tan Khai and have established a firebase, FSB Long Phi. They have 105s and 155s up there and are responding to fire support mission. The 33rd Regiment put one company in at Tan Khai, and the rest of the 33rd Regiment is moving through this forested area to Tan Khai but have been in a firefight most of the way. For right now, we're taking on these forces at the Tao O Bridge."

"What about B-52 support?" Hank asked.

"All that has been committed to An Loc and we get none of that. Even one load would do wonders for us, but we can't get any of it." As Willey spoke, Moose continued to attempt to get Hank to scratch his ears.

Hank was given a guide to take him to the 2nd Battalion, which had been pulled out of the line and was in reserve while the new battalion commander and executive officer became acquainted with the unit. Hank's guide, who went by the name of Tuo, couldn't do enough for Hank. He was eager to carry his own equipment and Hank's as well. Hank refrained from allowing the young man to carry his rucksack, and Tuo accepted that. Reaching a command track, M113, Hank sought out the battalion commander.

Major Nguyen was short, even for a Vietnamese officer, lean as most were and much older than Hank had expected. He had been in the Vietnamese Army for over fifteen years and had spent all his time in the Delta, born and raised there. His service time had seen him in numerous firefights but always small-unit operations, nothing bigger than a platoon-size engagement typical of the fights in the Delta and always against the Viet Cong. Fighting a combined-arms fight with artillery, infantry, and close-air support all mixed and employed together was something totally new to him. And fighting hard-core NVA was even more daunting.

"Major Nguyen, I am Major Sabine. I was told to join you and serve as your advisor," Hank said in his best Vietnamese. Major Nguyen turned slowly from the map he had been studying and said nothing, looking Hank over from head to toe. Then a broad smile broke on Major Nguyen's face and he thrust his hand out, grabbing Hank's hand before he could fully extend it.

"Major Sabine, I glad you come. I told you come. You help me, yes?" Nguyen asked, vigorously pumping Hank's hand.

In Vietnamese, Hank replied, "Yes, Major, I will help you all I can. I will advise you, and you make the decisions." Too many Vietnamese officers felt that the American advisors were injecting themselves into matters that were strictly Vietnamese affairs and taking over command decisions. Hank wanted to dispel that fear right away.

"Major, you speak good Vietnamese. I no speak good English. I need practice. We speak English, okay?" Major Nguyen said.

"Okay, Major, we speak English," Hank responded with a chuckle.

"I make bad decision, you tell me. Right?" Nguyen asked.

"I will advise you of how I think something can be done better, but you must decide. You're the commander," Hank said, a bit fearful where this conversation was going. Nguyen said nothing for a moment, lost in thought.

"Okay, we work good. Kill many enemy. You live my bunker," Nguyen ordered and turned to Tuo. He told Tuo to take Hank's stuff to his bunker, which Tuo was happy to do. Hank suddenly realized why Tuo was so enthusiastic. Being Hank's aide kept him out of the frontline fight, and Nguyen was Tuo's father. Hank made a mental note not to endanger Tuo.

"Come, I show you enemy positions," Nguyen said, picking up his steel pot, which appeared so big on him that he could have sat down and crawled under it like a turtle. Out the door of the bunker, Nguyen led the way with Hank right behind him. They moved about fifty yards and entered a trench line that the ARVN soldiers had dug. This trench line, unlike the enemy trench line, had few bunkers with overhead cover. It was intended to serve as a fighting position from which to support an attack, not to repel attackers. Moving at a crouched run, Nguyen and Hank turned a corner into a trench line that was parallel to the enemy, about fifty yards away. Nguyen started pointing towards the enemy positions. At first Hank could only make out a slight rise in front, but as he looked closer, he began to see openings in the concealment. *Damn, that's some fine camouflage. No wonder the FAC can't see shit*, Hank was thinking. As he studied the enemy position, he began to see the pattern that Colonel Willey had drawn out for him. This was truly a formidable position.

"Major Nguyen, the first problem we have is the enemy is too close to employ close-air support. If the Air Force drops bombs, they're liable to hit us or we'll have casualties from the concussion wave," Hank explained. "Our best bet is artillery or mortars." The expression on Nguyen's face told Hank that wasn't sitting well with the little guy. He wanted close-air support and napalm if he could get it. To lift his spirits a bit, Hank offered, "Let me see if we can get some attack helicopters on these frontline positions and close-air support further back where his supplies and his reinforcements are."

"Oh, that be good," Nguyen beamed. "Make soldiers happy to see bombs over there."

"I've seen enough. Let's get back and I will get on the radio and see what we can get for tomorrow morning," Hank said as he led the way back to the 2nd Battalion command post.

## 52

# MOVE TO TAN KHAI

**17 MAY 1972**
  **33rd Regiment**
  **Tao O**

The day before, orders had come down for the 33rd Regiment to move from its current location in the vicinity of Tao O to Tan Khai. The 1st Battalion, 33rd Regiment, would fly to FSB Long Phi to replace the 2nd Battalion of TF-15. Moving the remainder of the regiment was not going to be a piece of cake, Colonel Charlie Butler was thinking as he entered the command post and saw Lieutenant Colonel Nguyen Viet Can studying a map. The staff was packing up the command post.

"Charlie, we fly 1st Battalion today. Regiment is to move on ground east of Highway 13 through this forested area to Tan Khai. The order of march will be the Reconnaissance Company, 2nd Battalion, Regimental Headquarters, and 3rd Battalion will be last," Colonel Can outlined.

"Sir, may I recommend that the battalion mortars split into two sections? This way, one section will always be available to fire while the other displaces. In addition, if a fight ensues, the entire mortar platoon won't be engaged by enemy fire," Butler recommended.

"That makes sense. We do it your way," Colonel Can said and turned to his operations officer to issue the orders. Turning back to Charlie, Can said, "We should be at Tan Khai a few days."

"Do you think so? This is pretty tough terrain. We have a forest to move through, some hills and swamps. Intel hasn't given us much of a picture as to what we're going to find moving through there. I would plan on at least a week to move up," Charlie said. He noted a look of concern drift across Can's face.

"This is the same route that TF-15 used to initially get to Tan Khai and they met no resistance to speak of. Why should it be different for us?" Can inquired.

"Sir, the enemy wasn't expecting anyone to come up this way. Now that he knows it's possible, he may have moved some troops into the area. In this forest it won't take much of a force to slow us down. I would expect we're going to see hit-and-run tactics as we move through there. He isn't going to stand and fight, but he will harass and delay our movement," Charlie pointed out. His words, he saw, didn't fall on deaf ears.

* * *

The previous day, Lieutenant Colonel Ho Ngoc Can, TF-15 commander, greeted the 1st Battalion 33rd Regiment commander.[1] "Welcome to Firebase Long Phi, Major. Have you completed your exchange with the 2nd Battalion?" he asked.

"Yes, sir, the linkup and exchange have been completed. His battalion is moving to link up with the 3rd Battalion of your task force," Major Nguyen Dai Chien said. Major Chien was another Delta warrior experiencing his first time fighting in such terrain against a formidable enemy.

"Good, you battalion will be located on the eastern side of our perimeter for now. Tomorrow, we will move forward with your battalion on the right flank. The 9th Armored Squadron will be reinforcing the task force on the left flank. My operations officer will provide you with further instructions later at the command brief tonight. See my logistics officer if you need anything. Any questions?"

"No, sir. If you will excuse me, I will see to my battalion," Chien said. He had never worked with Colonel Ho Ngoc Can before and thought he should keep it as formal as possible until they got to know one another. He was looking forward to getting back to his usual commander, Colonel Nguyen Viet Can. Major Mandela Craig monitored the conversation.

After Chien left, Craig said, "I spoke with Colonel Butler, the advisor for the 33rd Regiment. He said that they sent their best battalion and battalion commander to you."

"That is good, I think we will need good commanders," Can said, motioning towards the map. "We just received some intelligence on the enemy. It appears that the 7th NVA Division is controlling this fight in our area. Its headquarters is located somewhere in this area, seven kilometers southwest of An Loc. The 165th Regiment of that division has a command post under the railroad tracks approximately here at X-Ray Tango Seven-Six-Seven, Eight-Three-Five. Intel says they constructed a reinforced bunker under the tracks on this abandoned railroad line," Can pointed out.

Craig looked at the map before he pointed to a line of hills three kilometers north of Tan Khai. "Sir, I would expect that his defensive line will stretch from this hill or ridge at seven-five-eight-zero eastward across Highway 13 and into this area around Dong Phai and along this high ground south of Dong

Phai. I think along this line is where we're going to get the most resistance. Where Highway 13 crosses this line is a very narrow gap that he can easily mine and register artillery on. We're going to have to envelop that gap before we attempt to push anything up the road through there."

Can considered what Craig had just said. With a spread-out hand, he measured the frontage that they would be covering. "We can cover about four kilometers moving on line northward. I will position 3rd Battalion and the reconnaissance company on the west flank across Highway 13 with an objective of this high ground to the west of Duc Vinh 1 and be prepared to continue to Duc Vinh 2. The 2nd Battalion will move to link with 3rd Battalion west of the highway. 1st Battalion, 33rd Regiment, will seize his hill mass at seven-seven-zero, eight-zero-eight. The 9th Armored will move up Highway 13 once the 2nd Battalion and 1st Battalion 33rd have secured their objectives. What think you, Major?"

"Sir, I think you have a plan. From here at Tan Khai to Duc Vinh is only four kilometers, so 2nd and 3rd Battalions should be able to reach there within a day if they meet no resistance as it does have some hilly country. 1st Battalion should also take about the same amount of time," Craig pointed out.

"Yes, but we both know that the 165th Regiment is in this area and they are not going to let us just walk in, as you say. We will just have to see."

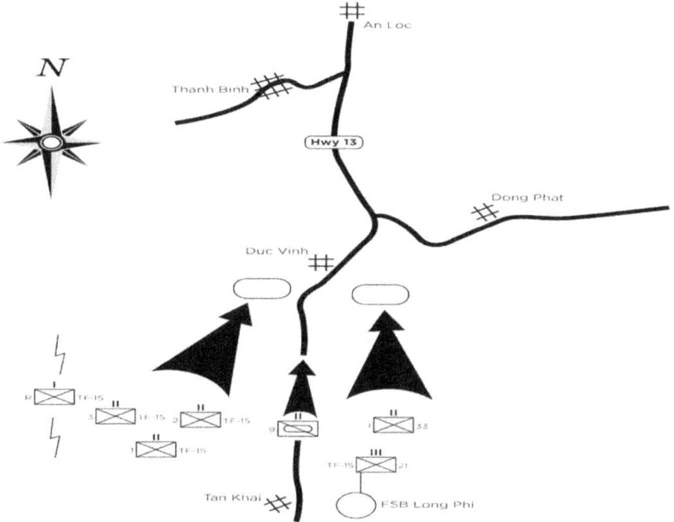



**Task Force 15 Assault, 18 May 1972**

The next morning, 18 May 1972, Task Force 15 moved out under incoming artillery fire. Everyone was glad to be away from FSB Long Phi as it was receiving the incoming artillery. Colonel Can and Major Craig moved behind the 9th Armored Squadron, seeing to it that it didn't move too quickly ahead of the infantry battalions and lose its security as the NVA frequently did.

"Major Craig, have you spoken to Colonel Butler today? How is the 33rd Regiment doing and when do they expect to arrive?" Colonel Can asked.

"Sir, I have, and truthfully I wouldn't expect them anytime soon—probably late today at the soonest. Colonel Butler says they're being harassed by sudden ambushes and firefights along the way and have made little forward progress," Craig informed the colonel.

"Does not surprise me. I think the enemy is beginning to realize that he has a dangerous situation developing with our forces north and south of his forces. I think he is going to be pulling forces away from An Loc and committing them against us to prevent this road from being opened. If this road is opened, reinforcements and supplies will flow into An Loc and he will definitely lose the town. Taking the town now is not as important as keeping this road from being opened," the colonel explained as his operations officer handed him a note. He smiled as he read it.

"Good news, sir?" Craig asked.

"Yes. It seems that 3rd and 2nd Battalions are only finding empty enemy positions. It appears that their troops have pulled out. At this rate, we may be in An Loc in a couple of days."

Colonel Can and Major Craig monitored the progress of the 2nd and 3rd Battalions of Task Force 15 and received intelligence reports from the Task Force Reconnaissance Company. The 9th Armored Battalion was moving up the road with no difficulty and almost no resistance. 1st Battalion, 33rd Regiment, also was progressing smoothly. The four kilometers to Duc Vinh were uneventful, to everyone's surprise. As the lead elements approached the Duc Vinh the next morning, the enemy showed himself. Reports began to flow into the command post of the enemy engagements being less than twenty-five meters away and opened with an initial salvo of mortars, RPGs and machine-gun fire. They were so close that close-air support could not be employed.

* * *

Charlie was glad to finally get into Tan Khai. The frequent ambushes and hit-and-run tactics of the enemy had deprived everyone of some needed sleep. As the regiment closed into FSB Long Phi, sectors were assigned for the defense of the firebase. 2nd and 3rd Battalions and the recon company assumed positions on the perimeter.

"Colonel Butler, you are needed in the command post," the young soldier said, waking Charlie as gently as possible. Charlie could tell it was still dark out. He was so tired that the incoming artillery hadn't bothered him. He was snug in his bunker and warm under his poncho liner.

"Okay, I'll be right there," Charlie said, grabbing his boots. Old habits died hard, and so he shook each boot to make sure no scorpions had taken up residence during the night. Once ready, he waited for a lull in the artillery to hurriedly move over to the command bunker. When he entered, Colonel Can was studying a map of the area and a sketch of the perimeter.

"Evening, sir. What's up?" Charlie asked.

"Sorry to wake you, but I think we need air support. Our OP/LP are reporting movement all around the perimeter. I think we are in for ground attack," Colonel Can said. "Intel, how you say, weenies, say two battalions from the 141st Regiment of the 7th Division with tanks are approaching our position. It is good for defenders at An Loc as we are drawing the enemy away from them. Bad for us," Can concluded.

"Sir, I'll get Sundog on the radio and see if we can get a Spooky gunship overhead. This may increase our priority for air support," Charlie said.

"Can we get Spectre gunship?" Colonel Can asked. He understood the more sophisticated systems in the AC-130 US Air Force Spectre gunship versus the C-47 Vietnamese Air Force Spooky gunship.

"I'll request it, sir, but I doubt if we will get it. They're up supporting An Loc," Charlie said.

"Don't they understand that the fight is now here? You ask for Spectre, okay?" Can ordered, his voice tinged with apprehension.

"Will do, sir. The worse they can do is say no and send us Spooky," Charlie said. Moving back to his bunker where his radio was, Charlie was concerned. *Colonel Can has never before shown stress or apprehension. This situation has him worried*, he was thinking when he picked up the hand receiver.

"Sundog Two-One, Beagle Six, over," Charlie transmitted. He had to think what his call sign was today as they kept changing the call signs to confuse the enemy. *Hell, all they're accomplishing is confusing me*, he thought, unsure if Sundog's call sign had been changed.

"Beagle Six, Sundog Two-One, over."

"Sundog Two-One, Beagle Six has movement around our entire perimeter. Request a pass by Spectre, over," Charlie transmitted and crossed his fingers.

"Beagle Six, I'll see what I can do but they're pretty much working over An Loc. How about Spooky if I can't get Spectre? Over," Sundog offered.

"Sundog, beggars can't be choosy. I'll take whatever you can send me," Charlie replied.

"Roger, stand by."

Charlie waited by his radio for a response, which he knew would not be coming quickly. With time on his hands, he contacted Lieutenant Colonel Willey.

"Bulldog Six, Beagle Six, over."

"Beagle Six, Bulldog Six, over."

"Bulldog, how you doing?"

"Beagle Six, we're beating our heads against a wall with this position. They've dug in like ticks on a hound's back. Well fortified and interlocking. They really don't want us coming up this road. How are you? Over," Willey asked.

"We've closed in here and will be striking out in the morning. Some movement around the perimeter now and waiting on Sundog to confirm my request. Have you heard from Big Dog?" Big Dog was the call sign for Ross Franklin.

"Big Dog was in here yesterday and said he was heading your way tomorrow. Has some concerns that he'll address with you. Over," Willey said, which got Charlie's attention.

"With our hosts? Over," Charlie transmitted.

"Affirmative," Willey replied. The sound of a heavy aircraft didn't go unnoticed by Charlie.

"Bulldog Six, I think my package from Sundog has arrived. Need to go. Take care." And Charlie quickly changed frequency. Hitting upon the correct frequency, he immediately heard, "Beagle Six, Sundog, over."

"Sundog, Beagle Six over."

"Beagle Six, thought I lost you for a moment there. Your request has been approved, but not Spectre. They'll be contacting you on the host frequency. Over."

"Roger, Sundog, and thanks. Beagle Six out." Charlie gathered his weapon and helmet and headed for the command post.

Colonel Can had just been informed that Spooky was coming on station. He was resigned to the fact that he wasn't going to get Spectre, but Spooky was better than nothing and he knew its presence would raise the morale of his soldiers.

The explosion woke Charlie from his early-morning slumber. Spooky had been overhead all night and small-arms fire had punctuated the night silence, but this was the first of the incoming and it wasn't mortars. These rounds, unlike mortar rounds, announced their arrival, and they were loud. *Shit, that's artillery*, Charlie thought from in his confined bunker where he and his radio assistant lay. Charlie's radio assistant had been assigned to him by Colonel Can as the young man spoke passable English. Besides carrying Charlie's radio, one of two, he took care of general housekeeping as well. Vietnamese soldiers liked serving as batmen, as the British would describe these soldiers, since the Vietnamese soldier knew that if things got bad, the American would be extracted by helicopter and there was a chance they would be too.

For the next three days, Charles Butler got little sleep as the 141st NVA Regiment pressed its attack and pounded FSB Long Phi with artillery fire.

## 53

## PRESS THE ATTACK

**20 MAY 1972**
**TF-15**
**Thanh Binh**

Major Craig and Colonel Can patiently moved behind the 3rd Battalion. Everyone was moving slowly, and as quietly as possible. The task force had gotten through the enemy positions around Duc Vinh. It had been a tough fight, but close-air support had been more generous than in the previous months, senior leaders having come to the conclusion that the enemy had given up on taking An Loc but now wanted to prevent any reinforcements from reaching the besieged town. The plan was to move the task force at night, silently cross the Xa Cat Creek to seize Duc Vinh hamlet. Slowly, forward movement ground to a halt.

"Colonel Can, why the hold-up?" Craig asked, feeling like a sitting duck exposed in the creek.

"The point elements are hearing tanks," Colonel Can said in a whisper. An hour later the lead elements started forward and the remainder of the task force followed. No major engagements occurred, but an occasional rifle shot or a quick burst of machine-gun fire penetrated the silence of the night. At first light, the first explosion from a mortar round was heard and several more would be received as the column moved north. The task force made progress, however, and morale was raised with each step closer to An Loc. Reaching their designated objective, the lead elements began to dig in, preparing to support the unit that would bypass them and continue the movement forward. This slowed the progress but offered more security. Known as bounding overwatch, it placed maximum firepower on an enemy force that engaged the point elements. Can directed this technique and it appeared to be working, until it didn't.

Approaching the hamlet of Thanh Binh, the lead elements reported sporadic contact. Can could hear the small-arms fire increase in intensity. As the intensity increased, it increased not only in the front of the task force but on all sides. TF-15 was surrounded. The task force was well equipped, having been resupplied the day before by a parachute drop of supplies.

"Major Craig," Can called out.

Craig made his way over to the colonel. "Sir?"

"Major, can we get a B-52 strike now?"

Craig was a bit surprised at the request as close-air support was engaging. Can wanted this fight over and over quickly.

"Sir, I can request it, but the chances of getting one anytime soon are slim. We might get one by tomorrow morning," Craig offered.

"Please request," Can said. "We need to get a medevac aircraft in here and cannot with the ADA that the enemy has surrounding us. A B-52 strike could open a corridor for the medevac aircraft to get through."

Major Craig returned to his radios and contacted Sundog and Ross Franklin to pass on Can's concerns and request.

"Hound Six, I doubt if Danger Seven-Nine is going to approve your request for an ARC Light immediate. I'll send it forward, but don't hold your breath, over," Ross transmitted.

"Roger, Big Dog Six, but we can ask, can't we?" Craig asked Franklin.

"Roger, I'll forward your request. Is the situation that bad? Over."

"Big Dog Six, we're mounting casualties fast. We're giving as good as we're getting and an ARC Light would greatly help. Sundog is working overtime for us right now. It appears that we have a regiment reinforced with tanks attempting to overrun us. Over," Craig stated.

"Roger, Hound Six. I'll see what I can do. Big Dog Six out." And Ross cut off the transmission.

As Craig handed the hand mike to his assistant, a voice called from the command post, requesting his presence. *What the hell now?* Craig thought as he put his steel pot back on and sprinted across the firebase to the command post.

"Major Craig," Can said, "I have been in contact with the commander of the opposing forces." Craig's heart stopped. *Son of a bitch is going to surrender!* Craig had heard about the regimental commander in the Quang Tri area that had surrendered his entire regiment and firebase without much of a fight. Was this going to happen again?

"Yes, sir" was all Craig could say, anticipating the next shoe to fall.

"He and I have agreed"—*Here it comes* flashed through Craig's mind—"that commencing at 1400 hours we will have a cease-fire so that we both can extract our wounded from the battle area," Can said, noticing a significant change in Craig's facial expression. "Major, did you think I was going to say something else?"

"Oh no, sir, I'm just relieved that we will be able to extract the wounded. How long does the cease-fire last?"

"It lasts until someone starts shooting again," Can said with a simple smile. Someone started shooting again, and not in a small way.

The rain of mortar and artillery upon the task force was almost too overwhelming. Once the wounded were extracted, Can and the task force spent their time improving their positions, digging deeper foxholes, preparing interlocking firing positions and resupplying their positions. It all started at 0600.

"Sir, 1st Company is reporting tanks," the young soldier on radio watch stated with a bit of apprehension in his voice. Can and Craig were hunched over a map. Outside their bunker, the sounds of a battle were clearly heard. Reports from the companies indicated that a fierce battle was raging. The sound of A-37 jets could be heard departing the area with an immediate deafening explosion following. Sundog had gotten the little jets up early and they were making a difference.

"Sir, 1st Company reports a tank has broken through his lines and is advancing towards us," the young man reported, the level of apprehension very evident now.

"Sir, I'll take a look and see if I can get Sundog on this," Craig said, picking up his weapon and moving to the opening in the bunker. He didn't want to get too far from the bunker as he might be needing its overhead cover if the mortars or artillery commenced again. The enemy employed a tactic that they referred to as "grabbing their belts," which meant getting close to the friendly so their close-air support couldn't be used. That also implied that the enemy's artillery and mortars couldn't be used either. Craig heard it before he saw it. Looking in the direction of 1st Company, he saw a track vehicle approaching, but too small to be a tank. A moment later, he realized that he was looking at a PT-76 amphibious vehicle with a small turret and a 75mm main gun, and it was rolling straight at him! *Shit, what now?*

"What now" turned out to be an ARVN sergeant with an M72 squatting in a foxhole right next to Craig. Craig hadn't seen him and wasn't aware of the sergeant being there. The report from the expended M72 startled Craig, who immediately threw himself on the ground, thinking that the PT-76 had fired its main gun at him. Lying there, he opened his eyes to the face of a grinning sergeant giving him a thumbs-up. The PT-76 was a burning pile of metal. Later that morning, the NVA broke off the attack right after the B-52 strike leveled Thanh Binh hamlet with NVA support elements and supplies located there. The secondary explosions lasted for most of the afternoon.

The air-defense threat around TF-15 continued. Medevac and resupply helicopters couldn't or wouldn't come into the area. Resupply and evacuation was being carried out by the 9th Armored Squadron running back and forth to Tan Khai. Helicopters were able to get to Tan Khai, the biggest threat being small arms and incoming artillery and mortars. Even water had to be brought in, although the Xa Cat Creek was less than fifty meters in front of the troops' positions. It was also less than fifty meters in front of the NVA positions. A stalemate settled in, with both sides slugging it out in the mornings, extracting wounded and dead in the afternoon and going back at it in the mornings.

## 54

# TAKING A TOLL

**24 MAY 1972**
**F/79th Artillery Battalion**
**Tan Khai**

Major McKay noticed the mood in the unit changing. No longer were the pilots carefree, happy kids. The past six weeks had transformed them into serious young men that were noticeably suppressing their innermost thoughts and feelings. At the club at night, they were consuming drinks as if there was no tomorrow, and many were believing that tomorrow would be the last. Nightly aircraft were returning with holes through the sides and mechanical problems caused by small bullets making big holes in the aircraft. To make matters worse, since the beginning of May, anti-aircraft missiles had appeared. Not effective against fast-moving jets, they were chasing helicopters. Resentment was building as the VIP helicopter units had all received and installed the new antimissile heat deflectors. These were attached to their exhaust stacks. The aircraft that were on the front lines didn't receive them. None of the aircraft that flew every day over An Loc, taking fire attempting to support the guys on the ground, were equipped with this system.[1]

"Today's operations will be supporting An Loc," the ops officer said. This didn't surprise anyone. "You will loiter at Lai Khe and wait for your mission assignments there. Any questions?" There were none. This had become routine.

Both John Henn and Isaac Hosaka were experienced Cobra pilots and both were chief warrant officers, second grade. Henn was serving as aircraft commander on this day, so he would be flying the back seat, with Isaac being the gunner in the front seat. The two were from opposite sides of the country with Henn from Massachusetts and Isaac from California. Here, however, they were family. They had graduated from flight school a month apart.

They flew up to Lai Khe along with two other Blue Max aircraft. The previous levels of jocularity between aircraft were absent. Pilots were having a hard time finding things to laugh at.

"Blue Max Three-Three, Blue Max Three."

"Blue Max Three, Three-Three, go ahead," Henn responded.

"Three-Three, contact Dustoff One-Ten on two-four-five-five Uniform and escort, over."

"Roger, understand contact Dustoff One-Ten on two-four-five-five for escort, over."

"Good copy, Blue Max Three out." Henn looked down and switched to the assigned contact frequency for Dustoff. "Dustoff One-Ten, Blue Max Three-Three, over."

"Blue Max Three-Three, good morning and glad to have you with me," Dustoff replied. Dustoff aircraft carried no guns for protection, so they always appreciated Blue Max aircraft surrounding them.

"Good morning, Dustoff One-Ten. What is your location and where we going?"

"Blue Max Three-Three, I'm just coming off Lai Khe northbound to vicinity X-Ray Tango Seven-Six-Eight, Seven-Six-Three for an urgent pickup, over."

"Roger, I think I see you now. We're a flight of three and will take up positions around you. What's the enemy situation?"

"The friendlies are holding a position just north of the pickup zone. The bad guys are occupying some low hills overlooking the Red Ball, over."

"Roger, we'll lay down suppressive fire as you go in and climb to forty-eight hundred waiting for you to come out."

"Blue Max Three-Three, sounds good," Dustoff One-Ten responded.

Henn switched back to his VHF and the flight. "Three-Eight, Three Nine, you two follow him to the landing zone and suppress. When he starts to come out, I'll dive down to cover him. How copy?"

"Three-Eight has a good copy. I'll take right side."

"Three Nine will get the left."

* * *

Nguyen Van Nam had been working in the rubber tree plantation before this mess had started. He remembered the days as a small boy when the Japanese had overrun his home in An Loc in the early 1940s. He remembered the French soldiers coming back through his town from Saigon in the mid- to late 1940s. The civil war had started after the French had left in the early 1950s, and the Americans had arrived shortly after that. Only one or two, and they were very friendly. Slowly over the years, more had arrived and they were all attempting to be very helpful, but never stayed very long. Some wore a green beret. Then the helicopters came in the early 1960s. Nam had never seen one before, until one day one landed in An Loc. It had a big glass bubble with a man sitting inside of it and another man jumped out. For the last seven years, however, many helicopters with many American soldiers were there. Some of those American soldiers were nice; some were always angry about being in Vietnam. Very disrespectful, especially towards the young girls. Nam had two daughters and kept them away from the Americans. Now, suddenly the North Vietnamese Army was here and they were much worse.

Nam had moved his family out of the small village on the south side of the rubber plantation as it had become a target, at first for the North Vietnamese and now for everyone. From his hillside observation, he could see the fighting around the village, which was mostly rubble now. At least hiding in the jungle where they were, they were safe, he thought.

He heard the helicopters approaching and looked skyward. Specks really, flying in circles, he noticed the four helicopters. Three were very skinny and he knew they were the gunships. The fat one would be carrying people, he knew. As he watched, the fat helicopter started to spiral down. Two of the skinny helicopters appeared to be chasing him downward as one stayed up high. Finally, the fat helicopter dropped out of sight behind the trees, as did the skinny helicopters. The sound of gunfire being exchanged between the NVA soldiers in his town and the helicopters was very distinct.

The new sound caught his attention—a sound he hadn't heard before. It was a dull booming sound and he looked skyward to see a white cloud climbing upward. Slowly the cloud changed its course slightly and seemed to go towards the one helicopter that remained very high.

* * *

"*Missile, missile, missile!*" was heard over the radio. Henn turned in his seat to look back as the nose of the aircraft was suddenly pitched forward and began to rotate. Isaac threw both hands up and was holding on to the side of the canopy as the spinning rotation increased and the aircraft began dropping rapidly. He glanced at the vertical speed indication as it passed through a fifteen-hundred-foot-per-minute rate of descent.

Nam was fascinated watching the helicopter fall out of the sky. The tail boom was falling away as the front half spun around. He watched for what seemed like a long time before the aircraft was out of sight behind the trees. The sound of the explosion was clearly heard, however. Nam didn't think anyone could have survived that crash. He moved back to the hide position he had for his family. He would see if he could find something useful in the aircraft when he felt it would be safe to go close to the crash site.

Back at Bear Cat that night, the mood in the club was very sober. Pilots drank but didn't display the jokingly morbid attitude that they had in the past.

"I'm telling you we made two passes over the crash site and saw no one. The wreckage was all engulfed in flames and the ammo was cooking off," Lieutenant Shields said, staring at the drink in front of him.

"Okay, listen up," Major McKay said upon entering. Everyone turned their attention to him.

"I spoke with General Hollingsworth. He said the aircraft went down in bad guy country and the ARVNs couldn't get to the crash site. He had the cav fly over the crash site late this afternoon, and from what they saw, they don't think they made it out. The aircraft was pretty much burned up and the surrounding vegetation was pretty much destroyed by the fire," McKay said, taking a long pause. "The general said that the ARVN commander will send in someone to the crash site once they push the enemy out of the area."

"Any idea when that will be, sir?" one of the pilots asked.

"He said he thinks it will be two weeks at least. The ARVNs are having a pretty tough time of it up there. Seems the enemy just does not want to let reinforcements or supplies reach An Loc by Highway 13," McKay said.

"Sir, could the cav send a little bird up and check it out again tomorrow? Maybe they got out before it blew and had moved off a bit in case the gooks came to inspect it," another pilot said hopefully.

"I'll ask the 229th if they would" was all McKay said as he picked up a shot glass with a brown liquid. *I'll ask, but I know what the answer will be and I understand* is what he was thinking. "Gentlemen," he said, raising his glass as everyone stood, "to absent comrades, Henn and Hosaka."

"To absent comrades, Henn and Hosaka," the group responded and chugged their drinks.[2]

## 55

---

# PUSH NORTH

**25 May 1972**
  **33rd Regiment**
  **Dong Phat**

The 33rd Regiment closed into FSB Long Phi and had spent their time resupplying and defending the firebase for three days against the 165th Regiment of the 7th Division. Only when the 141st decided it needed to stop the 9th Armored Squadron's runs from TF-15 to FSB Long Phi did they curtail the attacks on FSB Long Phi. They experienced some success in an ambush against the 9th, but not enough to change the course of events.

"Butler," Colonel Can said, gaining the attention of the advisor who was walking into the CP on FSB Long Phi.

"Yes, Can?" Butler replied. The formality of referring to each other by rank had fallen by the wayside.

"We have intelligence about the 165th Regiment. They are located in these woods. They have a command bunker at this location," Can said, pointing at the map. The location was along the abandoned railroad bed. "Intel says this is a reinforced concrete bunker, built into the railroad embankment. That is why it is not visible from the air. You think we could get a B-52 strike to destroy, please?" (Translation: get on the radio and get us a B-52 bomb strike on this location.)

"I don't know if it'll get approved, but let me request a strike," Butler said. Returning to his bunker, he made the call to Colonel Ross Franklin.

"Big Dog Six, Beagle Six, over," Butler transmitted.

A minute later and after two repeated calls, Butler heard, "Beagle Six, wait one." *Boss must be busy with something else.* Moments later, Big Dog was back on the radio.

"Beagle Six, Big Dog Six, over."

"Big Dog Six, Beagle Six. We have intel on the command post for the 165th Regiment. Any chance we could get a B-52 ARC Light on this target, or the positions at Xa Cam? Over," Charlie asked.

"Beagle Six, request seems reasonable. I'll run it up to Danger Seven-Nine and let you know. Anything else? Over," Big Dog asked.

"Big Dog, nothing further. over."

"Beagle Six, Big Dog Six, out."

*Well, that didn't sound too promising*, Butler thought as his Vietnamese assistant handed him a cup of hot coffee.

* * *

General Hollingsworth was sitting next to Ross when Colonel Butler made the call and overheard all that was said.

"Ross, I'm not going to approve that request. We still have a need to protect An Loc, which is doing better but isn't out of the woods yet. Minh was asking me this morning for some changes in the B-52 strikes and I told him no. He has got to ask the Vietnamese Air Force to start taking some of these bombing missions with the aircraft they have. They're the weak sister in this fight and once we leave Vietnam they're going to have to step up to the plate. If we keep covering their ass every time they need an air strike, then they're going to lose the next time the North attempts to overrun them. If it was a case where the NVA were overrunning the 33rd, I would probably approve it, but that's not the case," Hollingsworth explained.

"Sir, I understand" was Ross's only comment as he saw the frustration across Hollingsworth's face.

"Hell, Ross, he even asked if we would commit C-130s to air-drop supplies to his units along Highway 13. One, we can't waste aircraft hours when his own helicopters won't supply them a lot more accurately and easily than an airdrop. Two, he needs to start putting pressure on the VNAF to fly those missions and stop asking us to fly them. We've been giving them helicopters as we downsize, and they aren't even flying them. Damn waste of good equipment. Worst mistake we made was allowing the Vietnamese Air Force to have all the helicopters and sending them Air Force pilots to train them. We should have had experienced Army pilots training them and advising them. Get back to Butler and tell him request disapproved," Hollingsworth ordered.

* * *

General Minh was not happy. When Minh received a request through his channels for a B-52 strike on the 165th CP, he took it to General Hollingsworth. Earlier, when Colonel Can had been told by Colonel Butler that the request for a B-52 strike hadn't been approved, Can had gone directly to General Hau, the 21st Division commander, who'd passed the request to Minh. Hollingsworth couldn't or wouldn't explain why the request had been denied. Minh was going to attack this problem his way.

General Huynh Ba Tinh, 3rd Air Division, and his deputy, Colonel Nguyen Van Tuonh, had been summoned to Minh's office. "Gentlemen, please come in and have a seat," Minh welcomed them. Once they were settled, he commenced outlining his problem. "We have identified the location of the 165th Regiment command bunker. It is well fortified and located here southeast of An Loc," he said, pointing to the location on a wall map as he spoke. "There is also a defensive position here at Xa Cam. We requested B-52 strike to destroy both but the request was denied. Do you have the capability to destroy this target?"

Both officers exchanged looks before General Tinh answered. "Sir, the first issue that must be resolved is the US Air Force assigned zone. It was agreed months ago at the start of this campaign that the US Air Force would work the area around An Loc and we would work south of there. This appears to be within their zone, so we would have to meet with them to get clearance to bomb in that location."

"Well, if we got a clearance from them, do you have the aircraft and the weapons to employ on this target? No point in fighting the battle with the US Air Force for clearance if we don't have anything to use on the target," Minh said with some frustration.

General Tinh looked over at Colonel Tuonh and nodded his head, indicating he should now speak. "Sir, besides being General Tinh's deputy, I am also the commander of the 3rd Air Division Fighter Squadron. I have some CBU bombs that the Americans gave me that we could use on the Xa Cam position. I could deliver them using our AD-6 Skyraiders. The Americans do not operate after 1800 hours, so we would not have an airspace management problem after 1800 hours and thus no need for coordination and permission from the Americans. I just need someone on the ground to talk to and mark the target for us," Tuonh said.

Minh's face lit up. His problem was about to be solved.

"I will need a few days to train my pilots on the use of the CBU as well train as the ground crews on how to mount the bombs. I don't want to initiate an attack only to find we didn't have the training we needed nor the proper rig. Can I get back to you when we are sure we have everything correct?" Tuonh asked.

"Colonel Tuonh, that will be most satisfactory. When you are ready, please inform my staff. Good day, gentlemen," Minh stated, indicating the meeting was over.

**56**

---

# XA CAM

**7 June 1972**
  **33rd Regiment**
  **FSB Long Phi**

Colonel Butler and Major Craig had been up until the wee hours the night before, going over the plan for this day's events. There was an air of anticipation over the firebase. Everyone felt that today would be a long day and great things were expected. Three days before, the 6th Airborne Battalion had arrived by helicopters and bolstered the defenders of FSB Long Phi. The 6th Battalion had been in Lai Khe, reconstituting from its retreat from Windy Hill. Not only had the airborne battalion arrived with its six hundred assigned personnel, but an additional group of replacements had come as well to bolster the 33rd Regiment and TF-15. Additional replacements were flown into An Loc. All told, the friendly forces were increased by two thousand more soldiers.

"Morning, Lieutenant," Colonel Butler said as Lieutenant

Ross Kelly, senior advisor for the 6th Airborne Battalion entered the advisor bunker. "Want some coffee?"

"Yes, sir, and a good morning to you too," Kelly replied, "and to you as well, Major Craig." Craig responded with a nod as he sipped his coffee.

"Is the 6th Battalion set to go this morning?" Butler asked, handing Kelly a canteen cup of coffee.

"Yes, sir. After what has been felt as a defeat being forced off the hill back in April, the battalion is determined to kick some ass this time. The firefight since the day before yesterday at Duc Vinh was its revenge. We came away with pretty light casualties," Kelly offered.

"What were your casualties?" Craig asked.

"Sir, we had one KIA and sixty-four WIA. The NVA didn't fare as well. We policed up thirty-one dead along with two crew-served weapons and twelve individual weapons. Not a bad haul," Kelly said with some pride.

"Good job. Today when we're done evacuating some wounded and finish the resupply, everyone is going to move out and continue the push north. TF-15 will be on the left flank, 33rd Regiment in the middle and 6th Battalion on the right flank. At about 1800 hours, the VNAF will be conducting a bombing run on the Xa Cam chot complex in front of your unit, Kelly[1]. Expect that you may be ordered to launch an assault right after the bombing, so you may be going in at night. Be sure your commander has planned accordingly for some illum, and I'll see that we have Spectre or Spooky up to cover us. I think we can get Spectre as we're under the US Air Force airspace once we hit Xa Cam," Butler pointed out.

"Sir, he and I discussed the possibility of illum. His mortars are packing a lot of illum rounds," Kelly said.

"Let's be sure and stay in touch. My call sign for today is Comanche Six. Craig, you take Apache Six, and, Kelly, you will be Cherokee Six. Ross sent these down earlier. His call sign, I know he picked this one, is Big Chief," Butler said with a smile. Craig just rolled his eyes.

"Sir, do you know what time we'll move out today?" Craig asked.

"I think the colonel was shooting for 1300," Butler said, looking at his watch.

"In that case I best get back to the task force. I want to go over a couple of things with Colonel Can before we kick off," Craig said, draining the last of his now-cold coffee. "Y'all be safe now, you hear?" were his departing words.

"I best get going too, sir," Kelly said, standing and returning the canteen cup to Butler. "See you on the other side, sir," he added, rendering a proper salute.

"Be safe, Lieutenant," Butler said as he returned Kelly's salute.

* * *

The attack continued at 1300 hours as planned, and almost immediately, small-arms fire and an occasional mortar round were heard. As the afternoon wore on, slow progress was made moving north towards An Loc. So close to the finish, no one wanted to be the last casualty. High above, the popping sound of a UH-1H's rotor blades could be heard. General Minh wanted a bird's-eye view of the planned air strike. He didn't hold the Vietnamese Air Force in high regard as far as their helicopter service was concerned. Their Skyraiders, however, were highly regarded, orbiting at eight thousand feet to stay out of range of the SA-7 missiles. Seated next to him was General Tinh. Tinh had his fingers crossed that this air strike would be executed flawlessly. He had spoken with Colonel Tuonh earlier in the day about the need for this to be success-ful. Tuonh would be flying the lead aircraft.

As they orbited, Minh looked towards Bien Hoa and

caught a glimpse of a reflection in the sky. Scanning, he spotted the AD-6 Skyraiders. He didn't see the two A-37 Dragonfly jets, one flown by Colonel Tuonh, until they started their strafing runs over Xa Cam positions. Once the Skyraiders were in position, the A-37s broke off their attacks and allowed the Skyraiders to hit the target.

Sitting five hundred meters from the Xa Cam chot position, Lieutenant Kelly watched as the first Skyraider approached the target with the remaining three right behind the first. Coming in low, the first aircraft released his solitary CBU and pulled up, followed by the other three. Kelly watched as the first bomb was released and flew parallel to the aircraft before it slowly dropped away. Before it hit the trees, the remaining three were also in their respective descents and the aircraft were quickly turning and bearing away from the area. Kelly understood why they turned away so quickly when the first CBU exploded. The concussion wave hit Kelly with such force that his head felt like someone had hit him with a fist in his helmet. Kelly hadn't been this close to a CBU drop and was startled to see the damage that it was causing. Unlike the B-52 strikes, where whole trees were thrown two hundred feet in the air, trees were being cut down and chopped up. In fact, anything standing was being cut down as if a giant sickle had passed over the land. When the last bomb exploded, the battalion commander's radio operator handed him his hand mike. It appeared that General Minh was wanting to talk. Kelly stepped back so the colonel could talk without Kelly crowding him. If it was important, he would tell Kelly. When Kelly turned to step back, his radio operator was handing him his hand mike.

"Comanche Six," the radio operator said.

Taking the hand mike, Kelly responded, "Comanche Six, Cherokee Six, over."

"Cherokee Six, Comanche Six. Your counterpart is getting

an order to assault the position now. If you need illum, artillery at Long Phi is standing by. Over," Colonel Butler informed Kelly.

"Roger, Comanche Six, I believe he's getting the order now. Good copy, over."

"Cherokee Six, let me know what you find in the complex. Comanche Six out."

Kelly gave the hand mike back to his operator and noticed the colonel was on the battalion command net now. He also, with his limited Vietnamese, understood what was being said. They were assaulting right away.

As the battalion covered the five hundred meters to the enemy positions, artillery fire was falling on the enemy positions with delay fuze so the rounds would bury themselves in the ground before detonating. Delay fuze was most effective against well-prepared bunkers with overhead cover. Sporadic small-arms fire engaged the paratroopers, but an organized resistance didn't materialize. As they entered the trench network, it became increasingly obvious that the air strike had accomplished the intended results. The prize was the reinforced concrete bunker of the 165th Regiment command post. The colonel received a call and picked up his pace.

"Kelly, we go quick. Company commander for 61 Company has found regiment command post. Wants us to see," the commander said with some excitement in his voice.

As they approached the entrance to the command bunker, the pace slowed and they were greeted by a smiling company commander who simply motioned for them to enter with an arm wave and a slight bow. He performed the gesture so smoothly and with such polish, he would have made the doorman at the Saigon Hilton proud. Kelly entered and immediately noticed the room was well lit and large at three hundred square meters. Nothing appeared to be disturbed and all was orderly. He then noticed the bodies. They were lying on the floor or sitting at their desks, heads down as if sleeping. But they weren't sleeping as the blood seeped from their eyes, noses, and ears. All two hundred had died from the massive pressure released by the CBU bombs. The 165th Regimental commander was among the dead. The last enemy position before An Loc was eliminated.

## 57

---

# LINKUP

**8 June 1972**
  **6th Airborne Battalion**
  **Thanh Binh**

Clearing out Xa Cam positions took a full day, and the decision was made that the battalion would move out first thing in the morning. Remnants of the 165th Regiment had other ideas, however. Small-arms fire was heard almost immediately as the battalion began to move. Wrong move for the enemy, as the ARVN paratroopers quickly fired and maneuvered to overwhelm the enemy attempting to block their progress.

A yell from the commander got Kelly's attention. "Close-air support?" It was a question and not a directive or statement. They were operating in the airspace of the US Air Force now, so calling upon VNAF aircraft would be pointless.

"Yes, sir," Kelly responded, but he wasn't sure where it was needed. There was no significant fighting going on and it was all close in, so TACAIR wouldn't be able to deliver ordnance unless the battalion broke contact and pulled back. "Do you have a target for an air strike, Colonel?" Kelly asked.

"No, not now. Just wanted to know" was the response Kelly received. *Suddenly he's getting cautious.* Kelly did notice an uptick in the intensity of the small-arms fire, however. *Maybe I'll check in with the FAC just to be sure*, Kelly thought and looked skyward to see if he could spot a FAC orbiting. When none was noted, he made the call.

"Sundog, Sundog, Cherokee Six, over." He waited, listening to the squelch on the radio. "Sundog, Sundog, Cherokee Six, over," Kelly called again.

"Cherokee Six, Sundog Two-One, good morning. Over."

"Sundog Two-One, and a good morning to you this day. I have no targets for you but just wanted to check in with you. Over."

"Cherokee Six, I'm over your location. It'll be another thirty minutes before I have any packages arriving, over."

"Roger, Sundog, understood. I'll see if I can find something for you."

"Much appreciated, Cherokee Six. Sundog Two-one standing by."

Since the major fight over An Loc had ceased in the middle of May, there was no need to keep a commanding FAC on station, so King FAC was no longer coordinating multiple air strikes. A single FAC could handle the requirements. By midafternoon, Kelly still didn't have a need to call upon the services of Sundog.

"Cherokee Six, Comanche Six, over."

"Cherokee Six, Comanche Six, how goes it? Big Chief wants to know your status, over."

"Comanche Six, we had a bit of contact earlier. Last count was seventy-three November Victor Alphas, Kilo India Alpha and two crew-served weapons. We came away with eleven Kilo India Alpha and thirty-one Whiskey India Alpha. They have all be evacked," Kelly reported. "We're moving now up to Thanh Binh, and at the pace we have if we meet no more resistance could be there in forty-five minutes. Over."

"Roger, understood. Let me know when you reach Thanh Binh, over," Butler directed.

"Roger, Cherokee Six out."

* * *

Lieutenant Winston Cover was tired. It had been a long day starting at 0400, when the NVA had decided to wake everyone with an artillery and mortar barrage. Since mid-May, ground attacks had been limited to probes and ambushes executed by both sides. The threat of tanks was still a real possibility, but none had been seen or had approached the perimeter of the 8th Airborne Battalion. The 8th Battalion had been in the same location since early May and had over time turned the position into a well-fortified defensive position with overhead cover, cleared fields of interlocking fire, target reference points, concertina wire and mines. Right now, Cover was preparing a cup of hot coffee loaded with caffeine that he hoped would carry him through the rest of the day.

"Raven Six, Hawk Six, over," Cover heard coming from his radio. *Wonder what Colonel Taylor wants*, he was thinking as he put his coffee down and picked up the hand mike.

"Hawk Six, Raven Six, over."

"Raven Six, Hawk Six, contact Cherokee Six on four-two-point-five-oh. Coordinate a linkup with him. Make sure your counterpart is aware of the situation and talking to Cherokee Six's counterpart. Let me know when linkup is effected, over." Cover almost couldn't believe what he had just heard. He thought about asking for a repeat but decided that he'd heard correctly.

"Hawk Six, Raven Six, roger. Will do right now," Cover

said with enthusiasm dripping off each word. *Damn, this may be over*, he contemplated as he switched frequencies on his radio.

"Cherokee Six, Raven Six, over," Winston transmitted when he had his radio tuned. He waited.

"Raven Six, Cherokee Six. Understand you're going to meet me. I'll be waiting for you at Bravo Mike One-One Seven. How copy? Over."

Winston immediately pulled his map out of this pants' cargo pocket and laid it on the ground, flattening it. As he did so, BM 117 practically jumped off the paper. Looking up, he could see that location not five hundred meters down Highway 13 in front of his position as it was a major road intersection.

"Cherokee Six, Raven Six, what time do you want to link up? Over."

"Raven Six, Cherokee Six. How about 1730 hours? Over."

"Raven Six, I'll see you then. Cherokee Six out."

Lieutenant Ross Kelly had moved up to join 61 Company along with his battalion commander. They were joined by the company commander as the unit moved north, keeping Highway 13 on the right flank. The move up to Thanh Binh had been executed smoothly, with what little resistance that was met quickly dispatched. Thanh Binh itself was almost completely destroyed. The rubber-processing plant was a burned-out shell. As they moved into the town, a young soldier came running up to the company commander and said something. Kelly was too far back to hear the conversation, but the young man was very excited. *Oh please, Lord, don't let it be a damn tank*, Kelly silently prayed.

The commander turned to Kelly with a broad smile.

"Lieutenant, we have people at the linkup point. We go now." And the pace picked up. As they moved out of the town on the road connecting with Highway 13, Kelly could see soldiers wearing traditional US helmets. On the Vietnamese soldiers, these "steel pots" almost looked ridiculous as the soldiers appeared to be eight-year-olds playing with their GI fathers' helmets. A small security element surrounded Kelly as they moved down the road. Standing at the crossroads, BM 117, stood another small group. As they approached, Kelly recognized the tall American soldier standing off to the side of the group and approached him.

"Winston, how the hell you doing?" Kelly asked extending his hand, which Winston accepted.

"Right now I don't think I could be much better," Winston replied. The two Americans watched as the 6th Battalion commander and Lieutenant Colonel Tran Tien Tuyen, executive officer for the 8th Airborne Battalion, exchanged salutes and warm handshakes.

Word quickly went out that the linkup had taken place. Lieutenant Colonel Ho Ngoc Can, commander of TF-15, was informed that a member of the press was present at the linkup. Can wanted to be included in this momentous event and, grabbing Major Craig, immediately headed up Highway 13 to join the celebration. He was met by Colonel Nhut, who had left the province headquarters in An Loc to greet the first forces approaching the town. When the two commanders met, Nhut presented Can with a bottle of cognac, the last bottle in An Loc. The immediate threat to An Loc was over, but not the fight.

# 58

# EMOTIONS

19 June 1972
**Lieutenant Colonel Butler**
**Tan Khai**

Charlie had been out with the troops for the normal first light stand to follow by the trip down Highway 13 to bust the latest ambush put in by the NVA. It was becoming a daily ritual. Done the same way, same time, same troops every day and nothing changed. *How stupid is this? Nothing changes and they wonder why they get the same results*, he was thinking as he entered his bunker and surprisingly found a letter on his air mattress. Mail was sporadic at best and only came when Ross brought it up to the firebase. If Ross was on leave or over in Thailand, then you didn't get mail. After he read what his wife, Jo, had written two weeks ago, he decided the war could take a break while he wrote back to her.

*Dear Jo,*

*Another day of the same way of doing things that accomplishes nothing. The mail just does not flow into this place. Ross attempts to get it to us, but he has to bring it himself or it doesn't get delivered. He did give some to a VNAF flight crew. We never saw it as that never arrived. Some packages that you sent arrived, after the VNAF guys opened them and picked out what they wanted. I have talked to Ross about it and he promised not to send any packages forward unless he brought them.*

*Today is Vietnam Armed Forces Day. No parades scheduled locally but plenty of action. The 1st Airborne Brigade is trying to move south from An Loc to here to extract by helicopter. They got to our area last night but are now in contact. All kinds of air strikes are going in as well as Cobras and artillery—what we term as a real "rat fuck" or "Romeo Foxtrot" if you prefer the sanitized version. All this was to start early but nothing seems to happen on time whether the US or the VNs are controlling. Well, if the airborne gets out, they'll go back to Saigon Barracks to refit before joining their division in the Battle for Hue, the last suspenseful event of the 1972 campaign! I expect to watch that one on TV!*

*Our frustrated, fatigued, fouled-up 32d Regiment is to finally be relieved of their millstone, the roadblock at the 72 grid line. A fresh force from the 18th Division is to replace them. LTG Minh is brilliant: he finally noticed that regiment with over a thousand casualties wasn't getting any better, and what's more, he astutely observed that some of the troops had had insignificant combat in the campaign. For this great strategy he'll probably get another medal—he should have been fired before!*

*So, Burr Willey and crew will be going to Tay Ninh Province to, hopefully, get rested up.*

*Yesterday Ross was fed up and said he quit giving advice to Gen Hau. And miracles never cease, Hau actually moved his CP nearer to the battlefield! But Ross sent no one with him! Jack Conn, the replacement, is due in Saigon on the 25th, so we'll be saying farewell to Ross soon after.*

*Got orders not to aid the 4th Estate at all with rides, etc. Still OK to speak to them. It seems that LTC Benedit, one of the originals from An Loc, got a helo lift for some newsmen who then did a really negative story on the situation of the troops and civilians. The LTC was expecting a praise job for the survival of An Loc!*

*Ross says he's trying to get my Xuan fired—my living Buddha has completed seven days in the TOC bunker—only goes out to do his "duty." His poor calf is still infected. I don't dislike Xuan, he is an agreeable man but he is not getting the job done. But, if Hau doesn't fire the 32d CO, then everyone ought to be safe.* [1]

"Incoming!" someone screamed, followed by the sound of a freight train rapidly approaching. Butler was on the floor of his bunker as the round exploded. *Damn, that was close,* he thought as he lay there. His radio operator had also taken a supine position on the floor. With a sheepish grin, the radio operator slowly raised his thumb. "We good," he said as the next round landed but a bit further away.

*I'll finish that letter later. For now I best track down Can and see what he needs,* Butler thought as he started to pick himself up. His radio operator started to move as well but Butler motioned for him to stay where he was. "No need to get us both killed running to the command post," he mumbled as he headed out the door. It would be a long night.

**59**

---

# HUNKER DOWN

**19 June 1972**
  **32rd Regiment**
  **Tao O Bridge**

The 32rd Regiment had been slugging it out for the past month almost on the NVA position. Little by little, the regiment was making some progress, but not enough. Air strikes by the VNAF didn't seem to faze the defenders. The position had been well prepared by the NVA, and the stubborn resolve of the NVA soldiers was a major contributing factor. In addition, every third day, the defenders were rotated out through a trench system back into the jungle and fresh troops took their place.

General Ho Trung Hau, commanding general of the 21st Division, was beside himself. The pressure he was under to accomplish his one mission of opening Highway 13 did nothing to ease his rude and arrogant personality. Ross Franklin needed all his self-control to maintain a rapport with the man. Hau's subordinate commanders could do nothing but take the verbal abuse that Hau dished out. Today, Colonel Nguyen Van Biet was going to be the recipient of the tongue-lashing. Ross decided that he didn't need to listen to this, so he sought out Biet's American advisor, Lieutenant Colonel Burr Willey.

Burr was sitting in his small bunker along with Major Sabine. Naturally Moose was present, looking for any scraps of food that might fall his way. Somehow, Willey always managed to have a dog biscuit handy, compliments of his wife sending frequent care packages through the mail that Ross would bring up. When Ross entered, Willey and Sabine started to stand.

"Keep your seats. Got any coffee?" Ross asked.

"Matter of fact we do, sir. Just made a pot this morning and figure it's still good. Can't stand a spoon up in it, so not quite strong enough, but it'll keep you up until this evening," Willey said as he poured the black sludge into Ross's canteen cup.

"Did you hear about Ed?" Ed was Lieutenant Colonel Ed Stein, advisor to the 31st Regiment.

"No, what happened? He's okay, isn't he?" Willey asked with a bit of concern as he handed Ross the cup of coffee.

"Yeah, he's fine. Was driving up Highway 13 back on the 6th and was ambushed. He was able to flag down a couple of A-37s that provided some close-air support and saved his ass. General Hau heard about it and nearly shit a brick. He's catching hell from Saigon because this road isn't open completely yet." Ross took a sip, smiled and said, "Good enough." Pausing for a moment, he then asked, "Okay, what's been going on? Why no forward progress?"

Burr and Sabine exchanged looks of disbelief that the question was even being asked. Looking back at Ross, Burr said, "Sir, haven't you been getting Biet's reports? We're getting the crap pounded out of us with artillery and mortars every day. TACAIR hasn't been able to keep the tubes off our backs. We have VNAF support, so there's no FAC for us to talk to and direct. The VNAF boys show up and drop where they want. They don't go hunting for the artillery or mortar positions, so they're shooting at us with impunity. When we kick off today's assaults, I hope you and Hau are here to witness for yourselves what happens."

"What's the plan for today?" Ross asked.

Sabine immediately pulled out his map and spread it out on the ground at their feet. In addition, he had a sketch.

"Sir, this sketch is what we've been able to make out of his defensive positions. Whenever we launch an attack, Colonel Willey and I note where we're taking fire from to confirm if we've plotted a position or add a new position that we haven't found before. Then at night we sit with Biet and develop a plan for how to go about attacking the next day. Each day we expand and fill in the sketch. I would really like to get in and see how they laid out this place," Sabine said.

Ross studied the sketch and compared it to the 1:50,000 scale topographic map that was in use. When he was satisfied, he nodded his head. Willey took that as the go-ahead to address today's mission.

"Sir, this morning we're attacking on the right side, or what we think is the right side, of this complex. We have thirteen tanks that will accompany the infantry. We will precede the attack with an four-minute artillery prep from Long Phi and then move across this open ground as quickly as possible to get into their trench line. The 1st Battalion will be the main effort with 2nd and 3rd Battalions providing support. If 1st Battalion gets into the trenches, then he will hold the shoulders while 2nd Battalion and 3rd Battalion exploit the breech," Willey explained.

"Where are you going to be?" Ross asked.

"Sir, I'll go with Colonel Biet and he plans to follow 1st Battalion," Willey answered.

"And you?" Ross asked, looking at Major Sabine.

"Sir, I'll be with 2nd Battalion," Sabine answered.

"You know, Major, I have a General Brooks breathing down my neck to get you back to Saigon to write your report. He has been very understanding, but I'm not sure how much longer I can hang on to you. General Hollingsworth has argued to keep you, but I'm not sure how much longer he can make the case. Have you got enough material to write your report now?" Ross asked.

"Sir, I have more than enough to write my report. I thought, as I'm sure my compadres thought, that we were going to come over here, spend a month driving around and watching drills and ceremonies. We didn't expect to have this kind of opportunity to see just what has been accomplished with the Vietnamization Program," Sabine responded.

"What do you think has been accomplished, if I may ask?" Ross asked, not wanting to violate the rules about the inspectors being in-country.

"Sir, I see some hard, determined soldiers that will stand and fight when properly led by competent commanders. I have seen well-trained junior officers that are eager to take the fight to the enemy, especially in the Airborne and Ranger units. I have witnessed a logistical system that's supplying the soldier in the field as well as can be expected under the circumstances. I have also seen a VNAF that couldn't fly two helicopters in anything closely resembling a formation arriving on time. The VNAF will tuck tail and run at the first sign of trouble. Army aviators should have been the advisors for those helicopter units. Aviators that knew how to fly combat assaults, not Air Force advisors that have never flown a combat assault. And I've seen some senior commanders that were just plain cowards," Sabine said, expecting pushback.

Ross sat for a moment, staring at the map and taking in what Sabine had said. Finally, he looked up and then stood. "Major, I hope you write it up just that way."

* * *

An hour later, the 1st Battalion moved out two minutes under the cover of the four-minute artillery prep. Biet wanted to get as close to the enemy as possible when the artillery stopped. He wasn't too concerned about his soldiers being within the probable kill zone as he felt they would be safe if they only reached the fringe of that zone. Willey concurred with Biet's assessment and so stated to Ross. As the battalion crossed the open ground in front of the enemy position, Willey, Ross, Sabine and Moose jogged from one covered position to the next. The first indication that the enemy artillery was firing was the fountain of dirt rising up. More rounds began impacting around the assaulting force. The attack was starting to falter.

*This cannot happen*, Willey thought as he saw a few soldiers run past him, towards the rear. He knew this action could be infectious and had to be stopped. Ross and Sabine were several yards away from him when the next mortar round exploded. Ross appeared to be hit and on the ground. *Got to get Ross*, he thought as he jumped up. Running towards Ross's position, Willey was firing his M16 from his hip. Moose loped along right beside him, enjoying the fun of chasing his master. Ross started to stand to stop Willey but was too late. The artillery round landed right next to Willey and Moose. The attack faltered and failed.[1]

**60**

---

## TWO SNAKES DOWN

20 JUNE 1972
  3rd ARVN Airborne
  Tan Khai

For almost two months, the 21st ARVN Division had been hung up attempting to move north to relieve An Loc and link up with the 3rd ARVN Airborne Brigade. The NVA had been seriously crippled but like a wounded snake, still very dangerous. Tan Khai, a small village, seemed to be the focal point of their resistance at this point.

"What we got today, sir?" asked Lieutenant Stephen E. Shields as he approached Lieutenant Colonel Lew McConnell, commander of the 229th Assault Helicopter Battalion. They had met up at Lai Khe, where aircraft coming up from Bien Hoa would stop to refuel. Lieutenant Shields was the designated air mission commander on this day for the Blue Max flight. His copilot was a relatively new officer to the Blue Max family, Captain Ed Northrup. Ed had a previous tour in Vietnam as an infantry officer. A West Point graduate, he'd decided that if he was going to stay in the Army, he wanted to do it as a pilot.

Also present were First Lieutenant Louis Breuer and CW2 Burdette Townsend from F Troop 9th Cav. Mr. Townsend was the flight leader for a cav team consisting of two Cobras and two LOH aircraft.

"We are covering the extraction of elements of the 3rd ARVN Airborne Brigade. They're being extracted and brought back to here. C-130s will be picking them up in the morning and taking them north to Quang Tri. The 229th is conducting the extraction; the cav will screen the flight route and Blue Max will provide support," McConnell said, laying out his map on the floor of the UH-1H aircraft he was flying.[1]

"So the VNAF is absent again," Shields said with sarcasm dripping off each word. Others just exchanged looks of agreement.

McConnell continued, "They're located here at X-Ray Tango Seven-Seven-Eight, Seven-Seven-Eight in this clearing. The slicks will be going in low-level with Smiling Tigers flying escort and us at high cover. F Troop 9th Cav will lead the flight and clear the flight path by five minutes," McConnell said, looking at Shields and Northrup. "They have two little birds and two Cobras, but we might get calls from them to support, so let's position ourselves between the cav element and the lift." McConnell paused for a moment. "Between us ladies, I suspect this will be a hot extraction, so be on your toes. Any questions?" There were none, and the crews returned to their respective aircraft after exchanging call signs and frequencies.

As Shields and Northrup put on their flight gear, they noticed the slicks sitting in the refuel point taking on fuel. Northrup had filled their tanks when they landed, so they were ready to depart. Copilots generally occupied the gunner front position in the Cobra and had the dubious honor of being the refueler for the aircraft as the Cobra didn't bring a crew chief with it on missions. The cav aircraft were the first off by five minutes ahead of the lift as planned so they could recon the flight route.

Speaking on the internal FM frequency for Blue Max, Shields questioned if everyone was ready and got a positive response from the other two aircraft. "Roger, Lead is on the go."

And with that, a swirl of dust enveloped the aircraft as it moved forward and gained speed and altitude off Lai Khe with the other two aircraft right behind him. The morning was fairly clear with the anticipated afternoon rain showers hours away. Some clouds had formed but were scattered at six thousand feet. Ever conscious of both the SA-7 threat and the threat of anti-aircraft fire, Shields held the flight at two thousand feet to avoid the anti-aircraft fire, which had been posing the biggest threat. The two Cobras from the cav were operating at about fifteen hundred feet, covering the two little birds that were at treetop level. Shields was monitoring the cav frequency on his VHF radio, his own aircraft on the FM radio and the lift ships on their UHF frequency. It took a developed skill to mentally monitor three radio transmissions at the same time, tuning in what was important and ignoring the unimportant.

"Taking fire" was an overriding call, and it came from the slicks.

"Smiling Tiger, engaging."

"Blue Max flight, Smiling Tigers are engaging, Anyone have eyes on?" Shields transmitted.

"I got them," Shields's wingman said. Shields turned in his seat to see his wingman break to the right and enter a dive. Shields followed. As he did so, he could see the flight of Hueys engaging a tree line as they passed. Shields's wingman was punching rockets into the tree line and Shields was determined to cover his break. As the wingman began to turn and climb, Shields began punching rockets and Northrup began engaging with the duel miniguns in the nose of the aircraft. Adrenaline was running high in both as Shields commenced to turn out of his dive. The first sound of trouble was a sledge-hammer blow to the side of the aircraft, followed by a second.

Immediately the master caution light came on, the master caution horn was blaring and the master caution panel lit up, indicating a multitude of damaged systems from the heavy anti-aircraft weapon that was engaging the aircraft. The rapid fluctuations in the engine RPM, rising engine oil temperature and decreasing engine oil pressure told Shields that he had to put the aircraft on the ground because the engine was about to quit.

"Hang on, we're going in" was all Shields could tell Northrup before the engine did quit at almost treetop level. Northrup had time to place both hands on the forward instrument panel before the aircraft was on the ground with smoke billowing out of the engine. Not needing to be told, Northrup was out of the aircraft and drew his pistol as small-arms fire began hitting the smoking aircraft. Crouching down, Northrup began returning fire with his .38 Special pistol, the only weapon issued to pilots. Shields dropped down beside him and also engaged where the shooting was coming from, but in the dense foliage, they couldn't see anyone.

High above, McConnell watched the gunfight unfold, with the other two Blue Max aircraft engaging the tree line that now revealed not one but multiple heavy anti-aircraft weapons arrayed in triangle settings to better engage an aircraft that entered the triangle unknowingly, as Shields had done.

"Blue Max Six, Sabre Lead, this is just too hot to get in there with the little birds," the flight leader for the cav called. McConnell could see the tracers raising up to meet each aircraft. *Son of a bitch, they've set traps for us and we walked right into it*, McConnell was thinking as he watched the events unfold below him.

"Run for the tree line across the clearing. I'll cover you. Go!" Shields yelled at Northrup. Northrup was out of bullets and didn't wait for a second order. He turned and in a low crouch started to run. Shield fired the last of his bullets and commenced to do the same when the machine gun in the tree line they were running towards opened fire.

McConnell could only watch as the two pilots were cut down. The other Cobra pilots had witnessed that action and with all the anger they could muster entered into steep dives, engaging the tree line where the fire that cut down the two pilots had originated from.

Lou Breuer and Mr. Townsend were at fifteen hundred feet and witnessed the death of the two pilots. Townsend began to line his aircraft up to engage when over his radio he heard, "Missile, missile, missile!" With their heads on swivels, both began scanning to see where this new threat was. Townsend immediately put the aircraft into a dive, when the missile slammed into the exhaust pipe of his aircraft.

McConnell watched in horror as the Cobra exploded in flight, with pieces descending to earth. A decision was necessary, and he made it. "All elements, abort, abort. All aircraft return to Lai Khe." Every crew member in the operation breathed a sigh of relief that someone had made to call to stop the operation.

**61**

---

# MORE INCOMING

**20 JUNE 1972**
 **33rd Regiment**
 **Tan Khai**

Lieutenant Colonel Charles Butler sat in his bunker and decided that he needed to write to his wife, Jo, and his son. The kerosene lantern provided a soft glow to see by and the humming sound of the burning mantles was almost comforting. The radios were quiet and the evening was almost pleasant, with no incoming—or outgoing, for that matter —artillery.

*Dear Jo,*

*A little sunshine this morning. I got up at 0600 for a change as things are supposed to happen today. Clear weather would be helpful. The 1st Airborne Brigade finally got through the bad guys and are to be picked up today by helicopter. Unfortunately, the pickup place is too near to my bunker. I plan to stay under cover all day—even more so than usual. The NVA will undoubtably try to interfere with the operation. If they were smart, they'd let the airborne go peacefully and save their ammunition for us, but they won't.*

*I know some of the airborne advisors—hope they fare well on their next assignment. (Drunk in Saigon!)*

*President Thieu announced, on the occasion of the Armed Forces Day, that the NVA invasion had been stopped and that all SVN territory would be taken. Expect this counteroffensive will exceed my tour of duty.*

*Just had a severe setback—we lost two Cobra gunships to the Russian heat-seeking missile. One was hit only about 300 meters from my bunker. Some people saw the whole thing. The Cobra blew up in the air. We have had such a weapon for several years, but the Russians have only recently furnished it to the NVA. The other Cobra is missing—no one is sure yet what happened to it. So the extraction of the airborne is delayed.*

*On top of the losses is the announcement only the other day that the 3rd Brigade, 1st Cavalry Division, is to leave VN. These guys are all close to going home. Tough conditions for them to work under. When they announced a stand-down of a unit, I thought they took it out of action. But maybe these air cavalry guys are to stay awhile.*

*Some really sad news. Burr Willey, the 32nd Regt advisor, was killed yesterday. He and Ross were with the attacking elements at the roadblock when rockets or mortars began to fall. They all took cover in foxholes, but Burr thought that Ross was hit and ran towards him only to be hit himself. He was always too brave under fire. Ross had already recommended Burr for the Silver Star. I am certain Ross will seek a DSC for this act of bravery.*

*The irony of Burr's death is twofold: he was to have gone to*

*Lai Khe yesterday afternoon to pack for 2 weeks leave. And what's worse, yesterday was the last day for the 32nd at the roadblock! Today a new outfit is to relieve them. Ross takes casualties really hard. I have seen him speak at two memorial services—last September when his Sergeant Major was killed. Ross was very close to the Sergeant Major as they were together all day while visiting units with General Nghi. Ross was deeply moved as he tried to express his feelings for the man. The Sergeant Major was obviously the best liked person on the team because he genuinely cared for others. And his job was totally oriented toward helping the team—from the CO to the specialist.*

*Burr was in a different category. He joined us in March after having served six months with the Bac Lieu Province Team. As a regimental advisor he was known really only by the few on his team. I never heard him mention his family except that they lived in Virginia. He had asked for a job near his house and planned to retire soon.*

*I do not mean to upset you by writing about Burr's death. I do not pass on all the war stories which I hear or experience personally. Burr's passing should be picked up by the press because of the correspondents who have covered this campaign have interviewed him either at his CP or at the roadblock. You see, this was the only battle scene which the press could visit. So Burr's enduring roadblock symbolizes the Highway 13 campaign.*

*It is late, so I best get some sleep. We heard of another ambush site being put in along the highway and will be going out early to destroy it. Good night.*

*Love,*

*Charlie*[1]

* * *

The linkup with the forces in An Loc had been accomplished. Lieutenant Colonel Nguyen Viet Can was a bit frustrated and disappointed that his regiment was not the force that made the initial linkup but recognized that this fight was still not over. The forces in An Loc had been able to push out as reinforcements flowed in to reinforce and replace the beleaguered defenders. On 13 June, the 2nd Battalion, 31st Regiment, was flown into An Loc to reinforce those forces from the 5th Division. Additionally on that day, the 48th Regiment, 18th Division, was brought into An Loc. Remnants of the 5th and 7th NVA Divisions as well as the 9th Division were still in the area and could at any time mount probing attacks. Tanks were no longer feared by the ARVN soldiers and none had been seen. What bothered everyone, however, was the mortars and artillery that were still in the area and harassing the ARVN forces. Frequently, the NVA would set up ambushes along Highway 13 that had to be rooted out. These frequent events usually included artillery or mortars from enemy guns.

Lieutenant Colonel Butler decided to accompany the battalion commander this morning. The road would be dusty and hot as they moved up. The first thing Butler noticed was the fact that the little girls that were normally on the side of the road selling warm Cokes were not there. *This is not good*, Butler was thinking as they moved forward. His internal antenna went up when he noticed very little traffic on the road moving in the opposite direction. *Where are all the overloaded buses, oxcarts and motorcycles?* He scanned his map, looking for potential ambush sites. The brush and vegetation on both sides of Highway 13 had been moved back in previous years when the 1st US Infantry Division operated Rome plows the area, but that was four years ago and it had not been done since. Heavy brush lined the sides of the highway offering good concealment. Scanning the roadside up ahead with his field glasses, he was hoping that the battalion's lead company had out good security. He was about to find out.

The sudden and violent sound of intense automatic weapon fire told Butler that they had just walked and driven into an ambush. The only sounds he initially heard were from AK-47 assault rifles, PKM machine guns and 75mm recoilless rifles. Slowly the sound of M16s and M60 machine guns were heard, indicating the ARVNs were responding, but too slowly for Butler. *I need to get up on the point and see if this is moving in the right direction*, he was thinking as he began making his way forward. The closer he got to the head of the column, the more intense the sounds of ARVN weapons came to dominate the firefight. After an hour, the ambush site was cleared and the battalion returned to Tan Khai.

Arriving back on the firebase, Butler first went to talk to Colonel Can and told him of his favorable impression of the action by the battalion. FSB Long Phi/Tan Khai was the target of NVA artillery forward observers. The enemy had been badly mauled in their effort to take An Loc, but they weren't yet defeated. Hidden artillery and mortar positions still ringed the town. Since FSB Long Phi was a major firebase with artillery supporting both An Loc and the

action at the Tao O Bridge, Long Phi was an important obstacle to the NVA. For the past two weeks since it had been established, it had received ground probes and incoming artillery. Butler's face was a common sight to the ARVN soldiers. He was frequently seen walking the perimeter, talking to the soldiers and checking on their welfare even during the frequent attacks and barrages.

"*Moi den!*" someone yelled as the first artillery round slammed into the center of the firebase. Butler, being fluent in Vietnamese, mentally translated the term—*Incoming!*—about the time the round exploded. Small-arms fire commenced as well, indicating that some coordination was behind this attack.

"Colonel, I'm going to see if we can use some close-air support on this," Butler said, heading for the door of the command post. His radio was back in his bunker. Sprinting across the short distance from his bunker to the command post, he quickly ducked into the shelter. As he began to exit, he was met by an artillery round.

## 62

---

## WRITE YOUR REPORT

**21 June 1972**
  **FSB Long Phi**
  **Tan Khai**

Hank had received word through the ARVN command late the previous day that he was needed at FSB Long Phi, but no reason for the need had been provided. The previous day, FSB Long Phi and the 33rd Regiment had been under artillery fire, but during the night, Spectre had been busy removing the enemy artillery and mortar positions. Thus far the morning had been quiet, so the VNAF helicopter that was dispatched to get him flew him over. Once on the ground he was met by an ARVN soldier that grabbed his rucksack and asked Hank to follow him to the command post. When Hank walked through the door, his senses told him something was wrong.

"You, Major Sabine," Colonel Can asked, approaching Hank.

"Yes, sir. How can I help you?" Hank asked, looking around for Colonel Butler.

"I am Colonel Can, battalion commander. I was told to expect you. Please come with me," Can asked walking past Hank and heading for the door. Hank stepped off right behind him with some trepidation.

As they moved outside, Hank asked, "Excuse me, sir, but where is Colonel Butler?"

Can stopped and turned to face Hank. "I am sorry," he said, and his face showed some pain. "I am taking you to him." And he turned and kept walking toward the first aid bunker.

*Shit, Butler has been hit*, Hank immediately thought as he followed Can towards the aid station. Can didn't enter but walked behind the bunker. Rounding the bunker, Hank stopped. The line of six bodies covered in ponchos froze him in his steps.

"We very sorry, Major. He was good advisor. I leave you for moment. Colonel Franklin is coming with a helicopter to pick you up and Colonel Butler," Cam said, placing his hand on Hank's shoulder and repeating, "We very sorry."

Hank stood for a few more moments, staring at the line of bodies. He noticed that one body had a US dog tag laced into the boot, reinforcing this thought that this was an American. Finally, he had to be sure and knelt down next to the body. Slowly he pulled back the poncho to reveal the face of Lieutenant Colonel Butler. He noticed a second dog tag and, wiping the blood off it, read, "Butler, Charles." That was all he needed to confirm it was Colonel Butler. *Damn Hollywood tells us that the recently departed look peaceful. Hollywood hasn't been on a battlefield since Korea and has no idea what a soldier looks like in death*, Hank was thinking when the sound of an approaching helicopter broke his thoughts. Looking skyward, he quickly noticed the nose insignia of a 229th aircraft escorted by two Smiling Tiger gunships. Moments later the UH-1H landed and then quickly departed, climbing to altitude. Lost in thought, he didn't hear Ross approaching.

"Major, Sabine," Ross said as he walked up behind Hank, who simply turned to acknowledge him. "Is this Colonel Butler?" Ross asked. Hank looked back at him and noticed that Ross's eyes were red and puffy.

"Yes, sir, I can identify him and his dog tags confirm as well," Hank explained as he stood. Ross took his place, kneeling beside the fallen colonel. Slowly Ross peeled back the poncho. For a moment he just stared at what lay before him, and then he laid his right hand on Charlie's cheek and looked upward.

"Oh Lord, May he soar with the Angels on the Wings of Eagles; May he watch over those he loved and those who loved him; May he Rest in Peace until we all gather together again on Fiddlers Green for the final formation," Ross prayed while Hank hung silently repeated the prayer. Placing the poncho over Charlie's face, Ross stood and turned to Hank.

"Major, are you okay?" he asked, noticing a slight bit of emotion from Hank.

"Yes, sir. I had only met him once but heard a lot of great things about him. Did you know him well?" Hank questioned.

"Both as a fellow cadet at the Point, as an infantry officer in Korea and as an advisor on my team. He was a damn fine officer and a good man, but that's the way it always is, isn't it? The good die young," Ross said, quoting a popular song. "I have an aircraft inbound to take you and him back to Bien Hoa. Medevac doesn't take the nonliving. I want you to escort him back. That bird will then take you on to Saigon. You're wanted back at MACV headquarters. General Brooks himself called me to get you back there. Time for you to write that report." Ross paused for a moment. "I know I'm not supposed to ask, but what are your thoughts, for your time here?"

"Sir, my thoughts..." Hank did not answer immediately

but thought. "Sir, I think the only reason the county has not been overrun with Communist tanks is because of three factors. First, the guts and determination of the ARVN soldier when properly led by good leadership at the lower levels and supplied properly. Second, and probably the most important factor, is the determination, dedication and courage of the American advisors at all levels. They're the linchpin in this entire effort. They serve with the ARVN, they live with the ARVN and they die with the ARVN. They're the connection to the third factor. They not only mark the targets for the close-air support, they designate and plan the targets for the strategic bombers. Without the support of the third factor, the US Air Force, Navy and US Army aviation, the North Vietnamese would have been sitting in Saigon a month ago. And the advisor on the ground on the front lines is the one that makes that support happen," Hank explained.

"That's all pretty positive stuff, Major. Any adverse comments to add to that?" Ross queried.

"Oh, sir, I have plenty of negative to add, starting with the senior leadership of the South Vietnamese Army, and it may be a cultural issue, but it's one that should have been recognized years ago. The senior leadership is corrupt, lacks initiative, is politically motivated, and has yet to recognize that reality that the US is not coming back to Vietnam to fight their battle.

"The Vietnamese helicopter force is plagued by cowards. I can't count the number of times they refused to land on a cold pickup zone, let alone a hot one, but remained at a hover and had the troops attempt to climb on or just left the grunts in a hot landing zone. We made a mistake not putting their asses in US cockpits to fly with US pilots or putting US Army pilots with them as advisors," Hank explained.

"I am afraid I can't argue with any of those points, Major," Ross said as his helicopter was on final approach to the firebase. He held out his hand. "It was good having you on the team, Hank. Take him home and write your report." Hand shook his hand and then rendered a proper salute. Ross returned it, then turned and walked towards his aircraft.

Hank turned towards Charlie. "Let's you and I go home, sir."[1]

# EPILOGUE

The North Vietnamese Army never was able to seize An Loc and establish it as the new capital, but after the siege was broken, there was almost nothing left of the town. Once a thriving community, it was now an inhabitable wasteland of broken homes, demolished buildings, open graves and death. The only structure not damaged, surprisingly, was a statue of Jesus Christ in the square in front of the church.

The North Vietnamese Army managed to secure Quan Loi, Loc Ninh and the surrounding hamlets to An Loc. Highway 13 was opened but never secured, with frequent deadly attacks on military convoys moving to An Loc as well as civilian buses and cars. Unlike Tet of 1968, when the goal was to win the hearts and minds of the people, the object in 1972 was to destroy the South Vietnameses Army and punish the people for not supporting previous actions to overthrow the South Vietnamese government. The North Vietnamese Army and leadership had to wait three more years to accomplish that task, which they did on April 30, 1975.

As a result of the collapse, the people of South Vietnam had untold suffering to endure as reeducation camps were established, property was seized, and imprisonment ordered for many. Many fled to other countries, only to be enslaved, robbed and even murdered. I highly recommend an excellent account of what they endured: *The Ground Kisser* by Thanh Duong Boyer, who recounts her experiences as a ten-year-old fleeing Vietnam.

* * *

**THE NEXT BOOK, Battle For Kontum, 1972, Volume 6
is *AVAILABLE FOR ORDER NOW.***

**FIND IT ON AMAZON**

*Keep reading for a look inside Battle For Kontum.*

# A LOOK INSIDE

BATTLE OF KONTUM, 1972

Undaunted Valor, Volume 6

By

Matt Jackson

# 1

## ANOTHER CUT



14 JANUARY 1972
   MACV Headquarters
   Saigon

Major General Carley, MACV G-3, found himself the bearer of bad news more frequently these past six months. Since the operation carried out by the South Vietnamese in April of '71, called Lam Son 719, the tone in Washington had changed. MACV was under more pressure to draw down American involvement and accelerate the Vietnamization Program. This latest message that he had just handed General Abrams was the last change to the plan. Abrams had read it once and said nothing but puffed harder on his cigar. The second reading increased his blood pressure, Carley was sure. Carley could tell he was about to explode.

"Sir, you recall that the President promised in the 1968 campaign that he would end our participation in the war and end the draft," Major General Carley said.

"I do recall all the promises, and I also recall that OPLAN

J208A was approved by him and Laird and that was the plan for the drawdown. What happens? Almost immediately, Laird starts telling us to screw the plan and start drawing down faster. We were supposed to draw down one division in '69, one division, and what happened? Six months into the plan and he says we need to have two divisions out by the end of '69. Two, regardless of the threat or the pace of getting the South Vietnamese Air Force up to speed. Why did we waste our time developing a withdrawal plan if they're just going to arbitrarily dictate the cuts?" Abrams replied. Carley watched as Abrams held the message in his hand and reread it for the third time. Each time, he was sure Abrams's blood pressure would rise a bit more.

"The plan supported the Vietnamization Program perfectly as it would transfer the equipment and fighting to the South Vietnamese forces, allowing for a gradual withdrawal of US and allied forces. It had to be a gradual withdrawal, providing time to train the South Vietnamese forces how to fight and how to use the new equipment they're receiving in their fight against the North. This phased withdrawal was outlined in OPLAN J208A and implemented on January twenty-ninth, 1969. Someone should have read it to Laird," Abrams said with an angry tone.

OPLAN J208A specified what the US troop strength in Vietnam would be on targeted dates based on certain criteria of the threat, pacification progress, and rate of South Vietnamese Air Force improvement. Since the plan had been initiated, monthly reports were sent to the Pentagon and the White House on the strength in manpower, equipment and units remaining in Vietnam and how much equipment had been transferred. MACV was charged with seeing that those target dates were met with the indicated reduction in US personnel.

Although the original plan specified criteria and withdrawal dates, Melvin Laird had his own timetable, and almost immediately, he had ordered the acceleration of withdrawals. This was just the latest change that was going to cause a knee-jerk reaction in the headquarters.

"Sir, I took the liberty of scheduling a staff meeting for 1600 to brief them on this and get them working on changes. Your calendar was open...," Carley pointed out.

"Fine, you're right. We best get the bad news out early. Let me work up some guidance for them as this one is really going to hurt," Abrams said, withdrawing his cigar and waving for Carley to leave him.

A staff meeting was called to discuss the impact on MACV. These unplanned changes were seriously disrupting the orderly flow of equipment, personnel and unit redeployments back to the United States.

When Abrams walked into the conference room at 1600 hours, it was immediately obvious he was not happy. As he entered, everyone stood.

"Sit down," Abrams bellowed. "Let's get this dog show on the road, General." General Carley did not take this growling personally.

"The purpose of this brief is to bring the staff up to date on the message we received yesterday on an unplanned reduction in the end strengths as outlined in OPLAN J208A and to receive your guidance on priorities for the force structure as we move to attain these new end strength figures, which are for May first, 1972. The President announced yesterday that there would be seventy thousand more troops out of Vietnam by May first," Carley said. The air in the room was almost sucked completely out by the staff in exasperation, replaced by murmurs that did not help General Abrams's mood. More than one pencil dropped on the conference table.

"I don't like it either, gentlemen, but we have our marching orders, so you all need to start getting out some meat cleavers and look at what we're going to be cutting in the next five months in addition to what we've already planned to cut," Abrams said, it being obvious to Carley that Abrams had just taken over the briefing. Abrams surveyed those seated around the table as well as the "horse holder" junior officers seated along the wall in the cheap seats. No one looked happy. He knew those junior officers were the ones that would be doing the work, with those at the conference table putting their heads on the chopping block if the numbers didn't come out right.

"Alright, let me give you some guidance for this. Plan on a force structure of sixty-nine thousand on May first," he started off and watched notes being taken. He could almost hear the unspoken cuss words as the original target of eighty-four thousand was out the window. A lot of work had gone into planning the cuts to get to eighty-four thousand and now more were going to be needed. These additional cuts were going to strain the personnel side as well as the logistical side, attempting to figure out what people needed to be removed from country versus who needed to stay in-country. This was going to be a morale issue, and morale was bad enough in the ranks now, as demonstrated by increased drug use in the lower ranks and higher alcohol use in the noncommissioned officer ranks. More racial issues were being reported as well, along with fraggings of officers and senior NCOs. Maintenance yards were already full to capacity as equipment was being turned in for turnover to the Vietnamese Armed Forces, which were insisting the equipment be in like-new condition.

"To reach this new goal, I want to maintain the following priorities for manning and equipping, in this order. Command and control of American operations must be maintained as well as installation protection. That is the number one consideration. We will continue to protect US forces and personnel as well as support and administer to our needs. To do this, I want us to keep two infantry brigades with an artillery battalion with each brigade. These will be for installation security and not active combat operations. Make that clear to those brigade commanders and their chain of command. We will provide minimal support in the area of intelligence gathering and analysis and minimal support in communications. The South Vietnamese can start picking up the ball on those two areas. We've transferred a significant number of helicopters and fighter aircraft as well as transport aircraft—they can now expect minimal helicopter and air support from us. I want us to keep three fighter squadrons in-country to be responsive to those two brigades if the need arises. We will continue to provide advisor support to the South Vietnamese forces but cut Army advisors back to one advisor at the brigade and higher levels except in the Ranger and Airborne units. They're the best that Vietnam has to offer, so we can keep a two-man advisor team at the battalion levels in those units. I understand the Marines want to keep an advisor at the battalion level as well—so be it for now. They can also keep two at the brigade and higher level. We will keep an advisor at the district level as well if that's okay with you, Mr. Colby," Abrams said.

"Yes, sir, thank you," William Colby responded. Colby headed up the Civil Operations and Revolutionary Development Support program, or CORDS as it was known. They were tasked with "winning the hearts and minds" of the rural villages and had Army personnel in the districts across Vietnam serving as advisors to the district chiefs.

"Alright, gentlemen, you know what has to be done, so let's get to it. General Carley, set a date to get back with me on the proposed cuts. That is all," Abrams concluded and departed.

* * *

Hours later, Colonel Irv Pahl the intelligence officer for Senior Regional Assistance Group, sat at MACV headquarters with his MACV counterpart, Major General William Potts. The two were discussing the previous meeting over a glass of scotch, imported.

"Sir, I heard what he said about intelligence operations, and it's going to hurt. We've already scaled back on assets and now we're scaling back on more at a time when every indicator is that the North is going to make a major push. The question 'is the North going to undertake a major offensive?' has been asked and answered. Yes, they are, in '72. But no one is asking the follow-on questions: where, when and how much?" Irv said with frustration dripping from every word.

"I hear you, and I've voiced the same frustrations, but right now Melvin Laird is calling the shots in Washington, and we can do nothing about it. Nixon promised to get us out of Vietnam and that's the Holy Grail to Laird. He thinks we have enough intel through the NSA to provide the early warning and picture that we need," Potts explained.

"Sir, we used to have the CIA here with their human intelligence networks, which have been reduced as most see the handwriting on the wall and have left the country. We had the various services reporting through the Defense Intelligence Agency, but as everyone's cutting back assets, the intel picture is minimal. The Air Force is providing stuff, but it's one over the world for us on the front lines. The YO-3 Quiet Star was providing good intel, but those were packed up and shipped home in December, so we have nothing except Air Force one over the world,"[1] Pahl said, standing to pour another drink. He motioned to Potts with the bottle, asking if he wanted a refill.

"Sure, what the hell?" Potts said. As Pahl poured, Potts continued, "You know that the guys in Ops that are responsible for identifying the units to be sent home first have already, based on the boss's guidance, identified shipping all the air cav units home by April."

"What!" Pahl said, in shock. "Sir, we cannot let that happen. They're the last of our eyes and ears in addition to providing some attack helicopter support. Hell, the damn Vietnamese Air Force is not going to conduct those missions. We can't even get them to conduct normal helicopter missions of resupply and combat assaults. Damn cowards and thieves," Pahl said before he slugged down that drink and reached for another. Potts said nothing but thought it best to let Pahl fume and vent. They had known each other for many years and frequently served together. A good deal of respect for each other was present.

"Sir, back in November, the Air Force spotted that large tank farm up in the vicinity of Base Camp 609, right next to Kontum Province, my area. The YO-3 flights confirmed the information. Sensors along the Ho Chi Minh Trail are indicating increased traffic coming south. What was once a footpath from Hanoi to southern Laos is now just short of being a paved road. Now with YO-3 gone, the cav is the only thing we have to keep tabs on the possibility of tanks moving into our sector. Hell, I can't convince Vann that tanks are up there or in our sector. He wants two sets of eyes on the tank from two different sources at the same time before he'll accept the fact that tanks are operating in our AO," Pahl said.

"What? What about the photos from the YO-3 and the Air Force? Didn't that convince him?" Potts asked, taking a sip of his scotch.

"No. He said two separate times...he wants two separate sources, at the same time, confirming tanks. I think he's putting his head in the sand on this one. Don't get me wrong, I like and respect him, but I think he's wrong on this," Pahl added.

"Well, he was the first to say we could expect a major offensive coming. Even sticking his neck out, predicting it would be after Tet and not during Tet," Potts said. "Argued that they'll wait until the weather favors them and not our TACAIR. Says that would be sometime in late March or early April. Pretty gutsy call," Potts indicated.

Having begun to feel the effects of his drinks, and having released his frustrations, Pahl sat back in the overstuffed chair. Looking up at the ceiling in resignation, he said, "Well, sir, the best we can hope for is that we're wrong and will be out of here before he does decide to launch an attack."

* * *

Le Tien Kien and his two companions had been in training for eight months since being drafted. Kien had always wanted to be a soldier and a good citizen, believing in the ideology taught in school. He excelled in his basic training and was soon identified as a natural leader. This brought him a promotion to squad leader, and he trained his squad vigorously. At last the long-awaited march to the south had commenced down the Ho Chi Minh Trail. Visions of glory passed the hours for him as they moved down the dirt road. As they did so, he saw hundreds of construction workers along the road, repairing and widening it. Some were working with shovels, some on bulldozers sporting such names as Mitsubishi, Caterpillar and Kubota. During the darkness, he noticed tiny sparks of candle-light marking the trail. The candles were placed inside notches that had been hacked into the sides of trees so the flame wasn't exposed outside of the tree but only the light emanated from the notch.

As they headed south on their one-month march, they would move off the trail to established rest camps. In the camps, they found warm food already prepared, latrine facilities and tentage to sleep under. They could exchange worn-out clothing and sandals as well. Occasionally, an entertainment troupe would be present and sing to them. At each, a political officer praised them for their courage and loyalty to the cause. Kien was proud that he was supporting the cause of ejecting the Americans out of South Vietnam, freeing the oppressed people from the corrupt government of South Vietnam and joining the two Vietnams into one.

As they continued to walk, Kien's thoughts of glory were interrupted when, without warning, the first explosion ignited, followed by a thunderous rolling sound coming loudly towards him. His dreams of glory were suddenly replaced by thoughts of survival as the earth erupted in front of him.

* * *

**Would you like to read more?**
Order your copy of, Battle of Kontum, 1972.
Available for order on Amazon.

MATT JACKSON
BATTLE FOR KONTUM, 1972
UNDAUNTED VALOR, VOLUME 6

# GLOSSARY

**AC**. Aircraft commander; also alternating electrical current.

**ADA**. Air defense artillery.

**ANGLICO**. Air Naval Gunfire Liaison Company. Usually deployed two to three man teams with a ground force commander to coordinate naval gunfire and close-air support.

**ARA.** Aerial Rocket Artillery, commonly referred to by the call sign, Blue Max.

**ARVN.** Army of the Republic of Vietnam. Soldiers of South Vietnam were referred to as ARVNs.

**BC.** Battalion commander.

**BOQ.** Bachelor Officers Quarters.

**C rations.** Canned food that could be eaten cold or hot, used by the military from World War II until the late 1970s or early 1980s.

**CWO.** Chief warrant officer.

**C&C.** Command-and-control aircraft.

**DC.** Direct electrical current.

**det cord.** White cord approximately 1/4-inch around that is highly explosive and used to quickly cut trees or blow up other objects.

**FSB.** Fire Support Base. Generally an circular constructed support area in the middle of the jungles approximately the size of a football field in circumference with a dirt berm five feet high. The berm would have fighting positions located at intervals. Located in the center would generally be artillery and mortars positions. In front of the berm approximately fifty feet or more from the berm would be three rows of bard wire, claymore mines, trip flares and other early warning implements.

**GCA.** Ground control approach, a technique used for landing aircraft, with a ground controller watching an approaching aircraft on radar and giving the pilots information as to runway alignment and altitude.

**klick.** Measurement of distance used by the military, consisting of 1,000 meters (one kilometer).

**LZ.** Landing zone, the designated location for the insertion of troops. Once an established firebase is present, it is named with the prefix LZ FSB

**MP.** Military police.

**medevac.** Medical evacuation.

**NCO.** Noncommissioned officer, those enlisted personnel in the military with a rank between E5 and E9; commonly referred to as sergeants in the Army, Marine Corps and Air Force and chief in the Navy and Coast Guard.

**NDP.** Night defensive position, usually established by company-sized or smaller units for their stationary position after dark.

**NVA.** North Vietnamese Army.

**PX.** Post exchange, the military version of Walmart.

**PZ.** Pickup zone, a location to pick up passengers or supplies.

**RLO.** Real live officer, a term applied to commissioned officers, versus warrant officers, who are appointed officers.

**SF.** Special Forces.

**S-2.** The title for the officer responsible for the overall planning, coordination, collecting and analysis of intelligence information.

**S-3.** The title for the officer responsible for the overall planning, coordination and execution of actions by an organization.

**S-3 Air.** The title for the officer responsible for coordination with aviation elements to support the actions of an organization.

**thermite grenade.** A grenade that is designed to destroy objects through heat rather than explode; burns at approximately 4,000 degrees.

**TOC.** Tactical operations center.

**WO.** Warrant officer, junior to CWO.

**XO.** Second-in-command of a unit.

# BIBLIOGRAPHY


Allen, Colonel Robert S. *Lucky Forward: The History of Patton's Third U.S. Army*. New York: Manor Books, 1965.

Andradé, Dale. *Trial By Fire: The 1972 Easter Offensive, America's Last Vietnam Battle*. New York: Hippocrene Books, 1995.

Brown, Mike. *Missile! Missile! Missile!: A Personal Experience*. Self-published, CreateSpace Independent Publishing, 2013.

Casey, Michael, Clark Dougan, Samuel Lipsman, Jack Sweetman, and Stephen Weiss. *Flags Into Battle*. Boston: Boston Publishing Company, 1987.

Clarke, Jeffrey J. *Advice and Support: The Final Years, 1965–1973*. Washington, D.C.: Center for Military History, U.S. Army, 1988

Davidson, Philip B. *Vietnam at War: The History, 1946–1975*. New York: Oxford University Press, 1988.

Dorr, Robert F. "The A-37 Dragonfly in Vietnam." Defense Media Network, September 13, 2013. https://www.defensemedianetwork.com/stories/the-a-37-dragonfly-in-vietnam/.

Fulghum, David, and Terrence Maitland. *South Vietnam on Trial: Mid-1970–1972*. Boston: Boston Publishing Company, 1984.

Hess, Gary R. *Vietnam: Explaining America's Lost War*. Malden, MA: Blackwell Publishing, 2009.

Hoang, Colonel Ngoc Lung. *Intelligence*. Washington, D.C.: U.S. Army Center of Military History, 1982.

Kroesen, Major General Frederick J. "Quang Tri: The Lost Province: An Identification of the Factors Which Culminated in the Loss of a Major Campaign to the Forces of North Vietnam in the Spring of 1972." U.S. Army War College Paper, 16 January 1974

Lavalle, Major A.J.C., ed. *Airpower and the 1972 Spring Invasion*. Washington, D.C.: Office of Air Force History, U.S. Air Force, 1985.

Leepson, Marc, and Helen Hannaford. *Webster's New World Dictionary of the Vietnam War*. New York: Webster's New World, 1999.

Lewy, Guenter. *America In Vietnam*. Oxford: Oxford University Press, 1980.

McDermott, Mike. *True Faith and Allegiance: An American Paratrooper and the 1972 Battle for An Loc*. Tuscaloosa: University of Alabama Press, 2012.

Momyer, General William W. *The Vietnamese Air Force, 1951–1975: An Analysis of its Role in Combat*. Washington, D.C.: Office of Air Force History, 1975.

Morrocco, John. *Rain of Fire: Air War, 1969–1973*. Boston: Boston Publishing Company, 1985.

Morrocco, John. *War in the Shadows*. Boston: Boston Publishing Company, 1988.

Nalty, Bernard C. *Air War Over South Vietnam: 1968–1975*. Washington, D.C.: Air Force History and Museums Program, U.S. Air Force, 2000.

Ngo, Lieutenant General Quang Truong. *The Easter Offensive of 1972*. Washington, D.C.: U.S. Army Center of Military History, U.S. Army, 1980.

Palmer, Dave R. *Summons of the Trumpet: A History of the Vietnam War from a Military Man's Viewpoint*. New York: Ballentine, 1984.

Ringenbach, Major P. T., and Captain P. J. Melly. *The Battle for An Loc, 5 April–26 June 1972*. Hickham AFB, HI: HQ PACAF, Directorate of Operations Analysis, CHECO/CORONA Harvest Division, U.S. Air Force, 1973.

Sheehan, Neil. *A Bright Shining Lie: John Paul Vann and America in Vietnam*. New York: Random House, 1988.

Smith, Major Mark A. "After Action Report, Battle of Loc Ninh, 4-7 April 1972.". *POW Network Biographies*. https://www.pownetwork.org/bios/s/s198.htm.

Sorley, Lewis. *A Better War: The Unexamined Victories and Final Tragedy of America's Last Years in Vietnam*. Orlando, FL: Harcourt, 1999.

Turley, Colonel G.H. *The Easter Offensive: Vietnam, 1972*. Novato, CA: Presidio Press, 1985.

Willbanks, James H. *Abandoning Vietnam: How America Left and South Vietnam Lost Its War*. Lawrence: University Press of Kansas, 2004.

Willbanks, James H. *The Battle of An Loc*. Bloomington: Indiana University Press, 2005.

# ACKNOWLEDGMENTS

Writing any historical novel that attempts to put accuracy into the story requires research. Unfortunately, there are only a few around who lived through these days. Those few that I was able to contact, I thank you for your time and input, Mike McDermott, James Willbanks, Mark Smith, Raymond Waite, Mike Henry, Allen Borstorff and Roger Fox.

I would be remiss to not thank my editor, Ms. Eliza Dee of Clio Editing, for putting up with me, and Infidium.net for my maps. As always, give Momir Borocki an idea and within an hour he presents you with a great cover. My newest member of the team and one who has freed my time to pursue my research is Mrs. Margret Daily of Rukia Publishing, US, for formatting and so much more. The one person that deserves a major thanks is my wife of fifty-two years, who has put up with my constant time on the computer.

# ABOUT THE AUTHOR

The author enlisted in the US Army in 1968 and served on active duty until 1993, when he retired as a colonel. In the course of his career, he commanded two infantry companies, one being an airborne company in Alaska, and commanded an air assault infantry battalion during Operation Desert Shield/Storm. When not with troop assignments, he was generally found teaching tactics at the United States Army Infantry Center or the United States Army Command and General Staff College, with a follow-on assignment as an exchange tactics instructor at the German Army Tactics Center. His last assignment was Director, Readiness and Mobilization, J-5, Forces Command, and Special Advisor, Vice President of the United States. His badges include the Combat Infantrymans Badge, Expert Infantrymans Badge, Master Aviator Wings, Senior Parachutist Wings and Air Assault Badge. His awards include the Silver Star, Legion of Merit, Distinguished Flying Cross, Bronze Star with oak Leafs and Air Medal with "V". Upon retiring from the US Army, he went into private business. He and his wife have been married for the past fifty-two years and have two sons, both Army officers.

Matt Jackson Books

Follow For Book Updates

# ALSO BY MATT JACKSON
## TO DATE 2023

**All titles are available for order on Amazon**

**Undaunted Valor Series:** Follow a young man from the time he joins the military in 1968 after two worthless years in college and watch his progression from a private to an accomplished combat instructor pilot over the course of two years. All events are true, and most of the characters are people he flew with.

*Undaunted Valor: An Assault Helicopter Unit in Vietnam 1969–1970*

*Undaunted Valor: Medal of Honor*

*Undaunted Valor: Lam Son 1971*

*Battle of Quang Tri, 1972*

*Battle For An Loc, 1972*

Battle of Kontum, 1972

**Crisis in the Desert Series (coauthored with James Rosone):** How much different would Desert Shield and Storm have been if Saddam had carried his attack through Saudi Arabia and into the UAE? This series examines the difficulties and challenges that would have faced the allied forces if Saddam had carried the attack as well as received assistance from the crumbling Soviet Union at the time.

*Project 19*

*Desert Shield*

*Desert Storm*

**The Cost of Valor:** A screenplay based on *Undaunted Valor: Lam Son 1971* and currently being offered to studios. Please visit

*Undaunted Valor* on Facebook for updates on the status of this effort.

# COPYRIGHT

# NOTES

## Introduction

1. Map. South East Asia, 1970, Created by Infidium LLC for Matt Jackson Books.

## 1. Prelude to Battle

1. Lieutenant General Ngo Quang Truong, *Indochina Monographs: The Easter Offensive of 1972* (Washington, DC: US Army Center of Military History, 1980).

## 2. Only an Observer

1. General Creighton Abrams was Commanding General, Military Assistance Command Vietnam.

## 3. First Signs

1. OPCON is a command relationship where one unit receives its missions from another and is under the operational control of the other unit. The controlling unit is not responsible for administrative or logistical support.
2. Rome plows were large serrated plows mounted on Caterpillar D7E bulldozers and used to clear the land. In 1979, legal arguments were raised that this clearing was a violation of international law.
3. Dai'uy (pronounced "die we") is Vietnamese for Captain.

## 4. Rumblings of Events

1. Major Mark A. Smith (Ret.). "After Action Report, Battle of Loc Ninh." 1972. https://www.pownetwork.org/bios/s/s198.htm.
2. Opinions vary on the quality of Vinh as well as other Vietnamese officers. From American authors, there is a low opinion of most of the

Vietnamese leadership. Lam Quang Thi, in his book *Hell in An Loc,* appears to present a more balanced critique of Vietnamese leadership.

3. Chinh is Vietnamese for Major.
4. There is some controversy about this engagement. The two infantry companies from the 2nd Battalion, 9th Regiment, and the 74th Border Ranger Battalion fought their way back to An Loc. The track vehicles were seen destroyed at the location indicated. The controversy concerns what killed the track vehicles—the ambush or the TACAIR. Lieutenant Colonel Duong, the squadron commander, was taken prisoner and claimed they fought to the end. If so, why was he not killed in the air strike or the ambush?
5. Advisor Team 47 remained with Colonel Nhut and had no intention of leaving. They worked closely with Team 70 throughout the battle.
6. Fox Four was a term for F-4 Phantom jets.
7. A combination of USAF and VNAF helicopters extracted 138 special forces defenders to include eight American advisors on 5 April. Paul T. Ringenbach and Peter J. Melly, "The Battle for an LOC, 5 April – 26 June 1972," (1973), p. 5..
8. Robert F. Dorr, "The A-37 Dragonfly in Vietnam," Defense Media Network, September 13, 2013, https://www.defensemedianetwork.com/stories/the-a-37-dragonfly-in-vietnam/.
9. Mike Brown, *Missile! Missile! Missile! A Personal Experience* (Amazon Press, 2013), p. 374.
10. Both Captain Spengler and Chief Warrant Officer Windeler's remains were recovered in August 1989.

## 6. Difficult Day

1. The 5th ARVN Division was made up of several battalions of Nung soldiers who moved to South Vietnam when the country was divided in 1954. Deep resentment towards the Communists still prevailed in the original Nung soldiers and their now-serving sons.

## 7. Loc Ninh Falls

1. What occurred in the 9th Regiment CP can only be determined by two people: Captain Smith and Colonel Vinh, who moved to the United States after the war. All others present were killed, as Major Carlson, Sergeant Lull and Sergeant Wallingford weren't present inside the CP. When asked about the events, Colonel Vinh had no comment. Captain Smith today resides in Thailand.
2. In actuality, Captain Smith did have a chance to get on the helicopter, but he drew his weapon and fired at the aircraft to wave it off so he

could take care of his people.

## 8. Escape and Evade

1.  Interview with Mike Henry, Tiger 36.
2.  Major Carlson, Captain Smith and Sergeant Wallingford all sat out the rest of the war in a POW camp for the next ten months, being released in February 1973. Sergeant Lull was captured moving south to An Loc close to Highway 13 and executed. His body was never recovered. He is listed as KIA. Major Davidson managed to make his way to An Loc, but the details have been classified and sealed for over fifty years now. Captain Wanat escaped for thirty days but was eventually captured and spent the remainder of the war in a POW camp. Interview Sergeant First Class Sean Everette, NCOIC PAO Outreach and Communications, Defense POW/MAI Accounting Agency, Washington D.C.

## 9. Command Decisions

1.  Lieutenant General Ngo Quang Truong, in his book *Indochina Monographs: The Easter Offensive of 1972* (p. 227), claims that this meeting took place on 6 April. Others claim 7 April.
2.  Despite this order, Lam Quang Thi claims, in his book *Hell in An Loc*, that the advisor team for the 8th Regiment didn't move forward into An Loc but returned to Lai Khe before the regiment moved up to An Loc. That is not correct as Lieutenant Colonel Benedit was the senior advisor and was in An Loc for the duration.
3.  It was a common belief among Vietnamese officers that the US would return with ground forces in the event of a major attack by the north. James II. Willbanks, *The Battle of An Loc* (Bloomington: Indiana University Press, 2005), 67.

## 12. Pack Up Airborne

1.  One source said it was 11 April when 1st Airborne reached Chon Thonh. A second source says 9 April. I chose 11 April as moving such a large force from the Vietnamese National Training Center to a location south of Lai Khe would have taken one day, 8 April. Moving from there to Lai Khe would have taken another day, and from Lai Khe to Chon Thonh another day.

## 14. Dustoff One-Oh-Seven

1. Major Allen Borstorff retired as colonel and resides in Jacksonville, Alabama, today. One source indicated that this individual was named Borstaff. I spoke with Colonel Allen Borstorff and confirmed his identity.

## 15. Rescue of Advisors

1. Captain Whitehead's aircraft was inspected by the unit commander, Major Lansky, who determined it needed to be sent back under a CH-47 aircraft. En route back to Long Thanh, it seems that the sling separated and the OH-6 aircraft plunged for three thousand feet into the Song Be River, never to be recovered. Captain John Whitehead and Sergeant Raymond Waite both received the Distinguished Service Cross for their actions. First Lieutenant Dave Ripley was awarded the Silver Star. Ray Waite returned to Maine, finished college and bought a lobster boat. He is still fishing for lobsters in Maine.

## 16. Preparing An Loc

1. Actual quote as related to me by Colonel Allen Borstorff, who was present for this exchange.

## 17. 8th Regiment Moves

1. ARVN deserters, unlike NVA deserters, didn't go over to the enemy side. Most just returned home, changed their names and joined the local RF/PF unit.

## 18. Airborne into the Fight

1. Officially, IFR stands for Instrument Flight Rules. Unofficially pilots sometimes refer to a navigation technique of following roads, thus IFR, "I Follow Roads."

## 21. Siege of An Loc

1. The hospital took direct hits, resulting in three hundred deaths and destroying most medical support for the duration of the siege. James H. Willbanks, *The Battle of An Loc* (Bloomington: Indiana University Press, 2005), 42.
2. There is a difference of opinion between Lam Quang Thi, author of *Hell in An Loc*, and Lieutenant General Ngo Quang Truong, author of *Indochina Monographs: The Easter Offensive of 1972*, as to the placement of boundary lines between the units. I have used those depicted by General Truong as they are supported by others.

## 22. 1st Airborne Brigade Airmobile

1. Doi Gio means Wind Change. American advisors called it Windy Hill.

## 23. Movement to Contact

1. It was noted on several occasions, to include Lam Son 719, that soldiers on heavy weapons would be chained to the weapon. This prevented them from running away.

## 24. Resupply

1. CARP stands for Computerized Aerial Drop System, a system that used a low-altitude container delivery method.
2. In March 1969, I experienced my first rocket attack here. It woke me out of a sound sleep, and about every fourth night for the next eighteen months, one or two would drop in at night. It got to the point that I would sleep through them.

## 26. Windy Hill Heats Up

1. Captain Doc Jensen and Major Leigh Pratt flew the plane south for as long as possible, crashing in a marsh area north of Lai Khe. Aircraft from the 229th Aviation battalion picked the crew up. They were back in the club that night.
2. Lam Quang Thi disputes this in *Hell in An Loc*, stating that Dinh was one of the survivors to be extracted by helicopter. James H. Willbanks states on p. 94 of *The Battle of An Loc* that "Dinh...had all but abdicated command...he jumped in and refused to come out. The battalion

operations officer told the American advisors that 'Dinh had made his peace with dying.'" This account is seconded by Andradéin *Trial by Fire*, p. 442.

3. Soldiers left behind hid in the woods for a week until the NVA turned their attention back to An Loc. They then walked for a week to an RF/PF compound at Song Be.

## 29. 5th Airborne

1. Mike McDermott, *True Faith and Allegiance: An American Paratrooper and the 1972 Battle for An Loc* (Tuscaloosa: University of Alabama Press, 2012), 63.

## 31. Resupply Problems Continue

1. The crew was declared KIA/Body Not Recovered on 5 May 1972. In February 1975, the remains of Kurt Weisman were recovered by North Vietnamese forces and returned. The remains of Harry Amesbury were recovered on 14 November 1991. I didn't locate any records on the recovery of the other crew members.

## 33. Commit the Strategic Reserve

1. Lam Quang Thi, on page 161 of his book *Hell in An Loc,* goes into great detail about the commitment of the 3rd Airborne Brigade in clearing Highway 13. This is the only publication I have found about the 3rd Airborne Brigade being committed in this fight. I did see a brief AAR from an advisor with 2nd Battalion, 3rd Airborne Brigade, that supports this reference.

## 34. Relief for An Loc

1. With the drawdown in Vietnam, promotions slowed down. Those selected for major in 1970 were in some cases considered promotable captains for four years. Unfortunately, this happens frequently in the US Army after a major conflict.

2. Communications-Electronics Code Instructions. This book contained all codes and frequencies as well as call signs for all units and was changed frequently. It was classified as a secret document and maintained by the battalion signal officer. Modern electronics today has made this paper book obsolete.

## 35. 229th Does It All

1.  The result was that each day, three to four medevac flights would get into An Loc to bring medical supplies and take out the most seriously wounded. Colonel Nhut placed soldiers around the landing zone each time for crowd control.

## 40. Major Push

1.  Colonel William H. Miller was slated for and assumed command of an infantry brigade in the 101st Airborne Division at Fort Campbell, Kentucky. He retired in 1981 after forty-one years of service. Major Borstorff was brought back to work in the operations section at 5th ARVN Division headquarters in Lai Khe.

## 41. Strella

1.  I was flight leader that day and personally witnessed the missile, reported it, and was told it didn't happen.
2.  All of the characters in this chapter were members of F/79 Artillery Battery. Each was shot down by either SA-7 missiles or anti-aircraft fire. Only Captain Brown survived, and he wrote about it in his book *Missile! Missile! Missile!*

## 43. #68-15009 Goes Down

1.  In *Missile! Missile! Missile!*, Brown reported that there were several versions of the story about what exactly shot down Williams and Strobridge. No one actually saw the aircraft take the hit, so no one can say if it was a missile or anti-aircraft fire. When the aircraft was hit, it was at altitude, so an accidental crash was definitely ruled out. Their remains were never recovered, although Williams's dog tags were.

## 45. Tao O

1.  Captain Harold Fridermeyer posthumously received the Distinguished Service Cross for his actions on this day.

## 46. Rapid Response

1. It was reported, but I could not confirm, that approximately eight women were captured while within the town, adjusting artillery fire on the town.
2. Both Captain Charles Huggins and Sergeant First Class Jesse Yerta were credited with several tank kills, for which they received the Distinguished Service Cross for their action at An Loc.

## 47. Small Reprieve

1. Hours later, the group approached an NVA position north of Tao Khai Bridge. After a discussion with the NVA commander, the villagers were placed in single file. As they moved forward, each was searched and anything of value was taken. Almost as soon as they were spotted, two NVA sympathizers came forward and volunteered to point out government employees, teachers and those vocally opposed to the communists. These people were separated from the group and eventually sent to a prison camp in Cambodia. The remainder were allowed to proceed south on Highway 13 and did eventually reach ARVN forces.

## 49. Move to Tan Khai

1. There is a discrepancy between Andradé and Lam Quang Thi as to who reached Tan Khai first and when. Thi claims the 1st Battalion reached on the fifteenth without incident. Andradé credits the 2nd Battalion air move with reaching Tan Khai and the 1st Battalion arriving on the eighteenth. The point is that, by the eighteenth, there was a sizeable force between enemy entrenched forces at Tao O and Xa Cam. The NVA had a new dilemma.

## 50. Standing Salute

1. Interview with Roger Fox.

## 52. Move to Tan Khai

1. He was no relation to Lieutenant Colonel Nguyen Viet Can, 33rd Regiment commander.

## 54. Taking a Toll

1. This has been an age-old problem between the rear echelons and the frontline fighting forces, even today. In Desert Storm it was boots. The first soldiers to deploy did so with jungle boots. By the start of Desert Storm, those boots were being held together with duct tape while the rear-echelon soldiers in Riyadh and Daharran were issued and wearing the new desert boots. Frontline soldiers never received desert boots until after they rotated back to the States some months later.

2. On or about June 2, friendly forces arrived at the crash site. Isaac Hosaka's body was recovered. John Henn's body was not found. Villagers reported seeing two bodies from the crash. https://www.vhpa.org/KIA/inident/72052430KIA.HTM.

## 56. Xa Cam

1. Chot complex was the term used for the reinforced NVA bunker complexes and road blocks along highway 13.

## 58. Emotions

1. Letter from LTC Butler to his wife, provided by Ambassador Larry Butler, his son.

## 59. Hunker Down

1. Lieutenant Colonel Burr Willey is buried in Forest Lawn Cemetery, Richmond, Virginia. He received a Silver Star for his actions.

## 60. Two Snakes Down

1. One source indicated they were there to extract a pathfinder element. I chose to use the account as indicated in *Missile! Missile! Missile!* by Brown.

## 61. More Incoming

1. Personal letter from LTC Butler to his wife. Provided to me by his son, Ambassador Larry Butler.

## 62. Write Your Report

1. Lieutenant Colonel Charles Butler was awarded the Silver Star for his actions from 6 June to 21 June 1972. He is buried at the United States Military Academy Cemetery, West Point, New York.


## 1. Another Cut

1. The YO-3 Quiet Star was an airplane built by Lockheed on the Schweitzer glider design, capable of carrying two, with an engine, for night reconnaissance missions. It was so quiet that it could fly at 1500 feet and not be heard. It was reported to fly at 200 feet and only be as loud as a bird in flight. Eleven were built, nine deployed. Only one exists today in the Vietnam Helicopter Museum, Concord, California.